Praise for Dan Chaon's

You Remind Me of Me

"Beautifully disquieting . . . This novel, his first, has elements of Stephen King's *Cujo,* Alice Munro's *Friend of My Youth* and Lucy Grealy's *Autobiography of a Face* all at the same time. . . . Emotionally complex and disturbing . . . Chaon's achievement . . . is to rescue his characters from oblivion and make their lives seem as real as our own."
—*The New York Times Book Review*

"In *You Remind Me of Me,* [Chaon] proves once again he's a writer worth watching." —*USA Today*

"Delicately hypnotic . . . haunting . . . a lovely, insinuating book with a special staying power." —*The New York Times*

"Chaon's remarkable first novel . . . is not only satisfying but devastating; a portrait of a Midwestern middle class struggling against the particular realities of a failed ideal, redefining family in a culture of absent and adoptive parents. . . . In the end, Chaon provides his characters a commodity they seem unable to acquire for themselves: grace."
—*Entertainment Weekly* (Top Ten Fiction of 2004)

"[A] remarkable first novel . . . It is a tribute to Chaon's considerable gifts that the truth, when it comes, deepens as many mysteries within the novel as it solves. . . . His vivid, unadorned prose . . . manages at once to be precise and dreamlike. . . . The book succeeds because it makes us feel its characters' pain and inhabit a world in which desperate measures often seem like the only ones available."
—TOM PERROTTA, *The Washington Post Book World* (Best Books of 2004)

"Pitch-perfect . . . Dan Chaon's meticulous and insightful novel *You Remind Me of Me* is such an important achievement."
—*San Francisco Chronicle*

"Sad, lovely . . . *You Remind Me of Me* is even better than [Chaon's] excellent stories." —*Chicago Tribune*

"Expertly written and crafted . . . one of this year's most involving and satisfying fictions." —Cleveland *Plain Dealer* (Best Books of 2004)

"[A] powerful first novel . . . [Chaon] moves relentlessly back and forth in time, touching upon one character and then the next, conveying their sadness and their good intentions, their solitary regrets and the sorrowful ties between them. It's an unnerving, poignant book that will make you think about love, and how lucky you are if you have it."
—*The Arizona Republic*

"Chaon is the master of the marginal, creating characters who through circumstance or personality or both are just barely getting by. He is also master of the minimal. . . . *You Remind Me of Me* allows him a broader canvas, and Chaon paints it up like Jackson Pollock. Blackly funny . . . *You Remind Me of Me* reminds us we are all marked by who we are; we can't outrun ourselves. And though we stumble around feeling lost, we are all connected, even in ways we wouldn't choose."
—*The Miami Herald*

"With deep insight and a fluid style that never calls attention to its considerable beauty . . . Chaon is writing about the irreducible mystery of human nature." —*The Christian Science Monitor*

"Chaon deftly reveals the quiet suffering of ordinary people in a way that can be uncomfortably realistic but is always compelling." —*People*

"A moving story of fate and family." —*The Oregonian*

"Meticulous pacing . . . controlled nuance . . . a quietly ambitious novel." —*Time Out New York*

You Remind
Me of Me

By Dan Chaon

Among the Missing
Fitting Ends
Await Your Reply

You Remind
Me of Me

a novel

Dan Chaon

Ballantine Books - New York

Thanks due: Noah Lukeman, Dan Smetanka, Elisabeth Dyssegaard, Steve Lattimore, Tom Barbash, Sheri Mount, Gilly Hailparn, Marie Coolman, Martha Collins, Sylvia Watanabe, Michael Byers, John Martin, Brian Bouldrey, Peggy McNally, Scott McNulty, Heather Bentoske.

You Remind Me of Me is a work of fiction. No characters in this novel are based on real people, and the author has taken some poetic license with the facts of law, history, medicine, geography, and weather. While there is, in reality, a city named Chicago, the Chicago of this novel, as well as the towns of St. Bonaventure, Nebraska, Little Bow, South Dakota, and others, exist wholly in an alternate universe of the author's imagination.

2005 Ballantine Books Trade Paperback Edition

Published in the United States by Ballantine Books, an imprint of The Random House Publishing Group, a division of Random House, Inc., New York.

Ballantine and colophon are registered trademarks of Random House, Inc.

Random House Reader's Circle and colophon are trademarks of Random House, Inc.

Originally published in hardcover in the United States by Ballantine Books, an imprint of The Random House Publishing Group, a division of Random House, Inc., in 2004.

Portions of chapters 3 and 9 are from "Where Is Your Mind," a story commissioned by Stories on Stage, a live dramatic short story reading series, produced by Chicago Public Radio.

The quotation on p. 104 is from *Ascent to Civilization: The Archeology of Early Man* by John Gowlett (New York: McGraw Hill, 1984).

Library of Congress Cataloging-in-Publication Data
Chaon, Dan.
You remind me of me / Dan Chaon.
    p.   cm.
ISBN 978-0-345-44140-9
  I. Title.
PS3553.H277Y68 2004
813'.53—dc22   2003063776

Printed in the United States of America

www.randomhousereaderscircle.com

9 8

Book design by Mercedes Everett

To Dan Smetanka
&
to my sons,
two good brothers
&
to my wife,
Sheila:
always, everything

PART ONE

1

March 24, 1977

Jonah was dead for a brief time before the paramedics brought him back to life. He never talks about it, but it's on his mind sometimes, and he finds himself thinking that maybe it's the central fact of the rest of his life, maybe it's what set his future into motion. He thinks of the fat cuckoo clock in his grandfather's living room, the hollow thump of weights and the dissonant guitar thrum of springs as the little door opened and the bird popped out; he thinks of his own heart, which was stopped when they got to him and then suddenly lurched forward, no one knew why, it just started again right around the time they were preparing to pronounce him deceased.

This was in late March 1977, in South Dakota, a few days after his sixth birthday.

If his memory were a movie, the camera would begin high in the air. In a movie, he thinks, you would see his grandfather's little house from above, you would see the yellow school bus coming to a stop at the edge of the long gravel road. Jonah had been to school that day. He had learned something, perhaps several things, and he rode home in a school bus. There were papers in his canvas knapsack, handwriting and addition and subtraction tables that the teacher had graded neatly with red ink, and a picture of an Easter egg that he'd colored for his mother. He sat on a green vinyl seat near the front of the bus and didn't even notice that the bus had stopped because he was deeply interested in a hole that someone had cut in the seat with a pocketknife; he was peering into it, into the guts of the seat, which were made of metal springs and stiff white hay.

Outside it was fairly sunny, and the snow had mostly melted. The exhaust from the bus's muffler drifted through the flashing warning lights, and the silent bus driver lady caused the doors to fold open for him. He didn't like the other children on the bus, and he felt that they didn't like him either. He could sense their faces, staring, as he went down the bus steps and stood on the soft, muddy berm.

But in the movie you wouldn't see that. In the movie you would only see him emerging from the bus, a boy running with his backpack dragging through the wet gravel, a red stocking cap, a worn blue ski jacket, stones grinding together beneath his boots, a pleasantly rhythmic noise he was making. And you would be up above everything like a bird, the long gravel road that led from the mailbox to the house, the weeds along the ditches, the telephone poles, barbed-wire fences, railroad tracks. The horizon, the wide plain of dust and wind.

Jonah's grandfather's house was a few miles outside of the small town of Little Bow, where Jonah went to school. It was a narrow, mustard-colored farmhouse with a cottonwood beside it and a spindly choke-cherry bush in front. These were the only trees in view, and his grandfather's place was the only house. From time to time a train would pass by on the railroad tracks that ran parallel to the house. Then the windows would hum like the tuning fork their teacher had shown them in school. *This is how sound feels,* their teacher said, and let them hold their fingers near the vibrating tines.

Sometimes it seemed to Jonah that everything was very small. In the center of his grandfather's bare backyard, an empty pint of cream would be the house and a line of Matchbox cars, Scotch-taped end to end, would be the train. He didn't know why he liked the game so much, but he remembered playing it over and over, imagining himself and his mother and his grandfather and his grandfather's dog, Elizabeth, all of them inside the little pint container, and himself (another part of himself) leaning over them like a giant or a thundercloud, pushing his makeshift train slowly past.

He didn't call to his grandfather when he came into the house that day. The door banged shut, the furniture sat silently. He could hear the television talking in his grandfather's room, so he knew his grandfather was there, dozing in the little windowless room, an addition to the house, just space enough for his grandfather's bed and a dresser, a small TV and a lamp with curlicues of cigarette smoke around them. His grandfather was propped up against some pillows, drinking beer; an old blanket, pilled cotton, silk edges unraveling, was thrown across his grandfather's middle, an ashtray balanced on it. Tired. His grandfather worked as a janitor, he went to work early in the morning, while it was still dark. Sometimes when Jonah came home from school, his grandfather would come out of his room and tell Jonah stories or jokes, or he would complain about things, about being tired, about Jonah's mother—*What's the problem with her now? Did you do something to get her mad? I didn't do anything to her!*—and he would swear about people that he didn't like, people who had cheated him, or maybe he would smile and call Elizabeth to him, *Babygirl, babygirl, what are you doing there, does a babygirl want a piece of lunch meat does she?* and Elizabeth would come clicking her nails across the floor, her bobbed tail almost vibrating as she wagged it, her eyes full of love as Jonah's grandfather crooned to her.

But Jonah's grandfather didn't come out of his room that day, and Jonah dropped his bookbag to the floor of the kitchen. There was the smell of smoke, and fried eggs, and the old food in the refrigerator. Unwashed dishes in the sink. His grandfather's door was half-closed, and Jonah sat at the kitchen table for a time, eating cereal.

His mother was at work. He didn't know whether he missed her or not, but he thought of her as he sat there in the still kitchen. She worked at a place called Harmony Farm, *packing eggs,* she said, and the tone of her voice made him imagine dark labyrinths with rows of nests, a promenade of sad, dirty workers moving slowly through the passageways.

She wouldn't talk about it when she got home. Often, she wouldn't want to talk at all, wouldn't want to be touched, would make their supper, which she herself wouldn't eat. She would go to her room and listen to old records she'd had since she was in junior high, her eyes open and her hands in a praying shape beneath her cheek, her long hair spread out behind her on the pillow.

He could stand there for a very long time, watching her from the edge of the doorway and she wouldn't move. The needle of the phonograph pulsed like a smooth car along the spiraling track of a record album and her eyes seemed to register the music more than anything else, her blinking coinciding with a pause or a beat.

But he knew that she could see him standing there. They were looking at each other, and it was a sort of game—to try to blink when she blinked, to set his mouth in the same shape as her mouth, to hear what she was hearing. It was a sort of game to see how far he could inch into the room, sliding his feet the way a leaf opens, and sometimes he was almost to the center of the room before she finally spoke.

Get out, she would say, almost dreamily.

And then she would turn her face away from him, toward the wall.

He thought of her as his spoon hovered over his cereal. One day, he thought, she wouldn't come home from work. Or she might disappear in the night. He had awakened a few times: footsteps on the stairs, in the kitchen, the back door opening. From the upstairs window he saw her forcing her arm into the sleeve of her coat as she walked down the driveway. Her face was strange in the pale brightness cast by the floodlights that his grandfather had installed outside the house. Her breath lifted up out of her in the cold and drifted like mist, trailing behind her as she moved into the darkness beyond the circle of porch light.

We won't be staying long, she would tell Jonah sometimes. She would talk about the places where they used to live as if they'd just come to Jonah's grandfather's house for a visit, even though they'd been living there for as long as he could remember—almost three years. He didn't remember much about the other places she talked about. Chicago. Denver. Fresno. Had he been to these cities? He wasn't sure. Sometimes things came in flashes and images, not really memories at all—a staircase leading down, with muddy boots outside of it; a man with a fringed jacket like Davy Crockett, asleep on a couch while Jonah looked inside his open mouth; a lamp with autumn leaves patterned on it; a cement shower stall where he and his mother had washed together. Sometimes he thought he remembered the other baby, the one that had been born before him. *I was very young,* she told him. That was all she would tell. *I was very young. I had to give it away.*

I remember the baby, he said once, when they were sitting together talking, when she was feeling friendly, holding him in her arms, running her fingernails lightly back and forth across his cheek. *I remember the baby,* he said, and her face grew stiff. She took her hand away.

No, you don't, she said. *Don't be stupid. You weren't even born yet.* She sat there for a moment, regarding him, and then she shut her eyes, her teeth tightening against one another as if the sight of him hurt her. *Jesus Christ,* she said. *Why don't you just forget I ever told you anything. I mean, I confide in you with something that's very private, and very important, and you want to play little pretend games? Are you a baby?*

She sat there coldly, frowning, and began to gather and arrange her hair, ignoring him. She had long hair that reached almost to the belt-loops of her jeans. His grandfather said she looked like the country singer Crystal Gayle. *Don't you think she looks pretty, Jonah?* his grandfather would say when he was trying to cheer her up, but she would only smile a little, not really happy. He watched as she shook a cigarette from her pack on the coffee table and lit it.

Don't look at me that way, she said. She took a sip of smoke from her cigarette, and he tried to make his expression settled and neutral, to make his face the way she might want it to be.

Mom? he said.

What?

Where do babies go when you give them away? He wanted to make his voice sound innocent, to talk in the way a child on television might ask about Santa Claus. He wanted to pretend to be a certain type of child, to see if she might believe in it.

But she didn't. *Where do babies go when you give them away?* she repeated, in a high, insipid voice, and she didn't look at him, she didn't think he was cute or forgivable. He watched the rustle of her long hair, her hand as she ran the head of her cigarette against the rim of the ashtray.

They go to live with nice mommies, she said. After a moment she'd shrugged darkly, not liking him anymore, not wanting to talk.

But he did remember the baby, he thought. He and his mother had seen it at the market, being watched by a lady he didn't know. The baby was pink-skinned, and had a tiny head without hair on it and it was inside something—a basket, he thought, a basket like apples came in at the grocery store. The baby was dressed in a green velvet suit with a Santa's head on it, and rested on a red cushion. It moved its hands blindly, as if trying to catch air. *Look,* his mother said. *There's my baby!* And a lady had looked at them, stiffening as his mother bent down to wave her fingers over the baby's line of vision. The lady had looked at them, smiling but also frightened, and she had spoken to Jonah sharply.

Please don't touch, the lady said. *Your hands are dirty.*

He remembered this vividly—not only because of the baby but because of the lady's eyes, the way she looked at him, the sharp sound of her voice. It was the first time he really understood that there was something about him that people didn't like.

He thought of this as he ran through the house that day, swinging a whisk he'd found in one of the kitchen drawers, pretending it was a magic wand he'd stolen. He thought about the baby, about his mother walking on the gravel road in the dark, and he stood at the edge of her bedroom door, looking up at the padlock she had installed there. It was the room that she'd had when she was a little girl, and then a teenager, and she had many beautiful things—there was a music box where she kept her jewelry, with a tiny ballerina that stood on a spring and turned around and around in front of a little mirror; there was a box like a little square suitcase with 45 rpm records in it; there was a photograph of her mother, who had died, in a small gold frame; there were seashells, and dried branches spray-painted silver, and postcards of paintings taped to the wall. Monet. Chagall. Miró. She'd named them for him once.

He had never even touched anything when he went in, but somehow she knew that he had been going into her bedroom while she was at work. She didn't say anything to him, but one day after work she came home with the lock kit, and he watched as she screwed the hasp onto the door frame, as she fitted the shackle of the padlock into the eye of the hasp and clicked it shut, neatly. She turned to him as he stood there watching, her eyes careful and hooded.

There are precious things in my room, she said softly. *I don't want a robber to get them,* she said, and now, standing outside the door, it gave him a lonely feeling.

After a while, he called for Elizabeth. He got a piece of lunch meat from the refrigerator and whistled for her. He called again, and he heard his grandfather's bed creak as she got down from the foot of it, where she had been curled up comfortably, sleeping while his grandfather slept. *Elizabeth!* Jonah said in a high, tempting voice, and she nosed his grandfather's bedroom door open and peered out at him warily, trembling a little, sidling sheepishly as if people were applauding and she were shy. But when he threw the piece of bologna, she caught it in midair.

She was a Doberman pinscher, older than Jonah by quite a few years. She was not just a pet, his grandfather said, she was a guard dog. The world was changing, his grandfather said, you couldn't leave your door unlocked at night like you used to. There was Charles Manson, a killer; there was the hitchhiker who murdered the man who gave him a lift over near Vermillion; there was the uprising at Wounded Knee. You couldn't trust people anymore, his grandfather said, and Elizabeth would chase a stranger's car down the road, she would frighten the

Mormon missionaries who wouldn't dare come to their door, and sometimes Elizabeth barked and barked from the kitchen, her voice raspy and wet even when there was nothing outside to be seen. *She's keeping them ghosts away,* his grandfather would tell him.

Years later, Jonah could still re-create the dog in his mind, perhaps even more vividly than he could recall his grandfather, or what his mother had looked like then. He'd spent so much time with the dog, the two of them sometimes just sitting on the couch as he petted her, playing quietly until she struggled to get away.

He knew her better than anyone but himself, he thought. He knew the plump shape of her torso, the particular, mottled pattern of her brown-and-black hair, the sinew and bones of her legs, the long, intelligent, pointed snout. Her head was like a noble bird with a long bill, solid, a dignified Egyptian statue that he liked to shape with his hands. He loved her rubbery black lips with their amphibious, warty nodes nestled near her back teeth, and he liked to make her talk, moving her lips with his fingers so that she told him knock-knock jokes or sang along with the theme songs of cartoons they watched. He loved the polished black of her hooked toenails and the mysterious, marrow-bone white stuff he found inside the shell of each claw; he loved the cracked, sandpaper texture of her footpads, the wiggly, recoiling meat of her tongue when he caught it and stretched it out, the freckled, pale, waxy skin inside her ears, the way she'd flap her head back and forth if he touched the right spot, as if a fly were bothering her. He loved the soft bare gray skin of her stomach, the two rows of nipples, which he would press, pretending they were buttons and knobs on a robot he had built.

Goddamnit, Jonah, his grandfather would call, when Elizabeth yelped. *Quit pestering that damned dog! I hope she bites you someday!*

Maybe there was something inevitable about what happened. When he tries to imagine it in his mind it always seems that there was something still and icy about the entire afternoon, something hushed, a kind of expectation, as if things had been prepared for him.

He remembers up to a certain point. He remembers the game they were playing, the fantasy he was in. They were being chased, and like a king in a cartoon he shouted "Guards! Seize them!" Soldiers with spears were running in small steps, single file, down a corridor lined with torches.

They were hiding in the bathroom, he and Elizabeth, and he feels that sometimes he can see it perfectly: his hand turning the lock on the bathroom door, which he loved more than any other lock he'd ever seen. A skeleton key in a keyhole. A doorknob made of cut glass like a jewel. You could pretend you were a king in a palace.

Once the door was locked, he breathed with satisfaction. Breathed, turned back to look at the dog Elizabeth, who stood uncomfortably next to the bathtub, her bobbed tail tucked down, ears laid flat, eyes wary and doubtful.

They're coming for us, he told Elizabeth, and she looked at him and then away, tiptoeing in an agitated half-circle in the tiny room. *They're going to kill us if they get in,* he told her, and he pressed his face against the door, listening.

It was a small room, not immaculate but tidy, chilly black and white tile on the floor, chilly porcelain tub, sink, toilet. A tall cabinet held towels and washcloths. There was a toilet with a fuzzy blue cover on its lid, like the hair of a puppet; there was the sink, a steady trickling drip from the faucet; a toothbrush holder, a medicine cabinet mirror above it. There was a small square of window with its glass textured like ice, Jack Frost designs. Below was the bathtub, clawfoot, deep-basined, the inside of an egg. An orange rust stain ran from the base of the faucet head to the drain.

It was his idea that this was the best place to hide. He remembers this clearly, too, the determination that they should hunker down inside the bathtub to get away from the soldiers that were hunting for them, but there was some difficulty in getting Elizabeth to join him in this plan. He stood in the bathtub and held Elizabeth by her front paws, so that she stood up on her hind legs. He tried to tug her forward, but she didn't want to come. She pulled away from him, and so he got out of the tub and tried to lift her by her hindquarters, but she was too heavy. He had a hold on the loose skin of her haunches, and he managed to lift her off the ground. *Get in!* he said, and gave her a hard shove. *Hurry, damnit!* And she made a sharp sound as he pushed her, as he fell into the bathtub on top of her.

He doesn't really know what happened next. There was a moment, a kind of wave, a blank spot during which the game fizzled away, during which Elizabeth became not-Elizabeth. The two of them scrabbled against the slick porcelain. Perhaps he was trying to hold her down, perhaps he pushed hard against a tender spot on her belly, perhaps she panicked, upended, disoriented, unable to gain a footing. Her thin legs struggled in the air, and her body twisted, trying to right itself, and she made a sound like she was vomiting up a string of yelps. She snapped with her teeth, twisted, lashed, and Jonah felt a spark in his mind that wasn't really awareness.

The first bite was one of the worst. The long front tooth, the canine, sank into the skin just below Jonah's left eye and tore in a line through his cheek to the edge of his throat. Blood shot up and stippled the window. The bottles of shampoo on the edge of the tub clattered as Jonah's feet kicked in a surprised spasm. When he jerked away from her, Elizabeth bit down on his ear and pulled a piece of it off.

Later he would try to think that Elizabeth had gone crazy. People would say that it might have been the taste of blood, that it might have been the noises he was making, the high-pitched sounds that instinctively made her think he was some kind of prey. People would say that attack dogs like Dobermans can be high-strung, that they can lose control of themselves. He didn't want to believe that she hated him. He didn't want to think that he was her tormentor, that whatever he'd done to her, she'd finally had enough. That she bit him and liked it, thinking *at last.*

But she didn't stop. Her teeth raked through his palms when he held them to his face, trailing through his forearms as he flailed at her, trying to hit. One bite cut through his lower lip as she tried to get to his neck, and another pulled the skin of his torn face into a flap. He remembers trying to press the skin back against his face, like it was a puzzle piece he was trying to fit. When he fell out of the bathtub onto the tile floor, he felt wet. He was aware of Elizabeth's front paws clawing fast against his clothes as if she were trying to dig a hole into him, her jaws, bites on his scalp, his neck, his chest as he curled and rolled and kicked, smearing blood behind him. *I'm sorry,* he said. *Mom, I didn't mean to! It was an accident!*

Maybe he doesn't really remember this. Maybe he only imagines it, looking at his body, his naked skin in the mirror. Most of what happened is outside of his memory. He can recall flashes of heat, of pressure, but not pain, exactly. Most people don't understand what it means to be an animal, to be killed, eaten. A quiet peacefulness settles in. The body relaxes, accepts everything.

———

That was all there was to it really. At a bar, years later, a woman says, *Tell me something interesting about yourself* and Jonah pauses.

I was dead once, he thinks. That's the first thing he thinks, though he doesn't say it. It sounds too melodramatic, too complicated and inappropriate. She is a smooth thinker, this woman, she will look at him skeptically, she will take a piece of ice from her drink and roll it in her mouth.

Oh, really, she'll say, after a moment. *So what's that like? Being dead?*

———

And he doesn't know, exactly. He is aware of a feeling of rushing forward. It is not unlike the way it felt on the expressway when suddenly, at sixty-five or seventy-five miles per hour, a pair of semi-trucks framed his car on either side, the rushing walls of their trailers creating a tunnel he was hurtling through. Ahead, a rattling garbage truck drifted into the lane in front of him; behind, a woman in a minivan pushed impatiently toward his bumper, sealing him into a coffin of velocity. Enclosed and yet hurtling forward.

At that moment, he felt a memory spin through his insides. The dog's teeth. The yellow house, the wide plain, seen from above. The skeleton key, the baby in the basket, the lady who said *Please don't touch, your hands are dirty.*

———

He was dead, or almost dead, when his grandfather broke open the bathroom door. He doesn't remember this, he just knows. He is aware of the blood, his own blood, all over everything. He feels the door splinter and fall open. He hears the sound of his grandfather's raw, smoker-voiced moaning. His grandfather caught Elizabeth by the collar, pulling her away, and then his grandfather began to kick her in the ribs and the head.

In the movie, the bathroom would seem to float in space, white and glowing fluorescently. In the movie, the ambulance men bend over him, the corpse of a small boy laid out on the bathroom's black and white tiles. The men are silent and gentle and godlike. He pictures them as kindly aliens, with round, interchangeable heads and large eyes. His grandfather must be there somewhere, off to the edge of things, but he can't see him. By this time, Elizabeth is dead. He can picture her, not far from where he is lying, Elizabeth on her side, her legs limp, paws turned inward, mouth slightly open, eyes staring as his own eyes are staring. A line could be drawn between their two eyes, his and Elizabeth's—two points, A and B, beginning and end.

Jonah's grandfather used to tease him all the time. It wasn't mean-spirited, he didn't think. Just something his grandfather did to amuse himself. He remembers the day before he died, the day before Elizabeth attacked him, an ordinary after-school afternoon, not long before his mom got home from work, when his grandfather called to him. *Jonah!* he called, in his wry, raspy voice. *Come quick! Come and look!* And Jonah had stood there eagerly as his grandfather pointed out the back window, toward the railroad tracks, where some boxcars were parked. *I see the carnival came through here last night,* he said. *Look at that! They left an elephant!*

Where? Jonah said, and tried to follow his grandfather's finger.
There! Don't you see it?
No.
It's right there—where I'm pointing. You don't see it?
No . . . Jonah said doubtfully, but he craned his neck.

You mean to tell me you don't see an elephant standing there? Jonah's grandfather demanded.

Well . . . Jonah said, not wanting to commit himself. *Well* . . . he said.

Jonah scoped along the lines and shapes outside the window again. He didn't see the elephant, but then, after a time, it seemed that he did. In his memory, there is still the figure of an elephant, standing at the edge of the train tracks. It curls its trunk, languidly, thoughtfully, and brings a piece of hay to its mouth.

2

Spring 1977, Spring 1978

Around the time that Jonah was being brought back to life by the paramedics, Troy Timmens was reclining in a beanbag chair in a trailer house on the outskirts of St. Bonaventure, Nebraska, watching some teenagers smoke marijuana. It was late afternoon, about five o'clock, but with the curtain drawn it could have been any time at all. Troy leaned back, settling more deeply, aware of the satisfying crunch made by the Styrofoam pills inside the beanbag chair as he applied his weight to them. He supposed that he was fairly content.

The trailer house he was sitting in belonged to his cousin Bruce and Bruce's wife, Michelle. Troy had gotten into the habit of stopping by their place after school, staying until dinner or beyond, staying until well past his bedtime. If she asked, he told his mother that he had been baby-sitting for Bruce and Michelle's two-year-old son, Ray, and often that was true. It didn't matter. Troy's parents were engaged in the final stages of falling in hate with each other, a stretch of many months that was leading toward their divorce, and everyone involved was pleased to have Troy elsewhere.

Troy was happy at Bruce's place. It was comfortable and exciting, a world he connected vaguely in his mind with California and rock stars.

He loved the things they owned: the black-light posters with their pictures of wolves and skulls and lightning bolts, the stacks of record albums and tapes, the beaded door that led to the kitchen, the refrigerator with an automatic icemaker built into the door, a possession Troy admired, along with stereo systems and microwaves and Corvette automobiles. They always had the newest kinds of chips and snacks that Troy had seen advertised on television, and he was welcome to eat as much as he liked. And the living room, he thought, was breathtakingly luxurious. There was the smell of incense sticks, drifting up from the glass-topped coffee table, and furniture you could sink into—not only the beanbag chairs but also a big sofa with giant pillow cushions. The living room carpet was a thick, brownish-gold shag that covered not only the floor but the walls as well, all the way up to the ceiling. Best of all was a beautiful fish tank, where dwelled an angel fish and a pair of kissing fish and a tiny frog, along with many, many black and orange mollies that constantly gave birth to amazingly tiny babies—babies that, to Troy's fascinated horror, the kissing fish often ate, breathing them into their large puckered mouths. But his favorite thing in the entire house was the plastic skeleton at the bottom of the fish tank, a sunken pirate who clutched a ship's wheel in his bony hands; beside him, a treasure chest belched out bubbles of air. Troy was the sort of child who spent a lot of his time at school drawing pictures of skeletons on his notebooks and onto desks—skeletons with sunglasses and Afros, skeletons laughing happily as they rose out of cartoon graves, skeletons piloting airplanes or driving cars or wielding machine guns.

He was sitting near the fish tank on that day, staring at the little underwater world, mesmerized by the way the pirate skeleton's arms fluttered in the current of air bubbles. He was pretending to be uninterested in the marijuana smoking, though in fact he was watching surreptitiously as a few older teenagers—friends of Bruce and Michelle—drew smoke into their mouths from the lip of a glass water pipe. They were all listening to a comedy record by Cheech and Chong, which was very funny. Everyone was laughing, and Troy leaned back, a bit shocked by the language the comedians were using. His eyes narrowed in the cloud of smoke that hung in a thin layer above their heads, but he was unobtrusive, smiling shyly. He was ten.

But he was different from most ten-year-olds. People at Bruce and Michelle's place always told him so. They said he was like a teenager—an honorary teenager, someone once said, which made him proud. No one minded having him around. He was never any bother.

And maybe it was true that he was unusually mature. There was an aura about him, Michelle told people, though she couldn't put her finger on it. *Old-souled,* Michelle said, and ran her hand through his hair gravely. Something about him, something in his manner and his face and even the way he carried himself that seemed eerily unchildlike. It was those pale blue, malamute eyes, the oddly alert, wary posture. It was the shy yet somehow wolfish grin he'd beam out sometimes, a grin that those teenaged girls seemed to think of as pre-sexy, imagining that in a few years it would evolve into something horny and devastating. And that deep laugh—a laugh that made the stirred-up girls lift their heads and stare for a moment. Troy didn't laugh often, but when he did, it wasn't like the laughter of any ten-year-old boy they'd encountered. He sounded like he was more experienced than he was—a whisper of male prowess, cockiness tinted at the edges with something like melancholy, and they flicked their eyes at one another, amused and yet uncertain: *Where had he learned to make a sound like that?* They exchanged private looks—suppressed turns of the mouth, slight widening of their eyes, almost imperceptible movement of brows. Troy noticed this, but didn't know what it meant.

There were three of them that day, three high school girls, along with a wiry mustached boy of about nineteen who was their leader, who had brought them to Bruce's place. Troy was aware of the subtle attention the girls were paying him, and it made him even more resolutely quiet. He observed them from his corner by the fish tank, thinking that maybe they were making fun of him for some reason, and he carefully glanced down to make sure his zipper wasn't open. He ran his hand across his hair, stroking it flat, and tried to listen seriously to what the comedians on the record album were saying. They were talking in funny accents about eating shit.

He had met these girls before, in a vague way. There was one named Chrissy, who had straight blond hair and a natural tan that made it seem as if she spent a lot of time on a tropical beach; another, Kim, was very skinny, and wore a tight T-shirt that said "I'm With Stupid," with an arrow that pointed in a general way toward whoever happened to be on her left—in this case a girl named Carla. He had seen this girl at Bruce and Michelle's a few times, and he remembered her: *Carla.* She was sixteen years old, a small, round-faced girl not much taller than Troy himself; she had large blue eyes, thickly surrounded with black eyeliner and mascara, and enormous breasts. She wore a scoop-necked T-shirt, and Troy could see the beginning of her cleavage, a slope of moled and freckled skin. He was aware that there was something about Carla's breasts that made them different from other girls', but he hadn't yet figured out that they looked different because Carla wasn't wearing a bra.

There were a number of important things he hadn't figured out yet, though he would before too much longer. For example, he did not know that his cousin Bruce was a drug dealer, and that these girls were customers. He didn't know that Michelle felt uncomfortable about him being there, watching these transactions, that later she would argue with Bruce about it. He didn't know that Bruce and Michelle were young—both of them twenty-four years old—or that they'd already begun a friendship with cocaine that they would spend a good portion of their later lives trying to escape from. In retrospect, of course, there was the way Bruce was fidgeting, his thumb and forefinger tapping against each other like anxious pincers; there was the nervous, walleyed gaze that Michelle fixed on him.

"Troy, Hon," Michelle said. "Would you do me a favor? Would you go check on Ray and see how he's doing?"

"Oh," Troy said, and straightened up as if he hadn't been paying attention. "Sure," he said, importantly, and clambered out of the bean-bag chair as the teenaged girls observed him.

This was his job when he was at Bruce and Michelle's place— he was supposed to watch the two-year-old Ray. He was supposed to make sure Ray was occupied, that his diaper was clean, that he wasn't sticking his fingers into electrical sockets or drinking from the bottle of pine-scented cleaner under the bathroom sink. It wasn't work exactly. Troy liked babies. He liked to take care of them, he liked their little toes and their soft, fleshy cheeks. Besides which, he was still young enough that he enjoyed playing with Ray's toys, the building blocks and the See-and-Say and the plastic yellow school bus with the miniature Weeble children that fit inside it. He still felt warmly toward the Dr. Seuss books that he read aloud to Ray. He didn't mind constructing games of pretend or hiding that Ray would find deeply involving. It was easy.

Nevertheless, Michelle was grateful to have him around. When he left the trailer at nine or ten at night and headed back to his own home, Michelle would often give him money. Five, ten, twenty dollars. "Thanks for coming by, honey," she would say, and as she tucked the bills into his hand, their fingers brushed in a way that made him wish that she were his older sister, or his mother.

The high school girls watched him as he sloughed out of the bean-bag chair he'd melted into, and the older boy made a face. Troy saw the boy raise his eyebrows in a not-quite-friendly way, making an "O" with his mouth as he centered his lips over the bong. *Get lost, kid,* the look said.

But the girl named Chrissy called after him. "Hey," she said, and as he got up he turned to look at her again. "Troy . . . is that your name?" He paused, awkwardly, and nodded.

"You're cute," she said. The other girls shifted their significant glances toward her, smirking as if she had made a mean joke. And then they broke into laughter.

———

That day was not a particularly important one in Troy's life, but it was part of a series of events that he thought of sometimes, part of the continuum of his life with Carla, those early days in Bruce's trailer when the two of them couldn't have ever known that they would eventually get married, that they would have a child together, that they'd end up years later separated and then divorced and yet, he thought, forever trailing this history behind them.

Twenty years later, when Troy was thirty and trying to decide whether or not he was still in love with her, he thought of that time in Bruce and Michelle's trailer. Carla had left him, was living with another man, their marriage was finished. Nevertheless, he had driven from Nebraska out to Las Vegas at her request, at the prompting of her late-night calls. "I just need you to come," she'd said, and he'd gotten into his car and driven for two days. "Will you please, please, just do this one thing?" she whispered, her voice raw and slurred, and he did as she asked, not least because of those long ago days at Bruce and Michelle's, when he'd stared at her chest.

———

Carla was not the first girl he kissed. The first girl was actually Carla's friend Chrissy, the permanently tanned blond girl, with her dusky arms and pale, lotioned palms. "She was disgusting," Carla said years later, when he told her about it. She didn't remember her times at Bruce and Michelle's as fondly as he did. "God!" Carla said. "How gross! I always knew there was something really wrong with her. She was just the kind of person who would try to seduce a ten-year-old."

And Troy had nodded—he was always convinced by Carla's vehement dislikes, even later, when he became one of them.

But the truth was somewhat more complicated than that, he thought; more than simple words like *disgusting* and *seduce*, though he didn't know what terms would be better to substitute.

It was all mixed up in his mind, twined up with his memories of that time in his life, with his love for Bruce and Michelle's place, with the history of his life with Carla, with the fact that Chrissy wasn't alive anymore.

It was a lot to process, he thought.

And to be honest, he didn't know what was really going on that day, or how it had come to be that Chrissy kissed him. A year had passed since they first encountered each other, and Troy was now eleven, almost twelve. It was the spring of 1978. He had been spending most of his after-school time at Bruce and Michelle's by that point, sometimes sleeping over on a Friday or Saturday night in a sleeping bag on the floor of Ray's room, falling asleep to the comfortable sounds of laughter and loud talking and partying, and then waking up to the dead silence of aftermath, the door to Bruce and Michelle's sealed tight, a blanket draped over a curtain rod to block the light from entering their room, a straggler or two asleep on the couch or curled up on the rug in front of the fish tank, beer cans stacked on the surfaces and the gray smell of stale smoke lingering in the air.

He'd wandered into the kitchen around six o'clock in the morning, hungry because he'd forgotten to eat the night before. Chrissy was sitting there at the counter, and at first he thought she was asleep. She had her head down, cradled in the crook of her elbow, and she didn't move when he got some sweetened cereal out of the cupboard and poured it into a bowl. But when he returned from the refrigerator with a carton of milk, she had raised her head.

"Hungry?" she said brightly, and he held himself still, wary. The pupils of her eyes were enormously dilated, so that the gray-green of the irises were almost swallowed up, a thin aura like the rind of sun around an eclipse. Her mascara was smudged: raccoon eyes, he had heard the other girls call it. But she was looking at him expectantly, and so he nodded. *Yes, I'm hungry.* A few strands of hair adhered to the sticky gloss on her lip, and she used the edge of her pinkie fingernail to dislodge them.

"I'll bet I look like shit," she said, in a musing, almost contented voice, and Troy wasn't sure whether she was addressing herself or him. He shifted as she lit a cigarette. She glanced him over lightly, then turned away to blow a line of smoke into the air above their heads.

"Oh, come on, Troy," she said after a moment. "You should know this. When the girl says, 'I look like shit,' the boy is supposed to say, 'No, you look great!' That's the way it works."

"Oh," he said, and fingered his spoon. The smeared makeup made her eyes inscrutable, and he couldn't gauge her expression. "You look great," he said softly.

"You lie," she said. She smiled secretively, then let forth another stream of smoke, her lips puckered like a child blowing soap bubbles. "You've got to be a better liar if you're ever going to get a girl to kiss you."

"Yeah, right," he said, and frowned. This was a game that people sometimes liked to play with children—"How many girlfriends do you have?" they would ask, or "I'll bet those little girls chase you all around the playground!"—and he didn't have much patience with this kind of teasing. He turned his attention to his cereal, sinking his spoon into the soup of milk and floating apple-flavored O's intently, ignoring her, expecting her to lose interest and move on to another room.

Around them, the trailer was silent. He could hear the hum of the fish tank's bubbler, the insistent awakening chirp of sparrows nested in the eaves and awnings of the trailers, or in the trailer court's single cottonwood tree. He made a slurping sound when he brought his spoon to his lips, just to annoy the quiet, and noticed that Chrissy was still observing him expectantly.

"Can I have a bite of your cereal?" she said at last.

He shrugged. "Okay," he said, but when he started to push the bowl toward her, she did something unnerving. She pushed her hair behind her ears and leaned forward, closing her eyes lightly and opening her mouth. She wanted him to feed her.

It was weird, he thought, and he hesitated. But she sat there with her mouth open, and after a moment he held his spoon out. He watched as she slowly closed her lips over it. Her eyes opened as she swallowed.

"Mmmm," she said. "That tastes good. Thanks."

"Uh-huh," he said. He set the spoon back on the counter, not sure what to do with it now that it had been inside her mouth. He had seen the inside of her lips, which were slick and pink and glistening. And her tongue. He wasn't sure what to think about it.

But she didn't act as if anything unusual had happened. He watched as she lifted her cigarette, blowing on the tip of it so that the ember glowed orange through the gray crust of ash. Then she stubbed it out. She smiled.

"Can I ask you a question?" she said. He just shrugged. Her attention was not particularly welcome, but it was also hypnotic in a way he didn't quite understand.

"I heard from Bruce that you're adopted," she said. "Are you?"

"Yeah," he said. "So?"

"So nothing," she said. "It's just that I was adopted, too, so I thought that was interesting. I mean, you don't meet many other people who are adopted, do you?"

"I guess not."

"You guess not," she repeated. She regarded him steadily for a moment, her expression hooded. Then she smiled. "You're funny," she said. Then: "So what do you think about it? About being adopted?"

"I don't know," he said. The truth was, he *didn't* think about it very much, and certainly never talked about it. He'd always regarded this fact about himself as both unimportant and private, like people's belly buttons. He was adopted. *We adopted each other,* his mother had told him. *God brought us right to you and put us together as a family.* He'd known this from an early age, and he'd been taught that it didn't matter at all, that he was no different from anyone else. His parents—Earl and Dorothy Timmens—were just as real as anyone else's parents. But still, it bothered him that Bruce had told this girl about it, and he felt uncomfortable imagining the two of them discussing him. He shrugged, eyeing her suspiciously. "It's not a big deal," he said. "Nobody cares about it."

"Huh," she said: a short laugh. "Oh, sure they do. You just don't know it yet." She made a wry face, her eyes glancing sideways slyly, as if someone might be listening, and she was going to tell him something secret, or dirty. "Don't *you* think about it? Don't you wonder about your mother?"

"Not really," he said. And what else could he say? He looked down, thoughtfully, tracing the fake wood-grain patterns of the counter's Formica surface. What could he tell her? Could he say that he'd always believed his mother when she told him that he was special—chosen, selected, his mother said. When he was little, he used to listen to a record "How Much Is That Doggy in the Window?" He would play it over and over, and in some ways he supposed that he'd always thought his adoption was something like that—that his parents had wandered through a corridor of glass cases containing babies, and that they'd suddenly halted, struck with certainty, in front of a bassinet that contained his infant self. They'd pointed, and a nurse had brought him bundled in a blanket into their arms, a clean and uncomplicated transaction. He'd never much considered what came before that. He knew about sex, about how babies were born, but the idea of being inside someone's stomach—of being expelled wetly from some woman's body—seemed grotesque and unreal. In his mind, that person was like a skin he'd shed, a cocoon husk he'd left behind.

"I guess," he said, "I guess I always figured that it wasn't very important." And he shrugged, shifting uncertainly. He was aware of the inexplicable and almost oppressive heaviness of her attention. It was an ability some girls had, he recognized, a power they could draw upon simply by focusing themselves on a single person. His skin prickled as she leaned closer, as her forearm brushed lightly against his and he could see the pale hairs just above her wrist, the rosy smell of lotion and moist, soft pressure of skin brushing against skin, the way her hair grazed his shoulder.

"Oh, well," she said. She let the pad of her forefinger touch the back of his hand, briefly, smiling at him in a way that wasn't really a smile at all, but something else—a swallowed sadness, a shudder. "I don't know," she said. "Maybe I'm just weird. I'm, like, probably sort of crazy or something. But . . . I think about it a lot. I think, you know, what is she doing now? Like, maybe she's a singer or a famous actress or something. And what does she look like? And what would have happened if she'd kept me? Do you know what I'm talking about? You could have had this whole other different life, and maybe you'd be different, and, well, *happier*. I mean, I know that I don't belong in the family I'm living in now, that's for sure." She made a face. "Maybe I'm the only one, I don't know. But do you really think your parents wanted to adopt a baby? Don't you think that if they'd had the choice they would have had a real baby? I mean, one of their own."

He didn't know what to say to this, and so he was silent. From the next room came the sound of thick male coughing, a throat cleared of phlegm. "Fuck," a sleepy voice muttered sharply, and her eyes shifted toward the sound.

"I feel sorry for you," she said. "You're a kid. You shouldn't be hanging out in a place like this."

And then, without warning, she kissed him. She tilted her head and pressed her lips against his. He felt her tongue move softly, a little flick along the line of his mouth, and he jerked with surprise. Her hands held his cheeks, and her lips moved against his for a moment before she released him.

"There," she said. "Now you'll remember me."

It was about 7:30 in the morning, Saturday, as he walked home, and he could still taste the dark, smoky pressure of her tongue as he hurried through the underpass with its walls of wet, dripping, rust-stained cement, past the little abandoned grocery store with its windows pasted over with newspaper, past the grade school, toward the rows of small houses that made up the street he lived on. As he walked down Dead-wood Avenue, a dog barked at him from behind a fence, and a pickup carrying a thin, ancient man in a cowboy hat pulled slowly by on the street. It had been a dry spring, and the yards of the houses were yellow-green, the tired-looking color of the sod that covered the prairie hills on the outskirts of town. St. Bonaventure was little more than a cluster of houses and stores in the middle of a dry plain of wheat fields, asphalt roads, bare, rocky hills. He didn't think of this often, but he was aware of it at that moment—the great expanse of the world beyond the borders, the woman, the mother he'd once been in-side of, out there somewhere. His stomach felt fluttery, and he felt in-fected by the sadness that Chrissy had given to him with her long, slow look, with the weight of her mouth against his. His heart was still light and quick and hollow in its beating.

Here was his house. Curtains drawn. The screen door with its alu-minum curlicue molding.

Inside, his father was asleep on the couch. His parents had been fighting again, and his dad was huddled there under an afghan, curled up, one pale bare foot uncovered, his face severe and drawn and pressed against the arm of the couch, frowning in his dreams. His hair stood up in stiff tufts, and his eyes shifted underneath their lids as Troy tucked the blanket over his exposed foot.

He loved his father. That was what he should have told Chrissy. He loved his mother, who was still asleep in the bedroom. He loved Bruce and Michelle and Ray, all his people, his family. He didn't want another life.

3

January 6, 1966

At the home for unwed mothers, Nora still holds out hope that the baby will stop growing, that it will die. Around her, the stomachs of the girls are swelling, becoming taut, and their souls are deflating. There is a smell of old fruit and eucalyptus, there is a large box television playing a game show, "What's My Line," a dozen expressionless girls staring at the screen, some of them smoking cigarettes or biting on their nails or clasping their hands in their laps. One of them is knitting. Knitting. This girl's hands move steadily and the skein of blanket or sweater or shawl is slowly, line by line, becoming a cloth that shrouds the lump of her belly. Nora wants to kill this girl, whose face is as blank as a rabbit's. Or she wants to kill the happy celebrities that the girl is watching as they tell their jokes. Or she wants to kill herself.

She moves along the hallway, walking, creeping, one hand cupped beneath her belly, the other on the wall. She isn't even showing yet, but still she holds her stomach uncertainly. There is a tickling feeling, like a spider spinning a web inside her, maybe she's only imagining it. The walls are cold, warty plaster, painted smooth, and she runs her fingers across them as if they are braille, supporting herself as she goes. Doors lined up. She suspects that the rooms are all identical, though she hasn't seen anyone else's. She knows: a single bed, a night table with a lamp and a Bible, a desk with empty drawers, a closet with identical cheap poly-cotton maternity smocks on hangers, a window with a bare, snowy tree in the center of it.

It is not quite a prison, not quite a hospital. A Home, they call it, in the way they call the repositories for the old and the insane "Homes." *They put her in a Home,* her father had once said about a neighbor woman who had lost her mind when she got old, and now Nora herself is in such a place. Being watched over. Taken care of. You cannot lock the door to your room in such a place, and her door won't even stay closed, she doesn't know why. The air pressure, maybe, the wind, something— she has no way of knowing, but sometimes as she lies in the dark the door will click open like an awakened eye, a shaft of light from the hall- way will fall across her face. It happens frequently enough that she has taken to leaning a chair against the doorknob when she goes to sleep.

In the dark, she can't keep herself from thinking that it is a ghost. She doesn't believe in ghosts, exactly, but if they did exist they would thrive in a place such as this. Girls have killed themselves here, she is sure of it. It is a deathly place. Silent. Cold. There is the kind of feeling you might have, walking alone through a park in late autumn, when a single leaf falls from a tree and twists slowly to the ground in front of you.

January 6, 1966. This is her fourth day of residence in the Mrs. Glass House, her fourth day of captivity, and it is beginning to sink in. There is no turning back. She should have accepted that fact a long time ago, but instead she still finds herself bargaining vaguely with her body, with God, thinking that it's possible that a mistake has been made. The long months stretch in front of her, and already it seems that she is los- ing herself. There is nothing to do here but wait, months upon months tunneled in front of her: June, they said, early June most likely. She sits in a chair by the window, reading her book, *The Collector* by John Fowles. It is inappropriate, she knows: "A brutal tormented man and the beau- tiful, aristocratic young woman he has taken captive," the back cover proclaims, and the story upsets her. *I hate the way I have changed. I accept too much,* the woman says, and Nora underlines this passage as small glimmering motes of snow pass by outside, as somewhere down the hall a transistor radio is playing AM love songs, the Monkees singing "I'm a Believer!" She reads: "I'm so far from everything. From normality. From light. From where I want to be." She closes the book and sits staring at her fingers, which don't seem like her own fingers. It is exactly the wrong book to be reading at the moment, she thinks, though on second thought, a happy book, an optimistic, escapist book would be even worse. If she's going to read anything at all it ought to be about suffering.

———

She thinks about things that she will never tell people, ugly memories that make her wince when they enter her mind.

Once, she punched herself in the stomach as hard as she could, hoping it would dislodge.

Once, she put something inside of herself—a knitting needle, which is what she had heard they used. But what, exactly, was she supposed to catch hold of with it? She imagined a floating piece of yarn with a glob of cells and blood at the end of it. Hooking it, pulling it out.

Once, she tasted bleach, but couldn't bring herself to drink it.

———

Have the others done such things? If so, they don't talk about it. They don't talk about much, these girls, as if they are all spies. Mostly, they glance at one another furtively—the scratch of silverware against plates, the sound of chewing, the television voices, the soft, private moan a girl will make when she walks down the hall. What is there to say?

"This is not a sorority," Mrs. Bibb tells them. "Let's keep our socializing to a minimum, shall we?" It is against the rules for girls to sit in one another's rooms and speak privately. It is requested that the girls do not reveal the names of the towns they come from, and it is best if they avoid speaking of their pasts at all—the fathers of their babies, the mistakes that have been made, the families they've disappointed. It is against the rules for the girls to tell one another their last names, and she suspects that most of the first names are pseudonyms as well. Like the girl who knits, who says her name is Dominique. *Dominique,* like the title of the popular song from grade school, the song by the Singing Nun.

"Oh, really," Nora says. "That's an unusual name." And the knitting girl looks down. She has dark eyebrows that meet in the middle of her face, right above the bridge of her nose, and her chocolate-colored eyes focus on the movement of the needles between her fingers. She is a girl who is used to being made fun of, the sort of girl who clutches her books tightly in front of her and plunges through the hallways of high school like she is walking into a blizzard. Nora knew of a girl like this back in Little Bow, a girl named Alice, which they all thought was funny. A Lice, they called her, and the boys sat behind her and flicked their boogers into her badly permed hair. A man who would make a girl like Alice or Dominique pregnant would have to be entirely evil, Nora decides.

"What are you knitting?" Nora says at last, but the girl keeps her head down stubbornly, as such girls will. Someone, their mother probably, taught them to *suffer silently*, taught them *sticks and stones will hurt my bones, but words will never hurt me,* taught them *a quiet girl is better loved.* Dominique pinches her lips as Nora looks at her.

"Well," Nora says, after the silence extends for a time. "It's pretty, whatever it is."

"It's a blanket," says Dominique, finally. "It's just a blanket. It's cold in this place."

"Yes," Nora says. "It's going to be a long winter!" she says, reminding herself unpleasantly of her father, his cheerful, commonplace chatter. For a minute she hates him, misses him, hates him, misses him, like flipping a coin or plucking petals off a flower.

———————

It will be a long time before she sees her father again. This is another one of the rules: relatives are not allowed to visit the girls at Mrs. Glass House, and she recalls her father's sorrowful, doubtful eyes as the matron, Mrs. Bibb, recited this to him. Mrs. Bibb is one of the horrors in a long list of horrors, with her orange hair and freckles and her cheerful, caustic blandness. A person incapable of either cruelty or kindness, Nora imagined, only an indifferent *nice.* It was terrifying, listening to her sweet voice, but what could be done? Nora was expressionless as her father looked at her shyly, as if she might advise him, as if she could tell him what to say or think. "Well, I suppose," he said, and Nora imagined that he was waiting for her to intervene, to lose her nerve, to cry out, "Daddy, don't leave me in this place!" Mrs. Bibb seemed to be preparing herself silently for just such a scene.

"Honey . . . ?" her father said, but Nora didn't say anything to him. She stared down at the ribbed upholstery of the easy chair she was sitting in. He knew what she thought, he knew what her decision was.

Originally, his own ideas had been quite different. "Just tell me his name," her father had said. "I'll talk to him, he'll do the right thing. I can promise you that."

But she shook her head. "No," she said.

For a while, he'd tried to argue. "It's his responsibility, too," her father said. "Believe me, he'd want to know what's going on. You just have to give him the chance. You think you know everything, Missy, but you know, I think that most men, they think that it's their baby, too. Men are not so different as you might think."

"Did he rape you, is that it?" her father said.

"Are you protecting somebody? He's married, isn't he?" her father said. "If he comes around here, I'll know it's him. I'll know it's him, and I'll kill him, you know that, don't you? I don't care about me, they can put me in prison, but I'll kill him."

"Did he hurt you?" her father said. "Did he threaten you? You don't have to be afraid to tell me."

"Don't do anything you're going to regret," he said. "A life lasts for a long time, you may not know that yet."

Of course, these conversations linger in her mind now that she's alone. Her father says, "Just let me help you, babygirl. You're my daughter. I'll do anything for you."

———

That is the worst part of it, she thinks sometimes: knowing that she has hurt him perhaps more than she has hurt herself. It aches to think of him, to picture him sitting in the mornings, hunched over his cup of coffee at the kitchen table, licking the lead of his pencil as he fills in the daily crossword in the newspaper, alone in the small house. She knows that he is already thinking of this baby of hers, that he won't let it go, that it will be on his mind for the rest of his life. She knows that the coldness and stubbornness she'd turned toward him will be like a cloak she has put on, which she can never take off.

But she cannot choose what he wants for her. Her father is a lover of babies, of families, of connection and structure, and she is not. She knows his stories, the events of the past that he's turned into little trinkets in his mind, telling them over and over, the same words, the same welling of emotion—wet eyes, constricted voice—at the same precise moments in the telling of his sad, sentimental tales. The orphan train, how they picked him up off the streets of New York City when he was only four years old and sent him all the way across the country to be adopted by a cruel farmer and his wife, who didn't want a child but a slave; how he'd run away at the age of fifteen. Or her mother, so beautiful and young, and him almost twenty years her senior, but they were soul mates from the start, his pretty little brown-eyed Sioux lady, how can he live without her now that she's dead? And Nora herself, his own babygirl, the way she used to follow him around and imitate whatever he did, *she even wanted to put shaving cream on her face and pretend to shave, just like her daddy!*

Oh, these stories—by the time she was fifteen they were almost unbearable. She would feel a smooth airtight window sliding up inside her, impervious to sympathy or pity. "I've heard this before," she'd say softly, but that wouldn't stop him.

Here at Mrs. Glass House, at least there is silence. At least there are no stories, and she is glad, because she can't transform what has happened to her into a romance. The boy, the father, is almost gone from her mind now, lingering only in her awareness of her own stupidity. Soon, the baby will be gone, too.

But until then, there must be punishment. Humiliation.

Here, at Mrs. Glass House, they are herded from place to place. They move, very docile, single file down the stairs to the basement cafeteria; they are preparing to walk down the hill toward town, where they will eat ice cream and see a movie. Mrs. Bibb distributes "wedding rings," cheap gold-painted strips of tin, which they are to wear on their left hand, third finger. The Home is said to be a convalescent house for expectant mothers. No one says words like *unwed*, or *bastard*, or *whore*. Certain aspects are pretended. Nora watches as Dominique is given a ring, watches as Dominique slides the ring on, over the chewed fingernail and ugly, wrinkled hillock of finger joint.

They line up. They will be led down the long winding driveway toward the town, young girls in various stages of pregnancy, ripeness, swollen and swelling girls marching single file from the doorway of this place that looks like a haunted house in movies or dreams—The Mrs. Glass House, with its three-story, turreted facade, with its loose gutters and peeling white paint, the long lawn and spike-tipped, curlicued cast-iron fence. If this were a picture, its caption would be: *Dread.* Its caption would be: *The undead stream forth in an endless torrent from the mouth of hell.*

She covers her mouth at the thought but doesn't laugh. She focuses instead on the steady crunch of Dominique's feet against the gravel, the girl's solemn, gracefully bovine trudge. She focuses on the clot of houses at the bottom of the hill, the tender, dirty nub of a prairie town, with its ice cream parlor and its movie house and its little post office and bank and gas station. There is a satisfaction in knowing that such places are dying their wretched deaths, in knowing that such towns are stumbling, wounded, their young people flowing out and away once they leave high school, draining out of the town like blood. Stupid people, she thinks. What kind of an idiot tries to build a town in the middle of the sandhills, a grassy desert where only sod will grow? These are the same people who would be pleased to act as if the fake rings make some sort of difference, the sort of people who will stare out their windows, deeply content, as the girls drift into their streets. After a moment, Nora slips the tin ring off her finger and lets it fall to the ground. She can imagine a soft "ping" as it hits the gravel driveway. She can picture it rolling down some groove in the ditch, through the dry weeds and mud, off toward some adventure. She thinks of the gingerbread man in the fairy tale. *Run, run, as fast as you can, you can't catch me, I'm the Gingerbread Man.*

If she lives long enough her life will have a story, and the story will begin at this moment. Once upon a time, there was a girl who didn't want to have a baby, but she did. Once upon a time, there was a baby who lived in the body of a girl, and there was nothing that she could do about it. Once upon a time, there was a girl who thought her life would be different.

4

June 4, 1997

A child disappears from his grandmother's backyard on a morning in late spring. He is there one minute—the grandmother glances out the window while she is washing the dishes and she sees him standing by the cyclone fence near the copse of lilac bushes, his hands clasped behind his back, talking to himself, as he likes to do.

And then he is gone.

It is a morning in early June, tranquil and warm, and the town of St. Bonaventure, Nebraska, has reached its greenest moment. By July the prairies that surround the town's clutch of houses and trees will have faded to a grayish-tan, the color of lichen, and even the fields of corn and alfalfa will seem artificial, desperately verdant beneath huge, insectlike irrigation systems that stride over the fields on long metal legs. Dust devils as high as churches will rise up in the stubble fields and churn their way across the roads and highways, right into the walking sprinklers as if attacking. Dust will settle on the crops' damp leaves.

But this particular morning the hot, dry, rainless days still seem far away. It is truly, purely spring. School is out. Children play in yards and ride bikes on the sidewalks. Discount City has set up rows of bright pink and blue kiddie pools, in three sizes, along its outside wall. Farmer's

Co-op displays planters full of seedlings—tomato plants and jalapeño peppers and watermelon vines and garden flowers—spreading them out on folding tables in the sun.

On such a day the grandmother is not particularly concerned that she doesn't see the child when she looks out the kitchen window. He's playing, she thinks. The boy, Loomis, is six years old, and in fact is a kind of miracle of restraint and politeness for a child of the late twentieth century. He's the type of child who still consistently presents himself to her to ask, "Grandma, may I use the rest room?" and who will pause to take note of the time on the plastic wristwatch his father has given him because he likes to be in bed at exactly eight-thirty. When she looks out again and sees that he is no longer by the fence she doesn't think much of it. He is a quiet boy, almost aloof in his elaborate pretend games, and she likes that about him. She respects his sense of privacy.

Another twenty minutes pass. The grandmother, Judy, finishes the breakfast dishes, dries them, puts them away in a cupboard. She is watching—half watching—an old musical on the small television she keeps on the counter for company. *Carousel,* very sad. "You'll Never Walk Alone," a woman sings, and she purses her mouth against a welling of sentimental emotion.

She is tired today; she didn't sleep well. Recently she's been troubled by strange fluctuations of her pulse as she lies down to sleep, and then, once her pulse stops accelerating and she begins to drift off, her heart seems to stop. It is as if the body has suddenly forgotten that it is necessary to keep blood pumping, and she rises with a jolt into consciousness, like a cork from the bottom of a bucket of water. Her whole body tingles for a moment.

This happens irregularly, but it had frightened her badly last night, and she had paced gingerly through the kitchen with a cup of warm Ovaltine. She wondered if something was wrong with her. The doctors would blame her weight, she thought. Her blood pressure, probably—she had escaped it up until now, but she saw ahead a whole series of adjustments: pills, diets, tests. She would begin the slow and futile ritual of staving off her own mortality. She had seen this happen with her own mother—the way the maintenance of health began to occupy more and more of her mother's daily life, until most of her waking hours were consumed in a kind of endless tennis match with her own body. Prevent one thing and the ball would come whizzing back over the net: a cold she couldn't shake, another organ failing, another limb hard to move, or painful. Eventually her mother died from shingles—a ridiculous and almost comical-sounding ailment that had beaten Judy's mother simply by virtue of her weakened immune system.

Judy had been thinking of this, pacing through the darkened house, when a noise came from outside—a rattling, the soft echo of a jar rolling over a hard surface. She heard what at first she thought was a high-pitched, raspy voice—a voice not unlike her mother's in her last years—and she shuddered. Out the window, she saw the raccoon. When she flicked on the porch light, it stood up. It held its front legs against its chest like palsied arms, hunching there, cringing. Its eyes glinted, and when she opened the screen door to holler at it, the creature stared at her like a malevolent and senile old person—like one of those old men who glare from their wheelchairs as you pass them at the nursing home. Abruptly, the raccoon dropped from its standing position and trotted to the corner of the yard. On all fours, the animal looked grotesquely swollen, its wide hindquarters jiggling as it ran. She watched as it smoothly slipped through a gap under the fence, near the lilac bush, and vanished.

It is this image that comes to her when she opens the back door to call Loomis. An image of that creature loping, waddling, into the bushes, like a heavily drugged person trying to crawl quickly. Its body was too slow and casual to express terror, but she could tell that it was actually quite desperate. "Loomis," she says, and for a second she thinks she sees a flash of movement, a tail, a swatch of dark pelt disappearing under the lilac foliage.

This image unnerves her at first. She actually shudders—a shadow passes along the nape of her neck—and then there is the emptiness of the yard. "Loomis?" she says, uncertainly.

The yard behind Judy's house is not a place a person could hide in. It is a simple square, a clean patch of grass with some dandelions and clover in it, enclosed by a metal cyclone fence. In the northwest corner is a lilac bush, near the end of its blooming; to the east, along the wall of the garage, is her small garden plot: two tomato plants, two zucchini, four rows of yellow wax beans, a cantaloupe vine she is experimenting with. There are some hollyhocks along the side of the house. But mostly it is open yard. A few of Loomis's toys are scattered there— a Batman doll, a blue rubber ball with yellow stripes, a plastic bag full of dinosaur figurines and soldiers and matchbook cars.

"Loomis?" she says. There is a moment of disorientation, eyeing the yard again, when she thinks somehow he *must* be here, that there's something wrong with her perception, her vision.

He could have climbed the fence, she supposes, though that seems so unlike him. Maybe he tossed something over the edge by accident and went to retrieve it? The wire of the fence crisscrosses in a diamond pattern, easy enough for him to fit his tennis shoes into the holes and hoist himself over. It seems foolish—he is not a particularly athletic or adventurous child, not liable to run off.

Still, she walks across the yard toward the north end of the fence, her thongs snapping under her bare feet in the warm grass. Here is the narrow alleyway that separates the rears of the houses on her block from the rears of the houses that line the block to the north, just wide enough for the beeping garbage truck to lumber down on Monday mornings. She looks to the right and left—nothing, just trash cans of varying shapes and sizes, plastic and corrugated metal, a few with stuffed garbage bags beside them. Weeds breaking through the cracked cement. Trees and poles, the branches and wire lines interpenetrating. At the far end, where the mouth of the alley opens into a street, a red truck drives past and vanishes. No sign of Loomis.

She is aware, for the first time in many years, of the way the world might look from the point of view of a small child. The largeness of it, the way a common alley might seem to be a mysterious tunnel, the way the back fences and gates of houses have an ancient, abandoned quality. She notices—remembers—the narrow strip of space between the fence and the rear of her garage: another tunnel, but one that doesn't seem maneuverable even for a child, since logs are piled up there—pieces of an old tree that she'd had removed several years ago. For some reason she must have thought the wood would be useful, though now she can't remember why. Now it is spotted with lichen and shelf fungus, wet, rotten, perhaps full of termites or ants.

"Loomis!" she calls, raising her voice for the first time, now not embarrassed for the neighbors to hear her. She lets herself bellow, once: "Loomis! Where are you?" And the dog in the neighbor's back-yard to her left begins to bark. He wouldn't have gone there, of course. He hates and fears the dog, a moody and thickly muscled pit bull named Pluto. Nevertheless, she goes to the edge of the fence and peers over, and Pluto runs at her. He is leashed to a clothesline, and the eye-let of the leash makes a hollow sound, like a marble rolling down a pipe, as it passes along the length of the clothesline rope. At the sight of her, Pluto lets out a series of angry, territorial barks, his ears pinned back and eyes bright with outrage.

"Shut up!" Judy says sharply, and claps her hands, a gesture she re-members from childhood, from her mother, when they lived on a farm outside of town and sometimes encountered strange stray dogs. "Git!" she says, and claps her hands again. "Go on now!" And Pluto, im-pressed, stops barking and watches her warily. The neighbors, the Woodwards, are a childless and cordially unfriendly couple of whom she knows little. They are perhaps in their thirties. The woman, Bonnie, a secretary at the courthouse; the husband, Sherman, a worker at the feedlot outside of town. He is a hunter, and nearly every fall will bring home a deer that he skins and dismembers in the backyard. Beyond this, she knows little about them, and she is glad that they show no in-terest in her. She is an older divorced lady: *Mrs. Keene,* they call her re-spectfully. She suspects that they have probably heard some gossip about Loomis and his parents, some version of that unpleasant story, but they have said nothing, and she appreciates that.

She is beginning to get flustered now—somewhere between alarmed and annoyed. Where is Loomis? She is now of the mind that when she finds him she will give him a spanking, though she has never struck the child before. She unlatches the backyard gate—did he climb over it?—and walks into the driveway. The folding garage door is shut, but she peers in through the windows anyway, and then she goes into the garage and looks in the car. She remembers, in a suddenly vivid way, how her daughter Carla used to sit in the driver's seat when she was a child, holding the steering wheel in her small fists and pretending to drive. But Loomis is not in the car. She calls his name, very loudly and angrily now. "Loomis Timmens!" she calls. "If you don't answer me this minute, you're going to get a spanking!" And she strides down the drive toward the sidewalk, her thongs making sharp clacking sounds as she walks. Otherwise, the street is enormously silent.

She *will* spank him, she thinks. She will have to now. He has disobeyed, he has frightened her, and a lesson will have to come out of it. She thinks forward to this: dragging Loomis angrily down the street by his arm, turning him facedown on her lap in the kitchen and bringing the flat of her hand down on his bottom. Ten hard slaps, no more, no less. Sending him to his room without lunch. He may or may not cry— he seldom does, but she hopes that he will this time. Tears will mean that she has been effective, that she has impressed herself upon him and that he has repented. No tears will mean, what? Something to worry about.

That's the fear, she thinks, looking quickly to the right and left. That's the fear. He has been such a good boy, and the idea that this might change makes her heart sink. Loomis's mother, Carla, had been a good child, too, and look how she turned out.

Sometimes Judy tries to pinpoint the exact moment when things had gone wrong with Carla. Maybe it had been a simple moment, like this one with Loomis—willfully running off, without any concern for the consequences, without any concern for the feelings of others. She couldn't remember anything so specific, but she knew that Carla had started out like Loomis: quiet, bright, easily pleased. But then, outside of Judy's control, she had begun to transform. By the time she passed into her teenage years, she had become secretive, vindictive, addictive, in and out of alcohol/drug rehabilitation facilities since she was fourteen.

She pauses on the sidewalk. She has begun to perspire, and she looks up and down her street, Foxglove Road, the small one-story houses with their striped awnings and boxes of petunias and neat, tiny front yards. "Loomis! Loomis!" she calls, and her voice sounds like a parched hen crying for water.

Loomis has been in her care for almost a year now—the only stable year of his life, she thinks. Before that had been a series of trashy catastrophes, starting with his parents' marriage. Judy's daughter—Loomis's mother—Carla, had never been a mature or responsible person. Even at age twenty-eight, Carla was not ready to be married, Judy felt, but her choice of husband was even more ridiculous than Judy could have imagined. The husband's name was Troy Timmens, and he was some six years Carla's junior, twenty-two years old when they married but still an adolescent in Judy's estimation. Troy seemed to have no future plans beyond working as a bartender and turning his late father's home into a partying den on the weekends. When Carla found herself pregnant a year or so later, Judy had tried to tactfully suggest that Carla consider other options, such as abortion. But this had only led to another of their typical arguments—and another period of icy coldness between them.

But Judy was right, of course. Carla was no more prepared for motherhood than she would have been to pilot a jet plane, and Judy found herself called upon to baby-sit for the infant regularly while the nominal parents partied and fought. The marriage had dissolved under the pressures of young parenthood, coupled with a decadent lifestyle. Things grew worse and worse, until at last, when Loomis was three, Carla left town with a man she was having an affair with, taking Loomis with her and this man to Las Vegas, where she proceeded to become involved in drugs again. Troy retrieved Loomis and brought him back home to St. Bonaventure, and then was shortly thereafter himself arrested for possession of marijuana with intent to sell. At which time Loomis came into Judy's custody.

Thinking of these details, she is always surprised at how grotesque and depraved they seem. They are the kinds of things that happen to poor people—to trailer trash, to Indians on the reservations or black people in their ghettos—people whose environments put them at a disadvantage. Carla was raised in a solidly middle-class home. Judy was divorced, it was true, but she was college-educated, an elementary school teacher. Judy's life was supposed to be different. She had been the first person in her family to seek higher education; the first woman who didn't regularly spend her autumn canning food; the first, as far as she knew, who had seen an opera; the first who read literature. She had read Virginia Woolf's novels! And at the same time, she hadn't ignored her family in their times of trouble. She had loaned her brother thousands of dollars. She had spent much of her savings to pay for a nursing home for her mother, who had died with extreme slowness. She had gone into debt to commit her daughter to a decent rehabilitation facility.

Why should it be this way? Why should she have worked so hard to end up with so little, to end up fat and sixty-three, a divorced woman in a flowered shirt and tight shorts and flip-flops, a woman with a heart that palpitated irregularly at night and who was frightened by visions of raccoons? "Loomis!" she cried, and her voice broke, there was the edge of tears in it. There were times when she thought that this child, Loomis, her grandson, would make her life different, when she thought he was the child she should have been given all along, that he was a kind of reward for her hardship.

Why didn't he answer?

She hadn't yet let herself think of the bad things. The grown-up hand and the sack, the things she'd read about. The people who prey on children. The idea of disappearance.

But the more she thought about it, the more she remembered the last time she'd seen Loomis. She'd looked out the window, and he had been standing there by the lilac bush, his hands clasped behind his back, talking to himself, as he always did.

Talking to himself? She felt herself shrinking, even as she paced through the neighborhood, even as she hopefully expected to see him rounding a corner, running out of a bush in a yard, playing together with some group of neighbor children. In the alley, crouched behind a garbage can. In the house, somehow, sitting there and playing Nintendo and wondering where she was.

No, she thought suddenly. And then she could picture it, as if it were a memory. Loomis wasn't talking to himself.

5

1993

After Jonah's mother died, he took the old car and drove to Chicago, the city of his birth. It seemed as good a place as any in which to become a different person. He was twenty-two years old, and his intention was that he would never think of his past again. He would forget his mother, his grandfather, the shacklike yellow house; he'd forget the long humiliating desert of high school and afterward, a job washing dishes in the cafeteria of an old folks' home, a period of months and months and months when he felt certain that he'd finally reached the very bottom of his life.

All that would be erased, he thought. He remembered the way his grandfather had described the death of Jonah's grandmother, years and years before Jonah was born. "Excaping this world," Jonah's grandfather had said with wistful admiration, as if the grandmother's death had involved something masterful and Houdini-like instead of a mere car accident. It was an idea that Jonah felt friendly toward. "Excaping," he murmured under his breath as he crossed the Missouri River into Iowa. And then he corrected himself. "Escaping," he said. "*Es*caping."

He'd made a list of ways that he could improve himself, just to start out with. Grammar, posture. Training himself to say "library" instead of "lieberry," "picture" instead of "pitcher." Straightening his cowardly stoop and squaring his shoulders when he walked. Looking people in the eye when they spoke to him. Smiling. Easy stuff. As he drove along I-80, as glowing green-and-white signs caught his headlights and shimmered with the names of exit numbers and towns, he listened to a tape he had borrowed permanently from the Little Bow Public Library. *Fifteen Steps on the Ladder of Success,* it was called, and as he edged the speedometer up toward eighty, a man with a resonant, vowel-thick voice read aloud. Happiness and Unhappiness were choices that we made, the man said. They were states of mind. "'Problems' have no life of their own," the man explained. "'Problems' are mirages that seem to exist from a low state of mind, and they gain importance only because we choose to give it to them." Jonah listened, running his tongue over his dry lips, the glare of westbound headlights passing over his car, over his face, sliding up the body of the old Mustang like the palm of a hand, his mother's ashes in an urn in the passenger seat beside him. The stuff the man was reading sounded a bit like bullshit to him, but he hoped it wasn't.

Of course there were things he couldn't change about himself, things he couldn't slip loose of. There were, for example, the scars that had been left on him by the dog Elizabeth all those years ago, and every time he walked into a gas station or a wayside cafe, he was aware of the way people lifted their heads, turning their eyes sidelong to observe him, tracing over his skin. He tried to nod firmly at particularly frank gapers—an old farmer in coveralls, sipping his watery coffee, a tattooed motorcycle man, a little boy. He dipped his head, let his bangs fall into his eyes as he walked down the rows of vinyl booths, following a waitress he had flustered by his attempt to smile and make eye contact. There was a flutter among the people, as among grazing animals who sense a predator, and they glance away quickly when he nodded at them. *Jesus Christ,* they thought. *What happened to him?*

The scar they noticed first ran along his cheek from the edge of his eye to his lip. A keloid: a smooth, raised line of healed skin which they might associate with a cesarean section or appendectomy but not with a face. Not in America, not in the twentieth century. It made them think of a pirate, a thug from a pulp novel, a hideous blind beggar in a third-world country, and though there had been several revisions over the years, attempts at plastic surgery, the scar remained Jonah's most prominent feature. He had grown used to certain looks and their variations: the small-mouthed, wide-eyed gaze of frightened, judgmental middle-aged women who associated him with crime; the assessing once-over of macho worker guys who wondered if he'd had harder fights than they; the liberal-benevolent assumptions that he'd had a tragic life, and the subsequent game of pretend, the shifty act of direct eye contact, the ones who tried to make believe they hadn't noticed. But no matter where they looked they couldn't help but see damage: the nick of missing ear, the thin lines that ran along the backs of his hands, and others that pull down the side of his neck and past the collar of his shirt.

He had never known what to say to those looks. Sometimes he said cheerfully "Car accident," or some other lie. Sometimes he just smiled. *Take a good look.*

He hadn't decided what he would say to the wife of the building superintendent when she showed him the apartment. Sometimes it was better to gauge people face-to-face, to study their expressions, get a fix on them. But he knew he'd have to tell her something. He had called her beforehand and was prepared, he thought, for the kind of look she would give him. Even over the telephone there was an abrupt European-accented suspicion in her voice that made him act guilty. "Hello!" she said when she answered the phone, snapping through the receiver in a sharp, alarmed voice, as if addressing a shadowy figure who was slinking out of an alleyway toward her.

Jonah hesitated. He was calling from a pay phone, holding the folded and pen-marked newspaper in his hands while keeping an eye on his illegally parked car. Her voice unnerved him, and he tried to affect a very mild, harmless tone. "Yes," he said, and cleared his throat. *Don't mumble* was one of the items on his list. "I'm calling about the advertisement that was advertised in the *Chicago Reader*. There was an advertisement for furnished . . . eff-efficacies?" He winced. The newspaper actually said "EFFCY'S," which he knew was an abbreviation but he couldn't imagine for what.

"Efficiency?" the woman said in a booming foreign voice.

"Yes," Jonah said quickly. "Efficiency." He tried to imagine why people would use such a word to refer to an apartment, but all he could picture was the manager's office in the old folks' home where he had worked back in Little Bow. He pictured Mrs. Blachley, with her look of perpetual and almost painful delight, with her neatly arranged desk, the aligned display of in/out box, stapler, memo pad, pink paper clips, her hands folded restfully over each other. *Efficiency.* "Of course we're sorry to see you leaving us, Jonah," Mrs. Blachley had said, and beamed brightly, her eyes glassing with the effort of looking directly at him and pretending she didn't notice his scars.

The superintendent's wife, on the other hand, made no such attempt. She was already frowning when she opened the door, a small, thin, bedraggled woman with a mole like the head of an emerging earthworm at the corner of her eyelid and a pelt of gray-black hair on her head. Her jowls and lips were turned down in an exaggerated arc, which nevertheless deepened when she saw him standing there. She stared at him hard, her lower lip protruding and her nostrils widening as if she were furious, as if he were an enemy she were preparing to defend herself against. "Yes?" she exclaimed.

"How do you do?" he said. Despite his determination to the contrary, he found himself starting to adopt that slouching posture he hated so much, hunching, knotting his arms across his chest and tucking his fingers into his armpits. In high school, teachers would always ask him if he was cold, and other students used to imitate him, contorting themselves as if they were in the early stages of multiple sclerosis. "Yes," he said. " I called about the eff-eff-" and then he couldn't get the word out. "Apartments?"

"Efficiencies?" she said, and seemed to glare at the scar on his face. "Furnished efficiencies?"

"Yes, ma'am," Jonah said. He put his arms carefully to his sides, and tried to decide whether he was standing up straight. "I called you this morning," he said, and smiled at her, as he had told himself he would.

The woman paused grimly. Her name, he would later learn, was

Mrs. Marina Orlova, and she had grown up in Siberia. Later, she would tell him that she loathed the American custom of constantly smiling: "They are like chimpanzees," she said, in her bitterly exclamatory voice. She grimaced, baring her teeth grotesquely. "Eee!" she said. "I smile at you! Eee! It is repulsive."

But now she only looked at his smile with a sigh of disapproval, and he felt terribly self-conscious. "You wait," she said, finally. "I will get keys."

The efficiency surprised him. It reminded Jonah a little of a motel room, and he loved it immediately. There was a brown sofa that folded out into a bed, a small two-chair table with a standing lamp beside it, a seashore painting on the wall. In an alcove was a kitchenette with narrow counter space: a sink, a midget refrigerator, a microwave, a half-sized stove, a coffeemaker, some cabinets; and beyond that was a little bathroom, a tiny space not much bigger than a closet into which a toilet, sink, and bathtub had all been compressed. He was taken with the compactness of everything. *Efficiency*, he thought, and turned toward Mrs. Orlova, who stood in the doorway with her arms folded over her breasts.

"This looks great," he said. "Just . . . fantastic." He smiled at her again and looked her in the eye, as *Fifteen Steps on the Ladder of Success* had suggested. "I love it," he said. And he really did. It was the opposite of the house he'd grown up in, with its smoke-stained stacks of clutter, its thick cobwebs and faucets that ran yellowish, sulphuric water. He cleared his throat. "So, well then," he said. "Can I just—? How would I go about . . . reserving one?"

Mrs. Orlova raised her eyebrows, a single dark line that met over the bridge of her nose. "You have references?"

"References?"

"Where you live before?" She tilted her head and shrugged, tossing her hand. "You live somewhere, you have references."

"Oh." With effort, he prevented himself from assuming the submissive posture again. "I'm not sure," he said. "I'm from South Dakota. I'm just moving here."

"South Dakota?" she said, and moved the words in her mouth as if they were a new language. She frowned hard again, deeply and suspiciously, and he shifted from foot to foot. "It's . . . ah . . . west?"

"Yes," he said. "It's over—" and he pointed vaguely, though he didn't know the direction. In the city his mental compass didn't seem to work anymore, and he had no idea which way he was pointing. "Four—" he said, "five hundred miles or so?"

"Hm," she said. She seemed to consider this as if she didn't quite believe it. He watched as her eyes traveled again along the scar on his face, tracing an interstate on a map.

"I was in an accident at a factory," he said. "If you're wondering."

"I wasn't wondering," she said, though her expression softened somewhat. She moved her eyebrows in a complex way. "So what if this place is available? How will you pay?"

"I don't know," he said. "Will you take cash?"

Her face changed again as he took the roll of bills from his jacket pocket, a wad a little bigger than his fist. Her eyes sparked, and her lower lip protruded again as he peeled one-hundred-dollar bills from the stack with shaky fingers. One, two, three, four, five, six, seven.

"There was a settlement. From the accident."

"Ah," she said, and appraised him frankly. "They should have given you a million." She shrugged, considering him for a moment longer, but she seemed to have made a favorable decision.

He'd thought, originally, that the money would last for quite a while. Nearly fifteen thousand dollars, which at the time had seemed like a stunning amount, though he later discovered that houses in most other places, even dilapidated houses, sold for many times that amount. When he left Little Bow, he carried with him 234 twenty-dollar bills, and 100 one-hundred-dollar bills, which he'd tried to hide in various places in the car. A thousand in his wallet, another thousand in the glove compartment, hundred-dollar bills tucked into the pages of books and the pockets of the clothes he'd packed.

This was his inheritance. He had decided, even before his mother's death, that he would get rid of everything when it came time, and that is what he did. He sold the little yellow house in South Dakota, the plot of land, and all the furniture and possessions that he could get money for. Everything else—so many things—he had stuffed into garbage bags and left for the trash man. Gone were most of the photos of his family, letters, papers; gone were his mother's shell collection and worthless knickknacks, his own high school yearbooks and childhood drawings that had been saved, ragged quilts made by his grandmother, his grandfather's collection of Louis L'Amour paperback westerns; gone were piles of newspapers and junk mail and bank statements, canned pears and peas, ten years old at least, that had sat on shelves, never opened; gone were coffee cans full of pinto beans or nails or buttons, a whole closet full of unused cleaning supplies; gone were the horrible accumulations of the last years of his mother's life, when Jonah and his mother both had lost the energy to discard. He found a plastic mug, forgotten on a shelf in the laundry room, with a layer of dead mold floating on the surface of a half-inch of unfinished coffee. Who knew how old it was? It might have been sitting on that shelf for a year or more. He found a twenty-year-old grocery receipt in a desk drawer, along with a huge collection of pencil nubs and pens whose ink had long dried up. Seven-year-old telephone books. Ancient, pre tampon menstrual belts. Keys and key chains. Melted Tupperware. Worthless jewelry.

The auctioneer, Mr. Knotts, shook his head sorrowfully as the two of them picked through the clutter. He cleared his throat when Jonah pitched a packet of photos into the trash can.

"You should go through those," Mr. Knotts said softly, but Jonah ignored him.

"People can be rash when they are in mourning," Mr. Knotts said.

"Yes," Jonah said. He retrieved the pictures and set them back into a pile of things that he meant to keep, but he did this only for Mr. Knotts's benefit—as if he owed the old man something.

Mr. Knotts was a solemn little man with a high-pitched Arkansas accent, and Jonah had originally planned to dislike him. Which was to say that Jonah had not liked the way the man kept calling him "son," on the phone, and he had not liked the man's looks when they'd met to discuss the "auction process," as Knotts had called it—there had been something unpleasantly Christian about Knotts's softly resonant voice, Jonah had thought, and he had grimly noted the various accessories—

the cowboy shirt with its flowery pattern and pearly buttons, the string tie, the silver-tipped size-seven cowboy boots, the blondish toupee— all of which seemed to indicate a certain type of oily, Born Again smarminess.

But this wasn't the case, exactly. "I'm sorry for your loss," Mr. Knotts had said, but nothing else, no sentiment or piety beyond that. "I'm an honest businessman," he had told Jonah, surveying the ramshackle yellow house, "but I'm still a businessman, so I can't promise you much." Then he offered Jonah his hand.

He had a hand that was misshapen in a way that wasn't quite visible until Jonah shook it. Then Jonah realized that the pinkie finger was permanently stiffened, that the other fingers were oddly abbreviated and stubby, so that Jonah felt as if he were closing his hand over an ape's paw or a flipper. Mr. Knotts did not meet Jonah's eye with a serious, significant look; he did not say anything further. He simply let Jonah clasp his malformed hand, and something passed between them. Jonah had felt a rush of warmth for the man, a stranger.

Later Jonah thought it would have been good if Mr. Knotts had been his father. They would have had a steady, quiet, gently melancholic relationship, Jonah imagined. They wouldn't have been close, but he would never have felt unloved. Mr. Knotts would have been the kind of father who hovered, awkwardly tender, at the periphery of a son's life, attentive and formal in a folding chair at a band concert, lingering for a moment before he turned off the light at bedtime, the kind of father who closed his eyelids lightly as he kissed his child's forehead, the kind of father who would clear his throat often and grow misty-eyed. It would have been, what?, *lasting,* Jonah thought.

Mr. Knotts watched as Jonah stowed the urn containing his mother's ashes—her "Cremains," the man at the funeral home had called them—into the passenger seat of the car. Perhaps Mr. Knotts knew that Jonah had not given his mother a funeral. Who would have come to it, after all? There were no relatives, no friends. There was no reason to waste money on a casket and a gravestone and all the rest that the undertakers had tried to sell him.

But he couldn't tell this to Mr. Knotts. "Who doesn't deserve a funeral?" Mr. Knotts would wonder, though he wouldn't say it. Mr. Knotts would identify with Jonah's mother, of course. His eyes would grow gloomy and distant as he reflected upon his own funeral, presided over by his weeping children; his own gravesite, kept neat for years and years by his children and then by his grandchildren. He wouldn't speak of it, but the sight of the urn created an awkward space in the air into which all of these feelings rushed and solidified.

"Is that your momma?" Mr. Knotts said gently, and together he and Jonah stared at the urn that had been balanced on the passenger seat.

"Yes," Jonah said. And he wanted to come up with some sort of explanation. He wanted to say that she wanted her ashes sprinkled over some beautiful landmark, like the Grand Canyon, or the Atlantic Ocean. But he couldn't force the lie into his throat.

"Yes," Jonah said. "That's her."

"God bless her," Mr. Knotts said. "Poor woman."

"Yes," Jonah said.

In the weeks and months after he arrived in Chicago, Jonah found that he remembered that moment frequently—the two of them, he and Mr. Knotts, standing there looking at the urn, at his packed car at the end of the long gravel drive that led to the now empty house.

It could have been a nice memory, he thought, a *conclusive* memory: *God bless her, poor woman.*

But then he would also recall the way he'd stopped the car along the side of the road, only a few hours after he'd left Mr. Knotts behind. His heart was beating furiously, and he'd stumbled out of the car with the urn. He'd dumped the contents out into the weeds in the ditch.

Jesus, he'd think, as he sat in the dining nook of his efficiency, as he walked down a busy Chicago street, as he stood in line at a movie theater. Jesus, why had he done that?

He didn't know. Something had come over him, he guessed. A fear, a panic. He had been driving without thinking for a long while, his hands on the steering wheel and his eyes on the white lines on the road, dashes he was feeding into the body of the car like he was playing a video game. And then he had become aware, for the first time, of the music emanating from the radio. It was a wispy, somnambulant rock song, a high-voiced choir of men sighing disconnected phrases: "Time . . . to the sea . . . good-bye my love . . ." and his skin prickled. He was aware of how light-headed he felt.

The sun came out from the dark clouds with a kind of insistence, almost violent. There were stubble fields lined with barbed-wire fences and telephone poles on both sides of him, and he let the car drift slowly, ten miles per hour, on the berm for a while before he stopped. The tires went kathump, kathump against the uneven gravel shoulder and he thought he might be having a heart attack. There was a soft explosion that radiated from just beneath his breastbone, something like the pins-and-needles sensation of stepping down on a foot that has fallen asleep—only inside him, rippling outward. He felt the sensation wash over his eyes, blinding him for a second, his vision clouded by thousands of vibrating pixels, television static, and then the feeling slipped up his forehead to his hair, a scuttling of insects. A low-level buzzing remained with him as he brought the car to a complete stop, edged crookedly onto the side of the road.

He had remembered something that his mother once told him. "When I die, I want you to bury me under the floorboards," she had said. He'd been something like ten or eleven years old at the time, but even then he had known that this was her idea of a joke. "Cut me up in little pieces and put me in the crawl space," she said. "I want to haunt the shit out of whoever lives in this dump after we do." He remembered sitting there in the dark. She was angry because the power was out, and the tip of her cigarette bobbed. Outside, the rain came down in sheets, and the shadow of the rain and the windblown curtains moved on the wall behind her, a shadow like a giant jellyfish, waving its gentle tentacles.

The ashes sluiced out of the urn and onto the ground. Some of the ash drifted smokily in the air and powdered the leaves of the weeds. Jonah stood there, breathing, then carefully put the empty urn down on the ground beside the pile of ash, and it made a hollow, metallic tunk against the earth, like a coffee can. A single sparrow watched him from a telephone wire. He looked around, trying to identify the place—as if he might, in the future, come back here and try to retrieve the ashes. It was completely anonymous. A breeze rustled down a long field of corn, and he remembered his grandfather telling him once that as a boy he used to wake to the sound of the corn growing. "You could actually hear it growing," his grandfather said. "It made a creaking sound, like a rusty hinge." Jonah picked up the urn and waded through the high sunflower and pigweed toward the fence that surrounded the cornfield, walking cautiously in case of rattlesnakes. He put the urn upside down over the nearest fence post, fitting it over the top of the post like a hat.

No one would remove it, he thought. It would still be there, a marker of sorts, if he ever had to come back.

For a while, during those first months in Chicago, Jonah even considered calling Mr. Knotts to tell him about this. He wanted to explain to someone that he *had* to leave, that he *had* to throw everything away. He wanted to tell someone: *I am going to be a new person,* and to have them answer—

Yes.

Yes, of course you are.

Saturday, June 15, 1996

Troy dreams that his child has died, and he wakes up suddenly, suffo-
cating. He wakes because he has stopped breathing. His throat has
closed and he sits up abruptly, making a glottal sound like a dog chok-
ing on a strip of meat. His hands flail for a moment and he sucks in
breath, coughing, disoriented.

It takes him a moment to realize that nothing has happened. This
is his house, the house he has always lived in, and his son is not screaming. It is a morning in early summer. He puts his hand to his face, rubbing it dully. He is on the couch in the living room, where he fell asleep
the night before, still in his jeans and stockinged feet and unbuttoned
white shirt, blinking his eyes under a tent of mid-morning sunlight and
lazily drifting dust motes. The television is going, the sound of Saturday morning cartoons, and Little Man is in fact sitting cross-legged on
the floor eating dry cereal from a box, completely absorbed. Not
screaming. Not dead.

"Shit," Troy says, grimacing, and Little Man turns to look over his
shoulder as Troy clears his throat again. Phlegm.

"'Batman' is on," Little Man says. "It's a new episode. You're missing it."

"Oh, really," Troy says. "Cool." He sits there for a moment, staring slackly at the television as the superheroes and supervillains fight one another. He feels muffled, sluggish, fairly hungover. The long night comes back to him slowly—a party at the tavern where he works as a bartender, the honky-tonk music from the jukebox and the smoke that still clung to his clothes, sitting there drinking with his cousin Ray and some people Ray had just met, a girl from Denver who Troy had kind of liked, who kept covering her mouth with her hand; he remembers spritzing himself with Refreshing Citrus air freshener, trying to disguise the smell of alcohol and marijuana from the teenaged baby-sitter when he came in. He hoped he wasn't too wobbly. He was two hours later than he'd said he'd be, and he knew she was a little irritated as he counted money into her hand—he remembers that much, and then he'd been sitting on the couch after the baby-sitter had left, drinking one last beer and watching a late-night movie, *Vertigo*. He must have simply fallen asleep. He tries to remember. Had Little Man been screaming in the middle of the night? Things have begun to blur together lately: the days, the nightmares, and it takes a moment for the facts of his life to arrange themselves. It is the day after his thirtieth birthday. He is a father, a grown man with responsibilities. His bladder is full, and after a moment he stops casting about for solidifying thoughts and gets up, pads crookedly toward the bathroom.

He feels a little more oriented after he's patted some water onto his face, though he's still a little unnerved. There is something about the dream that lingers. It was as if the dream had been going on for hours before he woke, and it weighs heavily on him, a feeling of grief that weaves its way through his insides as he stares at himself in the mirror. In the dream he had been looking for Little Man, calling for the child through long hallways and rooms full of ominous hums and flutterings, catching glimpses of running shapes. He remembers that in the dream he had stumbled out into the open air. It was the backyard of the house.

This is what Troy recalls most vividly: the small backyard of the house, with its patch of grass, a curled garden hose, a child's shoe near the trunk of the old elm tree. There was a yawning roar of an airplane, a shadow pulling across the ground, and when Troy looked up, startled, he saw that Little Man was sitting at the very top of the old elm tree, perched in the netting of bare boughs. Little Man was crouched on his haunches with his arms around his knees, his feet resting on a thin, quivering branch barely strong enough for a bird. Yet somehow Little Man balanced on it. Somehow, impossibly, it held Little Man's weight, and the child's silhouette hung precariously balanced at the top of the tree. He would fall, Troy knew. Troy could sense that Little Man was already falling even as he tried to run, holding his arms out. Little Man was already plunging through the air, the thin branches snapping and whipping as his son plummeted. There was that awful sound that Little Man was making, a high, fading wail, a falling-scream, a death-scream, which now Troy has in his head and can't shake.

"Shit," Troy says. He gathers up some of the dirty laundry that is spilling out of the overflowing hamper behind the bathroom door and tries to stuff it in. Too full. He puts his foot inside the hamper and steps down hard, compressing, packing it in tighter, so there is enough room to close the lid. He stands there, frowning at it, and his face feels pale and cold with sweat.

He would like to think that things have been going well. He wants to be a good father, that's the thing, even though he doesn't always succeed. Little Man has been living with him for about three months now, and Troy tries not to think of the potential mistakes he's making. It's mostly good, he tells himself. It's mostly happy. They fit together, he thinks, not only as father and son but also as companions. Troy and Little Man, Little Man and Troy.

And really, despite his occasional bad dreams, despite his occasional fuckups and inappropriate behavior, he believes that single fatherhood has come pretty easily to him. Little Man is a quiet, uncomplaining child, and he doesn't seem overly traumatized to be separated from his mother, though of course the child misses her, thinks about her often. "When is Carla supposed to call?" he asks Troy, and "Do you think Carla will come see us this summer?" and he nods grimly when Troy says, "I don't know." He seems to understand, and Troy loves him for that. Troy loves the boy's stern expression, his deep-set, observant eyes,

his oddly upright posture. He loves the way Little Man takes things seriously, the way he will sit on the edge of a creek holding a fishing pole,
watching the motionless bobber floating in the water with a sharp gaze,
seemingly impervious to boredom, the way he appears to enjoy road
trips, out to look at cows and horses, his face turned attentively to
steadily passing fields and telephone poles and weed-filled ditches. He
loves the way Little Man will tell the waitress his order when they eat at
the old truck stop out at the interstate oasis, the way he will hold the
menu and pick out words he recognizes, like "egg" and "ham." He
loves the silent clutch of Little Man's arms as they ride Troy's motorcycle down the thin, rutted cowpath trails that run through the hills
north of town, the way Little Man presses his helmeted head against
Troy's back. It is even fun to go shopping for groceries, Little Man
pushing the cart proudly, despite the fact that it's taller than he is. Troy
taking various items off the shelves and holding them up for Little
Man's approval, juggling the boxes of macaroni and cheese in the aisle
or menacing Little Man with a package of plastic wrapped tripe from
the meat section. "Hey, Little Man, how about some of this stuff?" and
Little Man frowning thoughtfully, saying, "Dad, I don't think so!"

———

Little Man's real name is Loomis. Troy had been in favor of the name
when the child was born—his ex-wife, Carla, had come up with it, and
Troy had thought it was unusual and rugged-sounding, a cowboy
name, which was cool. The second choice was Marley, after Bob Marley, the reggae singer. That had been Troy's suggestion, and Carla had
said that she thought Marley would sound better on a girl.

But ultimately, Loomis did not seem to stick, not in Troy's mind at
least, and he liked it even less when Carla called the boy "Loomy,"
which for some reason conjured up the image of a slouching, drooling
ogre, with one eye bigger than the other. *Loomy*. They had argued about
it a little.

"Just don't call him 'Little Man,'" she said irritably. "You're going
to give him a complex," and he had frowned at her bossy, judgmental
tone of voice. "Why do you have to give everybody a nickname, anyway?" she continued. "It's like, you can't wait to get your hands on people's identities and mold them so you feel superior. I mean, it's like you

calling me 'Shorty' all the time, and now he's got to be 'Little Man.' So it's like, what are you? Some sort of giant? Are we supposed to call you *Big Man? Tall Troy?* How about *Humongous?* Maybe we should call you *Humongous.*"

He hadn't said anything. She seemed very hyper—cocaine, he thought, or crank—something like that, where you thought you were clever and your mind seemed sharp and taut as a guitar string. He hadn't wanted an argument, he hadn't wanted to say anything to make her change her mind.

The two of them were sitting in her kitchen, in her apartment, in Las Vegas. Little Man was in the next room, watching television, and her boyfriend, the one she was fucking now—there had been several since they had separated—was out somewhere. Troy didn't ask. The two of them sat at the table and drank coffee and stared out at a tiny desert yard filled with hard gray earth and scattered with dog turds. The cabinets in the kitchen were white, with gold edges around the molding; a gold-painted cupid statue sat on the table, presiding over a bowl of plastic fruit.

After almost a year of being gone, she had called him in the middle of the night. "Listen," she said, and her voice was heavily slurred. "I'm wondering if you could drive out here and pick up Loomis." She had paused, and he could imagine her trying to compose herself, her tongue working thickly. "This is not the right place for a kid," she said. "I was thinking about what you said. About custody and stuff."

"Yeah?" Troy said. "What are you saying?"

"I'm just wondering—don't be an asshole about this—but I'm thinking about whether you were willing to come and get him. Keep him for a few months. Maybe a year. Things are sort of . . . don't start in on me, Troy, but things are not so good here. I think he'd be better off with you." This was about four in the morning, and Troy had the vague idea that maybe everything would change, that eventually Carla and he would get back together, that after a while she'd come back to Nebraska and they'd become a family again, the mess they'd made of their marriage forgotten.

He even imagined this as he sat in her Las Vegas kitchen, as she stared at him grimly, her pupils swelling almost to the edge of her irises, so that it was hard to recall that her eyes were blue. "Look," she said, "if you're going to take him, you can't be dealing anymore. Not even pot, okay? He's a good kid, you know? And one of us has to try to . . . not fuck up, you know?"

"I'm not dealing," he said, which was mostly true. "I'm not even hardly smoking myself," he said, which was not. She laughed.

"Oh, for God's sake, Troy," she said. "Don't lie. You should see your eyes. They're like fucking bloodshot balloons. I wouldn't have even called you if I thought there was any other choice."

Troy thinks of this again, as he and Little Man walk along the dirt road beyond the house, the house that sits at the north edge of the town of St. Bonaventure, the road that leads up into the gray sod-covered hills. They are looking for fossils, which Little Man is very interested in, and Troy bends down to pick up a flat rock, imagining that it will be imprinted with the skeleton of a leaf or a fish, a trilobite. Troy has vague knowledge: At some point in the distant past, this dry plain was covered by a sea, thousands of miles across. Little Man is five years old, and they hold hands as they walk.

"You know what I'm wondering?" Little Man says. "If there was a sea here, what was the name of the sea? And also, were there sharks in it? Was it salt water or fresh water?"

"Hm," says Troy. It sometimes worries him that Little Man will become a genius. And then what will happen? He remembers how Carla used to tease him, when he would sit cross-legged on the living room floor, playing Nintendo with Little Man. "You know, Troy, in a few years he's going to be more mature than you are, and then what are you going to do?" He had grinned at her at the time, but now, remembering the comment, he feels grim.

"Let's see," he says. "I guess that it was probably fresh water, because, you know, there was the Ice Age, and all that? And then it sort of melted and evaporated, and all that was left was the Great Lakes, which are up by Chicago and so on." He thinks for a moment. He doesn't want to end up having the boy think he's an idiot. "Maybe we should go to the library and look it up."

"Okay," Little Man says.

"Do you want to ride on my shoulders?" Troy says. "Are your legs tired?"

And Little Man shrugs. "I wouldn't mind riding on your shoulders," he says, very politic, very formal and dignified as Troy lifts him.

"Uff," Troy says. "Either you're getting heavy or I'm getting old. I turned thirty yesterday, you know. I won't be able to carry you much longer."

"I weigh forty-two pounds," Little Man says, and hooks his heels into Troy's armpits like a jockey gently nudging a horse. "Happy Birthday, Dad," he says.

He's happy, sure. They're both happy, he and Little Man, the two of them together, and Troy knows he should be grateful for that. "Why do you worry about this shit so much?" Troy's cousin Ray asked him recently. "All you do lately is worry, and there's not any point to it."

And when Troy shrugged, Ray gestured expansively at Little Man. "Look at him, Troy. He's content, he's healthy, he's like a midget Einstein in our midst. What more do you want?"

"I don't know," Troy said. The two of them were sitting in the grass at the edge of the park, watching Little Man at play, cautiously passing a joint back and forth. Troy was more paranoid than he used to be, very careful now to pass the joint underhanded, thumb and forefinger, taking a quick hit and just as quickly lowering it. He didn't know why he should feel so uncomfortable. There weren't any other people around, and Little Man was fully focused on the slide he was working out on. Troy watched as Little Man climbed the ladder to the top and sat, hands folded solemnly in his lap, slipping down the metal pathway with the grim, determined expression of an accelerating race car driver. When he reached the bottom, he ran back to the ladder again. He didn't seem to tire of it.

"I need to start thinking about changing jobs," Troy said. "You know? I don't want to be a bartender forever. Besides which, it's a bitch trying to line up people who are going to sit for Little Man until I get off at two or three in the morning. You know, he's going to start school in the fall, and then what am I going to do?"

"Mmmm," Ray said, as if he were trying to sound thoughtful. He drew deeply on the joint and held the smoke in his lungs for a count. He tapped his chest with his palm, one . . . two . . . three . . . four . . . and then exhaled in a stream, his eyes watery and red-rimmed. "Shhhit," he said hoarsely. "What kind of a job are you talking about? Doctor? Lawyer? Senator?"

"Don't be a jerk," Troy said mildly. He was not in the mood for the teasing, affectionately insulting banter that usually passed for conversation when he and Ray were together. "Look," he said. "I'm serious. I thought about maybe going to college somewhere—or a technical school or something. I saw this one thing on TV where you can get a degree in, like, commercial art through correspondence courses."

"What's 'commercial art'?" Ray said, and the way he pronounced it made Troy wish that he hadn't brought it up. Ray was not really the sort of person to talk about making any kind of change. At twenty-three, Ray still spoke grudgingly about high school friends who had gone away to college and never come back. He still had a prescription for Ritalin, which had been prescribed for him when he was a hyper eight-year-old, and which he continued to take faithfully, believing that it helped him concentrate. To Troy, it wasn't clear why such concentration was necessary. Ray worked for the county Department of Roads as a laborer, and moonlighted occasionally for a company that contracted male strippers for bachelorette and birthday parties. It was a great way to meet women and get laid, Ray claimed, and besides smoking pot, his only other interest was working out with weights, an activity that was apparently greatly enhanced by Ritalin. "Commercial art," Ray said again, as if it was a French phrase. "What do you do? Draw pictures for commercials? It seems like you'd have to go to New York or something to get a job."

"I don't really know," Troy said. "It was just a thought." And he listened to the sound of birds in the bushes around them. He didn't feel like being disheartened, which was Ray's general mode of looking at the world, and so he simply shrugged. What else was there to say? He was embarrassed to be thirty years old and still without any clear sense of what most people did for a living. He'd seen a girl he'd known in high school at the grocery store not too long before—she was back in St. Bonaventure visiting her parents, she told him, she was working as an actuary at a company in Omaha.

"Actuary, huh?" he'd said, smiling and nodding. "That sounds interesting." Later, he'd had to go home and look it up in the dictionary.

Which was why the commercial he'd seen had caught his attention. "Tired of being stuck in the same old rut?" the announcer had asked, as on-screen a bedraggled waitress cleared a table of dirty plates with a depressed look on her face. "The Career Learning Center wants to help you discover new opportunities and actualize your potential!" The waitress then looked hopeful as a list of the many degrees you could get scrolled over the screen—computers, drafting, accounting, business. Commercial art was the one that stuck in his mind because art had been his only decent subject in high school. He could still draw fairly well—like the series of dinosaur skeletons he had drawn for Little Man on poster board and pasted on the wall above the child's bed. They were pretty good, he thought, pretty accurate. Even Ray had said so.

"I don't know," Troy said at last. "That was just one idea." Ray had stretched out on the grass and was staring up at the clouds. "It's just like, well, I feel like I need to get my act together. Maybe it's turning thirty."

"Word," said Ray, who sometimes used the slang of the rap musicians he listened to, aping their accents.

"You know what I ought to do?" Troy said. He watched as Little Man ran determinedly from the bottom of the slide back to the ladder again, still intent for the, what?, the twentieth time? Fiftieth? Troy sighed. "I ought to quit smoking pot all the time. And definitely quit dealing the shit."

"Oh, man," Ray said, sleepily. "Come on. What are you talking about? You're not a 'drug dealer.' I mean, how many people do you sell to? Like, twelve or something?"

"More than that."

"Yeah, well," Ray said. "That's stupid. It's not like you're some sort of Al Pacino *Scarface* cutting people's heads off with buzz saws and being evil, you know? I mean, come on. You're *you*. You can't change everything just because you have a birthday and you got a kid hanging out with you. Look, everybody loves you the way you are. Everybody's like, 'That's Troy, he's the man, we love him,' and you're going to be like, 'No, guys, I'm going to be all different now because I turned thirty and I'm having a crisis.' What the fuck is that? That doesn't make any sense."

"Mmm-hmm," Troy said. "Well, if you think everybody loves Troy, you should talk to Carla's mom."

"She's a bitch," Ray said, and stared up at the sky for a while longer before resting his thick, worker-brown hand over his eyes. "You should stay away from her. No way hanging with her is any good for Little Man."

Troy looked at him wryly. "So, what?" he said. "Can you watch him on Saturday night while I'm at work?" And he watched as Ray's slack expression tightened.

"Oh," Ray said. He sat up. "I would, but . . . I think I got a deal that night. Bachelorette party out in Greeley."

They looked at each other. "That's what I'm saying," Troy said. "I'm not so crazy about dealing with Carla's mom either, you know? But she can watch him. She wants to watch him. And I can't find anyone else to do it. That's what I'm saying. I need to make some changes if I'm going to have a kid around." After a moment, he stood up, brushing the grass off the back of his pants. From the top of the slide, Loomis gazed at him and waved, and he waved back.

"You know what," Ray said. "You need to get hooked up with a new woman. *That* is what you need. You don't need a new career. You just need a new squeeze."

"I don't think so," Troy said. He felt strangely heavy, thinking of Carla again, thinking of the old times at Bruce and Michelle's place. Great times. Ray's father, Bruce, was still in prison, serving a sentence for distribution of cocaine, and his mother, Michelle, was in Arizona now, living with an elderly real estate millionaire named Merit Wilkins. In some ways, Ray was still his responsibility, just as he had been back in the long-ago times when Troy used to baby-sit. Just as he had been when Bruce went to jail and Michelle had started dating various old men. During his high school years, Ray had mostly lived with Troy and Carla, crashing on their couch—had more or less become their ward, and maybe still was. That was what this conversation was really about, Troy thought. *Don't leave me,* was what Ray was basically saying, and Troy felt Ray's eyes upon him as he stood up.

"Loomis!" Troy called. "We're getting ready to go!"

He thinks of all this as he drives toward Carla's mom's house with Little Man sitting calmly and silently in the back of the old secondhand Corvette that Troy had once been so excited about but which now suffers from serious health problems. He has to rev the engine at the stoplight to keep it from dying. Maybe something is wrong with the fuel pump. He hears the engine rasping, sputtering like a lung full of bile. He feels guilty and uncertain.

He's making a mistake, probably. Every time he drops Little Man off at Carla's mom's house, he thinks: Of all the ways in which he is probably screwing up as a father this may in fact be the worst. He crosses under the viaduct on Old Oak, turns left on Main toward the park, and turns again into the series of narrow winding streets—Meadow Lane and Sunnyvale, Linden and Foxglove, a little neighborhood on the far end of the park made up of small, pretty, boxy houses, all from the forties and fifties, all nearly identical, and which, when he'd first started dating Carla, he'd thought of as fancy. Sometimes he thinks that he should just turn around and go home, call in sick at work, forget about dropping Little Man off, make some other arrangement. He will see the little white house, with its red trim and shaded windows, with its neat lawn and sidewalk lined with dark petunias, and a stone will sink inside of him.

When he'd left Las Vegas with Little Man, this had been one of Carla's stipulations: "Just don't let him stay with my mom," she'd said. She'd looked at him fiercely. "You know, the minute she hears that Loomis is back in town, she's going to call you up, and she's going to be very nice, and she's going to make you an offer. Just do me a favor. Don't let him anywhere near her. You know what she's like. She can hardly wait to get her hands on him."

As far as he knew, Carla and her mother, Judy, had always hated each other. "Cunt," Carla said when they'd first started dating, when Troy was eighteen and Carla was twenty-four, and Troy had been scandalized that someone would use such a word to describe their own mother. "She's poison," Carla had said. "I don't want to have her anywhere near me!" He learned that Judy had once had Carla committed to a mental institution, that Judy believed Carla had a mental disorder:

borderline personality. And when he and Carla got married, it was a long time before Carla told her mother, arguing vehemently over the phone.

"I wouldn't mind if she were dead," Carla said, and he'd been shocked, just as he'd been shocked when Carla threw away the congratulatory card that Judy sent when Loomis was born; just as he'd been surprised when Judy had called him a "druggie little leech." Just as he'd been awkward when Judy called him to say that she could watch Little Man.

But as for Little Man, he has never complained. That's one thing. In fact, Little Man seems to like his time with Grandmom, and he seems unfazed when Troy drops him off at Judy's house. He runs down the front sidewalk and into the small one-story house, skirting around Judy as she stands on the front stoop with her arms folded over her chest. "Howdy," Troy calls to her, and she lifts her chin slightly in greeting. She is fat but not soft, a little bit over sixty years old, with short silvery-blond hair and leathery skin, bludgeon-thick arms and hands. She has the look of a woman who labors in the fields, in the sun, an old farm woman, though in fact she is a retired elementary school teacher—her look comes not so much from hard work as from relentless bitterness and anger. She squints at him and wrinkles spread out in judgmental rays from the edge of her eyes.

"Hello, Troy," she says, coolly and cordially, and Troy pauses several yards in front of her. Little Man is already inside the house, probably already perched in front of the television, setting up the Nintindo game that they'd decided to leave at Grandmom's house so he had something to do while he was there. Troy hesitates; he had meant to say good-bye to Little Man before he went off to work, but now it's awkward. Judy makes a point of not inviting him into the house.

And so now he just stands there for a moment. "So," he says, as Judy regards him. "Well," he says. "I guess I'll just pick him up in the morning as usual. Around ten or so." He makes a vague gesture with his open palms, but Judy's expression doesn't change.

"Yes," she says. "That sounds fine. I'll expect you."

"Okay," he says, and tries to smile. He clears his throat. Of all the things that he didn't expect from the world, this one perhaps surprises him the most. He has never been prepared to be hated, and maybe this is why he keeps coming back, this is why he smiles at her and offers Loomis up to her three times a week. He can't believe that she'll continue to dislike him forever, and standing there he wants to tell her about his plans for the future, about Commercial Art. He wants to say that he's changing his life. He wants to say that he had a terrible dream, he wants to tell her about Loomis at the top of the tree, getting ready to fall.

But he doesn't. He only clears his throat, politely, hoping that she's disliking him a little less than she did the last time he was standing in front of her. "Loomis!" he calls, vaguely, into the quiet of the house behind her. "I'm headed out, buddy! I'll see you in the morning!"

He shrugs as she stands there, her arms still folded.

"Okay, then," he murmurs.

7

Jonah was better off in Chicago, he thought, better off than he would have been in South Dakota. This was what he told Steve and Holiday, when they had him over for dinner. "Much better off," he said, and he meant it, even though he had been lonely much of the time since he'd arrived. He did not want them to know that he didn't make friends easily, that he had spent much of the past year alone with his own mind, thinking. He didn't want to say that his life in the city so far had been more or less a void.

What did he do with himself? Well . . . He went to the movies a lot, sat at the very rear so he could feel the wall against his back. He watched many movies, film after unmemorable film, tracing the lines on his palm with his fingernail while various banalities played on the screen. He reheated carryout Chinese food in the kitchenette microwave, read various novels—Dickens, Tolstoy, Camus—while spooning up rubbery black mushrooms and tofu from his hot-and-sour soup; he sometimes drank beer at a bar where an extremely intoxicated woman once leaned herself against him and whispered, "Tell me something about yourself." He soaked in the small, efficient bathtub, curled into a space a little larger than a child's coffin—his knees up, filling and refilling it until the hot water was depleted.

He knew this was not what Steve and Holiday wanted to hear. They were a nice young couple, about his own age, spacey with bliss. Holiday had just had a baby, and they were both very excited and proud. Even though they'd had to drop out of college (they were both trying to take classes part-time); even though they seemingly had no more prospects for the future than Jonah did (Steve worked as a waiter at Bruzzone's, where Jonah also worked, but he wanted to be a filmmaker); even though it seemed to Jonah that having a baby would make their lives stressful and difficult—their faces shone with optimism.

So Jonah tried to think of positive things, too. There *were* positive things he could talk about, after all, and he had them all listed in his head as he got off the el train and walked the several blocks to Steve and Holiday's apartment. Good things, he thought. He liked his concise little apartment, and his job as a line cook at Bruzzone's. Boring, but okay. He could mention that he'd begun to take college classes—he registered for them at least, though he didn't always make it very far into the semester before he quit going—Composition 101, The Philosophy of Science, Introduction to Communication Studies. He could legitimately say that he'd sooner or later have a college degree; an associate's degree, at least, anyway. "It's a start," he could say, and shrug. He could tell them that he was saving money, that he was paying his bills ahead of time to develop a good credit rating. He *did* have some ideas about the future: trying to get some decent plastic surgery, for one, he could say. Thinking about different careers. Some kind of normal life: getting married, buying a house. Having kids maybe?

He had these talking points planned out in his mind, but when they were actually sitting there he couldn't bring himself to speak them. They didn't seem like very convincing subjects, really, and he didn't want them to get into the depressing fact that he frequently doubted the possibility of even these simple things. He didn't want them to know that they were the only people he'd had a real conversation with in almost a year. Eventually, he ended up doing imitations of Mrs. Marina Orlova, with her hatred of smiling Americans. He showed them how she grimaced like a chimpanzee and tried out a version of Mrs. Orlova's voice: "I smile at you! Eee! It is repulsive." They laughed and laughed, and Holiday said, "Jonah, why are you so shy? You're blushing. You're so hilarious."

———

Jonah had noticed Steve before Steve noticed him. He had gotten into the habit of watching other people whom he imagined to be about his own age, just because he was curious. He wanted to know what he should be like. He would walk behind a trim young executive, observing the short haircut, the dark blue squared-off suit and bright red tie, the brisk, purposeful stride; he would linger in a music store to examine a sloe-eyed employee, with pierced nose and tattooed forearms, an attitude of bored, pouting superiority; he would follow two grinning sailors in their anachronistic uniforms, stumbling and laughing loudly as they emerged from a bar. For a moment, he could almost imagine himself into another life. He could exist for a second inside of these people—a flash in which his own skin sloughed off and he turned down a different path, as if he could pass through the membrane of their bodies and suddenly find himself looking out through their eyes.

At first, Steve had just been another vessel he could project himself into. Steve was a waiter—one of those distant, vague figures who moved in and out of the kitchen; a blond, round-faced person with a charmingly earnest demeanor that Jonah vaguely associated with teen idols of the 1970s. There was a way that Steve would widen his eyes and say "Wow!" that seemed to Jonah particularly notable. He tried it out when he got home from work, standing in front of the bathroom mirror. "Wow," he said, and put on an imitation of the sleepy, knowing smile that Steve used. "Cool," Jonah said, in the odd way that Steve did, so that it sounded like: "Coo-el." He and Steve would look very much alike, he thought, if it weren't for the scars. They both had a similar type of straight, blondish-brown hair, a similar round-cheeked boyishness in the face. They were even about the same height—a little under six feet—though Steve's body was better constructed, all smooth lines, like a swimmer. Jonah's own body was more angular, odder—pale-skinned, reddish at the hands and foot soles; broad shoulders and chest and ropy muscled arms, which led to a round, slightly plump belly, and then to narrow legs and long-toed, nobby feet. He was like three different bodies grafted onto one person, he thought, though he also was aware that posture made a difference. He tended to hunch and to let his belly stick out, and if he straightened up and sucked in his gut he looked better. He tried his version of Steve's smile again, looking at himself in the mirror from first one angle, then another, covering up the scar on his face with his hand. *Not bad,* he thought. *Really. Not bad.*

Steve was more present in the kitchen than most of the waitstaff. Mostly, the waiters and waitresses would rush in and out—they would thrust pieces of paper at the cooks, scribbles of food requests, cry "Order!," and then hurry away. And Jonah was even more peripheral than the other cooks—mostly, he was in a corner at a cutting board, chopping mushrooms or celery or carrots, the tips of his fingers at the very edge of the rapid movement of the knife in his other hand.

But Steve had noticed Jonah. Steve was always coming in to chat up the heavyset black woman, Ramona, and the older Mexican man, Alphonso, the two main cooks. Steve would tell them about his pregnant wife, keeping them abreast of the developments, saying "Wow," and "Cool!" to them, and then he brought in photos of the baby's birth, which he passed around in the late afternoon, when the lunch crowd had cleared out and the work had lulled. He was grinning, very pleased with himself, and he gave people cigars as a kind of joke. Even the women.

Jonah watched him with cautious interest. He admired Steve's ease with people, the genial, natural way he would flirt with Ramona, or tell a joke (in Spanish!) to Alphonso, both of them laughing deeply, their eyes narrowed slyly. But it was disconcerting, too, because Steve kept catching Jonah's eye, noticing Jonah's staring before Jonah could drop his gaze. On the day he brought in photos of the newborn, he'd looked directly at Jonah all of a sudden.

"Hey, man," Steve said. "Do you want to see?"

Jonah shrugged awkwardly. "Sure," he said, and Steve came around the divider and passed a few pictures into Jonah's latex-gloved hands. In one photo, a bloody infant, with a body like a skinned squirrel, opened its wide mouth and scrunched its eyes; in another, the infant, now swaddled in a blue blanket, was pressed against the bare breast of an exhausted girl in a hospital gown.

"That's Henry," Steve said. "That's my son!"

"Huh," Jonah said, uncertainly. "Nice."

Steve grinned and extended his hand. "I'm Steve," he said. "I see you looking sometimes, but we never connect."

Jonah started to insert his slick, latex-covered hand into Steve's palm, and then realized how rude and odd it was. "Oh, sorry," Jonah said, and he took off his glove, wiping his damp palm on his shirt.

"I'm Jonah," Jonah said. He felt very self-conscious. *I see you looking at me sometimes,* he thought, and he wasn't sure what else to say. He'd thought his watching of Steve had been quite subtle.

But Steve didn't seem upset about it. "Hi, Jonah," he said. "Nice name."

"Thanks," Jonah said, and he gave Steve the grin he had been practicing, before he realized that Steve might recognize it as an imitation. He looked down at the pictures again, at the wife's expression of wonder as she held the infant—Henry—her face wan and shell-shocked and yet, Jonah thought, quite beautiful. He was embarrassed that he could see her breast, even though the infant's mouth was covering the nipple. "These are nice, really nice pictures," he said, holding the photos out for Steve to take back.

"I've been meaning to introduce myself," Steve said. "I always see you looking over at me, and I'm thinking, 'Wow, I must be getting on that guy's nerves!' You know, coming in here and talking to everybody and kind of like, not talking to you. I must've seemed annoying!"

"Oh," Jonah said. "No, no. Not at all. I didn't mean to . . . give the impression that I was annoyed." He smiled again, and made an effort to look Steve in the eye. "It's probably something about my face. I think my expressions are weird." He cleared his throat, wincing inwardly. Why did he feel the urge to draw attention to his face? It was no wonder he didn't make friends, he thought. He was always making people uncomfortable.

"Actually," he said, "I was just noticing you because you look a lot like someone I know." He didn't know what he was doing, except that he felt the urge to explain his staring. And then, for no reason he could figure out, he said: "You look almost exactly like my brother."

"Oh, really?" Steve said.

"Well," Jonah said. "He's dead now. He was killed in a car accident. But you . . . you look almost exactly like him. I'm sorry for staring."

Steve's eyes widened, and he took the photos Jonah was trying to return to him. "Geez," Steve said. "Wow! How weird!"

"Yeah," Jonah said. "I'm sorry, I didn't mean to say that."

Afterward he was terribly flustered. Why had he said such a thing? He paced his apartment, moving from the kitchen to the bathroom's medicine cabinet mirror; he stood at the window looking down at the empty street, the traffic light at the end of the block blinking yellow in soft breathing beats. It was a very freakish thing to do, he thought, and he sat down on the fold-out sofa and tapped his forehead with the knuckles of his fist, staring grimly down at the carpet. *You look exactly like my dead brother,* he thought. How ridiculous.

But the lie had come to him almost supernaturally, like a premonition, that was the thing. Lies often did. He could actually picture the brother who looked like Steve. He experienced the car accident, a slow-motion slide into a semi-truck on a slick interstate, he pictured the way his brother would throw up his arms in front of his face as the seat in front of him loomed and turned into a thundercloud, an onrushing darkness. He heard his brother's final gasp, which was strangely delicate. "Ah," his brother breathed, and then everything went dark. The whole thing had burst forth with such vividness that it had almost seemed real. He thought of the fairy tale in which one sister is blessed to cough up diamonds, while the other is cursed to spit out toads— that's what it felt like.

Whether this was a diamond or a toad, he wasn't sure. The truth was, the lie had effected exactly what he wanted it to. It had established a connection between them, a bond, and suddenly Steve was interested in becoming his friend. Steve was pleased in some way, flattered that he looked exactly like the brother who had died.

Steve told Holiday about Jonah. Jonah was invited to dinner at their house.

He had been thinking a lot about relatives lately, that was one thing. About the baby his mother had given up for adoption, about his father, who was still out there somewhere, presumably. About his mother and grandfather and Elizabeth. There were times when he thought that his past was more present now than it was when he was living it. He had not kept a single photograph or memento, but memories would constantly float up and create a scrim over his daily life.

He had been thinking about his father, for example. His mother had always been very coy about this—many times she had told him that she didn't know who his father was, and it had always been awkward to ask, since more often than not even a vague hint in that direction would send her into an irrecoverable mood.

"Why do you do this to me?" she would say. "It doesn't matter. Whoever it is, he doesn't care about you anyway. He doesn't even know you exist!" And her teeth would clench together. *"Jesus Christ!"* she would murmur to herself, the plaits of her long hair pulling dully across the surface of the table as she lowered her head.

His grandfather had been more sympathetic. "Son, you know I would tell you if I knew anything about it," his grandfather had said. Jonah had been about twelve then, and had finally gotten up the nerve to speak to his grandfather in private. They sat together, in lawn chairs out behind the house, and his grandfather took a long drink of beer. "I think," his grandfather said carefully, "that it wasn't someone she knew real well. She was living out in Chicago at the time, and I imagine that he was from there, but I really couldn't say."

Not long afterward, on a Saturday, his grandfather had driven him over to the Pine Ridge Reservation, to visit some of Jonah's grandmother's relations. There was Jonah's grandmother's sister, Leona, an enormously fat Sioux woman who stood aside grimly as Jonah and his grandfather sheepishly entered her house. The living room had a cement floor with a thin, faded red rug on it, and they sat there on an old sofa that was draped with an old bedspread, his grandfather and his great aunt Leona smoking cigarettes and saying little. She told them a story about a rattlesnake that had gotten in the window, trapped between the pane and the screen, and how they'd killed it. Some boys who were identified as Jonah's cousins came in to look at them, bronze-skinned, dusty kids, two plump and one narrow, and then they left, ran outside to play, and Jonah didn't follow. He sat there, with his hand across the side of his face, while his aunt observed him heavily. Jonah didn't know why they had never gone back, and when he had asked his mother once she had only shrugged. "That's just what you need," she said, glaring at him. "Go loiter around that dirty Indian reservation. Aren't you close enough to the bottom as it is?" And that, as far as she was concerned, was the end of the discussion.

Jonah's mother *would* talk about his brother sometimes—the baby she had given up for adoption when she was in high school. She would joke sometimes about it. Whenever she saw a lady with an infant, she would say, "Oh, look, there's my baby!" and she would smile at Jonah, as if they were sharing a bitter joke. After Jonah's grandfather died, when she started taking drugs more and more, she would occasionally grow sentimental.

"Don't you wish I'd given you up, Jonah?" she would say, full of slurry self-pity, in a haze of her own angry thoughts. "I'll bet he's a lot happier than you are."

Jonah, a teenager by then, thought about how to respond to this. He sat at the kitchen table considering, watching as his mother's head dipped abruptly, as if her neck muscles suddenly gave out and then recovered. "It doesn't matter," his mother said, and caught her hair in her hands and gave it a sharp tug, testing the strength of her scalp. "Don't even listen to me, just . . . go play somewhere." And she waved her hand vaguely, as if shooing Jonah off toward some carefree existence she imagined he lived. Jonah sat frowning at her. Hating her. Of course he'd have been happier if she'd given him away, he thought, but that wasn't even the point. The point of her obsession, he thought, the reason she kept going over and over it in her mind, was that *she'd* be happier. Her life could have been different, that was the point of everything: the axle around which the dull wheel of their life had turned for as long as he could remember.

He wished he could tell someone these stories. He could imagine telling them to Steve and Holiday at some point, for example, though the lie he had told would make that enormously complicated. He would have to insert the imaginary brother who looked like Steve into the fabric of his past, somehow, in the way that special effects were added to films; he would have to alter or modify certain stories to include his imaginary brother in the action, or at least to explain his absence from the scene.

He thought of this as he sat at the dining table in Steve and Holiday's apartment, but he discreetly avoided mentioning the dead brother again, whose name (he had decided, just in case they asked) was David. "I was glad to get out of South Dakota," he said. They were eating linguine and drinking red wine, Chianti, Steve told him. As he spoke, Holiday leaned her hand against her cheek and smiled, her eyes warm and attentive, as if he were dear to her. "I wanted to . . . find a place with more opportunities. I thought about Omaha, you know, because that's not so far away from Little Bow, but Chicago just seemed, well, more exciting. Sort of like going to New York, but not so . . . scary." And both Steve and Holiday nodded. They were both from Wisconsin, so he guessed they had some idea of what he meant.

"It was brave of you, to set out like that on your own," Holiday said. "Don't you think so, Pie?" she said—she called Steve "Pie" as an endearment—and Steve raised his eyebrows and nodded.

"Absolutely," Steve said. "You'd never been to a city or anything before?"

"Not exactly," Jonah said. "My mother and I lived in Chicago and Denver when I was really little, but I don't really remember it."

"Does your mother still live in South Dakota?" Holiday said.

"Not exactly," Jonah said. He took a small sip of red wine, blushing a little. "She's dead, actually."

"Oh," Holiday said. "I'm so sorry."

"That's okay," Jonah said. He shrugged, feeling himself blushing again. "I'm not . . ." he said, "I'm not sensitive about it."

But there was a respectful silence. There was an awareness that Jonah had experienced tragedy that Steve and Holiday had not, and the two of them looked at him thoughtfully. His brother's name was David, Jonah thought. Maybe his mother had been killed in the same car accident in which David had perished?

They talked about things like movies—which was great, which was fine. One of the things that Jonah had purchased with his newfound wealth was a VCR, and so he had seen both *Carnival of Souls* ("Brilliant!" said Steve) and *Choose Me* ("Highly underrated," said Holiday). Steve talked about the script that he was working on, which was based upon a children's book called *Louis the Fish*, a book Steve had loved as a child and which he thought was a "work of genius."

"It's not going to be a film for children," Steve said. "There are a lot of adult themes that I want to stress. It's going to be kind of surreal and disturbing, but not inaccessible." And when Jonah admitted that he hadn't read or heard of the book, Steve exclaimed enthusiastically, "Jesus, Jonah! You won't believe how incredible it is! I have to give you a copy!" He got up to look for an extra copy of the book, and as he did he gave Holiday a kiss on the side of her face.

"Four hundred and fifty-five!" he exclaimed. He told Jonah that he wanted to give Holiday one thousand kisses before the end of the week, and so he was counting.

Jonah laughed. They were funny together, Steve and Holiday. Delightful. Sometime later, he would realize that they were the kind of people who were at their best when they had an audience. They were happiest when they had someone they could dote on, someone who in turn could bear witness to the way they were in love.

It was not a role he minded playing, of course. Maybe they were interested in him because he had a dead brother, because he had ugly scars and a shy demeanor, a whiff of tragedy. When they talked about other friends, he got a sense of it: Allison, who had been homeless for a while and who was struggling to stay off drugs; Javier, an illegal immigrant from El Salvador who had worked at the restaurant for a time before Jonah got there; Dallas, the bartender they knew who had been divorced twice and hadn't even turned thirty, who once stayed with them for almost a month after his wife kicked him out, sleeping on their couch and rotating through the same three changes of clothing. Listening to the anecdotes they told of these friends, Jonah could imagine himself becoming part of this menagerie, another stray they'd brought home and loved for a while. But he didn't care. All that really mattered to Jonah was that they were interested in him, and their interest—their focused, smiling attention—was wonderful.

After dinner, Jonah and Steve cleared the table and washed the dishes while Holiday sat at the kitchen table, nursing baby Henry. Holiday was a small-boned girl, with short, dark hair and a long face and nose, but her breasts were enormous for such a thin figure. *Of course,* Jonah thought. *They're full of milk.* But he made a conscious effort not to look over at her as she sat, with her blouse lifted. He was drying the dishes, and the first couple of times that Steve handed him a rinsed plate he stupidly said "Thank you!" as if he were being given a gift. Steve and Holiday both thought this was very funny and made a little joke of it: "Here, Jonah. A colander for you!" And Jonah played along. "Thank you so much," he said. "I really appreciate it." In a clownish mood, he did his imitation of Mrs. Orlova for them, and they laughed once again.

"You should be an actor, Jonah," she said. "Have you ever thought about it?"

"Not really," Jonah said. "Not with—" He started to say "Not with my face," but then stopped himself. According to *Fifteen Steps on the Ladder of Success,* one of the signs of a losing mentality was to disparage oneself in front of others.

"I'm surprised," Holiday said. "You didn't even act in high school? You seem like one of those guys who seems shy until they get up on a stage."

"Ha," Jonah said. "Not hardly. High school was like—" And he cleared his throat, accepting the big, dripping pot that Steve handed him. "Well," he said, "let's just say that I wasn't the type to be in plays."

"Were you athletic?" Holiday said.

"No," Jonah said. "I wasn't . . . I wasn't anything really." And he tried to think back. The few friends he'd had were like him, at the bottom of the social ladder: Mark Zaleski, whose IQ didn't quite qualify him as retarded, but who was nevertheless two years older than everyone else in their grade, a friendly but humorless boy who liked to trade comic books and talk about various types of cars; Janine Crow, an intelligent girl, part Sioux like his mother, a girl who developed so early that she looked like a middle-aged woman by the time they were juniors, the sad outline of her bra visible through the dowdy blouses she wore; she was picked on so constantly that she automatically flinched when people spoke to her. And even with these people, he hadn't been close. He was ashamed, sometimes, to realize how little his teenage years had involved anything that other people would recognize as normal rites of passage.

"My brother did a lot of that sort of stuff," Jonah said. "He was in—what do you call it?" He glanced surreptitiously at Steve, trying to imagine what sports Steve might have played. "Track," he said. "And, well, *he* was in a play." He scoped his mind for a minute. *"The Glass Menagerie."*

"Oh, I love that one," Holiday said. "I'll bet he played Jim didn't he? Jim O'Connor, the gentleman caller."

"That's right," Jonah said. He cleared his throat—he would have preferred it if Holiday hadn't been so familiar with the text, which he'd read but didn't remember very well. "How did you know?"

"It's funny," Steve said, wiping his hands on a dish towel. "Actually, *I* played Jim when we were in high school. And Holiday played Laura. The crippled girl."

"That's almost spooky," Holiday said, and Jonah felt his face reddening.

"Well," Jonah said. "He did a lot of things, my brother. He was involved in a lot of stuff." And he was silent as the two of them grew solemn; silence expanded in the kitchen as he continued to wipe the pot that Steve had given him even though it was dry. He wished that he hadn't said anything.

"You must miss him very much," Holiday said, respectfully.

"I do," Jonah said. He averted his eyes as Holiday unplugged Henry from her nipple and lowered her shirt. "We don't have to talk about it, though."

"Oh, no! Of course not!" Holiday said. And when Jonah looked at Steve, Steve was observing Jonah's hands, the thin tooth marks that left scar trails from his wrists to his knuckles. There was a silence, and then Holiday said: "I'll bet Henry would like it if you held him, Jonah."

———

It was a significant moment, he thought later. It was maybe the first time he'd held a baby. He sat down in the kitchen chair and Holiday lowered Henry into his arms, and he actually felt weirdly shaky. Steve and Holiday smiled benignly, watching, but he almost forgot about them. He was caught up with the amazement of it, the warm, squirming weight that settled into his arms and grew still.

The baby stared at him, steadily gazing. There was a weight of the past. It made him think of the way his grandfather used to sit and look out at the horizon. He thought of his mother's bitter joke: *Oh, look, there's my baby.*

The baby's large eyes settled on him, and though this had been one of his happiest nights in his whole life, it made him melancholy. He had read somewhere that babies are instinctively drawn to faces, that they will fixate even on drawings or abstract, facelike shapes, and round objects with markings that might resemble eye-mouth-nose. It was information that struck him as terribly sad, terribly lonely—to imagine the infants of the world scoping the blurry atmosphere above them for faces the way primitive people scrutinized the stars for patterns, the way castaways stare at the moon, the blinking of a satellite. It made him sad to think of the baby gathering information—a mind, a soul, slowly solidifying around these impressions, coming to understand cause and effect, coming out of a blank or fog into reality. Into *a* reality. The true terror, Jonah thought, the true mystery of life was not that we are all going to die, but that we were all born, that we were all once little babies like this, unknowing and slowly reeling in the world, gathering it loop by loop like a ball of string. The true terror was that we once didn't exist, and then, through no fault of our own, we had to.

8

June 20, 1996

After his fall, Little Man cries for a while. He is going to have a black eye—"A real nice shiner," Troy says—and Little Man touches the swollen area gingerly.

"I can see my cheek," he says, bitterly. "And I'm not even trying to look at it."

He rests his head against Troy's shoulder, nuzzling a bit, sniffling. He seems okay, and Troy tightens his grip around the child's middle. Troy's hands are trembling, and he hopes that Little Man doesn't notice the shuddering of his palm as he presses it against his back. He keeps smelling Little Man's hair as they hurry down the sidewalk.

It freaks him out a little. He thinks of his nightmare, of Little Man falling from the tree. And here Loomis *had*, in fact, fallen from a tree!

"What were you thinking, man?" Troy whispers, soothingly chiding. "Are you going to become a daredevil on me? The Evel Knievel of tree climbing?"

"Those kids lied," Loomis says grimly. "They said there was a bird nest with eggs in it, and I believed them. They boosted me up there, and I fell." He presses the good side of his face against Troy's shirt. "What's Evel Knievel?"

"Oh," says Troy, distractedly. "He was this famous motorcycle guy. He did, uh, daring things." But he isn't thinking about Evel Knievel. He is thinking about the other kids, boosting Loomis up into a tree. "Bastards," Troy says, and his dislike for the other children hardens into something like hatred. Scotty and Davey, little white-trash pieces of shit from down the block. What were they? Eight or nine? Taking advantage of a five-year-old. He had known it when they came running up to the screen door, faces flushed, eyes bright. "Mr. Timmens! Loomis fell! He's hurt! He's crying!" gleeful, he thought, almost shining with excitement. He should have known not to trust them from the beginning, with their ugly shaved heads and their dirty white T-shirts, sockless feet in thrift-store basketball shoes. They'd started coming over to play, to eat his good cookies and potato chips, and when they'd offered to take Little Man over to their house, he'd had a moment of weakness, thinking it would be nice to have an hour or so to himself, he'd do the dishes and wash a load of laundry, stuff he'd been neglecting for several days. He should never have trusted them, he thinks now, and his mood darkens, he bites the inside of his cheek. He tries to think of ways he could scare the crap out of them. Teach them to screw around with his son. *Mr. Timmens! Loomis fell! He's hurt!* Jesus Christ, he had never felt that kind of dread before, running down the block, imagining blood, broken bones. An ambulance.

It wasn't as bad as that. He puts Little Man down in a kitchen chair and holds up three fingers.

"How many fingers am I holding up?" he says, and Little Man looks at him warily, puzzled.

"Three?" he says, and this makes Troy feel a bit better. Troy takes an ice-cube tray from the freezer of the refrigerator and cracks it over a dish towel. He bundles up some chunks of ice into the cloth.

"Here," he says. "Hold that over your eye. It's going to be cold but it will make the swelling go down."

Little Man does as he's told, but winces as he presses the balled, ice-filled dishrag over his eye. "Why will this make the swelling go down?"

"I don't know," Troy says. "Trust me. It just does."

He sinks down into a chair across the table from Little Man, looks him over for a moment. He's okay. Troy reaches into the small glass

ashtray that sits in the middle of the table and plucks up the dead marijuana joint, half a finger long, and flicks it toward the sink. Good shot:
It lands in the basin where the garbage disposal is, and he leans his
forehead against the ham of his hand. He should not be smoking pot
in the middle of the day, he thinks, and then he picks up the portable
phone, which is also on the table, and puts it to his ear. No sound. He
had been sitting there, smoking a joint and talking to Ray on the phone
when Scotty and Davey came racing to his screen door, and he supposes that he should call Ray back eventually, just to let him know
everything is all right.

But he doesn't feel like it right now. Ray has been in a neurotic
mode lately, and they had been talking about Ray's fear that he might
have some mental illness, like Tourette's syndrome. "I have these
urges," Ray had been saying. "You know? Like, urges to do bad things.
I mean, like, suddenly I have the urge to shout profanity in the supermarket. Or, like, I'm at a restaurant, and the waitress is coming down
the aisle carrying a load of plates, and I'll have the urge to trip her. I
mean, really bad. Like an evil urge. And, you know, I think about ex-
posing myself to, like, old ladies and shit. It's very disturbing."

"Ray," he said. He'd begun to roll a joint automatically, sitting at the
table with the phone tucked in the crook of his chin. It's natural to
want to get high when he's talking to Ray. "Ray, man, does it ever occur
to you that you're just an exhibitionist? I mean," he said, "you're a stripper. You take off your clothes for dozens of women week after week
and you think that's, what? Normal?" He drew deeply on the puckered
end of the marijuana cigarette, just as the children appeared at his door.

He puts down the phone. Ray has other people to call, other people to
complain to. He examines Little Man's black eye again.

"How are you feeling?" he says. "Are you feeling okay?"

"I guess," Little Man says. The area around his eye is black and
blue, fairly bad. Falling out of the tree, he'd struck his face against the
bark of the trunk. He'd lain there, huddled in the sparse grass, holding
his face and crying silently. He is the kind of kid who plays dead when
he's hurt. It wasn't until Troy came charging into Scotty and Davey's
backyard that Little Man had lifted his head. Jesus Christ, Troy thought.

Where was their mom? No sign of her—the windows of their house were blocked by tacked-up sheets patterned with football logos. A naked engine was sitting on cement blocks near the tree, the grass around it dead from shade and motor oil. *He could've been killed,* Troy thought, and drew breath. He tried to suck the thought back into his brain and out of existence.

"You're really okay?" Troy says now, and Little Man shrugs.

"I'm a little upset," he says.

"Those kids," Troy says. "I'm sorry that they fooled you."

"They didn't know what they were talking about."

"Fucking idiots," Troy says.

Little Man purses his lips and presses the ice against his eye. "I agree," he says.

Troy has been having lifestyle issues, or something. He feels vaguely guilty all day, with Little Man so subdued and quiet. Poor kid, he looks terrible. The side of his face around his eye is bruised brownish-black, and a swollen knot has risen up on his cheek, and he seems very blue.

"I wish I could talk to mom," Loomis says, and Troy actually blushes.

"I'm sorry, kiddo," he says. "You can talk to me, if you want."

But Loomis just turns back to the television. He's been very moody ever since his fall, frowning gloomily at children's programs like "Sesame Street," "Barney," "Mister Rogers' Neighborhood," stuff that usually would have been much too babyish for him. Nevertheless, he sits there, listening as Mr. Rogers sings, "You'll never go down, you'll never go down the drain . . ." holding his old blanket against his face, rubbing the silky lining between his fingers. It's a habit from when he was a toddler, and it worries Troy enough that in the afternoon he calls a nurse he knows, a woman named Shari who is also one of his regular marijuana customers. He has her run over the symptoms for concussion with him: headache, dizziness, confusion, nausea, vomiting, vision change—none of which Loomis is presenting.

"What about tinnitus?" she says. "Ringing in the ears?"

Troy puts his hand over the phone receiver. "Loomis," he calls. "Are you experiencing any ringing in the ears?"

"What?" Loomis says. He mutes the TV.

"Ringing in the ears?" Troy says. "Do you hear any ringing or strange humming?"

Loomis is quiet for a moment, listening attentively. Then he says: "No, I don't think so, " and turns the volume of the television back up.

"Well," Shari says, "keep an eye on him. If he still seems like he's acting funny in the morning, maybe you ought to take him in."

"Yeah? You don't think I should take him to the emergency room or anything?"

"I don't," she says. "It sounds normal." And then she clears her throat. "And how are you doing, Troy? We haven't talked in quite a while."

"I'm okay," Troy says. "Same old, same old."

"Uh-huh," she says. "Well, I haven't been out to visit you in a while, I'll have to do that pretty soon."

"Anytime," Troy says. "You know me. Always present."

And then, after he hangs up, he has the urge to call Carla. Something about Shari's voice, a kind of "wife" voice has reminded him of the ordinary, intimate conversations that men and women have when they live together—even he and Carla had such times, normal mundane stuff that he realizes now is what he misses almost more than sex.

Later, after Little Man is asleep, he tries to call her, and finds that her phone has been disconnected. "The number you have dialed is no longer in service," the computer voice says. "If you feel you have dialed this number in error, please hang up and dial again. If you need help, dial your operator." And then it repeats again, the same message, which he listens to in its entirety.

It's nothing he wouldn't have expected. Of course she'll call when she's ready, when she comes out of whatever new crisis she's found herself in, but he still feels a weird anxiety. A pathway has been severed, one of the last ones, and he curls up on the couch drinking beer, with the phone on the coffee table in front of him, flipping through channels.

He wakes up abruptly from a sound sleep and he is dreaming that he hears a voice from a children's program. Someone like Mr. Rogers says:

No escape for anyone, anywhere.

It scares him for a second. He can see the red light from his digital clock, which says 4:13, and there is a pale, pre-morning color to the darkness. Something inside his stomach makes a trickling sound. Yuck. He can feel himself flooding into his mind, gurgle, gurgle, like water rushing into an empty tub. Now he is hungover but blankly awake, blinking into the dimness, and whatever spirit world he had been touching is gone. He listens, and there is tinnitus, a thin metallic drone in his ear: no escape for anyone, anywhere.

He finds himself thinking about the phone call that came two nights ago, which he somehow associates with Little Man's fall from the tree and with his general anxiety.

Just the usual sort of telemarketing call. "May I speak with Troy Timmens?" the guy said, a woodenly awkward kid who Troy felt a little sorry for, since he seemed to be a lousy salesman.

"Yeah," Troy said. "Present."

"Oh," the guy said, and then wavered. "Oh," he said. It was late in the afternoon, and Loomis was watching cartoons in the next room: Spiderman, which Troy also enjoyed watching. Troy glanced in the direction of the television as the telephone guy got his act together: reading off cue cards, Troy thought.

"I'm speaking to Troy Timmens?" the guy said, at last.

"That's me."

"Oh," the guy said. "Okay." Then he seemed to fumble again. "Well . . . Mr. Timmens, I'm . . . I'm calling today as a . . . as a representative? Of the Mrs. Glass Institute? And we're . . . contacting people who were adopted through the Mrs. Glass House during the years 1965 and 1966. Is it safe to assume? I mean, that you are one of those people? Who was adopted from the Mrs. Glass House during the year 1966?"

"Who is this?" Troy said, and his voice hardened a bit. He didn't like to talk about the adoption thing. It was private information, he thought, and he felt a little uncomfortable to think that this stranger was in possession of some sort of list with his name on it, a file, a record. Stuff he himself didn't know. "Who is this?" he said, gruffly, and then, in his most formal voice: "To what is this concerning?"

"Ahem," said the awkward person. "My name is . . . David. David Smith. And I'm part of a project that's. A project who is interviewing various, various people. And, well. May I assume? That you are in fact *the* Troy Timmens that was adopted from the Mrs. Glass House in July of 1966?"

It was very bothersome. Troy frowned. "Listen, man," he said, "you can *assume* that I'm not liable to talk to someone over the phone about this. You need to send me a letter or something. I'm not going to talk to some guy that calls me up out of the blue."

"Oh!" the person said, now more flustered than ever. "You mean you haven't received a letter from us? A certified letter? It should have. Arrived."

"Never got anything," Troy said, sternly. "So, I don't know, maybe you've got the wrong guy or whatever, but you need to send out your letter again."

"Oh," said the guy. "Are you sure?" His voice sounded strained, as if Troy had somehow hurt his feelings deeply, and he was trying not to cry. God, what was the problem? "Can I . . . verify your address, then?"

"Fine," said Troy. "Look, I'm not trying to be rude. But this adoption stuff is private to me. It's not something I talk about with just some stranger over the phone, okay?"

"Oh," the guy said. "Of course. Of course! We understand completely."

After he hung up, he'd felt weirdly troubled. A little upset, as Loomis would say. And now, at 4:13 in the morning, he feels the same way. It was very uncool of them, he thinks, those adoption people, calling up and bothering folks. It reminds him of a story that his fellow bartender, Crystal, had told him once. One afternoon, an elderly couple had shown up on her doorstep. They were driving through, they said— they lived in Oregon, now, they said, but once, when the old man was a child, he had lived in St. Bonaventure. He had lived in that very house, where Crystal was now living, and he wondered if they might come in just to look around.

"Weird!" Troy said, not sure why he felt so repulsed. "And you let them in?"

Crystal shrugged. "They were just old people," she said. "They were, like, eighty or something. It was cute to think of them driving across the country. They were very sweet."

But once they had been admitted into her house, the old man became emotional. "It's so much the same!" he'd said. "I remember looking out of that window!" And then, when they walked into the living room, he started crying. "Oh!" the old man said. "I can picture mother sitting there in her chair, right there. I haven't thought of that in years." And he'd had to sit down, to get a grip on himself.

"Ugh!" Troy said. "How creepy!" And Crystal looked at him oddly, as if he'd missed the point of her story, or misinterpreted it.

"Not really," she said. "I just thought it was . . . interesting. You know, about the passage of time and all."

"I guess," Troy had said then. But now, thinking of it, he still doesn't think the "passage of time" is interesting. It's invasive and spooky, and he thinks he will tell that to the adoption people if they call him again. "Look," he'll say. "You guys gave up your claim on me a long time ago. Signed, sealed, and delivered. That's the end of the story, as far as I'm concerned."

Sitting at the kitchen table, sleepless, he writes this down on a scratch pad. "Signed Sealed Delivered. End of Story." He draws a cartoon talk bubble around the words, and then frowns, his tongue between his teeth, drawing a skull head, like he used to do when he was a kid. It's a happy skull, and he attaches the talk bubble to its smiling mouth. He gives the skull a bow tie and a porkpie hat. Then he crumples up the paper and throws it away. He gets up and fishes around in a drawer for a particular glass pipe that he likes. He takes his personal stash of marijuana out of the freezer, and sorts a pinch of it free of seeds and branches.

He has done nothing wrong, he thinks, but he feels like a bad person. He feels like *something* is his fault, something that he cannot even name but which sits like a heavy bird in a branch overhanging his mind, and he would know what it was if he only thought about it long enough.

9

March 1966

A girl has disappeared from the Mrs. Glass House. Escaped—that's what people are saying. Nora listens to the muttered bits of gossip in the cafeteria and the television room. She nods as Dominique repeats a version of the rumor, watching Dominique's cold-looking, red-palmed hands at work on her knitting. "I guess they've called her parents," Dominique says softly. "I hope Mrs. Bibb gets fired."

"Mm-hm," Nora says, and glances toward the window. Outside, the snow is knee-deep and dense, the first week of March, and no one seems to be able to explain how the escape was accomplished. They say, for example, that the girl left in the early morning, that her footprints were found in the snow, a soft series of indentations that led to the cast-iron fence, then ended. She must have climbed over the fence, people say—a six-foot fence with arrow-spikes at the top of each metal rail—and then perhaps jumped into the bed of a truck that was waiting for her, idling on the other side. Though there were no tire tracks. And though she was eight months pregnant, huge-bellied, not built for climbing fences and jumping into trucks.

"They don't know how she did it, that's the thing," Dominique says, and Nora can see the way doubt and hope are struggling with each other in Dominique's mind. "She must have been very clever," Dominique says, uncertainly.

Nora is quiet. What is there to say to such stories? They seem ridiculous but beautiful. Who wouldn't want to believe that a girl could plan such a gambit, worthy of a spy? Who wouldn't want to believe that there was a boyfriend out there, an eternally faithful boy perhaps with a flatbed pickup, the exhaust pouring out as you poised yourself over the sharp spines of the fence, the boy calling *Jump! Jump! I love you, baby!* as your legs coiled and you prepared to leap into the crisp snowy air like a horse across an impossible chasm.

———

Now that a month has passed, Nora finds that she is no longer surprised when she wakes up. There is no momentary gasp of unfamiliarity when she opens her eyes and discovers herself once again in this room, in this place. She lifts her eyelids: The pillow curves away from her vision like a landscape, and when she rolls over, the ceiling spreads out above her, a textured plaster ceiling with blurry yellow smoke stains running across it like the waves of a mirage; a tiny pill of cobweb quivers in an air current. She is no longer sick in the morning, no longer weak with fatigue or sudden gripping hungers. In the low, early-morning light her desk and chair have emerged from the shadows to become solid, and the bare walls are dim but visible. Outside, the blizzard continues unabated—not fierce, but relentless. Fat snowflakes the size of her thumb flatten themselves against the windowpane and pile up against the sill, and she tries to picture that heroic girl trudging determinedly, fleeing in nothing but her smock and a thin autumn coat. It doesn't seem likely.

The girl's name, the missing girl, is Maris. *Maris,* another wishful pseudonym, Nora thinks, the kind of odd, awkwardly lovely name that parents never really give to their children but that girls wish for when they are a certain age, imagining that a name will make them a different person, a princess, an exotic island. It is a good name for a girl who has, supposedly, vanished into the night.

After a while she finds herself drawn to the window. There is the bare tree and the fence beyond, dark charcoal etchings against the undifferentiated whiteness of ground and sky. Her fingers melt the ice at the edge of the glass, and she blinks slowly, thinking of that boy coming to Maris's rescue, his face eager with love, his cheeks ruddy in the cold.

She knows that it didn't happen.

It's more logical, Nora thinks, to believe that Maris committed suicide. Most probably, she has hung herself in her room or taken some well-concealed pills or slit her wrists. Mrs. Bibb and the other authorities have spread the rumor of her disappearance themselves so as not to upset or alarm anyone. They are trying to cover up the poor girl's death by creating a diversion, but the truth is that there is no "Maris," really. There is just another Ann or Kathy or Joyce, a parade of not very bright farm girls who are all in the process of realizing that their futures are sad and pathetic and ugly. They are not "Maris" futures. They are not "Dominique" futures.

Of course that's it, Nora thinks. The girl is dead. But still she has to admire the cleverness of the story, the image of those footprints leading out to the edge of the fence and then ending.

Still, the more she thinks about it, the more she realizes that it's just a myth, just an echo of a local legend that she has heard a number of times. She recalls reading about it in the newspaper one year around Halloween time—a ghost story of sorts that involved the disappearance of a child.

The legend itself is always presented, even in the newspaper, as a "true-life mystery." There are names, dates, places that suggest the sheen of fact. Apparently, for example, this incident took place on December 31, 1899, on a homestead located some seven miles east of Little Bow. The family who lived there was named Ambrose, a young couple with two sons.

On that particular night, a small group of friends had gathered at the Ambrose place to celebrate the coming new year. They sang songs and made toasts while the two boys, aged six and eight, popped corn over the fire. Outside, a heavy snow was accumulating.

At about ten o'clock, Mr. Ambrose asked his elder son, Oliver, to get some water from the well. The snow had stopped falling, and a gibbous moon was visible behind the breaking clouds, casting a pale light over the open yard and the fields beyond. Mrs. Ambrose watched as her son trudged out in his new Christmas overshoes, the silver bucket swinging lightly in one hand.

But the boy had not been gone more than a few minutes when the gathered party heard him cry out for help. "Momma!" he shrieked once, shrilly, as if he were being attacked, and then the sound stopped abruptly.

The adults rushed outdoors, Mr. Ambrose carrying a kerosene lamp, though the whole snow-covered prairie landscape seemed to glow, almost phosphorescent, in the moonlight. There was no sign of the boy, no sound, only the miles of treeless fields and snowdrifts, wafting into shadow. The boy's tracks ended about halfway to the well. There were no other marks of any kind in the fresh snow, only Oliver's footprints, and the bucket, lying there on its side. The wind sent a soft curlicue of powder around it.

According to the newspaper, a subsequent investigation only verified the adults' account of the incident. No further clues were discovered, and eventually the mysterious case was "quietly dropped" for lack of evidence. The last time Nora had seen the story recounted in the newspaper, they'd added a "human interest" element by consulting several experts, who suggested possibilities that ranged from the boy being carried off by eagles to being abducted by a UFO. One man, a private investigator from Denver, debunked the whole thing. He said that perhaps the boy merely made his way to the well in some playful way, so his tracks didn't show—along a fence, maybe—and then had fallen into the well and drowned.

When she was growing up, Nora herself had never thought too carefully beyond the chill left by those clear, abruptly ended footprints. There was an emotional reality to the story, a confirmation of what she'd always secretly felt—that there was something tentative about her own existence, something tenuous. She could remember her father sending her out to do some chore after dark—garbage she'd forgotten to haul, a sprinkler not turned off—and how the thought of that old story would spread across her skin as she hesitated in the doorway, the growing certainty, as she stepped out into the night, that she wouldn't ever come back from her errand.

Even now, sitting alone in her room, thinking of the story gives her an uneasy feeling. She looks at her wristwatch—6:40 in the morning, which is not a time to be superstitious and skittish. But still. The silence suddenly seems uncanny, and she throws back the covers and pads in her nightgown, barefoot, to the door, which is open just enough to be uncomfortable, just enough to feel as if someone could be looking in.

No one is, of course. The hallway is empty; it's still almost an hour until breakfast and the quiet is perhaps even normal. Many of the girls here sleep so much they seem to be barely alive. Twelve, fifteen hours a day, she calculates. There is one girl in particular, "Ursula," whom Nora has taken a vaguely scientific interest in—Ursula appears at lunch and dinner, groggy, eyes pinched, waddling with her enormous belly like a manatee. Nora thinks she is either carrying a grotesquely large infant or twins, but the point is that Ursula seems capable of sleeping anywhere. She sits in the TV room with her fat thighs spread open, her mouth ajar; she sometimes dozes over her food in the cafeteria, nodding with her fork and knife poised on her plate. Once, while they were in line to go out to a movie, Nora had seen Ursula asleep on her feet, waiting to be given her tin ring, her cheek nuzzled against her shoulder, her eyes fitfully closed, even as her feet shuffled forward in response to the other girls' movements. Sometimes Nora wishes that she could be like this girl, that she could accomplish the next dreadful months in a kind of coma.

But it doesn't work like that. Whenever she closes her eyes, there is something circling brightly, in the way that a june bug dive-bombs a lightbulb, swinging in unsteady circles and colliding with the side of the house, falling onto its back, buzzing wildly. There are thoughts of the dying girl in *The Collector*, thoughts of the other girls in the Home, Dominique and Ursula and the lost Maris, thoughts of Nora's own unimaginable future. She sits at the desk in her room and tries to draw faces on a piece of paper, girls with big eyes and bow mouths, modeling contemporary clothing.

Despite herself, she thinks of her father, back in Little Bow. At

6:45, he would surely be up by now, drinking coffee, ready to leave for work.

In 1914, when Nora's father was four years old, he was set aboard the Orphan Train. Nora's grandfather was a beggar who pretended to be blind, and he brought his three sons into the New York Children's Aid Society wearing gunny sacks, shoeless. Her father remembered that clearly: standing in a waiting room, aware of the stink of his own body, aware that the loose sack he was wearing was like a girl's dress. The boys' mother had died, but he didn't know how. Maybe in childbirth, he'd said, musingly, as if she were the forgotten name of a town he had visited. *It all seems like it happened to someone else,* he told her. *It's blurry in my mind.* He remembered, he said, that his father had hoped for money when he brought them to the Children's Aid Society. His father was a crafty, bitter man, and had imagined that his sons might be worth something. He argued for a while with a horrified lady in a heavy blue-gray dress, demanding that the boys show her their muscles, show her they could work! And at last, she gave him some coins and he went away.

The lady had turned to them. "Oh, my poor children," she had said. Nora's father had flinched when she touched his head, but he recalled that her hand had been tender and slow, and that she had brushed back his hair.

"Are you to be my mother?" Nora's father had asked, and one of his brothers had filliped him on the back of his skull.

———

As a sophomore in high school, Nora found the word *fillip* in *Webster's New World Dictionary, 2nd College Edition.* It was a find that pleased her with its accuracy, a word she hadn't known existed. "Fillip," she said, and thumped her own head like a melon. She sat staring at the dictionary, filled with wonder. It was a word that her history teacher, Mr. Bosley, himself would have to look up. Nora jotted this down. She was doing this as a project for his history class, an extra-credit project that Nora had wanted to do well on, since she had been given a B on the last test. Mr. Bosley was the president of the local historical society, and had offered them a reprieve from his cruel tests if they presented him with well-documented interviews of elderly residents of the community. She had known that her own father's story could help improve her standing in Mr. Bosley's estimation. She was aware that she would need to attain a grade point average of at least 3.5 if she wished to attend the college of her choice. At the time, she was of the notion that her future hung in the balance. She wanted to be a famous and remarkable person—different from the rest of her family.

She wrote:

> Starting in 1854, the New York Children's Aid Society began the "placing out" or "free home" programs to give orphaned and deprived children a chance at a new life in the West. Among these children was my father, Mr. Joseph Doyle. In 1914, at the age of four, he traveled by train to the town of Brussels, Iowa. He had been one of thousands of New York street children which were called "street arabs," but they were actually neglected and abandoned youths who roamed the city. The children made their way in the world by stealing, begging, and working as newsboys or bootblacks or coal shovelers. They spent their nights sleeping in alleys, doorways, and discarded packing boxes.

This is what she had been working on when she found out she was pregnant. The essay remains unfinished, a useless appendage, and she is aware that she will never know how it ends. She will never again interview her father about his experiences, she will never again get the chance to summarize his life and reach a conclusion.

But she knows she will always think about it. She will always wonder whether she would have discovered something about her father's history that explained everything and she will imagine the essay that she could have completed for Mr. Bosley, an A+ essay, she feels. Her mind will pace in a circle around these little mysteries: her father, and the legend of that disappearing Ambrose child, and the girl at Mrs. Glass House—Maris.

Outside it continues to snow. Whatever escaping tracks had been left by Maris would have been covered a long time ago.

10

October 12, 1995

When the packet came in the mail, Jonah didn't open it at first. He glanced over the brown manila envelope, and saw who it was from. *The PeopleSearch Agency* was stamped in smudged black ink in the upper right-hand corner. He saw his own name and address, not even typed, but handwritten in a sloppy, childish cursive, and his heart sank. It didn't look official at all.

He had waited almost nine months for this packet to arrive, long enough to be convinced that the whole thing was a scam. He'd tried calling them once, to check on the "progress" of his, what?, *his account,* he said at last, hesitating, and was immediately put on hold. The phone receiver grew wet against his ear as he waited, listening to crooning soft rock that was played to him through the telephone lines, running his fingernails up across his forehead, up through his hair. At last, after almost twenty minutes, an elderly-sounding woman came on to tell him that his case was still being "investigated."

"We're working on it, honey," she'd said soothingly. "These things can take *years,* I hate to tell you," and he'd nodded politely into the receiver. *Of course,* he said, *I understand,* though he felt his ears heating up, the sound of blood beating, hush, hush, hush. *Three thousand dollars,* he thought. He had given them three thousand dollars, nearly a third of the money he'd been able to save from the sale of his mother's house, the little yellow house where he'd grown up, the furniture—some antiques—and his grandfather's guns and coin collection. He thought to tell the woman this. *I gave you all my money,* he wanted to say. *I should be getting something back for it.* But he didn't. All he said was, "Well!" All he said was, "So! I guess you'll . . . contact me, when you know something?" And the woman had laughed warmly.

"Yes, we surely will," she said. "Just be patient, Mr. Doyle!"

And now, here in his hands was the result of his patience, the result of his savings. A thin nine-by-twelve envelope, not more than a few pages by the weight of it. He put it down on the coffee table, set his little statue of "The Thinker" on top of it. He was a fool.

That day had begun so simply. Jonah had a quick errand to run and he stepped from the foyer of his apartment building into the thick, chilly drizzle of a Chicago autumn day. October 1995: nothing significant happening in the world, or at least not in America, not in this city where Jonah had awakened to find himself alive and existent. Or *sort of* existent. Here he was, Jonah Doyle, aged twenty-five, no known connections, a wanderer in a major U.S. metropolis. Just an ordinary, anonymous person like the others who were moving grayly in the distance along the opposite street. He pulled the hood of his sweatshirt up over his head as droplets of mist speckled his unnecessary sunglasses. He stared down at the movement of his black, square-toed boots on the pavement as he walked. Tough, solid boots, and he was not afraid of stepping on broken glass, or someone's lost, flattened sock, or a bare, hideous chicken bone. Whatever. He crossed over the sad manhole cover that he liked, the manhole cover with grass growing in a ring from its cracks, beautiful baby grass, so new that the green was almost phosphorescent. He admired it again, wondering how it was possible for the grass to survive like that, how long it would last, with the frost coming. He turned up his headphones. The autumn leaves came spinning slowly out of the sky, sharp-edged Technicolor. His life wasn't so bad, he thought. The spike-tipped iron fences at the edges of the sidewalk seemed more vividly black, the three-story brick apartment buildings more solidly three-dimensional. The flap of a wayward newspaper page lifted its broken wing from the sidewalk and flew forward a few paces before settling, and he wasn't disturbed by it. Not really.

———

He was on his way to buy notecards. He would go to the drugstore and buy the notecards, and then he would go to the library, and then he would go to work, and then he would come home and begin to write the paper that had been assigned to him in his anthropology class. He would try to go to bed by one A.M.

He had been working very hard lately to keep things in order, to be very specific and goal-oriented. He was trying to make each day like a story he was telling about himself. He consulted the planner that he had begun to carry with him—his At-A-Glance calendar, his street map of Chicago, his train and bus schedules, his notes and memoranda. He would find himself shuffling through it even when he knew where he was going, dividing his day into neat segments, detailing it in his mind as he went. As he walked, he projected himself by increments into the future. He could picture the tattoo parlor two blocks away where he would turn left; he could see the aisle of the drugstore where the notecards and other paper products were kept, and the line at the cash register he would stand in. He had an idea of the particular table where he would sit at the library. At exactly one-fifteen, he would leave the library and walk to the el train, and he could visualize a map of the Howard Red Line, a seam that ran along the coastal edge of the city, and he could hear the crackling, murky voice of the train conductor calling out *Roger's Park. North and Clyborn. Loyola.* He could picture the locker room of the restaurant where he worked, his apron and checked cook's pants hanging there in the narrow metal hollow of his locker (#71); he could picture the table where he would stand chopping vegetables while the cheerful, aggressive Spanish of his coworkers passed over his head, and from there he would project himself even farther into the future—imagining his anthropology paper finished, typed neatly, handed in; imagining actually making it through the class to the end of the semester; imagining the college degree he was working toward. He could picture himself as a center point in expanding space—the other cooks moving past him in their hair nets and white aprons, the swoosh of waiters and waitresses passing through, the chatter of diners at their tables, the skyline of the city, the suburbs, the great silent fields that trailed their long emptiness all the way back to Little Bow, South Dakota, where no one who had ever loved him was alive.

And then, lifting his head from these thoughts, he found that he had not even reached the drugstore yet. He had, in fact, walked past it, or made an incorrect turn, or something. He was on an unfamiliar street, and he had to crouch down on the sidewalk at the edge of a building, irritated with himself and a bit shaky, too. He was lost again.

After all this time it should have been easier, he thought. When he first moved to Chicago, he had imagined that he would evolve, step by step, into a new self, a new life. But, though over two years had passed, he was not really a different person. Across the street, seagulls were alighting on discarded food in the Dunkin' Donuts parking lot, and people were hurrying or strolling along the sidewalk toward the el train station. At the end of the block, a bearded man reached toward him—a sun-browned yam of a hand, shaking a Styrofoam cup in which a few coins were lodged. Jonah straightened his sunglasses and moved past the man without speaking, though his back stiffened as the man stared at him.

By now he should know how to deal with these basic things. Most of the time he did. He knew how to avoid a crazy homeless beggar, he knew how to move headlong down the street with his face turned low, with the aura of a person who was busy and on his way to someplace important.

But it didn't come naturally to him. That was what he had been realizing. The pattern of his thinking was constantly being marred by intuition, by his imagination, by stories he told himself that soon metamorphosed into half-truths.

Now, standing on the el train platform, he could remember vividly how the PeopleSearch Agency had seemed like a wonderful solution to his problem. How enticed he'd been by the billboard that showed an elderly woman and a young woman embracing. "Are You Missing Someone?" it said. "We Can Help!" How gladly he'd written out a check after talking to them on the phone.

This had been only nine months ago, a day in late February not long after he'd been to Steve and Holiday's for the last time. Steve had quit his job at Bruzzone's, and the connections between them had become more and more tenuous. Jonah had lost his charm for them—he'd wanted, he realized, to be closer friends with them than they were prepared for.

He remembered once, sitting in their kitchen, playing with Henry while Holiday finished cooking the dinner. Henry was playing a game where he put his hand into Jonah's mouth, and Jonah pretended to eat it up. Henry found this hilarious. His mouth opened broadly, in toothless delight, and he laughed in that strange hiccuping way babies laughed.

"You know," Jonah said to Holiday. "If you guys ever wanted to go out on a date by yourself, or something, I could baby-sit for Henry. If you wanted."

"Oh, Jonah," Holiday said. "That's so nice of you. But . . . we have a really good baby-sitter."

"I'd do it for free," Jonah said. He smiled up at her, and then, when Henry again extended his fingers, he nipped them very lightly. "Arr Arr Arr," Jonah said, and Henry chuckled happily.

"Listen," Jonah said, after they'd played for a little longer. "Does Henry have a godfather? Because, you know, I'd be glad to do it. I mean, like, if you guys died in an accident, or something, I'd be glad to take him in."

Holiday turned from the stove and gave him a long look. Then she tried on a smile. "Well, Jonah," she said. "Both my parents and Steve's parents are still alive. So, I mean, if something were to . . . happen, I suppose he would go to them."

"Oh, of course," Jonah had said. "But they're old! They might not be able to take care of him."

"And I have three sisters. And Steve has a sister and a brother."

"Well, sure," Jonah said. "Right. I was just saying that if . . . it ever came up, I'm available. That's all."

"That's really sweet of you, Jonah," she said. But she'd stared hard as he chattered his teeth against the sour, rubbery flesh of Henry's fingers. "Rrrr," he growled, and her smile tightened, then faded.

Thinking about it later, he was aware that he'd crossed a line that he hadn't realized was there. He'd come on too strong, had tried to settle himself into the closest circle of their life where he wasn't wanted. They didn't say this, of course. But he could tell. They used to invite him places—they went to a festival of animated film, to a farmer's market, to a Korean restaurant where he fell in love with kimchi. But now they didn't call him anymore, and when he tried to telephone them, he always got their answering machine, even though he was certain they were there in their apartment, monitoring their calls. "Hey, guys," he said, awkwardly speaking as he imagined the bland slow turning of a recording tape. "I was just checking in . . . to see what was going on." And then he called an hour later, just in case. One week, he had left them fifteen messages, and not one of them was returned.

He had only been invited to dinner because he had run into Holiday on the street, on Michigan Avenue outside of the Walgreen's, and she'd hugged him and said, "Oh, it's so good to see you! We should get together sometime."

"Okay," Jonah said. "This week is good for me. Any night this week, actually."

"Oh," said Holiday. And then he'd realized that she hadn't meant it, though she immediately came up with a time and date. "It will be so nice to see you again!" she'd said. "We've missed you."

But it was clear, even as he arrived at their apartment, that this was to be the last time. There were silences even as they opened the door, and they would not show him Henry, who was of course asleep, and Steve and Holiday kept exchanging glances as Jonah tried to make conversation.

They used to like hearing him talk. They used to take pleasure in the various things Jonah saw as he wandered through Chicago, they used to say that he was "a brilliant observer." But now, it seemed, they could hardly wait for him to finish. He kept hoping that if he just continued on his observations would become brilliant again. But they didn't. He told a story about Mrs. Orlova, how every time he saw her she said "What's wrong? You look sick!" even when he felt happy. He tried to amuse them with talk about the people he saw from his apartment window, and the neighbors who shared the building with him who were always going in and out. Once, in the middle of the night, a shaggy, drunken young man had taken his trash to the Dumpster wearing only a pair of briefs, tiptoeing barefoot through the light snow with a garbage bag that, when Jonah had later out of curiosity slit it open, contained only beer cans and coffee grounds and grapefruit halves. Once he'd seen a man beating up a woman near the foyer, and the woman had put her hand over her mouth to muffle her own cries. People kissed in doorways, they hurried down the sidewalk or strolled slowly, they called to one another or sang. In the middle of the night, a pair of men had attacked each other, rolling around and gnashing in the street, and one of Jonah's neighbors had opened up a window and yelled at them. "Shut up!" his neighbor had called, throwing a stuffed animal down at them, and the men had both stopped fighting, rising up from their battle to shout angrily at the man who had thrown the toy at them. "Come down, you coward," they called, "Come down, come down. We'll kick your ass!" And they'd both begun to stomp on the toy before, finally, they stalked away together down the middle of the street.

In his mind, this had been a wonderful and hilarious account, one that would please them. But as he talked, he could feel the story faltering, becoming pointless and rambling, and Jonah was aware that they wished he would go home. Holiday was leaning forward as Jonah groped for words. The more painful it became, the more Jonah wanted them to laugh, or nod, or say "Ah!" in the way that they used to.

"I wonder how long we'll know each other," Jonah had said at last, after the pause in the conversation had seemed to settle over them like a layer of soil. He said it cheerfully, trying to sound as if he were just musing, but Holiday looked at him guiltily.

"Oh, Jonah," she said, reproachfully. "We'll always know each other! Once you meet somebody, you don't *unmeet* them."

"Jonah, Jonah," said Steve, as he always did, as if it were an old children's rhyme. "Jonah in the whale." He smiled sleepily, and Jonah thought of the Bible verse that he knew, that had once pleased them.

" 'Take me up and cast me forth into the sea,' " said Jonah. He smiled, speaking sonorously. " 'So shall the sea be calm unto you; for I know that for my sake this great tempest is upon you.' "

"That's so pretty," Holiday said, without enthusiasm, though the first time Jonah had recited it to her, she'd widened her eyes as if he'd performed a magic trick. "Why, Jonah!" she said then. "That's amazing! What is it? Shakespeare?" Jonah had told her that it was from the Bible, from the Book of Jonah. It was the only Bible verse he had ever memorized.

"The Bible is full of great poetry," Steve had reflected. "You've got a really excellent reciting voice, Jonah!"

But now Steve didn't say anything. Even discussion of Jonah's dead brother, David, the imaginary one who looked like Steve, didn't stir their interest anymore.

But Jonah continued to think about it. He had built a brother out of nothing—a brother who had acted in plays and ran track, a brother who had died in a car wreck. *David.* Without even meaning to, talking about it had brought Jonah toward a vague but constant awareness of the real brother who presumably existed out there, the male infant his mother had given up for adoption.

———

Nevertheless, when he saw the man on the el train, it took him by surprise. The intensity of it. It was the day after he'd been at Steve and Holiday's place for the last time, and he'd woken up late, with a headache from the red wine. *Take me up and cast me forth into the sea,* he thought as he opened his eyes.

He had been late for work that morning, which was unusual for him, and he actually ran the last block to the el platform, full of single-minded anxiety. He pounded up the steps just as the door to the train slid open and the waiting passengers began to funnel their way inside. Usually, he was right at the edge of the ramp as the train pulled up. He had become an expert at gauging the exact spot to stand, so that the doors of the train came to rest directly in front of him and he could be the first one inside. He prided himself on this skill.

But on that day Jonah was the last of the clutch of morning commuters to board. The seats were filled and the aisles were crowded, a thicket of raised arms and solemn faces, so packed that there wasn't even a handrail or support pole to grasp. When the train pitched forward, he stumbled against the bosom of an impassively frowning African woman in a brick-colored scarf. She said something horrible about him in her native language.

But he hardly noticed. For it was at this moment that he caught a glimpse of the man who might have been his brother. Or rather, he saw a face, floating some six or seven heads beyond.

Their eyes met for a moment, and an electric, rippling sensation slid over Jonah's skin. He felt it rise, tingling in his hair, and he was actually dazed.

It was him, Jonah thought. *Jesus Christ! That's him! That's my brother!* They might have been twins. They had the same blondish hair, the same brown eyes and short, blunt nose, the same wide mouth and broad cheeks. And more than that, the same . . . what? That old psychic feeling he'd had as a teenager. An aura, Jonah thought, something like a hallucination. Invisible waves emanated from the person he was looking at.

But the man didn't seem to notice anything. He narrowed his eyes to suspicious slits when he saw Jonah staring at him, then lowered his head deliberately to the paperback he was reading. A person moved, and then another, and then Jonah lost sight of him. Jonah tried to move forward, edging closer to the place where the man was sitting. But before he could even locate the person he'd seen, the train reached the next stop. There was a general, amoeba-like flow of bodies as people poured in one door and out the other. And the person he'd seen was gone.

For weeks after that, perhaps months, Jonah had gone to the el train platform and loitered there, in hopes of catching a glimpse of the person who might have been his brother. He went to the train later than usual and stood behind the waiting crowd, sweeping his eyes across the backs of their heads in his search. He tried to remain unobtrusive, slowly and casually strolling by in his white T-shirt and checked cook's slacks, a baseball cap with the brim low over his eyes. If someone caught him looking, he'd lower his head, staring down at his black scuffed sneakers for a while before resuming.

Maybe this was the child his mother had given up for adoption, he thought. Or maybe it was another child that his biological father had parented, a half sibling that he knew nothing about. Or a cousin. He was aware again of his father—who had lived in Chicago, according to his grandfather. He had never much resembled either his mother or his grandfather, and he considered the possibility that maybe there was a whole tribe of people who resembled him. Who thought like him. Who would welcome him.

But he never found the person he was looking for.

———————

On the day the package came from the PeopleSearch Agency, he had been mulling over a passage from one of his anthropology textbooks, *Ascent to Civilization: The Archaeology of Early Man.* He kept reading it over, trying to make it coherent, to make it fit his thoughts.

"*If,*" he had underlined. "If, as we commonly accept, the lives and values of the most 'primitive' people on earth today are worth as much as any reader of this book, then surely each moment of the past, each person, had equal value. Even in a book like this largely devoted to the Old Stone Age we cannot distinguish the difference between say 150,000 and 140,000 years ago. We do not know what the individuals of those two periods thought, felt, enjoyed, and suffered, or how different they were. But we can at least appreciate that to those people, their lives were as important as ours are to us."

It made him feel sad. Reading this made him feel worse than he had when he'd been reading novels in his literature class, where the characters were full of a purpose and meaning that had embarrassed him. They had motivations, and complexities, and their lives were full of systems of symbolic importance. They represented something. Various things.

The problem with his own life, he thought, was that he had not been born significant. He was like those primitive peoples whose lives left almost nothing—a few bones and flint tools, a charred circle where their fire pit had been. Unlike the characters in great novels, he had no connection to the major world of human endeavor—no relationship to politics, or sociology, or economics, or the great movements of his time. The stuff that would be remembered. What could he say but that his people were the detritus of various empires. Nothings upon nothing. Irish peasants, arriving at Ellis Island and wandering helplessly through the streets of New York; conquered Lakota, nomadic aboriginals, marched to the barren plains of their reservations and corralled there, to wait endlessly. Even the town where he grew up was a nothing town, not a place that an empire really wanted, but only a mile marker, a place that was necessary to own only because it existed in a great blank space in between significant coasts. The great pulse of the world, which throbbed vaguely in Chicago, grew silent as it irradiated out into the plains.

Jonah would not be remembered for anything. That, at least, was a certainty.

He thought of this as he walked home. Maybe his father, or his brother, had more to do with the larger world. Maybe it didn't matter. He didn't have an idea for an anthropology paper, not even a thesis, but only two quotes that circled in his head: *But we can at least appreciate that to those people, their lives were as important as ours are to us.* And *Take me up and cast me forth into the sea; so shall the sea be calm unto you.* There was a great essay in these two thoughts, if only he could bring them together. If only he could articulate it. Mostly, he experienced his thoughts as disconnected, as wobbly planets circled by moons, which were then themselves circled by little asteroids and space junk, all tilting around a central sun, which was himself. His literature teacher said his essays were "ambitious but muddled," and in the margins she wrote repeatedly: "Unclear." "Unclear." Or simply, "Hmmm. . . ."

Mrs. Orlova was outside their apartment building, sweeping the sidewalk with a broom, and he felt a bit better, knowing that she would scoff at everything that troubled him. Loneliness? Significance? Ha! She had grown up in Siberia. He smiled at her as she raised her head from her work to frown at him.

"You look terrible," she said. "Are you sick?"

"No," Jonah said. "Not at all." Even after several years, he was not used to Mrs. Orlova's bluntness—the gloomy exaggeration that was the exact opposite of the midwestern reticence that he'd grown up with.

"You must be depressed," Mrs. Orlova said, and peered at him. "You look sweaty."

"Oh, really?" Jonah said. He passed a hand over his face, which was dry, unperspiring. "No," he said. "It's nothing."

"Whatever you say," Mrs. Orlova said. "I can see with my own eyes that you have been fired from your job!"

"No, I haven't."

"It's worse then," Mrs. Orlova said, looking hard at him. "Someone has broken your heart."

He found the response from the PeopleSearch Agency curled up and crammed ungracefully into the narrow mailbox. It seemed unimportant.

But when he slit open the manila folder, he began to shudder. To actually shudder.

Here was the name of Troy Timmens. Troy's birth certificate. A photocopy of relinquishment papers. The address of the people who had adopted him.

Jonah stood there for a long time, his throat tightening, his breath seeming to harden in his lungs. He looked at the papers.

His life was changing. He could feel it.

11

June 30/July 1, 1996

On the night he was arrested, Troy was thinking that maybe things were okay. He was feeling better than he had in a long time. Pretty good! he thought. Calmed and almost happy, not worrying about anything. There was a little party—Troy and his old high school friend Mike Hawk and Ray. At eleven that night, they were playing Frisbee out in the road in front of Troy's house, under the streetlights. They were a little stoned, and a little drunk, but not so much as to be a nuisance. They kept their voices low, so the neighbors weren't disturbed; they kept their eye out for the infrequent car that might pull down the street; and they politely got out of the way when they saw headlights approaching. It was a friendly game—they didn't stand very far apart, and they passed the Frisbee between them in the same way that a marijuana pipe traveled in a circle from person to person. Troy enjoyed watching the bright green disk hover through the galaxy of insects that accumulated beneath the fluorescence; he enjoyed the minor prowess, the simple athletic movements that were required to snatch the Frisbee out of the air. Nothing special, or competitive: just a toy, passing from hand to hand. Troy, barefoot, in shorts, appreciated the warm, timeless summer air, the intimation of childhood vacation. Loomis was asleep.

Playing Frisbee was also fun because Ray was so notoriously bad at it. "Oh, come on," Ray complained. "Let's play cards or something."

"Cards?" Troy said scornfully. "Ray, how many beautiful summer nights like this are you going to get . . . in your entire life? I mean, if you live to be, say, seventy-five, the number of beautiful summer nights is a very finite number."

"Oh, good," Ray said. "Just what I need for my beautiful summer night. Morbid philosophy from Mr. I-Just-Turned-Thirty!" But he nevertheless followed Troy and Mike outside, and even, after a time, seemed to be enjoying his own lack of competence.

"Okay," he said. "I think I'm getting the hang of it." But the Frisbee, when Ray threw it, wobbled arthritically through the air, or fell on the ground, or spun forcefully in the wrong direction. Once, Troy told Mike Hawk, Ray had thrown a Frisbee and the disk had veered off behind Ray's head, striking an innocent young woman a glancing blow across the ear. It was weird, Troy thought, that Ray could work as a stripper—someone who had such control over his body's shifts and sways and gyrations—and yet he was ultimately so uncoordinated. Ray flung the Frisbee and it sputtered through the air, curving past Mike and landing with a thunk against a tree in Troy's neighbor's yard.

For his part, Ray was still getting a lot of mileage out of riffing on Mike Hawk's name. When they were at the bar, Ray loved to bring girls over just so he could say, "Ladies, I'd like you to meet Mike Hawk." No one thought it was that funny then, but he still kept at it.

"Mike Hawk is really going at it tonight," Ray said, in a sportscaster voice. "Mike Hawk knows when to get hard, and knows how to ease his way in!" This quip delighted him so much that he tripped trying to grab the Frisbee out of the air and fell onto the little patch of lawn between the street and the sidewalk, his long legs scissoring through the air as he fell. For a moment, it looked as if he might have hurt himself, but he bounced back up. "Jesus Christ," he said. "I really suck at this game. Can we light up another joint, please? I don't think I'll ever be able to beat Mike Hawk."

"Hilarity ensues," Troy said, making a wry face and curling his toes against the grass. Things were okay, he thought. Everything was normal. Happy. His life wasn't bad.

———

He had been feeling a lot of unplaceable anxiety lately. He was upset about Loomis's fall from the tree, and the fact that he couldn't reach Carla, and the call from the guy at the Mrs. Glass House. And just in general. A few days earlier, when Jonathan Sandstrom had shown up at the bar with the latest shipment, he'd been of a mind to refuse it—to quit, once and for all, as he'd told himself he would. He needed to change his life, and after this he thought he would have to start telling his various customers that they'd have to look elsewhere.

It was, relatively, a small delivery. "*Great* to see you, Troy," Jonathan Sandstrom said. He was a blond, glossily handsome guy in his late twenties, with a braying, artificial laugh and an almost disturbingly upbeat demeanor. He gave Troy an elaborate handshake when they met in the parking lot behind the bar. "Troy," he said, and paused dramatically. "You should maybe sit down, because you are going to be so *extremely* happy with the stuff I've got for you, you're not even going to be able to contain yourself."

"Okay, then," Troy said, and gave Sandstrom a quick, hard smile. "I'm glad to hear it." He sat down in the passenger seat of Sandstrom's BMW and opened the small, brightly colored paper tote bag that Sandstrom handed him. "The usual," he said, and grinned confidentially as Troy examined the contents: three large Ziploc bags of fresh, good-smelling Mexican marijuana, a container of hallucinogenic mushrooms, thirty-six tabs of LSD. This would tide him over for a number of months, and after that, maybe he would cut back even further.

"Listen," Sandstrom said. "I know you're not interested in cocaine, and I don't blame you. Very. Difficult. To. Deal. With." He underlined each word with a swipe of his hand. "But I think you really ought to think about Ecstasy. It's a nonaddictive substance. Not dangerous. *Very* popular. I know that some people are not interested in change, and I respect that, but maybe you . . ." and Troy watched as Jonathan Sandstrom built a kind of elaborate structure in the air with his hand gestures, "maybe you want to try a sample, just to test it out."

"I don't think so," Troy said.

"Something different. Just a suggestion."

"This ought to do me," Troy said.

"And that's fine, too," Sandstrom said. "You know what you want, and I respect that." He lowered the window and dropped the cigarette that he had just begun to smoke onto the asphalt. Then took another one out of his chest pocket, lit it, drew deeply.

"Listen," Sandstrom said. "Do you know the way to a little town called Beck? I'm supposed to meet someone there at—" He looked at his watch. "Jesus Christ. At three."

"Yeah," Troy said. "Sure."

They took out a map. Troy fingered the ropes of his tote bag handles, and pointed toward the northwest. He was getting tired, and wasn't thinking about much of anything. There was no way of knowing that the way to Beck would lead Jonathan Sandstrom to a ten-year prison sentence; there was no way of knowing that Sandstrom was being staked out by police, and that Troy was about to be swept up in the wake.

———

He didn't think of himself as a "drug dealer," exactly. It wasn't as if he hung around outside school yards, tempting children; it wasn't as if he were getting rich off people's addictions. He didn't believe in stuff like crack or heroin, and in fact he basically approved of the so-called War on Drugs, though he also thought that it was long past time that marijuana and other innocuous substances became legal. If the president admitted to trying pot—even if he supposedly "didn't inhale"— was it really such a big deal?

He liked selling marijuana, in the same way that he enjoyed being a bartender. There was a simple, cheerful camaraderie about it. He and the customer would be sitting together at the kitchen table, with the various objects spread out like chessmen in a friendly game—bong, lighter, cigarettes, baggies, the old pharmaceutical scale he used, with its checker-shaped weights stacked in a pyramid. He really did believe that marijuana was basically good for people, that it brought out what was benign in their hearts and heads. He believed the old line—who said it? Bob Marley?—that if only all the world's leaders would get high together, there would soon be peace on earth. Sitting there, talking to someone like the young lawyer Eric Schriffer, or the nurse Shari Hernandez, or Bob Boulder, a guy of about his age who taught tenth-grade history at the high school, or Lonnie Von Vleet, the fifty-year-old hippie guy who supervised the mentally handicapped people at the vocational center and who sat on the city council, it had seemed like he was providing a useful service. He had a place in the world, and at such times the notion that he was engaged in a criminal activity seemed distant and faintly ridiculous. A technicality.

Still, he did want to keep Loomis separate from it, and that was another reason he knew he needed to stop selling. He tried to complete most of his transactions at night, when Loomis was asleep, or, if during the day, when Loomis was out in the backyard, playing. But the time was coming when Loomis would begin to figure things out, if he hadn't begun to already. There had been a night, a few months after Loomis arrived, when the child had awakened and come into the kitchen where Troy and Lonnie Von Vleet were in the process of trying out some of the produce.

"Hi, Dad," Loomis said, standing in the doorway in his Batman underwear, and Troy had taken the bag of marijuana off the table and put it back in the old valise where he kept all his drugs.

"I woke up and I smelled a lot of smoke. I thought the house might be on fire."

"Well, it's not," Troy said. "You should go back to sleep, buddy."

"What's that?" Loomis said, pointing to the bong in the middle of the table.

"Oh," Troy said. "It's nothing. It's a water pipe that Mr. Von Vleet was showing me. That's where the smoke was coming from."

"You were smoking from it?"

"Yes," Troy said. "It was just . . . kind of a dumb thing we were doing."

"It's not very good for you," Loomis said.

"You're right." Troy glanced at Lonnie Von Vleet, who smiled.

"Hey there, Little Man," Von Vleet said. "Do you remember me?"

"Yes," Loomis said, seriously, and he shook Lonnie Von Vleet's hand when Lonnie held it out. "You do magic, right?"

"You've got a great memory, Little Man," Lonnie said, and though he was a bit small-eyed from the samples of produce they'd been smoking, he was still deft. "What's that behind your ear?" he said, and reached out, seemingly pulling a quarter from the shaggy hair that Loomis had tucked behind his ear. He offered it to Loomis, who took it, impressed. Back when Troy and Carla were together, Lonnie Von Vleet had shown a number of sleight-of-hand tricks to Loomis—pushing a pencil in one ear and out the other, making a coin disappear and reappear in his palm—and he seemed pleased that Loomis remembered him.

"You need to go off to bed now," Troy said, after Loomis had taken the quarter and thanked Lonnie Von Vleet. "I'll turn on the fan, so the smoke won't bother you."

"Okay," Loomis said, agreeably, and both Troy and Von Vleet had watched as Loomis disappeared down the hall and into his bedroom.

Troy cleared his throat. "Shit," he said, "I hate being a bad parent," and Lonnie grinned, patting him briskly on the back of his palm.

"What are you talking about?" Lonnie said. "He's a great kid. You must have done something right."

He thought of this again that night, as he and Ray and Mike Hawk sat around the kitchen table. He turned on the exhaust fan in the window above the kitchen sink, and opened the back door, and after they'd smoked a couple of bowls he wandered down the hall to check on Loomis. He felt uncomfortable as he stood in the doorway. Loomis lay there, his arms folded around his chest, a sheet covering the lower half of him. The pictures of dinosaur skeletons that Troy had drawn hung over the bed, as grim as gargoyles. Troy thought about adjusting the covers, but then thought better of it. Loomis was peaceful.

When he came back into the kitchen, Ray and Mike had taken out the old black leather valise that he uses to store his stash—the drugs he'd just bought from Jonathan Sandstrom. The valise was a memento that had once held his father's important papers—deeds, insurance, birth certificates, marriage license, will—all the formalities that made up a person's official life. Seeing Ray and Mike digging through it, he realized that it was probably reprehensible that he had used the valise to store his drugs in.

"Jesus Christ," Ray said, looking up. "Where have you been? We've been sitting here for, like, twenty hours."

"Just checking on the kid."

"You're such a mama," Ray said, and picked up the baggie of mushrooms, holding it up to the light critically. "Do you ever get any Ecstasy?"

"No," Troy said.

"Well, you should. It's a really cool drug."

"I'll take that under advisement." Troy took the bag of mushrooms from Ray's hand and put it back in the valise, then packed the rest of the new drugs on top, leaving only a small black film container full of pot, which Mike was going to take home with him.

"Let's go outside," Troy said. "I'm in the mood to play Frisbee."

It was around midnight when the police showed up. An ambush. Some kind of tip-off, a narc of some sort, and Troy wasn't prepared. He opened the door and three cops were peering back at him, standing broad-chested on the porch under a halo of insects—june bugs, millers, mayflies—that were circling ecstatically around the bare lightbulb. "Troy Timmens?" the first cop said, and Troy began to gesture behind his back at Ray and Mike, who were sitting at the kitchen table. Hopefully, they would recognize the desperation of his hand signals.

"Yes," Troy said to the cop. "Present. That's me. What can I do for you?"

"Mr. Timmens," the cop said, and put a thick hand on the edge of the door, as if to prevent Troy from closing it. "I have a search warrant for this home." He offered forth a folded sheet of paper, like a brochure, and Troy took it gingerly. He could feel himself blushing. He was very stoned, and he knew that the smell of marijuana smoke was rolling sleepily through the half-open door.

"Oh, shit," he whispered. He was aware that the amount of drugs in his house would almost certainly lead to a prison sentence. His chest tightened. There had to be a way out, of course there had to be, and he tried to make his mind move quickly as he stood there staring at the grim faces of the policemen. "Wow," he said. He felt like he could start crying.

Troy thought he knew what it would be like to die, what it would be like in that moment when you heard the retort of a gun someone had pointed at you, when your parachute didn't open, when you sank toward the bottom of the lake with something heavy attached to your foot. Even then, Troy thought, there would be a long, dreamlike pause where you imagined that there was still some way to escape. *Wait,* he thought. His mind moved rapidly through the hallways of a maze. Even as the walls grew narrower, even as the passage sealed in front of him, his mind yearned for that diminishing chink of light, still hoped for mercy, for wild luck, for reprieve or intervention.

"Look," he said, still trying to grasp at that alternate reality that existed before he opened the door, when he might have done something differently, trying to imagine a path into a future in which he might somehow escape. "You guys," he said to the cops standing there. He was aware that his life—the life he had been living, and the life he had been expecting for himself—was disappearing and there was nothing he could think of to do about it.

"Let me think for a minute," he said. But the cops were already pushing past him, with a jingle of keys and handcuffs. Two cops, then three, disappearing into the kitchen and down the darkness of the hallway. There was a clatter of dishes, as cabinets were opened, and one of the men pulled his hands behind his back and put a plastic tie around his wrists, reciting the Miranda rights. In the distance, he could hear one of the policemen shouting: "Come out from under the bed, sir. Come out from under the bed, sir! Sir, I order you to come out from under the bed!" *Ray,* he thought. *What an idiot.* And then he remembered Loomis.

"You guys, wait a minute," he shouted. "That's my kid. That's my kid! Don't hurt him!"

It was the worst moment of his life, and it wasn't until much later that he was able to make sense of the sequence of events, since everything seemed to happen at once.

The first was the sound of Loomis screaming as he was pulled by the leg out from under the bed, where he was hiding. "Loomis," he yelled, and tears sprang to his eyes, his voice cracking. "It's okay, buddy! It's okay, don't be scared!"

The second was the discharge of a pistol, an overanxious young cop, and Troy let out a cry.

And then there was silence. He didn't know at the time that Loomis had fainted at the sound of the shot, had curled up into a ball and gone rigid. He thought Loomis was dead, and the room distorted around him. He was weeping in a way he never remembered having done before, the way Loomis cried when he fell out of the tree: soundless, his contorted mouth trying to suck in air as tears ran down his face and out of his nose. His eyes wide as he tried to choke out words.

———

Dimly, in the distance, was the noise Ray made as he tumbled over the backyard fence, carrying Troy's valise. *Oof!* Ray grunted loudly, and he and Mike Hawk were running flat-footed up toward the hills behind Troy's house, leaving Loomis's screams, and the ricocheted gunshot, and Troy's weeping far behind them.

12

June 4, 1997

After she has searched for a little over an hour, Judy tries calling some of her neighbors. Her voice is hoarse from yelling, and she is extremely agitated. The presentiment that Loomis has been kidnapped has frightened her badly, and she is aware of a sharp thrum of panic at the edge of her perceptions. Something about her own, ordinary kitchen seems animate and watchful, as if the objects there might suddenly begin to breathe. Her forehead is wet with perspiration.

Nevertheless, her telephone voice remains, in the iron-clad custom of the Great Plains, pleasant and laconic, even as drops of sweat trickle from her forehead into her eyes. "Hi, Dawn?" she says brightly. "This is Judy Keene. How are you? . . . Well, I'm glad to hear it! . . . Listen, Dawn, I seem to have misplaced a youngster over here . . . little brown-haired fellow, six years old. A little small for his age. Wearing a red T-shirt and jeans? . . . No? Well, if you happen to spot him . . . All right . . . Thanks, I will . . . No, I'm sure he's around here someplace. These kids, I'll tell you! . . . Okay, then . . . Well, I'm sure I'll be talking to you soon . . . Yes . . . Okay, then. Good-bye, now . . ."

Her hands are shaking. Of the five neighbors that she is able to reach, none report any sightings. Dorothy Draper says that she heard that dog over at the Woodwards' barking and barking, but of course Judy knows that—she's the Woodwards' neighbor, after all.

"That's Carla's boy, is it?" Mrs. Draper says, and Judy has to suppress the urge to hang up the phone.

"Yes," Judy says. "That's right."

"Well, I haven't seen Carla in so long!" Mrs. Draper says. "How is she doing?"

"Oh," Judy says. "Fine! Just fine!"

"She was always a sweet girl. I remember when she used to come over here to play with Donald. She always had the most unusual games. Very involved. And I'd listen to them and I'd think to myself, 'she ought to be an actress.' Wasn't she in Los Angeles for a while?"

"No," Judy said, and cleared her throat. "Las Vegas."

"Oh," Mrs. Draper said. "Well, it must be good to have her home. Donald is in Saudi Arabia, can you imagine? He's in the navy, and that's where they sent him. I don't understand it, why they have to be over in those places. Has Carla been back in town for long?"

"No, no," Judy said, and pressed her hand to her chest, where another soft firework had erupted. "She's not in town. I'm just watching her boy. He's staying with me. For the summer."

"Is that right?" Mrs. Draper said. "Well, that really must be a treat for you. Do you know, I haven't seen my granddaughter since she was two—and now she's five! And I have said to Donald: Why don't you just send her to stay with her grandma for a few weeks? It would mean the world to me, I tell him. But to fly a child from the Middle East to the United States, and then to Denver, and then for me to drive over there to pick her up. It's very complicated."

"Yes," Judy says. And then she lightly presses down on the lozenge where the earpiece of the phone rests. Disconnecting. She hopes that Mrs. Draper will assume that they have been disconnected accidentally. She has rarely been so rude to another person in her life, but she is certain, at this moment, that she needs to call the police.

———

The dispatcher, Connie Cruz, answers on the first ring. "Communications," she says, and Judy tells her that she would like to speak to someone about helping her find a little boy.

Connie Cruz takes down the vital statistics. She asks for Judy's name and address, and leads her through a description of the child. "He's got brownish hair and blue eyes," Judy says. "He's wearing a red shirt and blue jeans. About three-foot-five or six. Maybe forty-five pounds."

"And he's a white male?"

"Yes."

"How old?"

"Six."

"Oh," says Connie, who has a six-year-old of her own. "A little guy."

"Yes," Judy says, recalling the repulsive nickname Loomis's father had for him. *Little Man.* "Yes," she says. "He is."

Like the rest of the country, St. Bonaventure had gone through a brief period of "missing child" obsession in the mid-eighties. This was the time when pictures of missing children began appearing on the backs of milk cartons, green-and-white photos of children with their vital statistics printed underneath: name, age, date of birth, hometown, weight, height, hair and eye color, last seen at _____. The photos themselves had a grainy, tabloid quality, the dots that made up the images clearly visible. Judy remembered being unnerved once while shopping, passing the dairy aisle and coming upon rows and rows of these faces staring out at her. Around this time the police department instituted a fingerprinting program in the grade schools, and she recalls the day her second graders had been lined up in front of a table where a sullen, elderly policeman sat with inkpads and thick paper cards. The children were thrilled.

But she herself had thought it was ridiculous. A kind of hysteria. No one she had ever met had actually known of a child who had been abducted. The supposed missing children were always from distant places—California, mostly, Judy noticed—and it was generally assumed that this was a problem in cities. Judy remembered hearing somewhere that ninety-five percent of these children had been taken by one of their own parents, the children mere victims of custody disputes rather than evil-minded strangers. By the time Loomis was born, the urgency of the syndrome had died down. The milk companies no longer printed the photographs, which apparently gave kids nightmares and hurt sales, and the disturbance seemed to fade away. By the time she retired from the elementary school, they were no longer fingerprinting children. Loomis had never been fingerprinted, as far as she knew.

The police car arrives at Judy's house a little more than five minutes after she calls 911. It has been a slow day, and Kevin Onken, the officer who answers the call, has had no reports to file since his shift began at nine A.M.

On a map, the town of St. Bonaventure vaguely resembles a pear or gourd. It is split down the middle by the railroad tracks and the main street that runs parallel. The police department has divided this pear-shaped collection of streets into fairly equal sixths, so that Onken's beat that afternoon is the upper eastern portion. It is primarily a residential area, framed on the south by the main street and to the west by a fairly well-traveled avenue called Old Oak Boulevard. To the north and east, houses trickle like ellipses into the open prairie.

Police Officer Onken, aged twenty-six, listlessly drives in slow concentric circles through this territory. He pulls down his stretch of main street—two gas stations, a motel, Discount Mart. A bit farther down there is a photography studio, a bank, and an old man's bar, The Green Lantern. If he waited outside the bar long enough, one of the patrons would stumble out, blinking in the summer daylight, and clamber unaware into his vehicle. Bam! An easy DUI. But Onken isn't in the mood for waiting. It reminds him, for some reason, of the many unpleasant early-morning autumn weekends he was forced to spend with his father, crouched with their shotguns in chill muddy duck blinds that smelled of dead earthworms and leaf-sludge, his father silently drinking Miller Lite and staring at the sunrise. The men who come out of The Green Lantern—divorced, unemployed, rapidly decaying through their forties and fifties—remind him of his father, and catching them brings him no more pleasure than it did to shoot a duck out of the sky.

And so he merely eyes the bar as he drives past. At the traffic light on the corner of Euclid and Old Oak Boulevard, he turns left and drives past more storefronts, past turn-of-the-century houses that have been converted into insurance and real estate offices and funeral homes, headed west toward the edge of town. He is bored enough that he almost stops to buy lemonade from a pair of little girls who have a stand set up on the sidewalk. They are also selling iced tea and "pretty rocks," which they've apparently picked up out of someone's gravel driveway, and this makes Onken smile. Though he is not married, not even close, he still has hopes to have a lot of children. Five at least. He especially would like to be the father to twin girls, he doesn't know why. He just likes kids, is all.

So when Connie calls in over the radio to report a missing child, the day suddenly seems more interesting. He responds in the affirmative and repeats the address. He imagines himself finding a frightened, weeping kid under a bush somewhere, picking him up, letting the kid wear his cap, letting him ride on his shoulders as he carries him back to his overwrought parents. The kid would hold tightly to him and give him a big hug. He'd be a hero for a moment or two. What other reason is there to be a cop?

––––

Onken turns into the driveway and a heavyset woman in a bright shirt and tight shorts comes hurrying out. She walks quickly over the grass toward him, flip-flops snapping, her face taut, frowning. And then Onken's heart sinks.

It's Old Lady Keene, his second-grade teacher. He feels himself blanching as she lumbers toward him. Second grade had not been the most pleasant time of his life, and even when he does happen to see Mrs. Keene—in the supermarket, or at the county fair, or somewhere accidental—he has always made a point of avoiding her. He doesn't know whether they've actually spoken since he was in elementary school.

But now, here she is. "Hello, Mrs. Keene," he says, stepping out of the car, and she stops to glare at him sharply.

"Hello, Kevin," she says, and gives him her old once-over. It's eerie to hear her say his name. It's the sound of a certain period of childhood: "Kevin," she says, and he is reminded again that he is not particularly bright or appealing, that he shouldn't hope for too much, that he will spend his life not attracting too much attention. She folds her hands behind her back in the way she once did when she was standing over his desk, not even disapproving but simply dismissing him, mildly, as another mediocre child who really wasn't worth her time.

"Kevin," she says, "I'm afraid I need your help."

They go through the usual steps. She has already canvassed the neighborhood, she says, both on foot and by telephone. She says that the child is not "the type" to wander off without telling her. He writes this down in his notebook.

"What about the," he says, "the parents of the child? Have you spoken to them?"

Mrs. Keene looks nonplussed. "My daughter is a drug addict," she says, flatly. "And she is also mentally ill." She clears her throat. "The last I knew was that she was in Las Vegas, but I do not know her current whereabouts."

"I see," Onken says.

"The father lives in town, but he is not the custodial parent. He was arrested about a year ago, and he's currently on probation. I'm the guardian ad litem."

"I see," Onken says. "And have you contacted him? The father?"

"No," she says. "He's ... under house arrest. Confined to his home."

"His name?"

"Troy Timmens," she says, with soft distaste.

"Oh," Onken says, and he feels an unpleasant weight settle over him. He knows the little boy, he realizes, and he feels inexplicably disturbed. He recalls the botched drug bust, the child's screams as he was pulled out from under the bed; the father, handcuffed in the kitchen, calling "It's okay, Loomis, it's okay," his voice breaking. The father had turned to Onken, his eyes stricken and teary. "Oh, shit, don't do this, please don't do this," he'd whispered, and Onken had said nothing. And then that horrible gunshot, the one that had gotten Ronnie Whitmire suspended, and him standing there, frozen, thinking the worst. Remembering this gives him a bad feeling, and he stands there for a moment, silent.

"So," he says. He looks blankly at his notebook. "Let's see," he says. "Are there any other relatives in town he might have gone off with? Or friends of the family?"

"No," Mrs. Keene says firmly. "Troy Timmens has some cousins or something—Ray, I think that's one of them. Ray Timmens, I assume, but no one *picked him up*. He was in the backyard. He was right in the backyard. He's not the sort of child to—"

"Can you show me the last place you saw him, please, Mrs. Keene?" Onken says. "And then we'll need to go through the house again. I'm assuming the child's room is exactly as it was before he, um, disappeared?"

"Oh, Jesus," Mrs. Keene says. And the part of Onken that still remains in second grade is deeply surprised to see that his teacher has begun to cry.

The last child to disappear from St. Bonaventure was found dead about six hours after he was reported missing. The child was a toddler, a little boy named Joshua Aiken, and there had been a short time when they had been dealing with his case as an abduction. The area had been secured, and a dog handler had come in to evaluate the scene for scents and make scent pads for his trail dog. Things seemed to be going smoothly at first—they had been able to cordon off the scene before family and neighbors had contaminated it too much, and the search was being conducted methodically. They had received tips on several reported sightings when the mother found the child's body.

It was in the basement. Police had searched the area previously but had neglected to look in the one place that, in retrospect, should have been obvious. A chest freezer, a Kenmore Quick Freeze, 24.9 cubic feet, approximately 3 feet high by 6 feet wide. The mother went down the basement stairs and noticed the little stool that was pushed up to the side of the freezer. It was a little three-legged stool that she'd almost forgotten about, which Joshua used to sit on while he watched TV and ate his lunch on the coffee table. *What is that doing down here,* she thought, and then her heart contracted. She put her hand to her mouth.

Later, the coroner determined that the child had suffocated, though it was also possible that he had frozen to death. It appeared that

Joshua had fallen into the freezer while trying to get a Popsicle, and that the lid had struck him a blow to the head, knocking him unconscious. Joshua's corpse lay there, stiffened atop a toppled stack of frozen diet dinners and plastic containers of summer corn and the white-paper-wrapped meat of a recently butchered deer. The child, in shorts and T-shirt and sandals, had already stiffened and begun to solidify in the cold.

———

Both Kevin Onken and Judy Keene remember this as they watch the dog handler putting his Doberman through its paces. The dog smells an item of Loomis's clothing, and then begins to explore the backyard area where Loomis was last seen, its bobbed tail stiff and quivering, its pointed ears erect.

He's dead, Onken thinks, suddenly. He has read studies. In seventy-four percent of the cases involving children, the child is deceased within three hours of being kidnapped. It's not just the studies though. It's an intuition.

Someone has him, Judy tells herself. Maybe he's with her daughter, who has performed a cruel trick. Maybe he's with Troy Timmens after all; they haven't been able to reach him by phone. Maybe he's simply inside someone's house, a friend, a neighbor, a stranger. But she is certain that he is somewhere. She has never been a superstitious person, but she is certain at this moment she can sense the presence of the child. His little soul. It is a small, steadily blinking pulse, like the light of an airplane moving across the sky at night.

PART TWO

PART TWO

13

April 16, 1993

A week before she died, Nora began to notice activity in the house again. Spirit activity. It was only little things at first: a pulse in the air, a feeling of being quietly observed, a quiver of movement behind her back. Late at night, she opened the door to the refrigerator and a cantaloupe fell out, rolling decisively across the kitchen floor as if guided, perambulating slowly across the tile before coming to a stop at the lip of the living room rug. During the day the telephone would ring and then stop—and not the usual sort of ring either, but strangely extended, the bell mechanism rattling and strangled, like an elderly singer trying to hold a high note for many measures. Of course, it stopped abruptly when she picked up the receiver. She stood there, holding the phone, and the bathroom door clicked open, hesitantly, as if a dog were gingerly nosing at it with her muzzle.

"Elizabeth," she said.

The past had been imposing itself heavily upon her lately, so it didn't seem so improbable that the dog might appear again in some form: a ghost, a presence. Or merely a feeling—tender, female, sad-eyed, tail tucked down with shy shame. Still sorry for what she'd done.

Nora supposed that if she had any decency she would be horrified by such a visitation. If she were a real mother, she would have hated Elizabeth. But all that came was a soft melancholy. "Elizabeth?" she murmured, as the bathroom door swung open. She was prepared.

But there was nothing. Nothing she could see, at least, and she was aware again of the foolishness, the perversity of her feelings. An ache had opened up inside her as she thought of Elizabeth, an overwhelming and unaccountable longing. There was no way to account for love, she thought, or for sorrow, no way to account for the ridiculous thought that in some ways Elizabeth had been her first baby. Her practice baby, she supposed. Even after all these years, she could vividly recall holding Elizabeth in her arms—a shy, lethargic puppy her father had brought home for her on her fifteenth birthday, and she had cradled the dog in her arms until it had gone to sleep, its paws limp and turned inward, the bare pink stomach heaving gently with breath. "Elizabeth" had been the name of a doll she had loved as a child, and also the name that she'd always hoped to christen a future daughter with. "That's not a name for a dog," her father had laughed, but she'd only shrugged.

"Well then, she's not just a dog," Nora said.

"She didn't mean to hurt you," she told Jonah after the accident. She sat by his bedside in the hospital, but she didn't look at his bandaged face, the single uncovered eye that glided vaguely in its socket, scoping the objects in the room indiscriminately. "She was just confused," Nora murmured, as if this would be a comfort to him. He may have heard her voice through the haze of painkillers, but ultimately she knew she was only talking to herself. Mumbling, reassuring herself. Years later, she would see a murderer's mother interviewed on TV, and she recognized that pinched quiver of sorrow and guilt and protective anger. "It was an accident," the woman said. "He'd never . . . on purpose," and Nora understood. She remembered the way her heart had clenched at the thought of her father beating Elizabeth to death, the way she'd sat dully in her chair in Jonah's hospital room, feeling her soul compressing into a wafer, a thin, meaningless cardboard lozenge. Jonah had looked at her—one eye covered, the other, roving aimlessly, raking a blur across her face. "It's locked," he whispered feverishly, and she would never know what he meant, though it ever after felt like an accusation. Her hands wavered over him, but she didn't know where—or if—to touch him.

Did he sense, in those first days that he was in the hospital, that at some level she hoped he would die? Did he know how fiercely she would have loved him if he *had* died, that he would have become a jewel she held inside her? Did he know that she could have endured his death more easily than his survival, his constant, living reminder of her failures as a mother, as a person?

Who knew? Who knew what Jonah was thinking—before or after? He was an eerie child even as a toddler: solemn, slow-blinking, big-eyed. In those few years after his birth when she was well, she was constantly having to reassure people—*No, there's nothing wrong with him. He's just spacey!* Very funny. Everyone laughed. Aged two, he trundled along in the child seat of a supermarket cart, talking to his own hand as if it were another child. A cute little act. He made his hand talk, flexing his fingers so the lifeline crease in his palm opened and closed like a puppet's mouth. People stared at them, smiling, but also a little unnerved. There was something forceful, odd, about his intensity of involvement with this game, and she remembered catching his hand—the hand he was talking to—and pressing it down, holding it tightly. *"Stop it,"* she said, through her teeth. "That's enough." And he hadn't protested. He looked blankly at the hand he had been talking to. "You killed my friend," he said, in his high, clear, toddler's voice, and it had actually made the hairs on the back of her neck prickle. He gazed at her, his eyes expressionless and owlish, and she said again, "Stop it. Right now." She knew it was wrong, but she dug her nails hard into the flesh of his limp hand. If only he had started crying—she would have picked him up, and held him, and stroked his hair, and rocked him against her shoulder. She would have said, "I'm sorry, I'm sorry, Jonah, Mommy didn't mean to hurt you." But he just stared.

"Ow," he said at last. "You're pinching me." And then she stopped. She let her grip relax.

Lately, the more she thought about finding a way to die, the more such memories came stalking her. She watched the bathroom door swing open of its own accord, stood there waiting, expectantly, and after a moment lit a cigarette. Her hands shook, but she managed it: brought the lighter flame to the tip, drew in breath, so that the ash began to glow. She breathed smoke, and that made her feel calmer. She didn't feel calm enough to actually enter the bathroom, but she could stand there, her arm folded across her chest, looking at the dim interior of the room dispassionately. Jonah would be home from his job at the old folks' home by seven-thirty. If he came into the house, the spirit activity would likely cease.

She was aware that she was trembling, shuddering like someone who had been out in the cold for a long time. She was forty-three years old. It was just after five in the afternoon.

Occasionally she tried to pinpoint the moment when she began to lose her mind. The psychiatrists she had talked to had wanted to discuss her mother's death; they had wanted to talk about what happened to her at Mrs. Glass House, but she'd always felt impatient with such conversations. Yes, it was terrible to lose your mother. Yes, it was very traumatic to give up a baby for adoption. But back then she had been doing just fine. For over five years she had managed, she had even been happy.

Look at the years 1966 to 1971. She aged from sixteen to twenty-one without any real problem. They might even be called the best years of her life—those years after she'd left the Home, those years before Jonah was born. It was easy to vanish into the world in those days, when the world was changing so rapidly, everything transformed and made new again. She had been discharged from Mrs. Glass House on a Monday, about a week after the baby was born, and she had known then that she wasn't going back to her father. She was already gone when her father's pickup pulled into the curving driveway of Mrs. Glass House, and when she called him from a pay phone in Omaha a few days later to say that she was okay, she had tried marijuana for the first time and her new friend Maris was standing beside her, the two of them giggling as she pressed her mouth to the receiver.

"You've always got a room here," her father said, earnestly, and she said, "I know, Daddy. Thank you, I know." She'd looked outside the glass wall of the phone booth to where a boy with a shaggy bowl of dark brown hair was leaning against his knapsack, waiting to take them to a place he knew, a communal house where they could stay for free. "I'm just going to be staying with a friend for a while," she told him. The glass of the phone booth was marvelously cool, almost liquid when she touched it, and the boy looked in at her and grinned. A few days later, she and the boy would hitchhike to Denver, and then she would ride with four girls in a blue 1955 Nash to San Francisco, and then she would live in Fresno for a while. She didn't call her father again, after that one time, for almost three years. She sent him postcards, little one-page letters decorated with cartoon flowers in the margins: She was happy, she wasn't thinking of anything, she was getting along fine.

Sometimes she tried to think about those years more specifically. She once collected a stack of notebook paper and tried to write herself a timeline. She wrote "July 1966" at the top of one page, and "August" at the top of the next, and so on. Then she sat there at the kitchen table with all the blank sheets of paper before her, a dozen thin threads tangling and unraveling in her mind. She couldn't put it in order, she realized. And even those things she thought she remembered, she found that she wasn't sure of. She started to remember, for example, that she'd met a girl named Maris in the bus terminal in Omaha, a sleepy-eyed, witty girl with plaited hair, sitting beside an overstuffed knapsack. But then she remembered that "Maris" was the name of the girl who had disappeared from Mrs. Glass House one day in early March. Would there have been two girls named Maris? It didn't seem likely, and yet she was certain that the girl she'd stayed with in the commune in Omaha was Maris. They'd been friends for . . . how long? When had she last seen this girl, what had become of her? She sat, staring at her blank sheets of paper.

It had troubled her all night. She'd been haunted, pacing the house at three in the morning, with the spirits sliding into place like shadows held for a moment under the beam of a flashlight. The house was full of ghosts, and she stood over Jonah's bed and trained her flashlight across his sleeping face.

"Don't . . . don't . . ." he'd mumbled, his eyes pinched, brushing at the light with his hand as if it were a cobweb. "Quit it! I've got to sleep." He didn't know how bad things were.

She could stand it when it was only at night. But now that it was during the day again, she didn't know. She stood outside the bathroom door for a long time, until her cigarette went out. Then she went back into the kitchen, thinking that she would make herself something to eat. She would feel better if she ate something, she thought. Some soup, maybe.

She found a can of soup in the cupboard and put it on the table. Then she found a can opener in a drawer and put it on the table beside the can. Then she found a pot and put that on the table, too. Here were three objects that were real. She didn't look over toward the bathroom, where the door was still open. She didn't hear the soft click of Elizabeth's black nails against the kitchen floor.

"Okay," she said. "Okay." She looked at her palm. She moved her fingers, and the joint creases opened and closed like the chirping mouths of baby birds. A terrible notion. Why should the creases between her fingers remind her of mouths? Why should a thing be like another thing? A word came to her from long-ago days at school— grammar school? Junior high?

Simile, she thought. You use the word *like* or *as*. My love is like a cherry. His cheeks were as red as apples.

It was a kind of craziness, she thought, that there were such echoes everywhere. It made the world indefinite, turning everything into a kind of cruel puzzle.

The handles on the drawer were like eyes.

The tree outside bowed its head like someone who was praying.

The top of a soup can was like a wrinkled, expressionless face.

Was it supposed to mean something? Was there a message in it? To receive these thoughts—similes, metaphors—was to draw closer to the spirit world. At least she hoped so. It was frightening to think that the world was simply a series of echoes, one object mirroring another randomly, emptily, a vast and multiform and mindless series of repetitions. The thought made her shudder, watching as a jellylike cylinder of cream of chicken soup slid into the little pot. She went to the sink and filled the now empty can with water, which she poured over the quivering gel of condensed soup. It eroded a little. There was a mouth she was thinking of, her fingers.

The question was, she thought, when had things started to go wrong? When had she started to lose hold of her mind?

In 1971, when Jonah was born, she had been okay. Twenty-one years old. Five years had passed since the first baby was born, and she was calmer. She was living with Gary Gray by that point, in Chicago. More or less stable. Gary had a job in construction, and they had a little place on the west side. She remembered her swollen belly, the difficulty she had kneeling down to plant petunias in the beds along the side of the house. She had been so big, she remembered, "a whale," she called herself, and that was how they had first come up with the name— as a joke.

"I feel like a whale," she said, and Gary Gray had made a quip about "little Jonah" in her belly. She'd called her father, to tell him that she was going to have a baby, and that she would probably be getting married. She just said this to make him happy. She wanted everyone to be glad for her. She wanted to be glad for herself. Being born, Jonah didn't hurt her nearly as much as the first one had.

14

September 3–4, 1996

Nebraska.

Utter blackness of the nighttime roads, space unraveling beyond the body of Jonah's car, emptiness. His headlights made the road signs glow like the eyes of animals, geometric shapes looming up abruptly.

Daytime wasn't any better, really. There were the towns, one after the other, spaced by a distance of ten or twenty miles, each with its grain elevator, a castle tower rising up out of the prairie. There were the flatlands and pastures that surrounded these outposts—round alfalfa bales like Stonehenge boulders in clean mowed fields; a single bare tree or ramshackle house in a barren lot of dirt-clod stubble; wide expanses of wheat, or corn, or sunflowers, with their thousands of heads turned east toward the sun. Blackbirds alit on the faces of the sunflowers, then rose up, flapping darkly. Bruise-colored clouds bunched up along the horizon that the road wove into, thunderheads with the pale sky above them.

Driving forward, he was aware of himself as a presence, a feeling, a sound track full of dissonance.

If this were his movie, here is where it would begin: foreboding scenery. He rewound the cassette tape over and over again, back to that same song, the distinct, plunking melancholy guitar, accompanied by the bone-notes of a xylophone. When the singer began to sing, he did, too. Staring out through the windshield at the onrushing highway, Jonah entertained himself by pretending that he could see the opening credits superimposed over the horizon.

He thought of his old friend—his former friend—Steve, holding up his palms, thumbs extended, framing the idea of a scene. "The story begins in late summer," Jonah said, imitating the thick, whispery male narrators who spoke in the previews for coming attractions. "It began in September, not quite six months after the boy turned twenty-five." But this didn't sound right, and so he'd gone back to the beginning. "The story begins . . ." he said. He liked the sound of it.

He found himself murmuring the same thing under his breath as he packed stuff into his mother's old car. Some books, clothes, compact discs. "It was September. He was twenty-five. No one knew he was leaving. Or where he was going." He packed some notepads. Some dishes he hated to part with. Clothes. A tent he'd ordered from a catalog.

The rest of his stuff—thrift-store bric-a-brac, winter coat, crappy old RCA radio/cassette/alarm clock, magazines and newspapers, laundry soap, cans of soup, ketchup, and a half-eaten jar of sweet gherkins in the refrigerator—this he left where it was, and he supposed that eventually Mrs. Orlova or her husband would have to clean it out; when they hadn't received a rent check from him in a while, they would open up his furnished room. Perhaps they would half expect to find him there dead, a suicide or a young-man heart attack. Sasha, Mrs. Orlova's husband, would mumble a curse in Russian, pulling at the keys that hung from his belt. Jonah had thought of saying something to Mrs. Orlova, he'd thought about calling his boss at the restaurant, but at the last minute he didn't. Better, he thought, to simply disappear.

And yet, when he woke that morning, he imagined that he was still in Chicago. He imagined the familiar framework of his efficiency, his bed, the dusty lamp and bedside table with its stack of books, the sound of the el train rattling beyond his window, the expectation of the restaurant sched- ule posted on a corkboard in the dark hallway of the restaurant's basement. The life he'd been leading for more than three years, to no avail.

He was in a tent. He saw a shadow shake against the canvas surface above him, a rustling shape, and after a moment he was aware of the memory of driving, of checking into the campground, a KOA park on the edge of St. Bonaventure. When he unzipped the tent flap and crawled out, the sun was rising low in the sky. There was his car, packed with his belongings; there was a long Winnebago parked across from him. A middle-aged couple—a woman with long brown hair and a fat man with a beard and a Hawaiian shirt—were sitting outside the Win- nebago in lawn chairs while their little girl played nearby. They were watching a small portable television and eating peaches, and they waved to him benignly as he looked over, as he limped barefoot over the gravel to his car. He opened his car door and sat down, staring at the road, putting on his shoes and trying to think.

This was not very cinematic. Sitting in the bucket of a car seat with untied shoes, looking at pebbles. The sun hung tentatively over the horizon, gelatinous and shivering like the yolk of an uncooked egg. He could feel an edge of mundane discouragement rising up again, as it often did when he was in Chicago. What now?

He sat there, looking at a map that he had ripped out of a tele- phone booth phone book, tracing through the puzzle of streets until he found, at last, the one he was looking for—all the way on the other side of town, on the very edge. He reached under the seat and found his pair of binoculars, which he placed on the passenger seat beside him. He listened as the little girl outside the Winnebago sang tune- lessly: "Tomorrow, tomorrow, I love you tomorrow," and he watched for a moment as she casually hit her baby doll with a stick in rhythm to the song. He tied his shoes.

For almost a year now, ever since that day in October when the packet came in the mail from the PeopleSearch Agency, he'd been trying to decide what to do. How to proceed. He'd gone over and over the information they sent him, tracing underneath each word, each individual letter with his fingernail, as if there were some encryption buried in it that he could uncover with careful study. Here was a name, an address; a credit report; some court documents.

He'd find himself waking up at night to go through this material, sitting there at the window of his third-floor efficiency, staring out at the empty street below, thumbing through the small sheaf of papers, aware of the strange, floating ache they conjured up, a kind of bottomless feeling. It reminded him of the time he'd found a reproduction of a landscape painting in a book for an art history class, a white house on a jagged seacoast that had struck him with the force of a forgotten memory. *I used to live there once,* he thought, though he also knew that it was impossible. Nevertheless, he could clearly remember walking up the gravel path toward that wooden, red-shingled house, could hear the sound of the waves against the rocks, the calls of gulls. He and his mother must have visited that exact place, he thought, and it was several days before he realized that the painting in the book was the same one his mother had on a postcard that she'd taped on the headboard of her bed. He must have stared into it so deeply that it had lodged in his mind as a memory. Even knowing this, he couldn't shake the feeling that this was a place he'd once been, that he'd walked along that path and into that house, where a friendly blind woman sat in a rocking chair, and the sunlight slanted against the blond wood floors. It wasn't a real memory, he realized, but it felt like one.

That same sensation came over him again as he read through the bare facts of Troy's life. He remembered the baby, the brother that his mother had told him about, her eyes turned sidelong toward him: *I was very young, I had to give it away;* and when he'd asked where the baby had gone when she gave it away, he could see again how her eyes had hardened: *He went to live with a nice mother.*

He had pictured his brother when she said this, very clearly—so clearly that he seemed like someone Jonah had met, a child Jonah had played with, who had perhaps lived in that Winslow Homer shoreline house, with the lighthouse in the distance. He never clearly saw the brother's nice mother and father, though he felt them not far away when he would come to the edge of the green square of lawn where his brother was casually throwing a ball high into the air, holding his hands out to catch it. Just beyond his brother's backyard was a cliff, with the sea below, the high tide lapping hard against the rocks. Jonah had stood there at the edge of the fence, with Elizabeth beside him, her ears pricked up and alert. The boy, his brother, had turned to look at him, and the ball had fallen into his open palms. Their eyes met. The boy had smiled, kindly, mysteriously, and tossed the ball across the fence to Jonah.

Years later, when Jonah and Mr. Knotts had been clearing out the old yellow house, he'd found that ball again, in a box of childhood things. It was deflated, almost flat, fading red with a yellow star in the middle. But it was a real thing. The ball existed, though the land that it had come from, the seaside house and the silent child in the patch of bright green grass, those were only his imagination.

———

He thought of all this as he drove through St. Bonaventure. He knew, of course, even before he came here that there would be no beautiful coastal house, no bright patch of lawn on a cliff overlooking the sea— none of the things that he'd imagined. And yet he still would never have believed how closely it resembled the place he'd grown up, Little Bow, South Dakota.

Like Little Bow, St. Bonaventure was the kind of town that people passed through on their way to somewhere else. A typical small Plains town. Here were storefronts: drugstore, cafe, barbershop, liquor store, bar. A Pizza Hut, a church. A Safeway supermarket set back from the road, with a half acre of asphalt parking lot in front of it, mostly un-occupied. The town was not quaint, exactly, though the buildings that some of the stores occupied had a turn-of-the-century feel to them, brick and stone, with high fronts like in Westerns. There was no doubt some history attached to the place, it had once been an outpost or way station along some great migration or another, the Oregon Trail, the Union Pacific Transcontinental railroad. Perhaps it was a fort from back in the time when the United States was busy with the project of wrest-ing the land from the native people who had dwelt there—wanting it very badly, but then finding it not very interesting once it was conquered. While the rest of the world was exploding with population, places like

St. Bonaventure were steadily shrinking, fading out. It was the sort of town that Jonah used to talk about bitterly to Steve and Holiday, the kind of town that Jonah had always claimed to have escaped.

He had been wavering now for months, almost a year of rising and falling urgency—an urgency that never went away, but simply tilted back and forth between anticipation and dread.

In the beginning, he'd merely taken pleasure in holding the information in his hands, feeling it take shape in his mind. He read his brother's name over and over: *Troy Earl Timmens.* He spoke it aloud, he read through the home address, *421 Gehrig Avenue, St. Bonaventure, Nebraska 69201*; the place of employment, *Stumble Inn Bar and Grille;* the credit report, basically quite good, a MasterCard and an American Express, a car payment, nothing else. He had a wife, Carla, and a son, Loomis, born December 18, 1990.

Jonah had been especially attracted to the adoption decree, with its odd, archaic language, like some olden-time bill of sale: *"IT IS THERE-FORE ORDERED, ADJUDGED AND DECREED that the right to custody of and power and control over said minor child and all claims and interest in and to the wages by said Mrs. Glass Institute shall and do cease and determine from and after this date, and the said Baby Boy Doyle is hereby declared the adopted child of the said Earl Roger Timmens and Dorothy Winnifred Timmens, husband and wife."*

He read this aloud sometimes, too, liking the sound of it. *Baby Boy Doyle,* he pronounced, redolent of some 1930s gangster-movie nickname, faint music of low piano keys and muted trumpet. "Baby Boy Doyle," he said, into the silence of his efficiency. "Troy Earl Timmens." A door thrown open with wind and a scuttle of leaves. Here was the history that moved outside of his mother's knowledge, a pathway tracing its way into the future. *Baby Boy Doyle:* his mother's son. *Troy Earl Timmens:* someone else entirely. The simplicity of it was the thing that stunned him the most. The exchange seemed so easy: a few words, and you were a new person.

————

At first he thought he was going to write a letter. *Dear Troy Timmens,* he wrote, and then he sat there staring at it for over a month. He wrote: *My name is Jonah Doyle, and I am your brother.* And then he erased it. He wrote, *You may not believe this, but.* He wrote, *I am writing to inform you that I believe that we are related, and I hope that you will be interested in perhaps meeting and.*

And what? The letter was on the table when he got up in the morning, along with a book he'd bought called *The Journey of the Adopted Child.* When he got home from work it would still be there, waiting, mute. A yellow legal pad: He would tear off the top sheet and write the new date at the top—December, January, February—and then he would write *Dear.*

Sometimes, he would get past the greeting, and he would even write the first couple of lines of the opening paragraph. He would open *The Journey of the Adopted Child* and flip through it irritably, looking for some clue about how to proceed. Then he might decide to go out for a walk, to clear his head, to think it over. He might go to a movie, and afterward, sit in the bar on the corner and have a few beers. Then, home again, his head a little fuzzy with alcohol, he'd find himself writing things that he could never send.

Dear Troy Timmens,

Once upon a time there was a woman who had two sons. The first son she gave away when she was a teenager, and she regretted it for the rest of her life. The second son she kept for her own, and she regretted that even more.

Or, even worse:

Dear Brother,

I used to think of you all the time when I was growing up. Our mother would talk about you and she would cry about how she hated herself ever since she gave you away. I'm the kind of woman who would give away her own baby, she would say, and I would sit there and think of you. I used to wonder why she had kept me. Why was I the one who got stuck?

It was not hard to find the street where Troy Timmens lived. He had to stop along the roadside a couple of times to consult his map, but the streets came together with an almost eerie inevitability, the way a wooded trail in dreams led closer and closer toward some unknown, waiting thing. A house, a treasure, a shape rising up with small eyes and bright claws among the dapples of leaves. When he saw the signpost, he slowed his car to a stop, pulled over to the curb.

Without warning, he had begun to tremble, and he held tight to the steering wheel. He was shuddering, as if inside him was a small motor such as powered an old lawn mower, his teeth humming against one another. Up to now, there had been only a steadily growing hollow pit of anticipation in his stomach, but abruptly it had grown huge. It was terror of a sort he couldn't even put his finger on—somewhere at the farthest end of stage fright with its limp-boned, consuming paralysis, and moving from there into something childish and primal, like the pure panic of a light being turned out, a door being closed and locked.

On the edge of Gehrig Avenue, Troy's street, he was momentarily overcome; a thin, thrumming wire stretched taut inside him. He fitted his palms over his face, breathing against his cupped hands.

He didn't know whether he could go through with it.

The first time Jonah had tried to call Troy was on his birthday, in March. He'd begun to realize that the letters he'd been attempting were never going to be finished, he was never going to find the right words that could be sealed up into an envelope and sent out into the empty world, utterly out of his control. Even if he did find the courage to send a letter, he knew that it would be unbearable to wait from a distance, to imagine for days and weeks the moment when the letter would fall into the mailbox, the moment when Troy Timmens would tear it open and—however eloquent Jonah managed to become—scan through the columns of words.

On the night of his twenty-fifth birthday, Jonah had bought a twelve-pack of fancy German beer, to prepare himself. He had drunk three of them when he telephoned Troy's house. It was ten P.M. in Chicago, nine P.M. in St. Bonaventure, Nebraska, and Troy answered on the first ring.

"Y'ello?" Troy said: A deep, country-accented voice, abrupt and thick. Jonah opened his mouth and silence unraveled out.

"Hello?" Troy said again, this time more formal, cautious. And then, after another long pause: "Carla?"

And Jonah had abruptly hung up.

Jonah had called again in late April, and then again in May, and both times it had been the same. Even though he'd written out a script for himself, he couldn't say anything. He would part his lips to speak, but he was only capable of hesitation. He pictured himself stumbling into that brightly lit pause, and his face grew warm with a blush. He would sound like an idiot, he thought. *Hi. My name is Jonah Doyle, and I . . .* He could imagine his hatefully befuddled voice, and his skin tingled with self-loathing. He hung up in April without saying anything. In May, he said, "Is . . . Is this Jonah Doyle?" And Troy said, "I think you have the wrong number."

When he called in June, he'd decided to take a different tactic. He'd decided that it might work better if he pretended to be doing a survey for the Mrs. Glass House Institute, and he'd felt calmer then, pretending to be someone else. But Troy was evasive, irritable in a way that got Jonah flustered. *I'm not liable to talk to someone over the phone about this. You need to send me a letter or something,* Troy said. And Jonah found himself inched into a corner, the conversation that he'd at first imagined was under his control—an interview, for God's sake, how could it go wrong?—had eventually collapsed under the weight of a simple lie: Jonah claimed that the Mrs. Glass Institute had sent a letter, and Troy hadn't received it. It was ridiculous, and he'd made plans to correct it, but he'd never been able to get ahold of Troy on the phone again. Thereafter, though he'd called several times in July and August, all he'd gotten was an answering machine, a hurried, wooden voice: *This is Troy. Sorry I'm not in. Leave a message if you want and I'll get back with you.*

When Jonah had heard this message for the tenth time, he realized what he had to do. He needed to go to St. Bonaventure. Whatever he was going to say, it had to be said in person.

So now here he was. He arrived at last outside the house that, according to all his records and maps, belonged to his brother: Troy Earl Timmens. He parked his car across the street, and hunched down in his seat. *The story begins,* he thought, but the romantic glow had faded from the phrase.

He had been hoping for something a bit better. He had imagined that his brother—with the advantages of a loving family, approved by the Mrs. Glass House and the St. Bonaventure County Court—might have made something more of himself. Even when he'd seen that Troy Timmens worked for a place called the *Stumble Inn Bar and Grille,* he'd thought that maybe it was a fancy place, maybe Troy was a burgeoning restaurateur; he thought Troy was perhaps an artist of some sort, working a bar job to make ends meet while he painted or sculpted or, like Steve, wrote screenplays.

Now, such imaginings seemed less and less likely. Troy's house was a shabby, simple white box, more or less identical to the others on its block—a lower-middle-class neighborhood at the very edge of St. Bonaventure, not far from the barren, hilly prairie that surrounded the town on all sides. It was the kind of home that made Jonah think of a child's drawing: two windows, a door, a triangle roof. Ancient bare branch of television antenna jutting out. There was a faded awning over the picture window in front. The curtains were pulled closed.

An unhappy place, Jonah thought. The unfenced front yard was overgrown—the grass unmowed and going to seed, patches of weeds thriving. There was a dying tree in one corner, half of the branches dry and bare, the others still leafy, but fading. The lot had the look of a property that had been up for sale so long that it could be considered abandoned, but then there was an aging Corvette in the driveway that signaled someone's presence, and there was the simple fact that the mailman delivered letters to this address. Jonah sat up and watched as the mailman, wearing khaki shorts and black socks and shoes, strode up the sidewalk and fit a packet of envelopes into the mailbox. He could imagine the letters that he had considered writing arriving in this way, at this sad house, and it made his heart sink.

The determination that had fortified him during his long drive seemed to leave him like a spirit lifting out of a corpse. All he had to do was walk up the sidewalk himself; all he had to do was summon the courage to stand there at the front door and touch the doorbell with his finger. He tried to project himself into that moment.

Here: Troy Timmens would come to the door, and he would look at Jonah with mild curiosity. They would resemble each other in some surprising way.

"I have some information that you might be interested in," Jonah would say, and he would hand over the packet from the PeopleSearch Agency. "I believe we have the same mother," Jonah would say softly, in a steady voice to buffer Troy Timmens from the shock. "We're half brothers, I think."

And then he would extend his hand for Troy to shake.

"My name is Jonah Doyle," he would say. "I've been wanting to meet you for a long time."

But despite his imagination, Jonah didn't do anything. He sat there, staring at the door, thinking of his mother. "I didn't even look at him," she had told Jonah once. "I didn't even get the chance to look." The nurses had taken the baby away while she was still under anesthesia, and he had pictured her drifting into sleep; he had imagined the thin trail of a baby's crying unraveling down a long blurry hallway while she drifted and dreamed, and then, finally, the infant's wails shrinking away into a dot of silence, blinking out as her mind went white with static.

"I'd be a different person if I'd have kept that baby," she said once, cloudy and blissful, and then her eyes focused and grew stern.

"I should have given you up, too," she said, and Jonah had rested his head against her as she'd stroked his face, tracing the pad of her finger along his scars. "You know that, don't you?" she murmured. "I could have let you be happy."

Even now, this struck him a glancing blow. He saw again the seaside house, the postcard landscape he'd entered as a child. Then he sat up abruptly.

A man had emerged from the house on Gehrig Avenue. He came around from the back, wearing a white button-down shirt and black pants, but Jonah got only a glimpse of him—a broad-shouldered guy, medium height, with a build like a high school wrestler, curly black hair, olive skin. A subtle, steady limp. Then the man was slamming the door of the old Corvette, revving the engine. Jonah was surprised at how calm he felt as he started his own car. Eased out from the curb. *I could have let you be happy,* he thought, and his teeth pressed hard against one another.

In a film, this moment would require some tricky camera work. For a second, the camera would float far above the town of St. Bonaventure with an ambient hum of chords, hovering and then banking down to follow the two cars in motion, almost two-dimensional from above. The red 1981 Corvette, heading toward the center of town and turning left, followed by the boxy, rattling, toylike Ford Festiva, Jonah's mother's old car, white with rust in the creases and cracks. The sky is gray. The leaves on the trees are still green, but it is clearly edging toward autumn. The camera slowly dips as the cars trace their way down the main street, through the few stoplights and finally to a side street—seedy, faded strip of storefronts beyond which the town begins to drift away into aging courtyard motels and trailer parks and fields. At last, the camera's eye settles onto Jonah's face. Troy's car slides into a parallel parking space, and then Troy emerges, unfolding himself from the low-slung bucket seat, limping tenderfooted into a bar that is lit by a blinking neon sign: STUMBLE INN, it says, the letters arranged vertically, and there is the outline of a thin neon cowboy leaning against the words.

In the movie, the camera would hold for a long time on Jonah's face. He would be expressionless, staring, but the music might hint at complex emotions, drifting into a minor key and some slight discord, pulling closer and closer toward his scarred face, toward his eye, with the pupil dilating larger and larger, as if he were moving into a darkened room.

Which he was.

He entered the dim barroom, with its softly damp, gravelike smell and its forlorn jukebox music. It was three o'clock in the afternoon, and the place was quiet. He hovered outside of himself, watching. An older lady, a bartender, busied herself at a chalkboard that listed the food that

could be purchased, busily erasing "Chili-Chicken Chimichanga—$4."
Two paint-freckled workers sat at the bar, staring at a muted television
mounted above the liquor bottles, watching studiously as a beauty
whom Jonah didn't recognize was being interviewed on an Entertainment News program. At the other end of the bar, a balding man in a
checkered sports jacket poked his finger into his drink and plucked out
a piece of ice, which he ate; at the far left, two stout, youngish, red-
haired women were playing pool while two red-haired toddlers dangled
their legs over the edge of a second, unused pool table and observed,
sharing popcorn from a bag. The booths that lined the walls and the tables that were scattered throughout the narrow barroom were otherwise empty.

None of these people looked at Jonah. Entering a place like this,
with a face like his, he anticipated the hostile curiosity of townsfolk,
but it didn't come. It was as if he was invisible, taking in the atmosphere, trying to locate the person he'd been following. He approached
the bar cautiously, and the bartender lady turned.

It was the usual reaction when she saw him—the quick, startled
gape and polite swallowing of response, the surreptitious trawl of her
glance across his scar, the question: *Jesus Christ, what happened to him?*
echoing murmurously against him as she blinked and regained herself.

"Can I help you?" she said, and Jonah cleared his throat.

I'm looking for Troy Timmens, he thought to say. But he just stared for
a moment, crossing his arms over his chest. "I was ... reading the
menu," he said, hesitantly. "Is the kitchen still open?"

"Oh, yes," the woman said, and flashed her kindly, silver-edged
teeth. She called over her shoulder. "Troy!" she shouted. "What are
you doing back there? Will you cook for awhile until Junie gets back? It
shouldn't be more than an hour. He had a doctor's appointment!" And
a voice, deep and affectless, said, "No problem."

In a movie, the camera would rattle for a moment. It would hover over
the outside of the bar, banking through the web of treetops and along
the flat tar-paper roof of Zyke's Roller Rink across the street, and then
it would begin to gather momentum, speeding up as it plunged toward
the Stumble Inn Bar and Grille, until it became the rush of a train as it

entered a tunnel—a blur of motion as it barreled through the bar, as the train went straight into the back of Jonah's head and right through him. Here, framed for a moment in the small window through which orders were passed to the kitchen, was the face of his brother, bobbing up and then disappearing. In a movie, there is only the glimpse of the face. Then the film strip breaks off abruptly, snapping and turning around and around in the reel as the projector shines blank light on the screen.

15

September 13, 1996

The parole anklet—the monitoring device—was always the first thing Troy noticed when he woke up. It was not heavy at all: a small black metal box, seemingly hollow, no bigger than a seat-belt buckle, attached to his ankle by a kind of thick plastic watchband. But still he could feel it there, even before he was conscious. It entered his sleeping mind as a discomfort, and then, slowly, his awareness solidified. Here was the anklet's weight against his skin. It was itchy. He reached down and scratched along the circumference of the plastic shackle, afraid to touch the thing, afraid that he would set off the tamper alert, which, he had been told, was extremely sensitive. He could almost feel the thing pulsing, sending out its radio signals to a station where someone sat in a swivel chair before a bank of blinking green and red lights. He was under "house arrest." He had been told that if he moved beyond the perimeter of his yard, an alarm would sound somewhere, and an immediate warrant for his arrest would be issued, and he would be tracked down and sent to prison.

It was sometime in the afternoon. He could feel the dull, steady heat of the sun as strips of it poured through the slats of the blinds, and the unhealthy film of daytime sleep clung to his skin. He stirred, restlessly, and felt a piece of paper crumpled beneath him. It was the T. rex skeleton he'd drawn for Loomis, which must have come untaped from the wall. He sat up and discovered that he had been sleeping in Loomis's bed. He didn't remember why.

In the two and a half months since his arrest, the house had been slowly devolving. It had never been particularly neat, but now as he padded in his underwear through the piles of dirty clothes and unwashed bowls of dried-up ice cream, the stacks of unread junk mail and bills, the jigsaw puzzle that he'd begun to put together as a distraction and then abandoned, the empty plastic bottles of soda—he was aware again that he had been overcome by entropy. "Son of a bitch," he said, as he stepped on the sharp plastic edge of one of Loomis's Legos with his bare foot. He limped into the kitchen and took a cola out of the refrigerator.

He'd been told that he was lucky. He was not in prison, where he would be easy prey for weight-lifting tattooed Nazis and angry Caucasian-hating black men. He had negotiated what was said to be an extremely light sentence—thirteen months of house arrest, with a parole anklet monitor, followed by two years' worth of regular parole. And his parental rights had not been terminated, exactly—though Judy had official custody of Loomis for an indeterminate period. He was still allowed to work as a bartender at the Stumble Inn, though he was subject to random drug and alcohol tests and part of his salary was garnisheed to offset the cost of the probation program.

His lawyer had convinced him that this plea bargain was the most favorable option. His lawyer, Eric Schriffer, had been one of his regular marijuana customers, and he'd assumed that this would mean that Schriffer would look out for his best interests. But now he wasn't so sure. It was true that they had photos of him purchasing drugs from the unfortunate Jonathan Sandstrom, but it was also true that they hadn't been able to accumulate a felony's worth of drugs from his home. Besides which a police officer had discharged a firearm in the direction of a helpless child. Now, thinking about it, he wondered whether a different lawyer, someone from out of town, might have been more aggressive. He might have had a good case to sue the police department.

Sometimes he thought Eric Schriffer had actually betrayed him, leading him into a plea bargain that mostly protected Schriffer himself.

Such ideas occurred to him now, long after he'd signed the myriad of papers, long after the anklet had been pinch-stapled to his bare ankle, long after Schriffer had stopped returning Troy's calls to the office of Goodwin, Goodwin, Schriffer and Associates. He was aware that he'd probably been duped. But what could he do now? Who could he call to complain—the Better Business Bureau? The ACLU? God?

It was over and done with. There was no one who could help him.

———

On the kitchen table was the black book—his "itinerary," as his parole officer called it. Stamped in gold leaf on the cover it said *Daily Planner* in an italicized, pompous cursive that he found offensive. This was #17 of the many conditions of parole that he'd agreed to: "Offenders will submit detailed hourly itinerary of their activities to parole officer"—and thus *Daily Planner* had become a constant, hated companion through the endless days and weeks of house arrest.

He sat down at the table and flipped it open. Friday the thirteenth: ha, ha. Each hour of the day, from one A.M. to midnight, had several lines next to it where he was to write down his "activities," and he took up his pen and wrote "SLEEP" in capital letters next to one A.M., and then below it SLEEP next to two A.M., and then down the row: SLEEP, SLEEP, SLEEP, SLEEP until he reached two P.M. He glanced at the wall clock, which said it was nearly three in the afternoon, and he was aware that he'd spent more than half his day unconscious.

His parole officer, Lisa Fix, would no doubt take note of this. She commented on patterns that she noticed as she read over the itinerary during their weekly meetings.

"You sleep a lot," she'd said the last time they had met. "Do you think you're depressed?"

"That's a keen insight," Troy said. "You ever thought of becoming a psychiatrist?"

She raised her eyebrows and looked at him over the rim of her glasses. For a bureaucrat, she didn't mind sarcasm all that much, and this was one of the things that made their weekly conferences bearable to him. She was in her mid- or late thirties, he guessed, a plump, freckled-faced, cynical woman with overly permed red hair—divorced, he would assume. She was a type he'd seen frequently in his years as a bartender, the kind of woman he could usually joke with or even flirt with a little as he served drinks, and she didn't seem to mind. She talked to him like she was his begrudging older sister, or a former lover who still liked him a little but knew his ways too well. There was something about her that made him think, for the first time in a long while, of Chrissy, that girl he'd met long ago in Bruce and Michelle's trailer, the girl who had kissed him when he was eleven. Lisa and Chrissy were probably about the same age, he thought.

"Of course I'm depressed," Troy said. "Wouldn't you be, given my situation?"

"Well," Lisa Fix said, "we've talked about various constructive uses for your time. Have you looked any further into the correspondence courses we spoke of?"

"Not really," Troy said. "Not yet." He shrugged. "Hey, listen," he said, "did you go to high school with Chrissy Hart?"

She raised her eyebrows at him. "That girl who committed suicide?" And now it was her turn to shrug. "She was a couple of years older than me, but sure, I knew her. Knew *of* her, at least. We didn't exactly run in the same crowd. Why?"

"I don't know," Troy said. "Just curious."

"A trip down memory lane," Lisa Fix said, and pinched her mouth a bit. "I knew your wife, Carla, too, as a matter of fact. She and Chrissy were seniors when I was a sophomore. I can't say that I remember ever speaking to them. Why? Is something on your mind?"

"I don't know," he said. He looked briefly at her eyes, which were sharply attentive, and then he looked back down. He thought to say *Chrissy was the first girl I ever kissed*, but what would be the point of that? "Just thinking about stuff," he said.

"Well . . ." Lisa said. "Look, Chrissy Hart slit her wrists in her mom's bathtub, and Carla has a serious drug problem and hasn't been heard from in months. I don't see much that's positive that can be gleaned from a discussion of those people." She cleared her throat, and her gaze hooked into him. "Why don't we think about the future instead of the past? Did you fill out that sheet I gave you?"

He grimaced. He still had the mimeographed piece of paper she had given him, onto which he was supposed to write down ten "short-term goals" and ten "long-term goals," but he didn't know where he had put the thing. He hadn't filled it out.

"What about Loomis?" he said. "You said last week that you'd look into seeing if I could talk to him on the phone. That's one short-term goal we can talk about."

Lisa looked at him heavily, as if he were a student who had given the wrong answer, even after she had coached and coached. "Well," she said, "I did look into that. *And.* Loomis's guardian has refused your request. She thinks that it's best if Loomis settles in awhile after . . . his trauma. I can't say that I don't agree."

"Fuck," Troy said, softly. He reddened—he could feel his temper growing, and as he swallowed it his eyes fishbowled with tears of frustration. He sat there, his face impassive, and drew his eyelids down slowly. He lowered his face and pressed his thumbs against his eye ducts for a moment.

"Okay," he said. "Okay. Well then. Let's move on."

———

At three-thirty he telephoned the headquarters, to let them know that he was traveling to his place of employment. The alarm on his ankle would be turned off for a brief time—ten minutes or so—to allow him to drive the few miles to the bar, to the Stumble Inn. Sitting in his car, he imagined himself as a red blinking dot, stuttering across the screen of someone's computer, watched, monitored. Early on, Lisa Fix had suggested that he think about another job—for example, working for the county's organization for the mentally retarded, for which he would be paid for thirty-five hours, minimum wage, with five hours going to his community service—but he'd stood his ground on this. He had worked as a bartender for years, he said. He was good at his job. It was his livelihood, the one thing he felt confident he did well, and this was the one thing that Eric Schriffer had done for him. They couldn't force him to change jobs. They couldn't completely unmake his life.

"Well then," she said. "I can put you on a cleanup crew for your community service. I was trying to give you a better option."

"I don't want to quit my job," he said. "And I don't like retarded people. What good is minimum wage shit work going to do me?"

"Okay then," Lisa Fix said. She gave him another one of her older sister stares, one that said: *I can't believe you're so stupid.*

Once he was at work, he called the number again, to assure them that he had arrived. He recited his offender number several times, and finally, the man at the other end of the phone said, "Okay. Check. I've entered you into the database."

"Thank you," Troy said, and glanced up to see a middle-aged drunk staring at him. The man had a craggy, oblong face, vaguely like Abraham Lincoln, and his drooping, dim-witted eyes examined Troy for what seemed like a long time. Then Abe smiled, his mouth turned up in a gentle, satisfied bow.

"They got you, huh?" the man said, and widened his grin to show a row of surprisingly large white teeth: dentures. "They really got you now!"

"Yes," Troy said politely, but didn't smile. "They got me."

Crystal was behind the bar, and glanced at him sympathetically as he slid open the cooler and began to count the bottled beer. "Hey, babe," she said. "How're you doing?"

"Mm," he grunted, and wrote on the back of a napkin the numbers of beers that he needed to bring up from the basement. "Slow day?" he said.

She nodded, her hands working in a bus tub of soapy water. "Terrible slow," she said. "For a Friday, especially." She brought up a beer glass and rinsed it under the tap.

"What's the situation with Honest Abe over there?" Troy said. He gestured with his chin toward the man with the dentures, who was sitting by the telephone, staring at it placidly.

"Oh, boy," Crystal said. "I don't know where he came from. He's been here since this morning. He's about eight or nine beers in."

"Well," Troy said. "Ring up his tab before you close out. I'm cutting him off."

She widened her eyes at him, as she always did when she thought he was being harsh or abrupt. She had large blue eyes, and straight, thick hair the color of cedarwood, a round pretty face. She was a nice girl. "The Mormon Chick," Ray used to call her, because her parents were supposedly Mormons from Wyoming. She wasn't religious herself as far as Troy knew—she worked as a bartender, after all—but she exuded a certain kind of goodness. There was a kindhearted innocence to her: She worried about other people's sadness and suffering and wanted to do what was right. She once confided to Troy that she thought people, all people, were basically good at heart, and Troy had looked at her wryly.

"I read that book, too," he said. "You know what? That Anne Frank—the Nazis killed her anyway."

She had argued with him a little back then, but now she said nothing. She cut off President Lincoln without protest, shrugging. "Vivian's here" was all she said, and Troy let out a slow sigh. Vivian was the owner, and she frequently got angry when Troy decided to refuse to serve a customer. "You're not the beer police, Troy," Vivian had said on a number of occasions. "If they're not causing trouble, they can drink until they're passed out on the floor as far as I'm concerned."

Troy slid open the ice cooler to check the status, to see if he needed to bring some more from the ice machine in the basement. "What's she doing here?" he said, frowning. "I thought she was taking the day off."

"She's training a new guy," Crystal said. "She hired a new cook. They're down in the office now, I guess, filling out some forms or something."

"Hm," Troy said. "Is something up with Junie?"

"He's sick again," Crystal said, and pursed her mouth. "I feel so sorry for him!" she said. "He's old. Do you know he's almost seventy? He shouldn't have to be working all the time."

"Oh come on," Troy said. "He likes to work." But the truth was that Junie the cook had been looking worse and worse lately, though he'd never looked exactly healthy. He was a small, wiry Sioux man, with deeply melancholy eyes and a permanent, exaggerated frown, and lately, every time Troy looked at him, Junie seemed to send out waves of pessimism. What if he ended up like Junie, Troy would find himself thinking. Junie, who had been in and out of jail, who smelled of old man b.o., tobacco, and stale beer, was now sick and probably dying. It occurred to him that Junie had once been his age. It occurred to him that a man could live out his last days in a bar like Vivian's Stumble Inn, that you could live for years and years and years with nothing at all, and still exist.

"Geez," Troy said at last, trailing these thoughts. "How sick is he?"

"I don't know. But he's in the hospital," Crystal said. "I might go visit him this weekend. Bring him some flowers or something. Do you want to come?" And then she stopped herself awkwardly. "Sorry," she said.

He was silent. These small, humiliating moments were not the worst thing about his "house arrest," but they were steady and goading, the most constant. He smiled at Crystal, but it felt more like a wince. "I have other plans this weekend," he said, ironically, even as she gazed at him with her large, sympathetic eyes.

"Are you okay, Troy?" she said. "I mean, I know you don't want to talk about it, but . . ." She sighed, made a flustered motion with her hand. "It must hurt you," she said. "You limp."

He felt himself twitch, involuntarily. "No, not really," he said. "It's not tight or anything."

"That's good," she said. She looked down at his pant leg, to where the anklet monitor was discreetly covered. "I just meant, well. Spiritually. It must be painful. It's a very cruel thing for them to do. To put that thing on you."

"Not really," Troy said, and he looked away from her, smiling tightly. The anklet felt warm and heavy. "It's not a big deal," he said. He shut the sliding door of the ice cooler, decisively. "I hardly notice it."

By the time Vivian came upstairs with the new guy, Abraham Lincoln had left peaceably and the bar was empty. Troy was reading the local newspaper, moodily thinking of his own recent appearance on page two. When someone went to jail in St. Bonaventure, everyone was aware of it. "Arrests" were written up on the same page as the obituaries and birth announcements and weddings. The write-up on Troy had been right under a big, grinning picture of a girl he'd gone to high school with. Beneath the descriptions of the girl's bridal gown and her proud parents, Troy had found himself summed up in a few sentences. "Area man. Possession of a controlled substance with intent to distribute.

Court date set." Today, he saw, there was another birth, another death, a drunk-driving arrest.

Vivian came up behind him. She stood there, her chin lifted, watching over his shoulder as he read. He finished the obituary before he looked up.

"Is there something you want me to do?" Troy said.

She made a wave of her hand, as if surprised. "Oh, I wouldn't want to take you away from your newspaper!" she said. She was a raspy-voiced woman in her late fifties, with a blond, steel-wool perm and a stout, shapely figure, which she accented with tight jeans and western blouses. Troy was used to her attitude of resigned suspicion and impatience, as if her main job was to keep him out of trouble, to ensure that he didn't slack off too much or sneak drinks when she wasn't looking. Mostly, he thought, this was just an act. He was a good employee, and she knew it. But it was a role she enjoyed playing, and to please her Troy began to take the liquor bottles off the shelf and dust them.

"I just hired a young guy to work in the kitchen," she said. "He's going to be starting tonight, so you'll have to keep an eye on him. You can manage that, can't you?"

"I hope it doesn't get too busy," Troy said.

Vivian cocked her head. "Well, if it does, it will be a good test for him. He has a lot of experience. He worked in Chicago for years."

"Is that right?" Troy said. Vivian's glasses hung from a beaded chain around her neck, and she lifted them to her face, hovering over the newspaper Troy had been reading, scanning it. "What's he coming *here* for, from Chicago?"

"Fed up with city life, he says," Vivian murmured. "There were some tragic circumstances, I gathered, but I didn't want to pry."

"Mm," Troy said. He continued to run his wipe over the glass bodies of the liquor bottles, frowning. "So what about Junie?" he said.

"Junie had another heart attack," Vivian said irritably, as if Troy were trying to make her feel ashamed. "What do you think I should do? I don't know when, or if, he'll be back. I can't close down the bar to wait and see if he gets well. And I'm damned tired of listening to you bitch every time I ask you to cook for me."

"Okay!" Troy said. "I was just asking." He watched as Vivian lit a cigarette and breathed a stream of smoke down onto the obituary notice.

"Just asking," she muttered. "I don't need you and Crystal guilting me about poor old Junie, that's for sure. I've got enough troubles as it is." She gave him a hard stare, but then they both composed themselves into politeness as the young guy she'd hired came up the stairs.

"Hello, Jonah!" Vivian cried, and Troy watched grimly as she switched into warm-and-friendly mode: the disarming, gold-tipped teeth in her smile, the crinkly eyes, the endearments—"honey," "sweetheart," etcetera. She did this with everyone she hired. For the first week or so, she treated them like she was a kindergarten teacher and they were her prized students. And then they lost their charm. She became a disappointed mother, ironic and long-suffering, tolerating their lack of competence and clucking critically even when she was satisfied with them.

"Hi," the guy said shyly. "I'm Jonah Doyle." He glanced at Vivian, and stood there awkwardly, his long arms limp at his sides before she introduced them. The guy kept his head down, not even looking Troy in the eye, but then when Troy offered his hand, Jonah clasped it in both his palms, squeezing it surprisingly hard. "I'm really pleased to meet you," Jonah said, with a nervous, earnest enthusiasm, as if Troy were someone he had heard of, someone famous.

"Yeah," Troy said. He shifted a bit, uncertainly. A narrow strip of raised scar tissue ran from the edge of the kid's eye, across his cheek. This might have seemed threatening on someone else. But with this guy it just seemed disconcerting. He had a freckled, boyish face, with round cheeks and carefully combed and parted blond-brown hair, and the scar was like an out-of-place appendage—a toe instead of a finger, a misaligned ear, an empty eye socket. It was hard to keep from staring.

"I'm really looking forward to working with you," Jonah said, and Troy nodded slowly, trying to avoid the guy's face. Jonah was dressed up like a churchgoer in a button-up shirt and khaki slacks, but then for some reason he had on heavy black work boots.

"Yeah," Troy said. "I'm looking forward to working with you, too." He glanced over to Vivian, who smiled benignly. If she noticed something strange in the air, her expression didn't betray it.

At least, as it turned out, the guy was competent. When things picked up around 6:30, Troy was fairly amazed at how much more efficient Jonah was than Junie. Troy would thrust an order through the little window that separated the bar from the kitchen and the next time he passed by a plate would have appeared—cheese sticks or Buffalo wings or nachos, arranged neatly and even garnished. He glanced back in the kitchen and watched briefly as Jonah's long, nimble fingers arranged deep-fried jalapeño poppers in a circle over a bed of greens—something Junie would have never bothered with. Junie would have tossed the poppers onto a bare plate once they had cooled off a bit. He certainly wouldn't have fanned them out like petals, or added a little side cup of nacho cheese in the center, as Jonah did. "You're getting fancy, eh?" Doug Lepucki said, grinning as Troy set the plate down on the bar, and Troy shrugged. "New cook," he said, and a popeyed young guy leaning on the bar with a clutched twenty-dollar bill ogled Doug's plate and said, "I'll take one of those things, plus a pitcher."

In his previous life, Troy would have been pleased. People tipped extra on food tabs, and he was under no obligation to share tips with the cook. It was surprisingly busy—the Stumble Inn had never been a particularly popular Friday-night gathering place, but by nine there may have been more than forty patrons packed into the small bar, and he was moving fast, pouring beers and pitchers and fixing drinks, a permanent sheen of sweat on his forehead. He had to empty the tip jar because it got too full.

But the truth was, he felt a little unnerved. It was a rowdy crowd, and the chimes of group laughter, the screams of delighted women, the bellows of asserting men, the general cacophony of drunken voices—the steady rising and falling of human chattering hooked into his spine.

The bar was too full of people for comfort, he thought. Too full of people who knew him, or who knew of him, or who had heard from an acquaintance about his situation. He didn't go out from behind the bar to clear tables of plates or glasses, feeling self-conscious of the monitor beneath his pant leg. A boisterous group of young men in their early twenties, apparently friends of Ray's, were the most troublesome. "Hey, bartender!" they called. "A round of bong hits for the boys over

here, bartender!" and a flock of har-har-hars rose up from their table
like crows.

— — —

What could he say? This was part of his punishment, this humiliation,
and all he could do was frown stoically. He thought of Lisa Fix: "I
wouldn't say that this is the ideal job for someone in your situation,"
she had said.

He was aware of Jonah, too. Jonah's eyes on him. He'd turn to look
over his shoulder and the prickly feeling on the back of his neck would
intensify for a moment. Here was Jonah, his nose and mouth shadowed, peering out from the kitchen as Troy tilted the edge of a glass
against the flow of beer. Troy filled the glass, letting the foam fall away
and slide down the outside edge of the mug. He looked over his shoulder again, just in time to catch Jonah gazing intently at his back. Jonah
smiled, shifted his eyes. "What?" Troy said, but Jonah didn't hear him
over the general noise of the bar and Troy was too busy to bother re-
peating himself.

But it continued to grate on him as the night wore on. Every time
he turned to look, there was Jonah, intent in his surveillance, then pretending to glance away as if he hadn't been staring. It made him aware
of himself as an object of observation, in general. There were the patrons who knew, watching as he limped along with his hidden parole
anklet, turning to their friends to remark, grinning with gossip, as he
passed. There was the monitor signal he was emitting, even now. There
was the black book, the "itinerary," which Lisa Fix would comment on,
prodding the mundane and intimate details of his life, as if it were all
typical, as if she could predict the rest of his life with a shrug of her
shoulders. All of this settled over him heavily, and when he looked over
to see Jonah with his neck craned and his lips parted, scrutinizing
Troy's preparation of a round of Jagermeister shots as if it were a
magic show, he turned with exasperation to face the guy. *What in the
fuck are you staring at,* he started to say.

But it was weird. He wheeled abruptly, irritably, and then said nothing. Jonah was looking at him with a kind of focused, unblinking concentration that seemed almost like a trance. It took him aback.

"Hello?" Troy said, loudly but uncertainly, and Jonah startled slightly, blinking at last as if he'd been asleep with his eyes open. "Hey, man, are you awake or what?" Troy said.

"Oh!" Jonah said. It seemed to take him a moment to lift out of whatever staring rhapsody he'd been in, and Troy shifted a little, uncomfortably. He noticed that there were even more scars etched along the backs of Jonah's hands, trailing along as if something had raked a claw across his skin. *What happened to him?* Troy wondered again, and for a moment a kind of shadow passed over him—something chilly, flapping like a sheet on a clothesline.

"Sorry," Jonah said. "I kind of spaced out for a minute."

"Yeah, well," Troy said. He cleared his throat. "We're kind of busy, if you hadn't noticed. Would you mind getting out there and clearing off the tables? If it's not too much trouble."

"Oh!" Jonah said, and Troy watched as he put on a kind of professional smile, like a mask. "Of course! Sorry!"

What was it? Troy thought. He watched as Jonah loped out onto the floor and began to collect empty glasses. Something was wrong with the kid, something beyond the scars, but he wasn't sure how to pinpoint it. A kind of actory stiffness? Troy had the paranoid idea that maybe Jonah was an undercover agent for the DEA or something, planted here to spy on him. Then he dismissed the thought—he had no connections, nothing worth spying upon, and in any case, whatever this Jonah was, he was no undercover agent. Troy observed as Jonah gathered the dirty beer glasses and arranged them neatly on the end of the bar, lining them up in a careful pyramid, like bowling pins.

"Thanks," Troy said, and Jonah looked him in the eye briefly, then nodded, as if they both knew a secret.

Closing time was approaching and the unexpected crowd began to thin out. The feeling of being watched faded as well, and every time Troy glanced behind him Jonah was busy with something or other. Not staring anymore—and Troy found himself wondering if he'd just overreacted, if he'd just imagined that Jonah had been watching his every move. He'd been feeling so self-conscious lately. He thought he'd get used to the ankle monitor, that it would come to be something he hardly noticed, but instead it seemed like it was worse, day by day, to the point that he sometimes felt like it glowed, or gave off waves of heat or radiation. He looked through the order window and saw that Jonah was dutifully scrubbing the grill with a charcoal pad, his head down, his hand moving like a painter. Troy cleared his throat, but Jonah didn't look up.

Troy leaned against the bar and rested his forehead against the ham of his palm. He heard the door to the bar open and slam shut several times as people left—headed out, headed home—and he didn't even look up. He imagined Loomis, asleep in Judy's house; Carla, somewhere in Las Vegas, tilting her head back as she drained a drink; Ray, opening a forty-ounce beer and tucking it between his legs as he drove home from some bachelorette party, his windows open, angry rap music tub-thumping from his speakers. *My life is ruined,* he thought, distinctly.

By the time two o'clock came around there were only two people in the bar: a man and a woman, French-kissing in a corner near the jukebox, their hands underneath each other's clothing. "Last call!" Troy said loudly in their direction, and the couple lifted their heads like animals surprised from grazing. "Last call!" Troy said, more softly, and the two of them got up and walked out wordlessly.

Troy turned back to look at Jonah.

"I think that's it," he said, remembering the official capacity Vivian had given him, to train Jonah. "Let me lock the door. Then we just finish up the side work, and we're done. Unless you have, like, questions or anything."

Jonah looked up from his sweeping and blinked.

"Questions?" Jonah said, and he had that unnerving, frozen expression again. It was almost like stage fright, Troy thought. His eyes flicked back and forth, like someone who was trying to quickly come up with a good excuse, and his expression tightened. It was as if he were hurriedly scanning for something inside his head, a panicked shuffling through stacks of blank pages on which he'd expected to find words.

"I mean," Troy said. "About the job? Do you have any questions about your . . . duties or whatever?"

"Oh," Jonah said, and Troy watched him hesitate, then relax a little. "No, not really. I think I've got a pretty good grip on it. I'm . . . I'm sorry I spaced out earlier. About clearing the tables."

"No problem," Troy said.

"I get a little . . ." And Troy watched as Jonah gestured, wiggling his fingers at the side of his head. "I space out, sometimes. When I'm nervous. But not, you know, often."

"No worries," Troy said. He gave Jonah an ironic half smile. "I do that sometimes myself."

"Oh, really?" Jonah said, and again there was that silent, disconcerting sense of inner struggle. "We're alike, then, I guess," Jonah said at last, and smiled broadly.

For a moment there was a glimmer of—what?—in Jonah's expression, and Troy hesitated. It was like that itch he got when doing crossword puzzles, that elusive flick of a word in the back of his mind when he couldn't quite think of it. It was like that feeling that is the opposite of a premonition: *Did I forget something? Something important?*

And then it vanished. Jonah turned and began to sweep.

parents were silhouettes against the slick, blue-black skin of the lake, and Troy was aware that the sky and the lake were both like deep water, depth upon depth.

At that moment, he had loved the world so much that it almost ached; he had loved his young mother and father with a kind of fierceness that he could feel in his muscles. His mother would enfold him in a towel, drying him, her nose brushing against his hair. Smelling him. His father, smiling, looking at the two of them, carefully setting another piece of wood on the fire, his face alit and noble and full of a stern, kingly pride.

Even now, after all these years, he still can't understand why they'd gotten divorced. For such moments to exist, and then to vanish seemed impossible, and he certainly couldn't fathom it when he was eleven, when he and his mother finally moved out of the house. Back then, he was certain that his parents would get back together eventually—how could it be that people who had experienced such happiness wouldn't want to return to it?

He remembers when he was thirteen, when his mother got married again, he still firmly believed that it was only a passing phase. His mother's new husband was a gentle, boring man named Terry Shoopman, a balding high school guidance counselor with a foreshortened, potbellied torso and incredibly long, spindly legs, and Troy couldn't imagine that it would last between them. He watched with skepticism as Terry moved in, ignoring his presence for the most part, weathering it.

A year later, when he was fourteen, Troy was still expecting things to go back to normal. Then Terry had gotten a job in Bismarck. Troy had refused to go, despite his mother's cajoling and promises. She wouldn't be able to stay away for long, he thought. He had moved back in with his father then, though the truth was he had begun to spend almost all his free hours at Bruce and Michelle's trailer, by that time smoking a lot of pot along with Bruce and Michelle and their parade of teenagers, while he waited for his mother to give up on Bismarck, to tire of Terry Shoopman and come to her senses. To come home.

He probably should have gone with her. Sometimes, thinking back, he is aware that he would have been better off. His father's drinking had grown quietly worse, more involved and ritualized, starting shortly after dinner and continuing, with steady determination, until he passed out. Meanwhile, Bruce and Michelle had begun to lose themselves to cocaine.

It wasn't until much later, not until after he'd been arrested and sober for several months, that he understood the sort of quiet, steady life that Terry had offered his mother. And he was aware that she had made a choice. She had let him go—had taken her own chance for happiness and comfort. He would have made her miserable, if she'd insisted that he come with her.

Back then, though, he thought she'd done him a favor to let him stay in St. Bonaventure, to let him settle into the life of a resourceful, unsupervised teenage boy. Back then he'd dreaded his visits to Bismarck, that anonymous bedroom they prepared for him: bed, dresser, desk, the pictures of sailboats on the walls, the books that some son of his mother and Terry might have read: *Treasure Island* and *The Flora and Fauna of North America* and *Jonathan Livingston Seagull*. At least they had cable TV.

Years later, when his father died—his heart finally, steadily poisoned by years of alcohol and cigarettes and self-pity—Troy probably should have gone back up to Bismarck with his mother. But he was twenty years old. He had started to date Carla. He told his mother that he was planning to go to college, or trade school, or maybe the military, but the truth was that he had taken over a large part of Bruce and Michelle's marijuana business—Bruce was in prison and Michelle was dating an odd, wealthy old man named Merit Wilkins, thirty years her senior, and moving to Arizona.

And then he'd married Carla. They lived on in his dad's old house, the house he'd grown up in, and there were wonderful, invigorating parties. Ray, aged fifteen, had run away from the place in Arizona where he'd lived with Michelle and Merit Wilkins, and he stayed with Troy and Carla, sleeping on the couch and irregularly attending high school in St. Bonaventure. It was another little family, Troy thought for a while, and shortly before Carla found out she was pregnant with Loomis, they even took a camping trip together, Troy and Carla and Ray. He'd made them wade around looking for crawdads with a flashlight.

But it wasn't real in the same way. Even after Loomis was born, it didn't feel as natural as it had when he himself was a little kid. His mother wasn't coming back—she couldn't come back now, of course—and when she, too, died, she hadn't yet had the chance to drive down to Nebraska to see Loomis. She'd only seen him in pictures.

They'd behaved badly at the funeral, he remembers. He and Carla and Ray, all of them stoned throughout the whole thing; the fourteen-month-old Loomis, solemn and intelligent even then, sat in the crook of Carla's arm as they toked up in the car outside the funeral home. The smell of marijuana must have wafted off them as they promenaded slowly past his mother's corpse in its casket, as they sat in the pew and listened to the preacher. He dully greeted a few of his old aunts and uncles, faces from his parents' long-gone parties, now scattered, now strangers. They went back to the house where his mother had lived out the last decade of her life with Terry Shoopman, and ate from relish trays of raw vegetables and dip, casseroles and cold fried chicken, pies and cakes. They sat together in a little cluster, he and Carla and Ray, talking about the idiotic things stoned people talk about, and when Terry Shoopman had come up and clutched Troy in a hug, he had seen Carla and Ray widening their eyes ironically from beyond Terry's shoulder. Terry had called Troy "son," and held Loomis tenderly.

"I still want to be a grandfather to this child," Terry had said, wet-eyed. "I hope you know that. I loved your mother very much. She was a very special lady."

For several years, Terry Shoopman had continued to send Loomis presents on his birthday and at Christmas. He had even called a few times. "Why don't you come up and visit me?" he'd said. "I'd love to see Loomis." And he had tried to remind Troy of the "fun" they'd once had, when Troy, as a teenager, used to spend Christmas or summer months with his mother and Terry in Bismarck. The truth was, Troy hardly remembered those times, he'd been so stoned; and after a while, after a few gentle rebuffs, Terry stopped calling, stopped sending cards and presents. Troy hoped that Terry had found another woman. Though he'd never wanted Terry as a stepfather, he didn't wish him ill.

His memory tunnels through these paths as he dozes under his mother's comforter, his mind a slow-moving dune. He opens his eyes long enough to see that it is after four in the afternoon, and then he is dreaming again, going over and over his own history. He can clearly see the places where he might have changed things, where he might have done a better job making his life, though most of those paths also lead away from Loomis's existence, and he can't bear that. Loomis, he thinks, is the one good thing he's done in his life.

As for the rest, he doesn't know. Can someone help him? He could call Michelle, in Arizona. She's forty-four now, she might have something wise to say, as she walks the golf courses with her wealthy husband; he could call Bruce, who is still in prison, denied parole after attacking another inmate; he could call Terry Shoopman, or one of the various relatives he once knew as a child—the aunts and uncles, the cousins he once played with on those long-ago childhood nights, to whom he hasn't spoken in years. But there is no real connection left, and he is aware that he is not even held to them by blood. He is the one who was adopted. His mother and father pulled him into their families, but now that they are dead, what remains? There is only Carla, who has left him; and Loomis, who has been taken away; and Ray, gone now, too, banished. *Get out, you moron,* he'd said.

He opens his eyes again, rubbing his bare feet against each other. God, God, God, he thinks, and lying there, he can picture his mother's body in the casket. She didn't really look like herself, and when Troy touched her hands they were as weightless as husks. They moved easily out of their folded position across her chest. He thought they'd be stiff, frozen into place, but in fact they were like dry branches and when he tried to press them back into their prayerful position they slipped farther astray. They hovered above each other as if they were trying to clasp something to her chest, and he had to ask the mortician for help. "I screwed up my mom's hands," he said, stoned out of his mind. "I'm sorry." He didn't cry for her until much later.

21

October 20, 1996

Even though it's almost sunset, Troy has to get out of bed to answer the doorbell. He hasn't been asleep, exactly, but he hasn't been quite willing to get up either. What is there to do, after all? Make coffee, this late in the day? Find something to eat? Watch TV? Continue to contemplate the unchangeable mistakes he's made?

But when the bell rings a second time, he finally slides himself out from under the covers.

He looks terrible, he knows—shirtless, barefoot, wearing only a pair of sweatpants, his eyes bleary with unsustained sleep, hair standing up in stiff tufts. He sees himself in the mirror that hangs by the doorway, tries to pat his hair down a bit as the doorbell bongs its three descending notes again. "Screw it," he whispers to his drawn, bleary face, and turns to throw open the front door.

It's Jonah—Jonah from work.

They both stand there, hesitantly. Jonah is holding a grocery bag in each hand. "Hey," he says, as if he is surprised that Troy has appeared at the door. "How's it going?" he says.

"Hey," Troy repeats, and then they are silent again. The chill wind ripples Jonah's hair and loose jacket as he stands there, and Troy crosses his arms tightly across his bare chest.

"I thought you might need some groceries," Jonah says at last.

"Some groceries?" Troy says. He tries to take this in, but can't quite gather what Jonah's getting at. It has the quality, he thinks, of some very dry-witted practical joke, and he feels himself wavering at the edge of a punch line. "You brought me food," he says. "From the supermarket."

"Yeah," Jonah says, and he gives the bags a little lift, to demonstrate. "I was going to, just, like, leave the bags on the . . . doorstep. But then I was worried that, you know, some animals or something would get into it. So."

"Okay . . ." Troy says, and raises his eyebrows. "And you're leaving food on my doorstep because . . . ?"

"Well," Jonah says, and looks helplessly down at the two bags as if he's handcuffed to them. "I wanted to make myself useful, I guess." Another gust of wind bursts across them, fierce, bending the heads of the trees and sending the leaves into a flutter of birdlike uproar and alarm.

"Dang," Troy says, flinching at the chill. "Listen, man, why don't you . . . Just come in, okay? Let me close this door before I freeze to death."

———

Jonah stands nervously in the living room while Troy slams the door shut on the weather. When Troy turns back to look at him he is red in the face, blushing noticeably, the long scar that runs from his eye to the edge of his mouth paler and more prominent.

"I hope I'm not . . . intruding," Jonah says. "I feel like this was a really stupid idea."

But Troy only shrugs. He finds a half-clean T-shirt draped over the couch and pulls it on with a shudder. The transition from the sleepy, overheated bedroom to the icy winds on the porch has left his mind and body in a little state of shock, and he peers at Jonah, slow-blinking. "So . . ." Troy says. "What's up?"

"I don't know," Jonah says, and then seems to consider. "I feel really stupid. It was just—I don't know, I was talking to Crystal. And she was saying how she was worried about you, and she didn't know how you were able to even do simple things like go out and get groceries with the ... the house arrest. And so I was out in the supermarket, and, so. I bought some food. I mean, I thought it might help you."

They look at each other.

"Crystal's kind of a fricking busybody, don't you think?" Troy says.

"Well," Jonah says. "Not necessarily." He stands there, still holding the two sacks in a posture that seems both hopeful and resigned to failure. What do you do with such a person? Troy wonders. What do you say? He has heard the story of Jonah's life—from Crystal, of course—all about the car accident. Jonah and his wife, eight months pregnant, driving on the expressway in Chicago, on their way to a movie. The semi-truck, boxing them in and then suddenly veering out of control, the crunch of metal, the sound of the wife screaming. He had found himself picturing it vividly, and now looking at the scars on Jonah's hands, Troy can't help but think of these images again. Here is a guy whose life has been even worse than Troy's own, and it's hard to be rude to him.

"Well, anyways," Troy says, after a pause. "Come on in the kitchen. Let's see what you've got there."

———

They don't say anything as Jonah sets the bags on the kitchen table. Troy glances at the stack of dirty dishes in the sink, the visible balls of dust that have collected at the bottom of the kitchen counters, the unsent letter to Mrs. Keene still propped between the salt and pepper shakers on the table. Yes, he thinks. It is the house of someone whose life is falling apart, the sort of person you'd bring charity groceries to.

"I don't want to seem like a jerk, or anything," Jonah says.

"Don't worry about it," Troy says.

"I mean, I didn't know what you really needed, so I just thought ..."

"I appreciate the gesture."

"I thought you might like some bread ... and cheese ... and some lunch meat ... and maybe, like, a cantaloupe?"

"Okay," Troy says.

"I bought a six-pack of beer, but I don't know whether you can drink it."

"Not really," Troy says. "That's probably not a good idea."

"So . . . I also bought some soda? Coke?"

And Troy sighs, softly.

"Coke is great," he says. "That's fine."

———

They are sitting at the kitchen table, with the food laid out between them like some complicated puzzle. Troy finds glasses and some plates, and a jar of mayonnaise in the refrigerator, then sits down across from Jonah, both of them shyly quiet, concentrating on their work, as they make sandwiches. Troy pours a Coke over the ice in his glass, and Jonah opens a beer.

"You know," Troy says, "I know that Crystal means well, but I really wish that . . ."

"It's my fault," Jonah says. "I'm sorry. It was a really dumb thing to do."

"That's not what I meant."

"I understand what you mean," Jonah says. He smiles apologetically at his sandwich before biting it. "But I'm not doing it because of that. I . . . just wanted to be friendly. You seem like a cool guy. And . . . I don't have a very easy time getting to know people."

And Troy isn't sure what to say to this. "Okay," he says at last, watching as Jonah takes another cautious bite of bread. It's strange to be sitting here with someone, after all the time he's spent alone. Jonah is the first person who's been in Troy's kitchen since he kicked Ray out, a month and a half ago, and despite the guy's edginess, it's not a bad feeling. Troy has spent a lot of time at this kitchen table—laughing it up with his customers, playing cards with Ray, eating cereal with Loomis in the morning—and he can feel the remnants of these old comforts hovering in the back of his mind.

"So," Troy says, after the silence has extended for a while. "You're from Chicago, right?"

"Yes," Jonah says.

"Is that where you're from originally?"

"Um," Jonah says. "Sort of. More or less." He shifts a little, regarding his sandwich. "Actually," he says, "I spent part of my childhood in South Dakota. Just a little small town."

"Ah," Troy says. "So you're used to this kind of small-town shit."

"Kind of, I guess."

"It's not that bad, I suppose," Troy says. "You get used to people, and it's comfortable. Not as hectic as Chicago, I imagine. Personally, I've never been east of Omaha."

"Oh, really," Jonah says, and Troy notices how his expression seems to tighten, focusing. "Didn't you—" he says. "Did you ever want to? Travel around or anything?"

"Oh, I don't know," Troy says. "Maybe at one point, I guess. But, you know. I had a kid, and all my family is from around here, and all that. And now . . . well, you've heard the story from Crystal. I would've liked to go to college, I think."

Jonah gives him another sharpened look. "Oh, really?" he says. "To do what?"

"I don't know," Troy says. He shrugs bashfully, thinking of his conversation with Ray, months ago, the skeptical look on Ray's face. "I thought about something like . . . commercial art? I didn't get very far into considering it, to be honest." He clears his throat. "But I guess you've been to college, yourself. That's what Crystal the busybody says, anyway."

Jonah wrinkles his nose. "Oh," he says. "Not really. I just, I took a few classes, here and there. You know. Just basic liberal arts stuff— American lit, history, math. Nothing very . . . focused."

"Uh-huh," Troy says. He's impressed by the way Jonah says "liberal arts," so easily—as if they both understand exactly what that means. "Lit" means "literature," Troy thinks, and he likes the sound of it. *American lit. Liberal arts.* He tries to picture what it would be like to go to college in Chicago, but all he can think of is a postcard one of his former customers had sent him of the John Hancock Building, with the antennae sticking up from its roof like two horns.

"So," Troy says. "Do you think you'll ever go back?"

"To Chicago?"

"To college."

"Probably not," Jonah says. He looks down at his hand, and Troy watches as he traces the pad of a fingertip along the upraised furrow of a scar, a rivulet that runs from wrist to knuckle. "I don't think I really have the . . . aptitude for it. I like the learning part of it. It's just . . . you know, the tests, and going to classes all the time, and that stuff. And besides, the things I'm interested in aren't actually going to be worth anything. Prehistoric civilizations? Or film appreciation? Or theories of mathematics? That's the kind of stuff I liked, and it's not going to be something to put on a résumé."

"Yeah," Troy says. "But then again, who cares, so long as it's interesting to you? If you like learning about it, isn't that all that matters?"

"Well . . . it does cost a lot of money."

Troy sighs. He's curious, he guesses; there's something foreign and vaguely romantic about the idea of a classroom full of students and an old professor expounding on something like "film appreciation," or "prehistoric civilizations." He can imagine great, arcane swaths of knowledge that he's never even heard about. "Okay," he says. "Tell me one piece of totally useless information that you learned." He smiles, and when Jonah rolls his shoulders sheepishly, he reaches over and pours him a little more beer. "Come on," he says, "take a drink and tell me something, college guy. I'm interested."

"All right," Jonah says. He draws on the beer, and for a moment it seems that there is a glint in Jonah's gray, flickery eyes that makes Troy feel as if they met a long time ago. "Okay," he says, at last. "Here's one," and he intones as if reciting. "The Swedish mathematician Helge von Koch hypothesized that an infinitely long line surrounded a finite area."

"Huh," Troy says, and he chuckles a little, because it is totally incomprehensible. "Do you understand what you just said?"

"I guess so," Jonah says, and he gives a little shrug, shy but proud. There's that glint in his eye again, which makes Troy think of the way Loomis looks when he knows an answer to a hard question. "I mean," Jonah says, "it's easier if you see it on paper. It's kind of like, you know how in grade school you made those snowflakes out of construction paper? You fold the paper up into a four, or an eight, and then you start to make jagged edges around it. You can keep making it lacier and lacier, and if you had the right tools, microscopic tools or whatever, you could go on making it more and more intricate. It could go on forever, that's the thing, because things can get smaller into infinity. Like you cut down to a molecule. And then you cut that down into an atom. And then you cut the atom into the particles that are smaller than an atom. And so on. So if you stretch out the edges around the snowflake into a straight line, it would potentially go on into infinity. Therefore."

"I get it," Troy says, pleased. "An infinitely long line surrounds a finite area. I can see that, sort of. It's kind of like one of those puzzles. Like one of those mind benders. Optical illusions. Right?"

"A little," Jonah says. And then he's silent. "I mean, it's abstract. You can't actually see something that's infinite, so it's just a puzzle in your mind." There's something in his solemn, calmly satisfied expression that makes Troy think of Loomis again. "It's interesting, though," he says. "To me."

⸻

Troy can't help but feel empathy for the guy. Jonah's life could have been something different, he thinks, if it hadn't been for that car accident. He can picture Jonah's wife: She wouldn't have been very attractive, Troy imagines, probably fat, but sharp and serious in her thoughts, the total opposite of Carla, and he thinks that they would have had a girl, a beautiful child. And Jonah would have finished college, and even if there weren't specific, practical applications to what he studied, the degree itself would have taken him somewhere. Something with computers, maybe, or a job at a library. And they would have had a happy life. He can imagine them all living in Chicago—in an apartment of some kind, with a coffee shop nearby, and they would push their daughter's stroller through some large city park, while Jonah talked about film, or math, or something else like that, and his plump long-haired wife looked at him with gentle admiration.

All of this comes vividly into his mind as they sit there, he and Jonah. He peers down, tenderly, upon his image of Jonah's happy family—and then his thoughts alight briefly on his own childhood, on his own mother and father and him at the lake, and finally on the life he should have provided for Loomis, if he and Carla had been different people, if they'd been able to overcome themselves.

"So, Jonah," he says at last, and tries to pinch off this last image.

"Be honest with me, man. What are you doing in St. Bonaventure? I mean really?"

He is surprised, even a bit taken aback, by how quickly Jonah looks up at this question. Jonah's mouth tightens, and something behind his eyes seems to flash.

"What do you mean?" he says.

"I don't mean anything negative," Troy says. "It's just, what are you? Twenty-three years old?"

"Twenty-five."

"Same difference," Troy says. "All I'm saying is that you're not going to want to work as a cook at the Stumble Inn for the rest of your life, right?" Troy pauses, purses his lips. "Don't you think you could do better for yourself?"

"I don't know," Jonah says, and his voice is a little brittle. "I like cooking for the Stumble Inn." He glances toward the dirty dishes in the sink, toward the black itinerary open on the counter. "Do you think you could do better for *your*self?" he says, softly.

"Ha," Troy says. "Not anymore, man. Maybe if I was twenty-five again, I would do things differently."

He's quiet then, embarrassed by his own self-pity. Because, of course, why should it be any harder for Troy to start his life over? Jonah has just lost his pregnant wife, his face is a mess of scars, his parents, according to Crystal, are dead. If anything, Troy thinks, Jonah's life has been harder than his own, and he feels a guilt settle over him. For some reason he thinks of his mother in her coffin, the way her stiff hands had come undone, his stupid, stoned efforts to put them back into place. He grimaces.

"I'm sorry," he says, after a moment. "You should do whatever makes you happy. I mean, if cooking at the good old Stumble University is what you want to do, more power to you."

Jonah looks at him inscrutably. His fingers touch the crust of uneaten sandwich, and Troy is surprised to see that the guy's hands are trembling.

"I'm looking for someone," he says.

"Uh-huh," Troy says, tentatively. "That's good." For a second he's aware of some unplaceable buzz in the air. "That's what you should be doing, man. You know, I know a lot of women. If you want, I could—"

"I mean," Jonah says, and he makes a sort of squint. "I mean, someone specific."

Troy watches Jonah's expression shift. The unscarred side of his face shudders a little, like the hide of a horse that is trying to shiver away a fly. Jonah tilts his head, leaning forward, and his hands tighten and then resolve themselves.

"I think we're brothers," Jonah says.

"Ha," Troy says. He tries to smile but an uncomfortable stiffness has settled over him. Jonah is shivering. His teeth actually chatter.

"I mean, really," Jonah breathes. "Your mom. Your biological mom. She's my mom, too."

And Troy feels his uneasy smile slip away.

22

October 13, 1996

It was a Sunday when they first met. It was the week before Jonah got up the nerve to go to Troy's house with the groceries. The weather was beginning to turn, and the wind ran in streams over everything, all day long. Tumbleweeds clogged the fences on the edges of town.

He'd found the street without any problem. Here it was, just a block away from the park. *Foxglove Road.* No doubt it was a pleasant place to live, Jonah thought, a quiet, curving little cul-de-sac with houses made to resemble English cottages, or so he imagined, each with bright-colored trim on the windows and eaves, with neat, yellowing lawns and fading flower beds, small statues of gnomes or fawns or the Virgin Mary. More tumbleweeds.

Jonah was sitting in his car when the boy and his grandmother came out, but they didn't glance his way. They continued down the sidewalk, the grandmother carrying a book and an unopened umbrella, a heavy woman, moving slowly. The child ran along in front of her, dashing and then, after a while, skipping, though with a thoughtful and even serious look on his face, as if skipping was a means of meditation.

There were other children in the park but not many adults. Jonah settled down in the chilly grass near some bare bushes, out of notice, but not enough to seem like he was hiding. He put his hood up and pretended to be bored, pretended that one of the milling children was his, that he was just another dutiful father. No one paid any attention: A pair of mothers talked avidly, sitting on the swings; Loomis's grandmother sat on a bench and bent her head toward her book.

As for Loomis, he was involved in some game of pretend. The other children held no interest for him, and he walked along the line of the play area, past the slides and bouncy horses and the monkey bars, his hands clasped behind his back, looking at the ground. He would occasionally say something to himself aloud. Jonah glanced over to where the grandmother was sitting. She wasn't paying attention.

Loomis was small for his age, Jonah thought, not skinny but compact, broad-shouldered, like a miniature adult. His hair was dirty blond and straight, and he had a round, solemn face. Jonah watched as he bent down and picked up something from the wood-chip playground bed—a piece of plastic, a forgotten toy. The child examined it, frowning, mumbled to himself. Then he put it in his pocket. He was about thirty yards from where Jonah was sitting, but drawing closer.

Jonah felt in his own pockets. A throat drop, a crumpled receipt from the pharmacy, a nub of pencil. And then: Here was the little rubber ball he'd picked up in the grass behind Troy's house, a bright Day-Glo orange superball that was made to bounce hard and high.

He looked over again toward the grandmother, at the mothers on the swings. And then, very carefully, he tossed the ball. It curved up, pinged against the trunk of a tree, and fell to the ground a few feet from Loomis.

The child's head turned, alert. Jonah watched as Loomis's eyes alit on the ball, watched as he walked cautiously toward it, as if it were a small strange animal that had fallen from a tree, stunned. Loomis stared at it, stroked his chin thoughtfully, then reached down to scoop it up.

"Loomis," Jonah said, in a short, husky voice. He kept his eye on the grandmother, but she didn't look up from her book. So he said it again, "Loomis," and the boy lifted his head sharply. They saw each other: Loomis's eyes fixed on him, wary and curious, and Jonah lifted his hand. He showed Loomis his palm, five fingers spread out. Then, deliberately, he got up and moved farther along the edge of the bushes, out of sight of the grandmother and the other adults, and the other children. And out of Loomis's sight as well.

After a moment Jonah heard the crunch of leaves. He was sitting in the dirt, half-hidden under the branches of a square-cut evergreen, his head down, his face shadowed. Loomis rounded the corner and peered at him.

"Hello, Loomis," Jonah said. He was very still, his sweatshirt hood pulled up, his hands resting on his knees—motionless, but prepared to hurry off if someone should notice him.

"How do you know my name?" Loomis said. He stood there, his eyebrows furrowed, nose wrinkled a little, his hands at his side like a cowboy about to draw pistols. Ready to run away.

"I just know." He spoke as if he didn't care whether Loomis came closer or not. "What are you doing? Are you solving a mystery?"

"I'm on a quest," Loomis said. "I'm looking for fossils."

"That's interesting," Jonah said. "Have you found any?"

"Not yet." Loomis took a step forward, then hesitated. "Are you a friend of my dad's?"

"Sort of," Jonah said. He shrugged, holding very still. "I'm sort of on a quest myself, if you want to know the truth."

Loomis considered this.

"What kind of quest?" Loomis said, angling himself so that he could get a look at Jonah's face. His mouth grew smaller.

"I'm looking for my brother," Jonah said at last. Why not? He dipped his hooded face, aware that Loomis was staring hard, uncertainly, at his scars. He brought his hands together, moving them with a slow, gentle, underwater drift, folding his palms together. "My mother had a baby before I was born," he said softly. "But she had to give him away. And now I'm looking for him."

Loomis frowned. "Why did she have to give the baby away?"

"She just had to," Jonah said. "She didn't have any choice."

Loomis narrowed his eyes thoughtfully. "Hmm," he said, at last, and Jonah took a quick glance to where the grandmother was still reading. "That sounds sort of like Moses," Loomis said. "His mother put him in a basket and into the river. Doesn't that sound dangerous?"

"A little," Jonah said. Loomis was looking at him seriously, an odd, stern little boy, his body still not relaxed. "Everything is dangerous in a certain way. But, well . . ." He was trying to pay attention to all of the elements at once. Here was the grandmother; here were the other adults, the screaming children; the slide and swings and merry-go-round spinning on its turnstile; here were the cars passing on the road in the distance behind him; here were the erratic movements of autumn leaves and branches. He groped in his mind: "But . . ." he said, "sometimes you have to take a risk. She put the baby in the river because she didn't have any other choice."

"It just doesn't seem like a good idea to me," Loomis said. "Couldn't you give the baby to a friend? Why would you put it in the river?"

"I don't know," Jonah said. He was struck by the image of his mother in the garb of the ancient Israelites, bending over the reedy, red-clay banks of a stream, the current drawing quivering lines in the water. "I guess people do things they regret." He considered.

"I think your father is my brother," he said.

He was surprised at how easily he was able to say this. After all the hand-wringing he'd done since he first came to St. Bonaventure, he found that it came out of his mouth without any of the doubts and second-guessing he'd been grappling with. It was just a fact.

"Do you know my dad?" Loomis said.

"Your dad is my brother," Jonah said. "I'm your uncle."

He expected, somehow, that this would have a greater impact than it did. Everything in his life had been leading to this moment. He pictured Loomis's eyes widening, a sudden rush of emotion, but Loomis only blinked, looking at him skeptically.

"Do you know my uncle Ray?"

And Jonah was silent, his heart beating. "I can't really tell you too much about it right now," Jonah said. He paused, thoughtfully. "I'm not sure if I can trust you to keep a secret."

"Oh," Loomis said. He seemed briefly taken aback by this. Jonah said nothing, just looked, very seriously, into Loomis's face.

"You don't want to get your dad into trouble, do you?" Jonah said.

"I can keep a secret," Loomis said, defensively. He paused, and for the first time turned to look over his shoulder, toward his grandmother. "Are you really my uncle?" he said.

"Yes," Jonah said.

Loomis stared at him dubiously.

"You have a scar on your face," he said.

"I know," Jonah said. "A dog bit me. When I was a little boy, about your age."

"Oh," Loomis said, and he seemed impressed and curious. He might have even come closer, but then in the distance, the grandmother lifted her head at last and looked around, scanning the playground. Jonah began to step backward, away.

"I'll talk to you again, maybe," Jonah said. "But only if you can keep a secret." He craned his neck, while the leaves disengaged themselves from the branches overhead. "You know, if you tell your grandma you saw me, your dad will get in a lot of trouble."

"I won't tell," Loomis said, softly. His face was pinched, solemn with worry, and he followed Jonah for a few steps as he walked into the shrubs and foliage. A leaf fell, and then another one, and Loomis stood there silently.

"Loomis!" the old woman called, and then, hesitantly, Loomis turned and walked back toward where she was sitting.

23

November 1996

Winter has arrived early this year. Temperatures have fallen abruptly, the little lakes and streams are frozen, there are storms and high winds all over the Midwest. Snow is coming down in Chicago, where Steve and Holiday are asleep, back to back, while their son Henry, now a toddler, sits up and stares at the blinking neon that pulses distantly beyond the closed curtains of his room; flakes melt against the window as Mrs. Orlova folds her hands against her breasts and frowns, waiting for a teakettle to boil in the darkened kitchen of her apartment; snow accumulates over the ditch in Iowa where Nora's ashes have settled, and on the South Dakota reservation where Jonah's grandmother's sister, Leona, lives, and on the yellow house he grew up in, now occupied by an earnest young evangelical couple and their children; on the edge of Little Bow, in the graveyard, fat, wet clumps of snow alight on the simple gravestone of Jonah's grandfather: JOSEPH DOYLE 1910–1984.

It is snowing in St. Bonaventure, Nebraska, as well. Ray the stripper is standing barefoot in the living room of a bachelorette party, undoing his shirt to the beat of rap music that blares from his boom box, a chilly sweat trickling down his back; and Junie, the former Stumble

Inn cook, opens his eyes briefly and fingers the plastic IV drip that has been inserted into his arm. The boy Jinx sleeps in his trailer with his little brother beside him in the bed, as his mother laughs at something on television in the living room. Police Officer Kevin Onken is cruising sleepily down empty streets, his windshield wipers flapping a slow metronome beat beneath the soft hush of his car's heater, and he perks up for a moment as the car carrying Jonah drifts by. Onken pays attention, watches the bright red radar numbers tick across the console. But Jonah isn't speeding. He keeps both hands on the wheel as he drives up Flock Road, along the contour of the park. The roads are slick. Jonah is cautious.

————

Crystal is just prescient enough to wake when she hears Jonah's old, rattling Festiva pass her house; her mind works in associations, and the distinctive sound of that car has lodged just firmly enough that she thinks *Jonah?* before settling back into the cushion of the couch, where she has fallen asleep.

Still, the ghost of him crosses through her subconscious: the shy slinking of his conversations, the radar of unspoken thoughts he had beamed out, some winking spark she couldn't quite catch.

She had been surprised at how abruptly he'd quit his job at the Stumble Inn. He'd seemed to be settling in fairly well by her estimation. He seemed to respond to Troy in particular.

But then, for no reason, he didn't show up for work.

"It just really concerns me," she said to Troy that afternoon, thinking that he might have some insight. "I honestly thought he was fitting in. Didn't you?"

But Troy only shrugged, moodily, his face growing unresponsive.

"Did he say anything to you?" she asked. "I didn't think he seemed unhappy here."

"I don't know anything about it," Troy said, and bent his head down to his crossword.

Crystal looked at him, sharply. "You guys didn't have an argument or something, did you?" she said, and he was silent, hesitant enough to confirm some event—disagreement? personality clash?—in her mind.

"Oh, Troy," she said. "He was a nice guy. What happened?"

"Nothing happened," Troy said, but she could feel the untruthfulness seeping out from him. "I hardly knew the guy."

"But didn't you feel bad for him?" Crystal said.

"Sure," Troy said. "Of course I felt bad for him. I feel bad for a lot of people." And then he moved off, abruptly, his back tight, out onto the barroom floor to straighten the chairs.

Vivian heard through the grapevine that Jonah had been hired as a cook by The Gold Coin. "That little shit," Vivian said, and Crystal lowered her eyes. "If he wanted more money he could have asked for it," Vivian said. "I don't appreciate that kind of behavior. Being left in the lurch like that. I guess he thought he was too good for us."

"I don't know," Crystal said, neutrally.

"I have half a mind to drive out to that banty-assed trailer of his and give him a piece of my mind," Vivian said. "I did him a favor, hiring him on the spot like that. I'll tell you, it goes to show what people are like in the world these days."

"Well," Crystal said, gently, "who knows what really happened?"

But Vivian wasn't a very forgiving person. She liked loyalty, and that was nearly all she liked about people. She had managed, over the years, to secure Crystal and Troy; and old Junie, the now-dying cook she had hoped Jonah would replace. There had been others, of course, workers who had stayed on for months or even years, but she resented them all, just as she resented Jonah, the little liar. That first day that he hadn't shown up for work, she had called him, and he'd feigned being sick.

"Oh," he'd said, when he recognized her voice. "Vivian. I was just about to call you. I've got a fever." And she was aware of the way he suddenly tried to make his voice sound frail. "I'm sorry I didn't call. . . . It was just, it really knocked me out. I've been practically delirious. I lost track of the time."

"This puts me in a bad situation," she said. "I've got a menu posted. What am I supposed to do with it?"

"I know," Jonah said hoarsely. "I'm . . . really sorry."

The next day, he called to say that he quit. He didn't even have the decency to come by. He just left a message on the bar's answering machine.

"This is Jonah Doyle," he said. His voice came out, boxy and full of static. "I'm just calling because . . . I wanted to let you know. I don't think I'll be able to come to work anymore. I . . . well." And then there was a long pause. "I'm sorry," he said. "Thank you for the opportunity to work at the Stumble Inn. I really appreciate it."

Vivian pressed the button marked "erase," very hard. But after a few weeks had passed, she didn't think too much about him, though she'd still look forward to catching him in the supermarket or some-place and telling him off.

———

Quitting his job at the Stumble Inn was a show of faith, Jonah thought. A sacrifice. To quit like that, so abruptly; to cut himself off from the people, like Crystal and Vivian, that he and Troy had in common. He hoped that Troy appreciated the gesture.

But it was necessary. Even as he struggled to tell Troy the facts of the story, he realized that they would need to put some distance between them for a while. He said as much.

"Look," he said, "I know that . . . maybe I didn't exactly go about this in the right way, and it's a little hard to . . . get your mind around. I mean, I want to give you some space, just to . . . think things over."

And Troy had stared at him.

"I don't want you in my workplace," Troy said at last. "I just . . . don't want people gossiping about this adoption shit. It's like the kind of thing they'd put in the fucking newspaper . . . for human interest or something. It's just too weird for me, you know?"

"I agree completely," Jonah said. He nodded earnestly, using the same grim frown that Troy was wearing. "That seems best," he said. "I mean, I realize that my taking the job there in the first place was, uh, probably not the smartest idea, but . . ."

"I'm serious," Troy said. "I want you to quit. Tomorrow."

"I understand," Jonah said.

"And I don't want you to tell them either. About this . . . this . . .

adoption stuff." He paused, heavily. "The last thing I need is to have Vivian and Crystal all *titillated*."

"You're absolutely right," Jonah said.

———

Jonah thinks of this again as he drives along the edge of the park, and he can feel the blush rising in his cheeks. He can picture Troy's pained, flinching look. "Jesus," Troy had said. "Why didn't you just tell me? This is— It's kind of a creepy feeling. I mean, it's like being stalked or something."

"Well," Jonah said, "that's not what I meant." And Troy had put his palms over his face.

"Jesus," he said. "This is not something I need to deal with right now."

"I know," Jonah whispered. "I realize that. I'm . . . sorry."

Beyond his windshield, the snow is a powdery mist. It turns the trees and houses and signs into the grainy, blurry grays of television static. The sky seems to be pressing down, collapsing, settling over ground.

Jonah slows. The heat coming from the defroster smells vaguely of carbon monoxide, and fits over his mind like a stocking cap. He presses his foot against the brake and squeezes his eyes shut for a moment.

———

At first Troy didn't seem to believe what Jonah was saying.

"Look," Troy said, "I'm not into this whole adoption thing. As far as I'm concerned, once the woman signs the papers, that's the end of it. I mean, I had a mom and dad that I was happy with. That's it."

"Okay," Jonah said. "But listen, let's just settle it once and for all. I've got the papers in my car. Don't you at least want to look at them? I mean, they could be wrong."

And Troy was silent for a long time. He knitted his hands together, hardening his mouth.

"Okay," he sighed. "Okay, let's see what you've got."

Now, as the snow comes down, Troy can't help but look again at the materials that Jonah has given him. The original birth certificate:

Baby Boy Doyle, it says, and he blanches again as he traces through the columns. Mother: Nora Doyle. Occupation: High school student. Father: Unknown. Occupation: Unknown. He feels his chest tighten, despite himself. This is not what he wants, he thinks. At first he'd really thought that he wanted this sneak, Jonah, and his adoption search nonsense out of his life forever. But now he's not so sure. A heaviness fills his diaphragm, and he draws breath, lets it out in a long stream.

Nora Doyle, he thinks. He doesn't much like her, this woman who had given him away, but now that she's in his mind he can't get rid of her. In his imagination, Nora Doyle vaguely resembles Carla—one of those unpleasant psychological tricks that a person doesn't want to think about too hard. He'd like to see a picture of the woman, if only to erase this creepy association from his brain.

And, well, he *does* have questions. She has been only the vaguest outline in his head up until now, a generic silhouette, like the picture on a bathroom door that meant "women." He might have been happy for things to stay that way. But now, without his even wanting it, this person, this mother, has begun to develop weight and contours, materializing into something that's almost solid. As angry as he was with Jonah at first, he knows that he's going to break down and call him after all.

He leans his forehead against the glass of the window, taps his cigarette against the rim of an ashtray. He's sitting there, wearing sweatpants and a T-shirt, a prisoner, and after a moment he reaches down and digs his fingers into the skin around the belt of his parole anklet. It itches, and he scrapes his nails back and forth, distractedly.

It's not long after eleven at night, and Jonah parks a few blocks away from the house. A blast of wind hits his face when he gets out of the car, and he keeps his head down, pulling up the collar of his coat, aware of the snowflakes settling over his hair in a thin layer.

By now he has gotten used to Foxglove Road. He knows, in general, when people go to sleep, he knows who has barking dogs, who has garage lights with motion detectors, he knows the yards with the best trees and bushes to cover him, though in this storm it's doubtful that even someone watching out a window could see him as he moves quickly down the sidewalk and up the driveway that leads to the backyard. He is a dappled shadow, passing through the swirl of snow, his hands balled up in the pockets of his jacket, his shoulders hunched, soundless. But even on a clear night, he would be invisible, he thinks. He knows the puddles of shade, the easiest way to beat a quick retreat, the places where he can stand still and blend into the background.

He knows the circumference of Judy Keene's house. In front, the large window is the living room, and the other, smaller, is Judy's bedroom. Another window into Judy's bedroom faces the driveway. At the back of the house, there is the kitchen, and then the back door, and then Loomis's room.

He has been thinking about Troy's letter to Mrs. Keene. *I realize that there are many good reasons why you have been reluctant to allow Loomis to have contact with me,* Troy had written, and Jonah recalls that precise block-letter handwriting, like the calligraphy in the voice bubbles of a cartoon. It was an earnest, heartbreakingly careful script, Jonah thought, neatly aligned on a page from a legal pad. *Although I know I have made mistakes I only want what is best for him,* Troy had written, and Jonah thought of Troy bent over his crossword puzzle at the bar, the tip of his tongue caught between his teeth as he filled in the squares; he thought of Troy hunched down, washing beer glasses, his eyes far away. Now he understands what Troy was feeling.

He has found himself looking at the letter over and over. He took it without thinking really—he had noticed it sitting on the kitchen table the evening he'd brought the groceries to Troy's house, had noticed it was addressed to Judy Keene. He had picked it up curiously when Troy was in the bathroom, and then, when Troy came out, he crumpled it into his pocket—all he needed was for Troy to catch him snooping! He had almost forgotten about it, as events had unfolded that night, and in fact it wasn't until the next day that he'd remembered, when he discovered the envelope balled up in the front pocket of his pants.

He had been feeling a lot of despair that morning, as he unfolded the letter and spread it out on the coffee table in front of him. He'd made a mess of their first real meeting—*I think we're brothers:* God!

How stupid!—and even after he had shown Troy the PeopleSearch information, even after Troy seemed to believe him, there was a chilliness that Jonah was afraid they'd never get over. *This is not something I need to deal with right now,* Troy had said, and Jonah had felt his heart contracting.

"I know it seems weird," Jonah had said. "But it's something that means a lot to me. I've been wondering about you for my whole life. I know that probably doesn't make any sense."

And Troy had looked at him bleakly. "It makes sense," Troy said. "I just don't know whether I can deal with it right now. To tell you the truth, I don't really need any more complications in my life."

"I can imagine that it's a lot to take in," Jonah said, but it wasn't until that next day, with the letter unfolded in front of him, that he truly realized what Troy meant. *Please, Mrs. Keene, I am Loomis's father and I love him. Have mercy on me.*

Jonah recognized that kind of desperation perfectly, and sitting there in his trailer, with the pale morning light slanting in through the smeary windows of his trailer, it was almost as if Troy was sitting there beside him. Confiding. It was almost as if the letter had been meant for Jonah rather than Judy Keene. *Have mercy on me,* Troy said, and Jonah pictured himself reaching out and closing his hand over Troy's wrist.

"I know you may not believe this," Jonah imagined saying. "But I understand what you're talking about." He had lain his palm across the words on the letter. Could he say, "I really want to help you"? Could he say, "I want to be a brother to you"?

Probably not.

———

But he likes to think about it. Standing in the steadily ticking snow outside of Loomis's window, he can vaguely see the shape of the child lit by a dim night-light, Loomis under the covers in his bed, his sleeping head peeking out of the spaceship-patterned comforter. Jonah puts the pad of his fingertips against the glass, watching the flowers of snow crystals catch against his knuckles and turn to water. He's aware of the accumulation on his shoulders and hair, and he likes to think that at some level Loomis knows that his new uncle is watching over him.

Have mercy on me, he thinks, and he wishes that the glass could turn liquid beneath his touch, that his hand could pass through, that the walls and windows of the world would give way to him. Just for this one time.

24

June 4, 1997

At three in the afternoon, four hours after Judy first noticed that Loomis was missing, the trail dogs arrive. There are several police cars parked in front of her house, and two heavyset men stand on the sidewalk with their arms folded hard against their chests, talking to Kevin Onken.

Judy is sitting on the steps in front of her house, very still. She feels a drop of perspiration slip from her hair and along the back of her ear, leaving a slow, cool track behind it like a snail. She shudders, watching as a man with a Doberman pinscher crouches on his haunches to look the dog in the eye, to speak to it, stroking its muzzle. Some of the neighbors have come out to stand on their front steps as well, shading their eyes; the few that have come up to inquire have been turned away, but she is aware of a circle of watchfulness around her. She observes as the dog man presses one of Loomis's T-shirts to the Doberman's nose, whispering to it. The dog's ears lift into triangles, and its bobbed tail vibrates enthusiastically.

Soon she is going to get up and walk over to the men and ask for information. But right now she just needs to sit here for a moment.

Her arm has stopped working. She tries to lift it and nothing happens. She stares at her hand and wills her fingers to curl and grip. They don't. The arm rests on her knee, and she reaches out cautiously to prod it with her finger. There's no feeling in it.

She tries to assure herself that it's just stress, that it's some odd psychosomatic reaction to the situation. If it was a stroke or a heart attack, wouldn't it hurt?

If she tells someone, they will call an ambulance, she knows. She will find herself in an emergency room, tended by condescending nurses. Whatever is happening back at home—whether Loomis is found, or whether he is dead, or whether clues to his whereabouts are discovered—all of this will be kept from her as she is poked and attached to monitors, as she becomes a body that is being examined and cared for. They will turn her into a willful child—as a grammar school teacher, she knows all their tricks, all the things about her personality they will want to control and subdue.

What is happening? A thick, balding man walks past her, stepping around her and into her house without saying a word, without a simple "May I?" And then she hears him talking to someone on a walkie-talkie.

"I guess they're bringing the father over right now. They don't have any take on the whereabouts of the mother of the child," he says. She can see his slacks, some kind of brown cotton with an ironed crease down the leg, made by an old-fashioned wife, no doubt, or a dry cleaner.

"No, it was just the grandmother who was watching him," the man says, and glances at her without much interest. His shoes are black and shiny, slip-ons, with leather tassels hanging from the tongue.

"I don't know . . . I don't know . . ." the man says. His eyes turn sidelong at Judy, as if he is considering asking her a question. "No, they didn't get divorced," he says, and lowers his voice a little. He must believe that she is hard of hearing, or that she is too confused to realize what he's talking about. "It sounds like she just up and left," he says, in a judgmental voice that makes Judy stiffen. "Drug addict of some sort, apparently," he says, and makes a short, snorting "heh" sound, as if the person he is talking to has made a snide remark. "No," he says. "I don't think so. I'm looking at her right now. She's just sitting there on the step. She looks pretty out of it."

She wants to respond to this, to glare at this buffoon and let him know she can hear his spittley voice, but she is afraid that her voice will come out slurred, like a drunk's. She is staring at the unresponsive arm, thinking very hard at it. Her brain sends a signal to her index finger, to lift, just a little, and she imagines that she sees it shudder. But maybe not. For some reason, she thinks of that famous Israeli psychic from the seventies, who was said to be able to bend spoons with the power of his mind. She focuses all of her brain's energy on the finger, and she can feel her face growing red, the flesh of her cheeks quivering a little. *Go on,* she urges it gently, *Go on,* she thinks, but nothing happens. A watery tremor trickles through her, and she closes her eyes.

———

She is struck by the premonition that Carla is nearby. There is, somewhere at the edge of the yard, the hint of Carla's voice, and Judy thinks: *Oh!* Her mind clutches loosely at the sound, and she imagines that they have found Carla, or that Carla has simply appeared, joining the circle of men and dogs on the sidewalk, introducing herself, flirting. Judy can visualize Carla standing there with her hip cocked, drawing on a cigarette, her hard mouth and sly eyes. "Why do you always look at me that way?" Judy can imagine her saying, and there is the high, shimmering tine of insect music from the trees, the sense of something encroaching. A pattern of sun beats against her eyelids through the dappled branches.

———

She is aware of herself dividing. There is a reasonable self, floating above her perceptions, a practical mind that observes the sensual organism. She is aware of herself as muscle and fat wrapped in damp skin, aware of herself as a dry, yellow-tasting tongue, aware of the matrix of sounds that spreads out from the center point of her body, the interstate of blood moving, the grasping tendrils of the spirit, seeking purchase.

The reasonable self knows that nothing at all is happening. She is just an old fat lady, sitting on a stoop with her eyes closed. Carla is not here, and besides, even if by some miracle Carla suddenly arrives on the scene, even if Judy opens her eyes and Carla is staring at her from across the lawn, there will be only enmity between them. She has known for a long time now that there will be no resolution or last-minute deathbed reconciliation; she has known that their relationship is a closed casket, sealed and buried and irretrievable. It doesn't matter if she opens her eyes or not. Carla, her real daughter, won't be there.

And yet there is still the hint of a voice, still the thick flutter of illogic, and she finds herself picturing Carla not as she would be today, but Carla as she was, Carla, aged fourteen or fifteen, her hair teased and moussed, her makeup overdone, wearing a shimmering silver shirt and faux leather pants. A silly, reckless girl, Judy thinks, a girl without qualities, a girl who needs a stern hand. Her child, and yet so different from her that it seemed as if a mistake had been made.

"Do you know how much it hurts me when your teachers call to complain about your behavior?" Judy used to say. "Do you like humiliating me, is that it?" And when Carla had said nothing, Judy had continued, as if to herself. "It really makes me feel so depressed," she said. "A lot of these people are my colleagues, do you know that? People I work with, people I'm friends with, and then to have you behaving in such a way in their classroom! It's so disrespectful, Carla, and you know, I don't feel like you love me very much, when you act this way. If you really loved me, you wouldn't keep embarrassing me."

Carla used to cry a little, after these incidents. She would go to sleep with her stuffed animals encircled in her arms, a blanket pulled over her head. Quick to blame others. *I never did anything. It's not my fault. They're lying. They're trying to get me in trouble.* And then shortly afterward, there were the drugs, and the arguments about that, and the concealment of the drugs, and the drug rehab clinic that she'd finally decided on.

"Mom," Carla said, "please don't make me go." That was the last time Carla had called her Mom, Judy thinks. "I'll do better," Carla said. "I swear I'll listen to you from now on."

———

Judy can say nothing now. She just sits there on the stoop with her eyes closed, with her arm motionless, pressing her tongue between her teeth, remembering that drive to the clinic—Carla in the passenger seat, her face turned toward the window, occasionally making the small, froggy sounds of swallowed weeping. Judy had believed, at the time, that the treatments at the clinic would remove the drugs and the alcohol and the recalcitrant desire for them the way chemotherapy burned away a cancer. She believed that her daughter would be returned to her, whole and clean and grateful, and thinking this she had hardened herself to Carla's whimpering.

She never would have expected that her daughter would, instead, become worse. In rehab, Carla would meet a new friend, a girl who'd teach her easy pathways to new types of drugs; in rehab, Carla would stubbornly refuse to admit that she was "powerless" against addiction, and the therapist would call Judy in, and they would both sit there, explaining and insisting and steadily beating her with their words, until she admitted, at last, her eyes blazing and puffy with tears, that she was "powerless."

For a flash, Judy can feel Carla's fingers against her wrist, her flushed face against Judy's neck. She holds a three-year-old Carla in her lap, reading to her, singing to her. Television is limited, in their house, to educational programs. They drive all the way to Denver, to go to art museums, listening to tapes of classical music in the car. Her IQ was tested—well above average, not quite genius level but close.

"You can be anything you want," Judy said. "I just want you to be happy."

And Carla, perhaps age ten, had gazed at her suspiciously. Even then, Judy had known that things between them would end badly. "You're capable of so much," Judy said. "That's what I don't understand about you. Why do you enjoy sabotaging yourself?"

"Mrs. Keene?" someone says. "Are you all right?"

She doesn't say anything. *Admit that you are powerless,* Judy thinks, and even now it is not something she could bring herself to do. She *will* get up, she thinks. She *will* tell them that Loomis's disappearance has nothing to do with her daughter, or, for that matter, her worthless son-in-law, who they are discussing in the living room, just at the edge of her hearing. She *will* open her eyes, she thinks. And maybe Carla will be standing there.

"Mrs. Keene?" someone says again, and she tries to pull her eyelids open.

She grimaces: a terrible headache. She is touching her left tricep with her fingers, and when she lifts her eyelids the light hits her in a sharp, painful flash. She is aware that her eyes are beginning to leak tears, blurring her sight. The left eye appears to be blind. A large black dot grows over her vision like an iris, dilating and dilating, a thickness of spots, like a swarm of bees. She shuts the eye and it seems to go away.

She can feel her body listing, slipping into the empty air beyond her shoulder.

What if she's dying? she thinks.

What if she never knows the end of the story? She shudders, and her mind continues to lurch forward into the future, that simple expectation of time passing—another moment, and another moment. It seems impossible that it will abruptly cease. It seems impossible that you will never know what happens next, that the thread you've been following your whole life will just . . . cut off, like a book with the last pages torn out. That doesn't seem fair, she thinks.

PART THREE

June 1966

Despite herself, Nora can't help but imagine names for the baby. She likes boys' names—old-fashioned, heroic ones: Agamemnon, Pyrrhus, Octavion, Aristedes. She has been reading a book about the ancient heroes of Greece and Rome, and it makes her sad that people can't be given such names anymore.

Octavion Doyle, she thinks as she walks down to the cafeteria for supper. *Jupiter Doyle,* and she smiles vaguely to herself. *Zeus.*

She is aware of the other girls moving with her down the hallway but she doesn't acknowledge them. They are dressed as she is in cheap smocks, their old perms and hairdos now growing limp and fading; they smell of sleep and old cigarettes, and the acrid musk of their private parts.

She has watched the girls who have gone before her; she has seen how it works. They fade and fade, until at last they begin to go into labor, and then they are never seen again. She knows: They give birth to babies, babies that childless parents are already waiting for. And then, pregnant no longer, they are returned to their former lives, or to new lives in distant towns, where they can forget. She knows this is what happens, but it's becoming harder and harder for her to believe. Once they're gone, it feels as if they are dead.

As they close in on the cafeteria, her baby tells her that he is hungry. She puts her hand to her belly as he lolls, moving his limbs inside her; she feels the anxious urgency of his squirm, his eagerness, and she whispers under her breath: *shhh*. For a moment, he quiets, though he continues to send tingles of anticipation through her, eager for the food.

She can't say why, but she knows that it's a boy inside her. *Hector? Alexander? Theseus?* Whatever his name, he is a clearly masculine presence, and in some ways that is a comfort. She wouldn't want to have a girl, she thinks. There's too much trouble, too much sorrow that goes along with it.

She eats in silence at the end of the table, not even thinking about the food, really—a patty of meat in gravy, a side of canned green beans, a dollop of whipped potato, applesauce—she shovels it in, automatically, and the baby's urgency calms. At the other end of the table others are chatting, something about rock bands, but she sits there with her face lowered, steadily spooning the potato whip and applesauce into her mouth, making small involuntary sounds, muted sighs of satisfaction.

Across the table one of the newer girls regards Nora warily, with a reserved air of disapproval. Table manners, Nora thinks. She's been making sounds in her haste to get the baby satisfied, smacking and chewing and grunting: disgusting. She lifts her head long enough to give the new girl a direct, baleful stare. She watches as the girl twitters silently, unnerved, but she doesn't maintain eye contact. The new girl looks down at her own food deliberately, her lips pursed, and brings a small spoonful of applesauce to her mouth as if she is eating a pearl.

Nora doesn't care. She has given up on even the simple basics of social contact. After Maris vanished, after Dominique had gone into labor, after the baby itself had become her primary human connection, she didn't feel the need to engage in the empty rituals of greeting and polite time-passing. It seems pointless, she thinks. She can spend her time more fruitfully reading, or simply communing with the developing creature inside her—its movements, its pleasures and displeasures, the early rudiments of its thoughts traveling through her body. It says, *I'm hungry. I'm restless. I'm happy.* She can feel these things as clearly as if it had spoken to her directly.

Sometimes she will open her eyes at night and she will be aware that it is awake.

You wouldn't really give me away, would you? it thinks, curled up inside her, its limbs moving softly.

And she stares into the darkness.

Why are you so stubborn? it murmurs, plaintively.

———

She doesn't know the answer to such questions. Only a few months ago she would have wished this thing, this baby, out of existence without a second thought. She remembers punching herself in the belly; she remembers tasting bleach, which she had heard could induce a miscarriage; she remembers how adamant she'd been with her father, who'd argued with her, gently, sorrowful, befuddled. He thought she should get married, and he'd wept when she admitted that she hadn't told the baby's father. "Honey," he said, "that's not right. That's not right. Believe me, he'd want to know what's going on. You just have to give him the chance."

And she'd looked at him sternly. Didn't he get it? What would the future be for her? Married at age sixteen, two high school dropouts, stuck forever in Little Bow, South Dakota, everyone's lives ruined. She felt her teeth clench. Why would she choose that for herself? Why would she force anyone else to accept that life? *I want what's best for the baby,* she'd told her father, *and that's not having me for a mother.*

———

But now, sitting in Mrs. Bibb's office, less than a week before her due date, she is less certain. She watches as Mrs. Bibb looks at some papers on the desk, and then up, frowning.

"I've been concerned about you, Miss ... Doyle," Mrs. Bibb says. Nora sits in the large wing-backed chair across from Bibb's desk, where once, long ago, Nora and her father had listened to Mrs. Bibb's recitation of the rules of residency. "There's been some concern about your comportment lately. Do you know what I mean by the word *comportment?*"

"Yes," Nora says. She lets a thick lock of her hair obscure one of her eyes like a patch, and lowers her head.

"You're a very bright girl," Mrs. Bibb says. "I've always known that. And I felt that I ought to talk to you, because these next few weeks are going to be extraordinarily difficult." She purses her mouth, folding her hands deliberately on the desk, left hand on top of right, so that her own, real golden wedding ring glints. "Your body is changing, Nora," Mrs. Bibb says. "You're going through a lot of physical changes that can also affect you . . . psychologically. And when that happens, very often girls will begin to have second thoughts."

"Well," Nora says.

But Mrs. Bibb clears her throat. "I wanted to say, Miss Doyle, that I admire your spirit very much. And I wanted to affirm once again that you are doing the right thing. I'm not at liberty to say much, but I can tell you that there are several very loving, childless couples who are waiting to give this child a real home. It's such an act of generosity, Miss Doyle. Such a gift for this child. But I know that it must be a struggle for you."

"Well," Nora says again, and her throat constricts. "What . . . what if I've changed my mind?"

Mrs. Bibb smiles, benignly. "You haven't changed your mind, Miss Doyle," she says. "You may be going through some changes in your body's chemistry, but that is natural, and it will pass, I can assure you. You'll be able to get on with your own life, and you'll have given this child you're carrying an opportunity that it simply couldn't have if it were being raised by an unwed teenager. We agreed on these points, I think, when you first came to the Mrs. Glass House. Didn't we?"

"Yes," Nora says at last, and the baby shifts reproachfully inside her.

Even though she has sworn to herself that she wouldn't, even though she continues to make a concerted effort, she has been thinking about the boy again.

Wayne. She lets his name pass through her mind, and his face comes trailing after, unbidden. Wayne. His dark curly hair; his long face, handsome for a farm kid—the prominent nose, the earnest eyes, the uncertain mouth—each detail emerging from the darkness like the smile of the Cheshire cat.

She hadn't thought that she was in love with him. Nevertheless, here he is again, a shadow leaning over her thoughts, a pang: Wayne Hill, sly-smiled wrestler boy who sat behind her in ninth-grade math. Younger than she was by almost nine months, not as tall as she was, unsophisticated. Why would she fall in love with Wayne Hill?

But she *was* in love with him, she thought. A little. At least it seemed so now, from this distance. Now, a hollow ache shudders through her as she thinks of him. It feels as if somehow he might have saved her, he might have saved her and their baby, if only she had told him.

She was not like her classmates, the other fifteen-year-old girls in her school who seemed to fall in love as if it were some sort of pastime, girls who spent hours and hours mooning over boys or photos of celebrities. She wasn't the type, she told herself. For one thing, she wasn't interested in the insular, clubby world of a small-town high school, with its after-school groups and cheerleaders and people "going steady"—all the fake rituals and social codes were vaguely repulsive to her; she preferred to remain outside such concerns, more interested in the lives of people she read about in books, more interested in art, in getting good grades, in the future—in which she might become an actress, or a painter, or a journalist. Each of these seemed like a real possibility, distanced from her only by hard work, and luck, and time. She had already begun to send away for information about various colleges, just so she could read their brochures and course catalogs.

Of course, she was outside of the world of high school whether she wanted it or not. Her life, her family, was too complicated—she and her father lived a few miles from town, and, since her mother's death, he was depressed; she took care of him, and even if she'd wanted to, she couldn't stay after school for the extracurricular activities. Her father came home from work and ate the supper she'd made for him. He was tired, and usually wanted only to drink his beers and sit in his room. He wasn't going to drive her into town for a football game, or a meeting of the Art Club, or to the movies where many of her peers went on their dates.

In any case, she wasn't entirely sure what boys she might have dated. She was the only person in their school who was mixed race, and she thought that this, too, put her outside of the main body of students. Indians and white people kept separate for the most part. They didn't date one another, certainly, and so, while boys of both races looked at her, appraised her, flirted sometimes, no one had ever asked her out. They weren't sure, she thought, what category she fit into.

The summer after she'd turned fifteen, the summer between ninth and tenth grade, she had persuaded her father to take her into town on his way to work so that she could go to the library, or the swimming pool. It was only one day a week. It was boring out in the country alone, and he hadn't objected too much to the idea. "Just stay out of trouble," he would always say, but he'd trusted her. "You're such a responsible girl, Nora. If it wasn't for you, I don't think I'd still be alive. That's the truth."

That was the summer she started seeing Wayne Hill. She knew who he was, of course. They'd had classes together, they even rode the same bus to and from school—Wayne lived on a farm a few miles beyond her house—but they'd never really spoken before. He was an athlete, somewhat of a smart aleck. The only thing that surprised her was that his name consistently appeared on the honor roll, along with hers.

And she was surprised, that day in June of 1965, to encounter him at the library. He didn't seem like the bookish type, but there he was, running his finger along the spines of books in the Fiction section, in the same concave of bookcases she was standing in. He looked at her curiously, and their eyes met for a moment before she glanced back to the shelves. After a minute, she was aware that he'd moved closer.

"You look like you could be dangerous," Wayne said, under his breath. "Did anyone ever tell you that? Like maybe you're a spy, or an assassin."

She didn't say anything for a moment. Then she shifted, irritably. "I just want to look at these books," she said, and he grinned at her, a wolfish grin, his lips jutting out a little, hearty and cocky and tinged at the edges with a hint of sadness.

"No problem," he said, and his eyes seemed to glint at her. "Have you ever read any Ray Bradbury?"

"No," she said, stiffly.

"You should," he said. And he reached down, right at the level below her waist, and pulled out a book. "Here," he said. "*A Medicine for Melancholy.* I bet you'll like it."

She hesitated for a moment, and then took it from him.

"I didn't mean anything negative when I said you looked like a spy," he said. "I just meant . . . you look like an interesting person. You look mysterious."

And she'd met his eyes, frowning. He was a compact, broad-shouldered, muscular boy. His eyes were a very strange pale, milky blue, like one of those Alaskan sled dogs.

For a few weeks they had met at the library, just to talk. Then they'd met at the swimming pool. Then they'd gone out, trailing their towels and street clothes, into the bushes just beyond the swimming pool fence. To kiss—to touch arms and brush their legs against each other— their skin still damp and warm and smelling of chlorine.

"I want to tell you something," he said. "I've been in love with you for a long time." And he laughed, beaming his grin at her. "Ever since we started riding the school bus together, I've been wanting to talk to you. You know? Every time you got on the bus, I would just get this . . . glow . . . in my heart. I know that sounds corny. You know, I meant it when I said you look mysterious. That's what I always thought."

In July he began walking to her house during the day. His family farm was six miles from the little yellow house where she and her father lived, and he would make excuses for his absence from chores that he was expected to perform. He would usually arrive in the early afternoon— trudging along the sides of gravel roads, crossing the long pasture be-hind her house.

Tuesday, Wednesday, Thursday. Her father was still at work, and she was home alone with the puppy, Elizabeth. Nora had been trying to train the dog, to teach it tricks. She would bark furiously when Wayne came up the driveway, but then when Nora snapped her fingers Elizabeth would sit. And after a few times, Elizabeth didn't bark anymore. She was used to Wayne.

He would sit there, stroking her fur. "She's a beautiful animal," Wayne said, and his eyes squinted as he smiled, cheerful half-moons. "You're lucky," he said. "I've never seen a dog like this."

And Nora had joined him in petting. "She's a Doberman pinscher. This man my father worked with gave her to him. They're very smart, supposedly. They're the smartest dogs—that's what the man told my father."

"Mm," Wayne said. They'd been petting the dog together, and their hands met as they ran down the sleek muscles of Elizabeth's back. The palm of Wayne's hand ran across her knuckles, over her wrist, up her forearm.

He looked at her. They kissed.

Before long they were in her bedroom, in her cheap, girlish four-poster, and Elizabeth the puppy was sitting anxiously outside the closed door.

That was the first time. It was not gross, like she imagined when she thought of her classmates and their activities. It was . . . something else. Like a part of her brain she hadn't known existed. Like discovering she could speak a foreign language that she had never heard before. She didn't know why she'd done it—she had been curious, she guessed, and whatever part of her was awakening, whatever part of her was impulsive and insane, caught hold suddenly. Her hand shivered as it made contact—a warm, pins-and-needles thrum, and Wayne Hill lifted his eyes to stare at her. Sharp blue eyes. She felt her hand underneath his shirt, brushing against his small, hard nipple, and he closed his eyes. "Hey," he said. His palms closed over her breasts, pressing against the cloth of her blouse.

The thing that surprised her the most was how easily she had become pregnant. In her mind, pregnancy had always seemed like a choice that people made, a switch that they might turn off and on. Birth control was a rumor that both of them had heard of, but they both believed the other things they'd heard as well—if she jumped up and down hard afterward, if she douched with Listerine, if she took a long hot bath that night—if she did that, if she didn't *want* to become pregnant, everything would be all right.

She must have become pregnant in late August or early September.

By then, school had started, and things had begun to cool between them. Not purposefully. It was just that they were both suddenly aware of the problems—of what people would say.

In gym, a Sioux girl named Elizabeth Tall had bumped hard against her shoulder.

"I hear you like that little white wrestler boy," she said, her eyes grim. "I guess you think you're too good for Indian guys, huh?"

And he must have gotten some version of the same thing, some ribbing from his peers on the wrestling team, because they didn't speak to each other in the hallway of the school.

In algebra, in late September, he passed her a note. It said: "We need to talk."

But they never did.

—————

This is something she thinks about more and more frequently as she sits in her room in Mrs. Glass House, waiting for her labor to commence. She is frightened, a little, though the nurses have tried to reassure them. They have explained what will happen, have told them about contractions, and about water breaking, and they say that there are tranquilizers, pain medications; it won't hurt as much as they fear, they are told, and there is a slide show about a procedure called a spinal, in which women can be numbed from the waist down. They will still be able to push the baby out, but it won't hurt as much.

Even as she listens to this, she finds herself wondering about Wayne Hill. Did he suspect that she was pregnant? She imagines him talking to her father, standing at the doorway of the house, wanting to know where she is. *I love her,* Wayne says, *I demand to know where she has gone.* They argue at first, Wayne and her father, but finally they come to an agreement. *We've got to save her,* they say. She closes her eyes, picturing the two of them, Wayne and her father, on their way to Mrs. Glass House, on their way to her rescue.

———

Years later, when she was incarcerated in the South Dakota Human Services Center as a mental patient, a young psychologist named Dave McNulty told her that this fantasy was probably the first manifestation of her illness. She had laughed at him.

"Manifestation," she said, and her cigarette trembled as she brought it to her lips. It was funny. Physically, McNulty looked like a wimpy, brown-eyed version of Wayne himself, Wayne with longer, shaggier hair and a tweed jacket, leather-patch elbows.

"Let's talk about the birth," McNulty said. "Let's talk about how you felt."

"I don't remember anything," she said.

———

And she didn't. She had a vague notion of the nurse saying to her: "This is Thorazine. It's going to calm you down a little." She had a vague notion of signing papers, and then asking to see the baby.

"Oh, honey," the nurse said, "your baby is already gone. He's already with his new family. Don't you remember? You said you didn't want to look at him."

"Is that what I said?" Nora whispered, and the nurse nodded.

"He's gone?" Nora said.

And the nurse just stared at her.

June 4, 1997

Loomis wakes and it's raining. He sees the droplets of water moving horizontally across the windshield, pulled unsteadily by the velocity, and he thinks of small fish moving through an aquarium tank, the aquarium that used to be in his father's house, with the mollies, and angelfish, and swordtails, and silver dollars. They have been driving for a long time, he thinks.

He is stretched out in the backseat of Jonah's car, covered by a blanket. It is okay not to wear a seat belt, Jonah had told him. He closes his eyes, and then opens them.

"Are we there yet?" he says, and he can see Jonah's eyes in the rearview mirror, glancing back at him.

"I don't think so," Jonah says.

Loomis rolls his shoulders, yawns. "Is it still a long time?" he says, and he watches for a moment as Jonah gazes out the windshield at the interstate, his face framed against the blur of passing telephone poles.

"Actually," Jonah says, "I think it might be a lot longer than I expected."

December 18, 1996

This is the day that Loomis turns six, and Troy can't stop thinking about it. He wakes up at four in the morning and sits in the living room, drinking coffee, listening to the radio, static-filled classic rock out of some faraway station in Denver. He wonders whether Loomis is going to have a birthday party. It is the last week before Christmas vacation, and perhaps the kindergarten teacher will lead the class in singing the birthday song to Loomis. Then Loomis will come home from school, and perhaps Judy will have decorated the house with streamers. Perhaps she will have baked a fancy cake in the shape of a dinosaur, or some other icon Loomis likes. Perhaps some of his friends from school will be invited over, to play games and watch Loomis open his presents. Troy imagines this; he doesn't know anything for sure.

He'd sent his own batch of presents to Judy's house three days ago. Mostly it was stuff that he'd ordered off the television: a special set of many-colored markers, and a set of books about animals, and a combination telescope-microscope, and some Batman figurines. He'd also sent a card he'd made himself: a grinning, cartoonish brontosaurus, with carefully inked letters that said: "Happy Birthday to Loomis. From: His Dad! With: Lots of Love!" He'd spent quite a few hours at the kitchen table working on that card, and as dawn light begins to filter in, he tries to decide whether Judy will give it to Loomis. He can imagine her just throwing it away. Maybe even tossing out the gifts, as well, before Loomis even sees them.

———

At eight in the morning, he dials Judy's number.

He has been very patient about this, he thinks. When she asked him not to call, back in August, she'd said that it was just "until Loomis got settled in." So he'd waited a month. But when he called in September, she'd been very curt with him. Loomis wasn't available to talk, she said. She would prefer it if he waited until she called him.

"Jesus Christ!" Troy said. "When is that going to be? It's been months since I talked to him," he said, and she'd given him a long silence.

"It will be when I'm ready," she said tightly, and the next day he'd gotten a call from his parole officer, Lisa Fix.

"Troy," Lisa Fix said. "Why are you harassing your mother-in-law on the phone?"

"I'm not," Troy said, but he felt himself blushing bitterly.

"Well," Lisa said, "I just got a complaint from her, and if you really want to end up off parole and in jail, this is a good way to go about it. You need to get a handle on yourself, my angry friend."

"What are you talking about?" Troy said. "I just called to try to talk to Loomis."

"That's not what she said," Lisa Fix said, evenly, in the voice of a woman who was used to being lied to. "She told me that you swore at her, and were threatening toward her, and I don't know or care what the actual truth of the conversation was. All I know is that this has absolutely got to stop. If you can't get some self-control, she's going to end up pressing charges against you, and then you'll never see that kid again."

———

Thinking of this, his hands shake when he hears her pick up the phone. It's risky, but he still can't believe that Judy would hate him that much. Surely, he thinks, she's not completely without a heart, and when she says "Hello," in her crisply friendly voice, he makes a conscious effort to sound as meek and gentle and repentant as he can.

"Hello, Mrs. Keene?" he says softly. "This is Troy. Troy Timmens." He hears her thin intake of breath and he squeezes his eyes shut, willing her not to hang up. "Mrs. Keene," he says, "I'm really, really sorry to bother you, and I'm not trying to disrespect your wishes or invade your privacy or anything. It's just that . . . I haven't heard from you in a while and I was really hoping that I might be able to wish Loomis a happy birthday. I really don't mean to harass you or anything. Honest to God. I just want to . . . open the lines of communication."

There is a long pause. He doesn't know what she is thinking, but he can sense that this is an unfriendly silence. The utter lack of sound is like a deep, toothy mouth that he is lowering his head into.

"So . . ." he says at last. "Did you get the presents? And the card?"

"Yes," her voice says.

"And . . . you will give them to him, won't you?"

He hears her throat clear, deliberately, and he can feel the hairs on the back of his neck prickle. She sighs. "No, I don't think so."

Her voice is firm and reasonable, reminding Troy of the years she'd spent teaching second-graders. "I want to be frank with you, Troy, and I'd like you to do me the courtesy of listening and trying to understand." She pauses for a moment, in the way a teacher might pause to underline a word on the blackboard. "Loomis doesn't need your gifts," she says. "Or your cards. Or your phone calls. He needs a stable life. He's happy in school, and he's a bright, thoughtful, caring child. The last thing he needs is to have you trying to bribe him with cheap toys and getting him all riled up."

Troy keeps his mouth shut, though he can feel the heat in his face. He is not crying, but his nose is running, and his chest feels tight and quivery when he tries to speak. "But . . ." he says, and then stops himself. He knows that it will do no good to argue with her, it will only make matters worse. He takes a breath.

"I understand what you're saying," he says, even as his hands tighten hard against each other. "But would it be possible for me to talk to him for one minute? Just to say 'happy birthday.' That's all." And he can feel his throat constricting. "I'm his father, Judy. I want to be a good father. I know you don't believe that, but if you'd just . . . give me a chance . . ."

"You want to be a good father," Judy repeats, and echoed by her, the words sound limp and pathetic. Troy stares out the kitchen window, where the tree swing is still hanging, encrusted, petrified with a layer of old snow and ice. What can he say?

"You're not a very reflective person, are you, Troy?" Judy says, very calmly and clearly, that neutral, therapist's tone that makes Troy flinch. "I don't know what your definition of being a good father is, but to my mind, you are the exact opposite of a good father. I would like you to think about the *facts*, Troy, the facts from my perspective. You sold drugs out of your home, while you had a child. You supplied drugs to my daughter, the mother of your child, who you knew was an addict. You opened your house to the very lowest scum of the earth, so they could purchase drugs, and these people wandered freely in and out of your house while your own vulnerable child was sleeping, or playing nearby, or maybe even watching while you and your cronies got high. Those are not the actions of a good father, Troy. I think you've gotten so used to charming people and maybe you've been lying to yourself for so long that you don't even know right from wrong anymore.

"But I do. I have a very firm grasp of right and wrong, young man, and this is something you need to hear. Do you know the most loving thing you could do for your son right now? Leave him alone." And then she repeats this forcefully, as if it is the answer to an important question. *"Leave him alone,"* she says. "Give your son a real gift, Troy. Show him real love. Don't make him miss you and yearn for you, because you know you will only ruin his life."

By the time he arrives in Lisa Fix's office, at one in the afternoon, Troy has calmed down somewhat. He even smiles at her, and she smiles back, adjusting the collar of her large yellow turtleneck as she types some things into her computer. It's a cold day. The parole office sits among a row of interconnected brick storefronts, directly across from the courthouse. A weathered cowboy is walking down the sidewalk and

Troy watches him pass, trudging with his hat pulled down over his face against the blast of snow sparks.

"So," Troy says, when Lisa finally turns to look at him. "Six months to go."

"Let's not get ahead of ourselves," she says, and she glances down into his journal, toying distractedly with her pen, clicking the retractable point of it slowly in and out. "You're doing fine, Troy, but let's do this a week at a time, okay?"

"It's my son's sixth birthday today," Troy says. "His grandmother won't even let me wish him happy birthday over the phone. Why don't you humor me? Give me something to look forward to."

She purses her lips, giving her pen another rueful click. "What do you want from me, Troy? I'm not here to predict the future. And I'm not here to humor you either."

"I just want to confirm the schedule of things," Troy says. He sighs, leaning his arm on her desk, his fingers brushing the little magnetic tube in which paper clips are imprisoned. "I just want to know— I mean, assuming that there are no glitches or fuckups on my part, or . . . *whatever*— She has to give Loomis back, doesn't she? That whole consent form that I signed for the probate court: Judy's guardianship of Loomis. It's temporary, right? Once I'm done with my parole, custody of Loomis reverts back to me, right?"

"Yes," Lisa says. "Technically, the custody would revert to you." Troy watches as she reclines back in her wheeled swivel chair, her eyes shifting, glancing out the window.

"Technically?" Troy says. "What do you mean by that?"

"Well," Lisa says. She looks at him for a long moment. Her round, freckled face grows solemn. "Listen," she says, finally. "I don't know whether I should tell you this or not. But you should probably talk to your lawyer."

And the look in her eyes sends the kind of thrum through him that he had felt, earlier that day, when Judy had said: *Leave him alone.*

"What do you mean?" Troy says.

"I mean that you should talk to your lawyer," Lisa says. "I'm not trying to get you riled up, Troy. But I think you should know. Your mother-in-law, Mrs. Keene, submitted a petition to the probate court to terminate your wife's parental rights. I just saw it yesterday. It's a pretty basic petition—nobody's been able to contact your wife for over six months, so it should be fairly easy to prove abandonment. I don't think Mrs. Keene will have a problem making her case."

Troy folds his hands together. Another person walks by the big window beyond Lisa Fix's desk, an elderly woman in a long wool coat and a pointed stocking cap. His hands are beginning to shake a little.

"And . . . ?" he said.

"And nothing," Lisa Fix says. "It's just— I think she has a good lawyer. I don't want to upset you, but if you think about it, once the mother's rights are terminated . . ."

"Then I would be the next hurdle, right?"

"I think it's a possibility," Lisa says. "But listen. I'm not telling you this to get you all worked up. Even if Mrs. Keene did petition against you, I don't think she could win. The law tends to favor biological parents. I'm telling you this because I think you need to be aware of it. What you need to do is keep your nose clean. Take your drug education class, do your community service, don't get into trouble. But if I were you, I would be prepared for the possibility that Mrs. Keene is going to challenge your custody."

Troy is quiet. He hunches his shoulders, staring down at the tile floor beneath his feet, his hands clasped tightly together. "Okay," he says at last. "Thank you."

As he drives back home he is aware again of that sense of entrapment he'd felt when the police had shown up at his door, all those months ago—that long, dreamlike pause where you imagine that there is still some way to escape. *Wait,* he thought. His hands were trembling as he clutched the steering wheel.

Do you know the most loving thing you could do for your son right now?

He could send his car swerving into a tree, he thinks. He could drive to Judy's house and strangle her. He could just keep on driving— cut off the parole anklet at the next intersection, head out to California, or Hawaii, or overseas—like Carla, disappearing into the vastness of the world.

You're not a very reflective person, are you, Troy?

No, he thinks as he turns down Deadwood Avenue. His windshield wipers tick insistently against the steady dots of melting snow that alight on the glass, asserting themselves briefly before being wiped clean.

Okay, he thinks. It is two-thirty in the afternoon, and he shudders as an old Guns and Roses song starts playing on the radio: a song that he and Carla had once liked, back before Loomis was born, and he almost starts to choke up.

———

Even before he turns into the driveway, he can see Jonah sitting there, perched on the hood of his old Festiva, right across the street from the house, waiting patiently. As he toggles the gear shift into park, he watches Jonah clamber off his car and stride up the driveway, and his muscles tighten. The old partying life he'd had with Carla falls away; the last chords of "Sweet Child o' Mine" cut off as he kills the engine.

"Hey," Jonah calls uncertainly. "Troy!" And Troy keeps on walking. He holds out his hand, like a traffic cop: *Stop. Keep your distance.* But Jonah shadows him as he walks toward the back door.

"Troy?" Jonah calls after him. "Troy?" And maybe he is so used to being ignored that he's oblivious, and Troy has too much ingrained midwestern politeness to simply keep walking. He turns to look over his shoulder, glowering, and Jonah widens his eyes.

"Hey," Jonah says. "I was, uh. I was just . . . stopping by? Like we talked about?"

Troy stands still for a moment, blinking. He remembers now that they'd made some kind of arrangement—"An appointment," Jonah had said. "Just to sit down and talk"—but it had completely slipped his mind. He thinks of excuses, pushes his hand through his hair. Though he has come to accept that the papers Jonah had given him are the truth, it's still a little hard to believe that this person is his brother. It's hard to know what to do with him. Where to put him on the list of things that need to be worried about.

"You know, Jonah," he says, "this is really bad timing."

And Jonah gives him a stricken look.

"Oh," Jonah says. "What's wrong?"

"Everything," Troy says. But this sounds melodramatic. "Nothing." Their eyes meet. What is he supposed to do with the look on

Jonah's face, which reminds him of nothing so much as the abused kids he'd known in grade school—that expression they'd get if you'd pay attention to them, a bleak hopefulness opening briefly and then shutting. What is he supposed to do with the fact that for a brief flash he can see the sort of younger brother Jonah would have been? He can feel a kind of shadow life pull across him like a cloud scudding across the sun, and he can picture Jonah: a grubby and wiry-tough little kid, beloved of no one but fiercely loyal nevertheless, and he feels oddly guilty, aware of all the ways he would have broken that imaginary younger brother's heart.

"Nothing's wrong," he says quietly. It's already more complicated than he wants it to be, even as he turns to go into the house to make his phone call to the monitoring device people. He sighs as Jonah hesitantly follows after him, but he doesn't say anything more. He just picks up the phone and dials.

Despite everything, Jonah *has* been on his mind—or at least the idea of Jonah. His brother? His biological half brother? A stranger he shares some genes with? It has occurred to him that, besides Loomis, Jonah is the only other person he's met in his life who is biologically related to him, and he's not really sure what to think about it.

At first, he'd simply been angry. Discovering that Jonah had spent those first six weeks spying on him had bothered him more than he cared to admit. He was already feeling vulnerable, aware of his own body being constantly monitored, and thinking of those weeks that Jonah had worked alongside him at the Stumble Inn actually made his skin crawl—the uneasy, dreamlike awareness that someone he barely knew was hovering at the periphery of his life, gathering information, pretending to be someone he wasn't. It was scary.

But he also found himself regretting how mean he'd been. He recalled the way Jonah had flinched like someone who was used to being hit, nodding in agreement when Troy had said, *I don't want you in my workplace. I don't even know whether I want anything to do with you.* Afterward, thinking about it, it had seemed cruel. It had connected in his mind with the way Judy had treated him, and Lisa Fix and his lawyers. When Jonah had called him a few days later, he'd held the phone in his hands for a long time without speaking, listening to Jonah's hoarse explanations.

"It was a stupid thing to do," Jonah kept saying. "I know I was a coward about it. I know that now, but I just . . . chickened out, every time I wanted to tell you."

"Yeah," Troy had said. "Well, maybe that was the right instinct."

"I don't know," Jonah had said, and there was a sandpaper edge of emotion in his voice that made Troy's heart tighten. "I know this sounds stupid," Jonah said, "but it was like you were the last person in the world I had any connection to. And I didn't want to come all the way just to have you slam the door in my face. I wanted . . . I don't know. To get to know you a little. I know we're not *really* brothers, but . . . I got caught up with the idea of it. The idea of connection. I'm sorry that I wasn't, braver, about it."

And Troy wasn't sure what to say. What do you do with a statement like that? *The idea of a connection.*

"Well," Troy had said. It came to him that everything Jonah had loved was gone: his parents, wife, his unborn baby, the future he'd imagined for himself. "Well," Troy said, "we should talk about it."

He thinks of this all again as he recites his information to the parole service. *Jonah is my brother,* he thinks, gazing over to where Jonah is still standing in the doorway, in his cheap, puffy ski coat and blue stocking cap, his arms crossed over his chest. *My brother. Biological half brother.* And there is a kind of uncomfortable wonder to this fact.

"You're clear," the monitoring device guy says, and Troy slowly depresses the receiver. Jonah's eyes skim over the surface of Troy's face, even as he wavers in the doorway, keeping a respectful distance, his head cocked like a sad dog.

"It's okay," Troy says. "You might as well come on in."

—————

Growing up as an only child, Troy used to have fantasies about having a brother. A little brother was what he always imagined—and in fact, back in the days when he was baby-sitting, he had come up with a game that Ray loved, in which they'd pretended to be siblings. Tim and Tom were their pretend names, and they made believe that Ray was only two years younger than Troy, instead of almost eight. It was a way to control Ray, he supposed, to keep him from wanting to play irritating kids' games or watch babyish movies that Troy disliked, but it also spoke to his own secret wish to have a cohort, a trusted follower in his adventures, someone to tease and argue with and hang out with.

He can't quite picture Jonah in that mode, exactly. Jonah would have been too much trouble, he imagines—and he has another guilty flash of that strange, fierce, large-eyed little brother he would have hurt and disappointed. Ray wasn't a good model, he thought. Ray had been too easy, too pliant, and in fact, he had probably done Ray a disservice, especially during Ray's teenaged years, when Ray was living with him and Carla. He'd let Ray do whatever he wanted, as if he was in his twenties, and had even encouraged him to drink beer and get high and drive without a license and basically join with impunity in the general hell-raising that he and Carla were engaged in. Ray could have used a real parent.

Still, he found himself wondering what Jonah would have been like if they'd been raised together. Would he have grown up so skittish and evasive, so spacey and unsocialized? Troy doesn't think so. He's not just a guy who had a tragedy with a car accident, Troy thinks. Whatever's wrong with him has been building up for years and years, and Troy can't help but feel that Jonah would have been better off if he'd been around to look out for him.

And maybe he himself would be different as well. Jonah wouldn't have been as malleable as Ray. It wouldn't have been a replay of the old Tim and Tom game—Jonah was much smarter, much more deeply involved with his own imagination, and maybe if they'd known each other earlier, Troy would have grown up to be, as Judy said, a more reflective person.

Of course, if they'd grown up together, they wouldn't be the same people at all. If and if and if— The little marks and scars they would have made on each other would have molded them in ways that were impossible to calculate. It's a little like that math puzzle Jonah had told him about: *an infinitely long line surrounds a finite area.* Fathomless.

"Do you want some coffee?" he says to Jonah, who has settled at the kitchen table.

"Well . . ." Jonah says.

"I'm going to have some myself, okay? So it's not a big decision. You want it or you don't want it. Whichever you choose is fine."

"Okay," Jonah says, and he holds his coat in his arms, fiddling with it. "I guess I don't want coffee, actually." His eyes widen and unwiden. "Is this a bad time?" he says. "I can come back later—"

"It's always a bad time," Troy says, and shrugs. How much does he want to say? "Listen," he says, and glances sharply at the phone. "I'm sorry I didn't turn out to be . . . what you were hoping for." He makes a laughing sound. "You drew some pretty unlucky cards when you came looking for me, didn't you?"

Jonah seems taken aback. "No!" he says, as if Troy has implied some bad intention. "Not at all." He purses his lips. "Is there anything I could do to help?" he says.

"You could kill me," Troy says. Then he shakes his head, disliking his own blithe sarcasm, his own self-pity, which he knows Jonah won't find funny. "Never mind," he says. "Nothing you can do, man. This is the hole I dug for myself, and I'll have to deal with it."

"Well," Jonah says, "even if it's something little. Like . . . going to the store for you . . . or whatever. There's probably something I could do."

"Not really," Troy says, and then they are both silent, listening as the coffee machine begins to gurgle and bubble.

"So how's things at work?" Troy says, and shifts his weight. "Ha! You know, someone mentioned the Gold Coin the other day and Vivian got all edgy about it. She's still pissed at you for jumping ship."

"Well," Jonah says. "I wish I was still at the Stumble Inn with you guys. I'm not very good at making friends with people."

"Mm," Troy says, and there is a twinge of guilt. "You're not missing anything," he says, and pours himself a cup of coffee from the still-filling pot, not caring that it spills a little. He sits down at the table, rests his forehead against the ham of his palm. He thinks again of his conversation with Lisa Fix. "Shit," he says, under his breath, and Jonah gazes at him cautiously.

"It's about Loomis, I guess," Jonah says, and Troy looks down. Is this the conversation he wants to be having?

"Sort of," Troy says. "Not really. It's not important."

"It's Loomis's birthday today, isn't it?"

And Troy looks up at him sharply. "How did you know that?"

Jonah shrugs. "You told me. Remember? We talked about all of this stuff. I just have a good memory for dates."

"Huh," Troy says, and it's another way in which they are completely different. Troy is aware again of the way in which Jonah soaks up information, that glint of gentle, steady computation in his eyes, which Troy had noticed when Jonah talked about his college classes, or when he talked about the details that he'd gathered about Troy himself—Troy had been amazed, and more than a little disconcerted, to look through the folders of court records and letters, certificates and credit reports, all annotated in Jonah's tiny cursive handwriting. He can picture Jonah alone in his trailer, transcribing their conversations into a little notebook or something. He's probably got shelves of notebooks, Troy thinks. He probably knows what he ate for breakfast three years ago on this day.

"That's right," Troy says at last. "It's his birthday. Six years old. Pretty amazing if you think about it. I mean, that's when you start to become a real person. You start getting, like, a *consciousness*, you know? You start getting this sense of yourself as a separate person in the world. I mean, your mind is more mature. You remember what it was like to be six years old, more than you remember being a toddler. And then after that, you're starting to become yourself. Your personality and brain. It's weird to think of that happening to a person you saw getting born."

"I guess," Jonah says, and watches as Troy sips coffee. Troy can see his expression moving through its shifts, the time-lapse-photography quality of a leaf, opening. "Did you get to talk to him?" Jonah says at last.

And Troy blushes. "No," he says. He shifts in his chair, grimaces, and he can't help but feel a little ashamed—a failure as a father, a man whose child would be better off without him, at least according to Judy. "That's actually a problem right now. I haven't been able to talk to him . . . for a while."

"Oh," Jonah says, and Troy watches as he processes this. "What are you going to do?" he says finally.

"I don't know," Troy says. "I don't think there's anything I can do, really. At least while I'm in this situation."

Jonah inclines his head, and his entwined fingers twitch lightly. Their eyes meet for a moment, and Troy is aware of . . . what? That odd, ambient sense of connection. He remembers the day Loomis was born, the moment when the nurse had lowered the swaddled infant into his arms, and it had struck him, suddenly, that Loomis was the first person he had ever met who was connected to him by blood, and now, as he looks at Jonah's eyes, he can feel a flutter of recognition in the pit of his stomach. That's the connection, he thinks. If Jonah and Loomis stood side by side, an observer would easily recognize that they were related. There are particularities of expression, something shared in the way their eyes flicker and then grow calm, a certain ruminative turn of the mouth. The resemblance is so clear for a moment that Troy feels a knot in his throat.

28

Winter 1997

Jonah drives around and around the edges of St. Bonaventure, but he can't seem to find a way out of his predicament. It has been this way always, he thinks—a long hallway, like the corridor of a motel or apartment building, and he winds his way along, checking the knobs, feeling his fingertips pulse with the dull electric current of all the people he might have been. He could have stayed on in Little Bow, working his way through the kitchen to a job as an orderly at the old folks' home. He could have tried to weather his way through Chicago—finishing college, maybe. Finding a career. Pursuing the tentative relationships that he'd made with more tenacity, maybe even *really* meeting a wife, having a family. He could have stuck it out at the Stumble Inn, too; he could have become friends with Troy, if not his brother; he could have been almost happy with Crystal and Vivian, making food for people. Almost.

But it is as if each possible life is just beyond his reach. He thinks of a fly against a windowpane, tapping steadily against a transparent barrier. He always gets to a certain point, he thinks, and then he fails.

And so it goes again: the worst one of all. He had the opportunity to make a real connection. He has shown bravery, has taken wild chances—is there anyone, he thinks, who would have taken such measures as he had to get close to Troy? Who else would have had such determination?

Yet he has let himself screw it up so easily. So stupidly. As many times as he goes over his life in his mind, he can't seem to find a way past the roadblocks that he has created for himself. He drives past the Discount Mart, with the great, dirty hills of snow plowed up in the corners of its parking lot. He drives to the edge of the interstate, to the truck stop with rows of sentient eighteen-wheelers lined up not far from the gas pumps. He drives along past country houses and sheds, posted at intervals along the rutted state highway, past winter fields and telephone lines hung with xylophones of icicles. White-faced Hereford cows alongside a fence, the snow accumulating on their backs. A blank billboard, with tatters of old advertising hanging from it in strips. He should be able to figure out a way to make this work, he thinks. He should be able to correct his mistakes somehow.

His biggest failures, he supposes, were the simple ones, the ones that shouldn't have caught him off guard. Like that day in November, when he'd brought in all the paperwork, and Troy had gotten to see his original birth certificate for the first time.

In the beginning, it seemed to be going well. Troy sat there reading the document over and over, and his hands actually shook as he turned the pages. Jonah watched as Troy's mouth tightened.

"Baby Boy Doyle," Troy said. He didn't look up for a long moment, and Jonah shifted, tense and respectful.

"I know it's kind of heavy," Jonah said, and cleared his throat. "It's a lot to take in at one time." He was trying to imagine what Troy might be thinking. Was he wondering about Nora, picturing his infant self as he was parted from her, his infant's eyes watching a blank ceiling unscrolling above him? Was he parsing the ways that his life might have been different? Did he feel, as Jonah sometimes did, the vast randomness of life spreading out in a long plain all around him?

But when Troy lifted his head, he was not overcome with emotion. He looked puzzled.

"Wait a minute," Troy said. "Why is your last name Doyle?"

"What do you mean?" Jonah said.

"I just mean . . . that's Nora's maiden name. I thought you said you had a father."

"Oh," Jonah said, and he could feel the blush spreading across his face, bane of liars.

"Actually," he said, and hesitated for a moment. "Well . . . my father's last name was Doyle, too. They weren't . . . related or anything. It's not that uncommon of a name. It just so happened that they were . . . lucky that way."

He smiled at Troy, who was looking at him with his forehead wrinkled—disbelieving?—Jonah couldn't be sure.

"Huh," Troy said. "Well, that was convenient, I guess."

"They used to joke about it," Jonah said. "That's . . . actually, that's how they met. He was getting her mail by mistake. His name was, um. Norwood. Norwood Doyle."

"*Norwood?*"

"Yup," Jonah said, and he looked Troy in the eye, steadily, smiling, hopefully sincere. "It was some sort of family name. He hated it. He went by Woody."

It still bothered him that he'd saddled himself with this imaginary, spur-of-the-moment father with the goofy name. It was such a mistake, he thought, because now he had to spend time inventing stories about this man, Woody Doyle, whom Troy had inexplicably taken an interest in.

"What kind of a father was he?" Troy said, one day in December. "Did you like him?"

"Hmm," Jonah said. "Well, sure. Of course. He was a carpenter. Like my grandfather. He built me a tree house when I was . . . I don't know . . . about eight. He was a pretty quiet guy, though."

"What did he look like?" Troy asked.

"Like me, I guess," Jonah said. "I mean, without the—" and he gestured lightly toward the scars on his face. "You know. Kind of blondish-brown hair. Round face. The same sort of build, basically."

"It's too bad you don't have any pictures," Troy said, and Jonah stiffened inwardly.

This had been an issue between them, this lack of photographic evidence. It was the thing that Troy seemed to find hardest to believe, even though it was perhaps the most truthful thing Jonah had told him.

"You mean you don't have *any* pictures of your family?" Troy said, incredulously, and Jonah thought of the time, all those years ago, when he'd been clearing out the old yellow house outside of Little Bow, the auctioneer, Mr. Knotts, watching him as he tossed the photos into an extra-large garbage bag. *You should go through those,* Mr. Knotts had said. *People can be rash when they are in mourning.* And now, of course, he was sorry.

"I lost them . . . in a fire," he'd told Troy, and Troy raised his eyebrows.

"That's *weird*," Troy said. "You mean there's no more pictures of them—period? I mean, there's got to be pictures of them somewhere. What about, like, other of your relatives? Or a high school yearbook?"

"Maybe," Jonah said doubtfully. "I wouldn't know how to get ahold of one."

And Troy had shrugged. "Well," he said, "you figured out how to find *me*. That's got to be harder than tracking down a few pictures!"

Troy didn't understand, Jonah thought. Troy had no idea how easy it was to disappear off the face of the earth, how easy it was for time to swallow you up. He thinks again of his mother's ashes, combining with the soil in a ditch somewhere in Iowa, shot through with the roots of small plants, which drew the nutrients from what remained of her body before dying themselves. Or his grandfather. More than fifteen years have passed since Joseph Doyle's death, and by now Jonah himself is perhaps the last living person on the planet who had loved the old man, who remembers his face clearly, who remembers the stories that he'd told about himself.

Maybe, Jonah sometimes thinks, he himself is fading out in the same way. He has spent so much of his adulthood wishing to be a different person, so many hours dreaming of exactly this sort of transformation. In the new self that he's portraying, Nora no longer walks through the rooms of the little house, muttering to herself, telling him that she wanted to die and then finding excuses not to; there is no Elizabeth, her bobbed tail tucked shyly between her legs; there isn't the sound of his grandfather's coughing phlegm into a handkerchief, there is no longer that morning when Jonah found him dead, his rigid fingers clutching the silky edging of an old blanket, pressing it to his half-open mouth.

There is hardly anything at all. His life is suddenly a large, empty house, with each vacant room waiting to be furnished. His made-up wife. His invented father. His pretend childhood.

He wonders if it is possible to unlie yourself.

———

Sitting in his trailer house, he tries to find a way to go back to the beginning, to that day in September when he'd arrived in St. Bonaventure, to do it over again. He draws diagrams in his notebooks, working backward, trying to fold up the expanding accordion of lies. February, January, December, November, October, September. He tries to walk himself through the dull dailiness of his new job at the Gold Coin Restaurant—burritos and chimichangas, tostadas and refried beans; through the days indoors, behind the shades, under a blanket on the couch, watching television, reading.

He finds himself driving a lot. Sitting in his car with the defroster on high, idling in the empty, snowy parking lot of Zike's Roller Rink, with its boarded-up windows. Puttering up into the hills behind Troy's house, where, months ago, he brought Rosebud, after he'd killed her.

The dog's body is concealed in a little alcove under a cliff of lichen-covered pumice rock, and he's not sure why he's drawn to check on it from time to time. Maybe he's just making sure it's still there—some kind of guilt or superstition pricking him. The body is almost skeletal now, crusted with snow, mummified, the skin pulled taut over bones, the lips shrinking back over the teeth in a kind of smile. Standing over the corpse with the wind and the dust of snow blowing up in whirlwinds, he thinks of that teenaged boy, Jinx, standing at his door. "I wonder if you've seen my dog," Jinx said, and he was no more than fourteen, though when they'd first met he'd seemed somehow threatening. Powerful with his group of stoned cronies. "I let her out last night, and she never came back."

And Jonah had looked at him, his forehead creasing, miming concern. "No," he said, and he was aware then that almost all of his life was a secret. The boy's eyes, undrugged, had an earnest, deerlike gentleness that reminded him a little of Troy, and Jonah had felt his heart blanch.

"Sorry," he said. "But . . . I'll keep my eyes open for her. I'm sure she'll . . . turn up."

December turned into January turned into February, and still Jonah would wake up at night and hear Jinx calling from the porch of his house.

"Rosebud," Jinx's voice would echo. His hands cupped around his mouth. "Rosebud! Rosebud!" And Jonah would press his face hard against his pillow.

———

Troy wanted to talk about the past, that was the worst part of it all. Troy wanted to hear stories about Grandpa Joe and the orphan train, about Joe and Lenore, their grandmother, who had died in a car accident before Troy or Jonah was born, and Jonah felt obliged to make up stories out of nothing. It was irritating that Troy was so interested in Lenore's relatives, the aunt Jonah had been to visit once, Aunt Leona, whose face Jonah could barely recall.

"Wow," Troy had said. "So we're part Indian. Part Sioux. That's really kind of cool."

Jonah sighed lightly. "I guess," he said.

And then he wanted to know about Nora. It was even harder to talk about her, since all the characteristics that Jonah most remembered about her were compromised by her imaginary marriage to the imaginary Woody Doyle. And it was even more difficult to talk about his own life, since he had to make up nearly everything. He had a Chicago childhood to invent, a house on the west side, with a pretend father and mother patched together out of projections: What would she have been like, if she'd been happy, if she'd been normal? What would he himself have been like? With that as his premise, he had to create an entirely new childhood, and from there, concoct a girl who would fall in love with him, and whom he would marry, and who would die in a car accident.

At first, this didn't seem so problematic. It was only when Troy began to talk about his own past, it was only when Jonah saw the photo albums that Troy kept, the stacks of pictures and mementos, each with a little anecdote or funny story attached, that he saw how thin and underdeveloped his own make-believe world was.

They looked at pictures a lot, at first. Dozens and dozens of Troy's "relatives"—the family he was adopted into. Here was Troy as a baby. Troy's adoptive mother and father, and Troy himself, aged about ten, outside a tent at a lakeside campground. Troy's cousins Bruce and Michelle, and their child, Ray, circa 1979. Troy's father, in an upholstered recliner, grinning, holding a beer. Troy and Carla and teenage Ray, sitting in the same kitchen that he and Troy now occupied. He looked at the photo, and Troy put his thumb across the bong that was prominently centered in the middle of the table. "Ignore that," Troy said, shrugging, flipping the page, and here was a collection of photos of Loomis as a baby. Even as a toddler, Loomis's eyes were recognizable: stern and serious and critical.

What could Jonah do in the face of such records? He had no such organized bank of history, nothing that tethered him to the facts of the world, not even something so small as a photo album.

Troy seemed so dauntingly grounded, so familiar with the story of his life, that Jonah found himself ashamed of the pitiful skeleton of his own.

He remembers the day of Loomis's sixth birthday, the way they'd sat there, looking at photo after photo of Loomis, the child's life mapped out year by year.

"You remember what it was like to be six?" Troy said.

"Yes," Jonah said. But he didn't know what else to say. "It's funny," Jonah said at last. "I'm not really sure if I remember anything correctly. About being a kid." He presses the inside of his lip against his teeth, trying to think. He should have stories about growing up in Chicago, about Woody and Nora Doyle, about the girl he'd married, but nothing came to him.

"I got bitten by a dog," Jonah said, and he could feel himself blushing as if this were a lie. "That's what I remember about being six. My mom's dog, Elizabeth. She was a . . . Doberman, and . . . she bit me pretty badly. I've always been kind of scared of dogs, ever since."

"Huh," Troy said. "Was that in Chicago?"

"In South Dakota," Jonah said. He could feel a pang against the surface of his eyes, a sharpness. "I had to go to the hospital."

"Wow," Troy said, and he seemed to muse on this, but not very sympathetically, Jonah thought. "We never really had pets," Troy continued. "I don't know why. My mom, I guess, didn't like the idea of having animals in the house." Then he smiled, as if remembering something fondly. "We had fish for a while," he said. "I really loved those fish."

"Ah," Jonah said. He hesitated. "I . . . like fish, too," he said.

He could have said it then. He could have said, "Look, Troy, I've been lying to you all along. I want to tell you the true story of my life." He even stood up for a moment, pushing his chair back from the kitchen table, sick of the single room that they seemed to have settled themselves into, sick of the weight of the false life that he kept on inventing. He stood there, helplessly. Each time he and Troy met, it felt as if he'd unraveled a little bit further from himself, from his true history. Each afternoon that they sat down at that kitchen table to talk, it felt like he was acting out a persona that was more false than the time before. It wouldn't be long, he thought, and he would be completely imaginary.

29

February 27, 1997

Troy has been thinking a lot about Nora lately. Despite everything, despite all the more pressing concerns, he finds her floating up from the back of his mind. *Nora Doyle,* he thinks as he trudges out the back door of the Stumble Inn, past the fat, unhappy Dumpster, pulling his stocking cap over his ears, the muddy slush of the parking lot beginning to solidify beneath his shoes as the little bit of sun sinks away. "You look a little pale," Crystal had told him as he was leaving. "Are you doing okay?" And he'd shrugged. "Just a cold," he said, and now, sitting in the car with the defrost on, he finds a crumpled piece of tissue and blows his nose grimly. Exhaust plumes thickly out from his muffler into the cold air, and he can imagine Nora, a teenaged girl five or six months pregnant with him, staring out a window of the Mrs. Glass House at the snow. He thinks of that long ago day when he was eleven, when Carla's friend Chrissy had talked to him about being adopted. *Don't you wonder about your mother?* Chrissy had said, and he recalls the small fissure that had opened up inside him at that moment, even though he'd tried to ignore it for years and years.

He has a vague image of her. A narrow face, Jonah had said, high cheekbones, dark eyes, a prominent nose. Long black hair, he thinks as he stands in his kitchen. "It was down to her waist when I was growing up," Jonah had told him, and Troy has a glimmer of her again, as if he has seen her before. The back of his neck quivers. He can see her face as she gazes out through her window, her mantle of dark hair, her features unclear through the layer of condensation on the glass. Would he have been moving inside her?

Probably not, he thinks, and he puts a pan of water on the stove to boil. He finds a package of powdered soup—yellow chicken-flavored dust, dehydrated noodles—and pours it into the pot, then changes from his work clothes into sweats while it heats. He looks in the medicine cabinet for some kind of cold remedy, and at last settles on a chewable grape antihistamine that he'd bought for Loomis sometime last year. He unrolls some toilet paper and blows his nose again.

She would have put her palms against the windowpane, he imagines. A sixteen-year-old girl. Water would have trickled down from the imprint of her hands.

The last few days have been pretty awful, and maybe that's what brings Nora into his mind. Monday had been the fifth anniversary of his mom's death, and he'd been surprised to find that it hadn't really gotten easier. The dull ache of grief opened up around him, exacerbated by his frustrating dealings with Jonah, by his worries about Loomis and custody. He'd learned that Judy had already, without any dramatic confrontation, managed to terminate Carla's parental rights, and he knew it was only a matter of time before a similar petition was leveled against him. He'd spent the better part of the day trying to reach his lawyer, Eric Schriffer, pressing the phone receiver to his ear as Nora and his mom and Carla circled through his mind in slow, lazy figure eights: dead, missing, lost. He listened to the soft, muddy bump as he was put on hold. Schriffer was "in a meeting," or "not in the office," or "on the other line."

They'd been friends once, Troy thought. They used to sit around and get stoned, and they'd had some pretty good talks, and even as he listened to tinny classical music being played for him through the phone lines, he could imagine confiding in Eric. He would tell him about Jonah and all the adoption stuff. He would tell him about the odd, elusive connections he could feel at the edge of his thoughts—his adoptive mom, and Carla, and Nora, these women he'd lost, pacing together in a wheel in his mind.

But when Eric finally picked up the phone, in the late afternoon, it was clear that they were friends no longer. He had only started to talk about the termination of Carla's parental rights when Schriffer cut him off.

"Listen, Troy," Schriffer said, in a bright, quick voice. "This is nothing to worry about. This is a fluke of your ex-wife's behavior that has nothing to do with you. I just got a report from your parole officer, and you're doing great. Even if she does present a petition, it will never in a million years make it to court. The law is on the side of the biological parent, man. You just need to take it easy and relax."

"Yeah," Troy said, and he could feel all of the things that he'd imagined telling Schriffer shriveling up. "Yeah, I understand, except—"

But Schriffer was already moving on. "It's really good talking to you, Troy," he said. "But I really have to get going. I'm sorry. It's really been hectic around here lately."

"Ah," Troy said. "Well then."

He paces through the house, drinking his soup from a coffee cup. He changes the sheets on his bed—the old king-size four-poster that had once belonged to his parents, and which he'd later shared with Carla. He checks on Loomis's room, the room that had once been Troy's as a child, and retapes some of the slumping drawings, loosened by the dry, forced-air heat. He sits down and sorts through some of his mom's things from the hall closet, her mementos and letters, her high school yearbook. Her jewelry box, where there is a little plastic baggie full of his own baby teeth, tucked alongside the earrings and necklaces. If he'd had a little alcohol in him, he might have even called Terry Shoopman, just to talk to someone who had known his mom, just to hear Shoopman bend his dull, steady high school guidance counselor voice to Troy's worries.

"You shouldn't feel guilty," Terry Shoopman would say. "Your mother always wanted you to find out more about your biological family. To tell you the truth, she was always a little troubled that you didn't show more interest in it when you were a child.

"It's true you've had a run of bad luck, Troy," Terry Shoopman would say. "But it seems silly to try to make these connections. Your wife, and your mother, and this woman Nora? They're all very different people. Surely you realize that."

"Yes," Troy would say. "That's true."

"I think you're spending too much time alone, young man," Terry Shoopman would say. "You need to get a grip on yourself."

"Yes," Troy says aloud, and curls his palm around the baggie of his baby teeth. He recalls what Jonah had said, a few weeks ago. They had been talking about Jonah's wife, Holiday, about the car accident, and Jonah had shrugged his shoulders abruptly.

"I really can't think about it anymore," Jonah said. "I need to move on." And then he'd looked at Troy plaintively, his eyes roving, scanning Troy's face. "You just . . . keep moving, right?" he said. "You're always . . . in the process of becoming a different person. Don't you think?"

"I guess," Troy said. He wasn't sure what to say to the strange, urgent conviction in Jonah's eyes.

There was so much that Jonah was evasive about, so many questions he skirted with general philosophical principles. He said that it was "hard to remember," that it was "not really that important," that there were "things he doesn't like to talk about."

"Jonah takes the Fifth Amendment once again," Troy would say, half joking, half irritated. "What is there to be so slippery about, man?"

"I'm just not that . . . interested in the past," Jonah had said, and lowered his head stubbornly. "I like to sort of . . . live in the present."

"Uh-huh," Troy said. "Well, for me the present kind of sucks, so we're a little bit at odds, don't you think?"

And Jonah had shrugged, moodily. "I'm telling you the truth," he said. "I just don't remember. I don't think about that stuff."

Nora was a particularly touchy subject for some reason, and Troy couldn't understand why. He knew there was something Jonah wasn't telling him. The silences grew longer when she slipped into the horizon of the conversation. Jonah's mouth grew small, reproachful, when

Troy asked a direct question. It was as if Jonah didn't quite recognize that Nora was what connected them, that Nora, at least biologically, was Troy's mother, too.

"Did she ever—" he had asked Jonah once. "Did she mention me, ever?"

And Jonah had shifted in his chair. "Well," he said. He brought his foot up and cradled it in his lap. "I think she thought about you," he said.

"What do you mean?"

"I don't know. It was just a feeling I got."

"But you knew," Troy said, after a moment. "You knew about me, that she'd given a baby up for adoption. She told you?"

"Well," Jonah said. "More or less." He cleared his throat. "You know," he said, "she didn't talk about anything personal with me. It was just like a . . . typical parent-child thing. Nothing special. I don't have any real insights or anything. You know? She cooked, and she kept the house clean, and she liked to read books. She liked art, I guess. She had lots of postcards of different paintings. And seashells. She collected seashells."

"Oh," Troy said. He watched as Jonah looked down at his hands. Unlike most people, Jonah tended to rest his hands with his palms facing up—maybe because of the scars that ran down his knuckles to his wrists—but it gave him an oddly religious quality. "You didn't like her very much," Troy said carefully, and Jonah glanced up, abruptly, startled.

"I didn't *dislike* her," Jonah said. His brow furrowed. His expression came near to annoyance, the closest that Troy had ever encountered. "We didn't always get along the best," Jonah said. "But she wasn't a bad person, exactly."

————

He had tried to be sensitive about Jonah's reluctance. He understood that there were things that were hard to talk about, and he had the vague notion that Jonah and Nora had some sort of falling-out, that there was some aspect that needed to be approached delicately. He even offered up his own adopted mother as an example, hoping that his stories about her would act as prompts to Jonah's recalcitrant memory.

Awkwardly, he had told Jonah the story of his mother's funeral—how stoned they'd been, how he'd undone the prayerful clasp of the corpse's nearly weightless branchlike hands. He had never told this anecdote to anyone before, but he gave it to Jonah, and they were both silent for a moment when he was done with it.

Troy shrugged, giving Jonah a sad, apologetic half smile. "It's fucked up," he said.

"A little," Jonah said. "Not— I don't think you did anything wrong, exactly."

"I don't know," Troy said. "I feel pretty guilty about it. I miss her." He waited, expectantly, but Jonah just sat there. His eyes shifted slightly, and he licked his lips.

"What was it like for you?" Troy said. "Was there a funeral for . . . Nora?"

Jonah seemed to freeze.

"Not really," he said. "Well, not in the traditional sense."

Troy raised his eyebrows expectantly.

"She was cremated," Jonah said. "So there wasn't a casket or anything. It was just . . . a quick thing."

"She died young," Troy said, after a moment. "I was thinking about that the other day. She was only, like, what? Forty-three?"

Jonah didn't say anything. Troy was aware of a whole map of memories moving through Jonah's brain, unspoken.

"She killed herself," Jonah said at last. "I don't really know why. But she, well," he said.

"Oh," Troy said.

"It was pills, basically," Jonah said. There was a long, ambient silence in the kitchen, and Jonah was motionless. Outside, the icicles that hung from the eaves cast reflected waves of light through the window, trembling yellow-gray shadows. "It was pretty straightforward. She took, like, a whole bottle full of pills, and then she died. I guess she was unhappy. I don't know."

———

It came as a blow, this information—this death.

Troy was surprised at how heavily it settled over him. This woman, this Nora, whose body he'd once inhabited, whose picture he'd never seen but whom he has put together from Jonah's hesitant descriptions. Suddenly she was a presence.

His mother.

Whatever he'd hoped for her crumbled a little.

"I'm sorry," he said softly, and hesitated. His hand felt shaky as he put it across his mouth, but Jonah's expression hardened.

"I probably shouldn't have told you that," Jonah said. "It's not like . . . something I dwell on. I'm not trying to make you feel sorry for me."

"I know," Troy said, and paused: a shudder. "But . . . I feel sorry for *her*, man. I mean, she killed herself! And you didn't tell me that?"

"I didn't want you to think she was a bad person," Jonah said, at last. "I didn't want you to think she was crazy."

"Jonah," Troy said. At that moment, there was something in Jonah's eyes that made Troy feel sad—a shifting, trapped look, the kind of expression you might have when you reached the dead end of a maze for the third or fourth time.

For a moment Troy half considered reaching across the table and touching the guy's hand. Okay, his brother. His mom had killed herself. His wife was dead. He was, Troy realized with sudden clarity, desperate.

"That's why you didn't keep any pictures, I guess," Troy said.

———

Troy goes through all of this in his mind as he sits there on the floor with his mother's jewelry box between his legs. It has been over two weeks since he last talked to Jonah, and it's weird. He's not sure whether Jonah will ever be back.

"I don't get it, Jonah," Troy had said. "Look, I thought the reason you decided to find me was . . . because she was our mother. I mean, if you can't be straight with me, what are you doing here? What's the point?"

"I don't know," Jonah said.

"What do you want from this, man?" Troy said. "I mean, let me ask you a question. What do you want from life?" And Jonah just shook his head, as if the question baffled him.

The house is dark now, and Troy doesn't bother to turn on the lights. He sits in Loomis's bedroom with the window open a little, breathing the freezing air, blowing smoke into it.

Here are the things that Troy wants from life: He wants to be a good father, to see Little Man grow up; he wishes he was the kind of dad who maintains the love of his son, over a period of years; he wants the adult Loomis to remember him fondly when he is dead. He wants to be the kind of man that Carla would want to come back to, sober and repentant, and if he can't have that, he wants to meet a beautiful, gentle girl he can make a home with. He wants great sex. He wants his old friends—Ray and Mike, Lonnie, all the guys he'd played cards with or got drunk with at the bar, the people who would sit out in the yard in the summer, the tiny bats dipping in the twilight above the branches, the stereo speakers sending stupid rock and roll into the yard, his bare feet in the grass. He wants to live next door to his parents. He wants them to be alive, still happily married and growing old together—and they would go on camping trips, his mom and dad, him and Carla, Loomis, maybe another kid or two not yet born. He wants to notice a piece of the world every day, something beautiful or funny or strange, that he can think about. He wants to be content most of the time.

He sighs. Across town Loomis is taking a bath, sitting with dignity among cloud peaks of bubbles, and maybe the time they spent together is already half like a dream; to the north, in Bismarck, Terry Shoopman watches a science program on public television, and a photo of Troy's mother is still centered on the surface right above the screen—Troy's mother and Shoopman on their wedding day; to the west, in Las Vegas or Reno, Carla runs her lighter under the glass of a pipe, her lower legs tangled in the sheets, a guy asleep beside her, and in a large house in Arizona, Ray's mother Michelle pours herself a glass of wine, stands in her kitchen, frowning as if she can feel someone thinking about her in the distance.

As for Jonah, Troy can't imagine what he's doing, what he's thinking. Maybe he's working at the Gold Coin, or sitting in his trailer, reading, solitary, an airtight wall between himself and his past. He remembers the blank look Jonah gave him. "I don't know," Jonah said at last. "I think . . . I guess . . ." Then he let out a kind of laugh. "I really don't know what I want," he said. "I really don't."

30

April and May 1997

When Jonah left St. Bonaventure, he didn't plan to come back. It was over, he decided. He'd made such a fool of himself—showing up drunk on Troy's doorstep, telling him, what? It didn't matter. It had been clear for a long time that things were never going to work out the way he wanted them to. Whatever hopes he'd had for Troy were gone now. He had screwed everything up again.

He packed only a few things before he left. He was very deliberate about it. Spartan, he thought, and liked the sound of the word. He laid all his clothes out on the bed: five T-shirts; three pairs of jeans; seven each of underwear and socks. These went into paper grocery bags, lined up in the trunk of the car. He put his cassette tapes into their little case and set them on the passenger seat. He put the envelopes with his money in the glove box, bundles of tens, twenties, fifties—everything he'd managed to save, plus what little was left of the original nest egg that he'd gotten from the sale of the house. He thought of that day, long ago, when he was clearing out his mother's belongings; he thought of the auctioneer, dressed like some old-fashioned Grand Ole Opry singer, shaking his head sorrowfully as Jonah stuffed trash bags full of photos and mementos. "Son, don't do anything you're going to regret."

There was a weird pleasure in it, though. That was what he realized. It reminded him of a time when he was a child, a day when he and his grandfather were trying to fly a kite in the stubble field out beyond their house. After a few failed attempts at getting the kite into the air, his grandfather remembered that a kite needed to have a tail. They searched around in the field for a while, looking for a bit of rag, and after a minute or two his grandfather said, "Oh, what the hell," and cut off a long strip from the bottom of his shirt—just like that!—with a pocket knife. Jonah recalled being a little shocked. "Oh, Grandpa," he said. "Don't do that!" But his grandfather just shrugged, and they knelt down in the dirt to work on the kite. He'd thought about that shirt for a long time afterward. He was impressed by the idea that adults could simply tear their own shirts on purpose, and there would be no repercussions. Later, he'd taken one of his own shirts out behind the house, cutting into it with a pair of his mother's scissors, frightened that someone would catch him but also exhilarated. He buried the ribbons of cloth in the garden, his face flushed, his shirt-murdering hands trembling.

He thought of this feeling again as he looked over his possessions: his victims. He had considered trying to hold a garage sale, but on second thought there was more satisfaction in sentencing this segment of his life to death. In thinking that there were still things in his life that he would live to regret losing. He stood with his arms folded in the living room of his trailer, considering, and then he began to stuff all the little flotsam that he'd cherished into garbage bags and cardboard boxes, filling containers one by one and hauling them out to the communal Dumpster in the alleyway behind the trailer court.

It felt good. He broke the base of a lamp against the metal side of the Dumpster. He slit open a bag of flour and let the contents slide in a curl of fog over some discarded shoes. He wavered only a few times before he befouled his well-thumbed old college textbooks and beloved paperback novels with the poured-out contents of his refrigerator—a bottle of ketchup, jar of pickles, cottage cheese, spaghetti sauce. Goodbye books. Good-bye term papers that he'd written when he was taking college classes. Good-bye stupid, desperate, self-pitying journals and diaries he'd been keeping. And finally, after a slight hesitation, good-bye packet of information that connected him to Troy, the photocopies of the birth certificate and court records. He crumpled these papers up very deliberately, shoving them into a two-ply plastic garbage bag full of household cleaning products that he'd bought when he first moved in. An electricity crackled across his fingers. Good, he thought, dragging bag after bag into the daylight, down the dirt path, to the alleyway. Good riddance.

It was a Saturday morning, and after a while the neighborhood kid, Jinx, came out to sit on the hood of a car. Still dogless, Jinx slouched back on his elbows, watching his baby brother playing in the dirt with matchbox cars, and when Jonah went past a third time, he lifted his head.

"Hey, Jonah," he said. "You throwing anything good away?" And Jonah smiled tightly.

"Not really," Jonah said, but on his next trip to the Dumpster he presented Jinx with a fairly new boom box that he'd bought at Discount Mart. "I was just going to get rid of this," he said. "Maybe you can find some use for it."

"Nice," Jinx said, mildly, and rubbed his hand over his incomplete mustache. "You moving out or something?"

"Something like that," Jonah said. He felt a small twinge of guilt, once again, for the death of the boy's dog. "I'm feeling the need to start my life over."

"Oh," Jinx said, "that's cool," and his grubby little brother gazed up at Jonah solemnly, crashing the fender of a matchbox car against Jonah's shoe.

"Yeah," Jonah said. He fingered the small framed photo in his pocket—the Polaroid snapshot of Troy and Loomis that Troy had given him. He'd thought about throwing this away, too, but now he thought he would keep it for just a while longer.

"Well," Jonah said, and held out his hand. "I guess this is good-bye."

Jinx smiled sleepily, regarding Jonah's extended palm for a moment, then at last inserting his damp teenaged hand into it.

"Good luck," Jinx said. "Have a nice life."

For a while Jonah wound his way along the interstate, stopping from time to time to glance at a road atlas. It was strange, he thought, to find the place he once lived, the towns he'd passed through, represented only as dots along great rivering roads. The maps showed the world spread outward from St. Bonaventure—from North Platte, from Omaha, from Chicago, from every center—spiderwebs, veins, nets that cast themselves across the open prairie. He recalled that day in the fall when he'd first driven to St. Bonaventure, when he'd stupidly imagined that his life was some kind of film—*the story begins,* he'd thought then. Now he wasn't sure what to think. *The story never ends? The story is pointless?*

Near the center of the state, he turned himself southward, past Red Cloud, where Willa Cather once lived, into a series of Kansas towns—Lebanon, Mankato, Belleville, Concordia—and into the larger world, which spread indeterminately outward. He could continue on this route, through Kansas, Oklahoma, Texas, all the way to Mexico City, or beyond, through Central and South America, to the tip of Antarctica. In between, there were many great cities, and millions of people, but that didn't comfort him very much. It didn't seem to matter really.

In Wichita he sat in a strip bar at the edge of the interstate, where a topless red-haired woman danced in high heels. He drank a gin and tonic, then rested in his car with his eyes closed. He traveled down I-35 through part of Oklahoma, stopping for gas in Broken Arrow. He ate a cheeseburger in Okmulgee. He crossed onto the Indian Nation Turnpike, on his way to Texarkana, before twining his way lengthwise across Louisiana to New Orleans, where he planned to live for a while.

But he hated it there. It was not the sort of place where you started over, he thought. On a block in the French Quarter, he watched a teenaged girl helping her friend throw up into a garbage can. A walking tour passed by, led by a man with a shock of black hair like a horse's tail, and curling stiletto fingernails, at least three inches long. The man was wearing a cape and a top hat, with dark makeup around his eyes, and he looked at Jonah's face suggestively as he passed, as if they were kin, as if Jonah was yet another curiosity he might point out to the docile people following behind him.

Jonah slept in his car that first week, trying to decide if he really wanted to rent a room. At night he sat with the map light on, reading the various brochures for attractions that were scattered across the city, listening to the radio and the street sounds. One night he woke up and a couple were having athletic sex while braced against his car. He sat there in the backseat, blinking, watching the man grin fiercely as he thrust himself against his partner, a woman bent double, with her face pressed against Jonah's hood. Jonah wasn't sure what to do. The man seemed to be looking directly at him, his gritted, gilt-edged teeth glinting under the streetlight, and Jonah didn't move. Did the man see him? Jonah wondered. He felt for a moment as if he were disappearing, ceasing to exist, and in the morning, he wasn't sure if it had really happened.

It reminded him a little of that March morning after his birthday, the stuff he'd been trying not to think about. He'd awakened on Troy's couch, and at first he didn't remember much of anything. Hungover. His head was too fuzzy, too painful, and when he tried to sit up he could feel his equilibrium swinging around him in a nauseated, wobbling circle. His shoes and socks were on the carpet, next to a plastic bucket that had been placed near his head. He sat up, rubbing his hands against his face, and it was then that a little flash of the night before came to him. He remembered the bottle of bourbon he'd purchased for his twenty-sixth birthday, and then showing up at Troy's back door. They were sitting at the kitchen table, as usual, but he didn't remember what exactly they'd said. All he knew was that he'd slipped up. Told more than he should. (*I don't have a wife. There wasn't any car accident.* He remembered that much for sure.) Called Troy names. (*If I had your life, I wouldn't have fucked it up as bad as you did.* Had he said that?)

What had he done? There were large, unpleasantly blank chunks throbbing in his memory, but it didn't matter what he'd actually said. It was clear to him even in his hungover state that the damage was irreversible. He picked up his shoes and socks and limped, barefoot, along the cold cement of Troy's driveway to his car.

For the next few days he slept. He unplugged the phone, didn't bother to go into work. He lay in the dim bedroom and tried to piece together the conversation they'd had. The alcohol had fragmented it into dozens upon dozens of tiny shards—some nearly clear, some blurry, some utterly dark. He could picture Troy's face, grim, silent, listening. Ultimately, he had no idea what he'd told Troy—how much of the truth, how many new lies he might have layered on top. But he knew that he'd ruined things.

For a few weeks he tried to imagine himself into New Orleans, but it seemed less and less probable—like a bad rerun of his first days in Chicago, without the eager, hopeful belief in the idea of becoming a different person. He didn't know what to do with himself. From a phone booth on Bourbon Street he called Steve and Holiday's number, and listened to Holiday's voice on the answering machine before hanging up. He called Crystal about an hour later from the same phone booth, listening sadly to her surprised, stiffening voice.

"Oh! Jonah," she said. "How nice of you to call!"

"I'm in New Orleans," he said, and Crystal exclaimed as if impressed. "That must be exciting!"

"Yes," Jonah said. He could feel the people moving around him on the sidewalk as Crystal hesitated awkwardly. "How is everybody doing?" he said. "I've missed you guys."

"That's so sweet of you," she said. And he wavered there in the brittle politeness of her silence.

I don't have anywhere to go, he imagined himself saying. *I want to go home but I don't know where that is.* He winced at how pathetic it sounded, how self-pitying. What could she possibly say to that? What could she do to help him?

"So," he said at last. "How's Troy doing? He must be just about done with parole by now."

When he finally arrived in Little Bow, South Dakota, it was the middle of May. Over four years had passed since he was last in this, his hometown, but nothing much had changed. Main Street was still the same sad cluster of shops. The movie theater where he'd spent so much of his time was still there, and so was the high school, the football field, the clump of bushes beyond the chain-link fence where teenagers were still standing, furtively smoking cigarettes and joints.

A few miles outside of town, the little yellow house where he grew up was still there as well. He passed down the long gravel road where once the school bus would drop him off; here was the same metal mailbox with the red latch-flag that you could lift to tell the postman that outgoing mail was contained inside; here were the stubble field and prairie, here were the kitchen windows and the white door, the weeds beginning to grow in the flower beds on either side.

He sat there for a while, his car idling, and at last a woman came out of the house holding a baby against the crook of her hip. Another child, about three, a girl child in a purple smock, followed behind.

"Hello?" the woman said cautiously. She was a homely little woman, about Jonah's age, with short brown hair and a pointed, witchy nose. "May I help you?" she said. Her voice was gentle and musical.

Jonah rolled down the window. "I'm sorry," he said. "I'm not here to bother you. I used to live here once."

"Oh, really," the woman said, pleasantly. She glanced in the backseat of Jonah's car, where a stack of dirty clothes was covered by a blanket and pillow, and an old flashlight was wedged alongside a smattering of books and magazines. "Just passing through?" the woman said. She didn't seem to notice—or at least, she didn't respond to—the scars on Jonah's face. "Do you want to look inside? It's a little messy, but I'd be glad to show you."

At the edge of his vision, Jonah could see Elizabeth loping along the side of the house, her paw lifted because of a thorn. He could see the clothesline where his mother hung the wash, draped with billowing blankets.

"I know what it's like to want to come back to your old house," the woman said kindly. "I think about doing that myself. I grew up in Boise, and I know someday I'm going to do the same thing you are. I'll just park in the driveway and take a long look. I think that's an important thing to do."

"Yes," Jonah said. The little girl looked at him from behind her mother—a thin, hollow-eyed child, her blond hair lifting in the constant wind, her brow furrowed.

"We love this house," the woman said. "We're so happy here."

After a moment, Jonah returned her smile. "I'm glad," he said.

Later that same day he found his grandfather's headstone in the cemetery. There were some plastic flowers next to it, very old—the color in them had faded, and the plastic itself had become weathered and brittle. They were meant to resemble orchids, and he picked them up and put them under his arm. His grandmother's grave was alongside: Lenore, who died in a car accident when his mother was a girl. There should have been a gravestone for his mother, as well, he supposed. But of course there wasn't.

He'd been dreaming about her lately. He dreamed about her walking, the way she walked when she was taking Thorazine, the jerky, deliberate steps of someone who doubted the solidity of the ground in front of her. He could see her contracted eyes, the pupils about the size of the head of a pin. He remembered walking with her in the supermarket when he was a teenager, dreading the moment when she'd see an infant in a stroller and go into her routine, her old, bitter joke. *Oh look,* she'd say, *there's my baby!* and he'd flinch as she tottered forward, her once beautiful hair now stiff and unruly, cut in a shag style, her mouth small and dry and trying to make an exaggerated smile for the infant. Jonah stood there stiffly as the woman pushing the stroller recoiled at their approach. *There's my baby!* his mother crooned. *There's my baby!* His mother was only thirty-five but looked much older. Her body was wiry, monkeylike, with ropy arms and stumbly, stick legs, wearing clothes from the children's department at Sears, girly jeans and a pink T-shirt, and he sometimes thought that if he grabbed her wrist, her hand would come off and the thin fingers would curl and shrivel around his thumb.

He dreamed that she was leaning over him as he was sleeping, shining a flashlight into his eyes. He dreamed that she was singing to him, a song from one of her records, slow, terribly sad: *I wish I had a river I could skate away on,* she murmured, her alto voice throaty and thin in the darkness above his bed. The damp pads of her fingertips passed along his face, along the ridges of his scars, and when he groaned and tried to push her hands away, she winced, then smiled.

"Don't worry," she said. "I'll be gone soon enough. Then I won't bother you anymore."

"Good," he said, and when he tried to close his eyes again she bent down and kissed him firmly on the mouth.

"No one will ever love you again," she said softly, as if to herself. "You know that, don't you?"

And he squeezed his eyes shut, pressed his face to the pillow, just wanting to get back to sleep.

"Yes," he said.

And he supposed that it was true. He drove around town one more time, past the old folks' home where he'd once worked, past the Harmony Chicken Farm, where his mother had once spent her days, packing eggs, and in the late afternoon he even drove out onto the reservation. His grandmother's sister, Leona, would be in her middle seventies, he guessed—if she was still alive—and after a few passes down the rutted dirt roads, a few angry dogs snapping and chasing at his tires as he rolled through their territory, he found at last the boxy, prefab house his grandfather had once taken him to, years before. The bare, grassless yard was scattered with toys—a purple bike, a basketball, a naked Barbie, some plastic building material—and when he knocked at the screen door a Lakota boy a few years younger than he came to the door. The boy was wearing a white T-shirt and jeans, and his hair was cut very short, as if he might have been in the marines.

"Can I help you?" the boy said.

Jonah cleared his throat. "Well," he said. "Actually, I was looking for Leona Cook. I don't know whether she still lives here."

The boy was silent, his eyes passing over Jonah's face and body with a heavy, neutral look of appraisal. Behind him, Jonah could see a boy and a girl, aged about six or seven, sitting on a couch, watching television. He could hear the bloinks and xylophones of cartoons.

"What do you want her for?" the boy said.

"Well," Jonah said, "I guess she's my great-aunt. Her sister, Lenore, was my grandmother, and I just thought . . . well, I just . . ."

"She's not in very good shape," the boy said. "She had another stroke a few weeks ago." He didn't open the screen door.

"Are you her son?" Jonah said, and the boy blinked at him.

"Her grandson," he said, his voice uninflected.

"Well," Jonah said. "I guess that means I'm your cousin. Your . . . third cousin? Maybe. My name is Jonah."

"Oh," the boy said. He glanced down at Jonah's palm, which was extended as if to shake hands, the scrim of the screen door still between them.

"You know," the boy said. "It's probably not a good time. She can't really talk or nothing. She just sits there, you know? With her fingers moving? I don't think it would be good for her to have a stranger in the house." He peered uncertainly at Jonah, and of course he must have wondered about this pale blond guy with the scars on his face, claiming to be his cousin. Maybe, Jonah thought, Leona would confirm their relationship, but maybe she wouldn't remember him at all. Maybe, he thought, there was no one left alive who really knew who he was.

At last, he traced over the route he took, years before, along the edges of South Dakota, Nebraska, Iowa. Here was the old two-lane highway he'd traveled down once. He watched along the edges of the road the fence posts, the growing weeds, the barbed wire. He had to drive past, a few times, before he finally saw the place.

Miraculously, the urn was still there, upturned over a fence post, weathered and rusted, but still present. Four years had passed. Nothing remained of her body, of course.

He felt his hand against the gear shift, putting the car into park, and then he turned the key in the ignition and the idling car went dead. A weight settled over him. Even after all this time, it was still only the two of them, just as she had said.

He was a little past his twenty-second birthday when she died. He had been working at the old folks' home, washing dishes, and when he came into the house everything was silent.

"Mom?" he'd said. "Mom?" For years he had been rehearsing

the moment when he would come home and find her dead. His shoulders tensed; the skeletons of expectations began to erect themselves around him.

He'd pressed his hand against her door, and rattled the knob. "Mom?" he said, and for some reason he knew that it was real this time. He could feel her inside the room, the flick of a fishtail, a muscle spasm before the fish was cut open, its mouth closing on dry, useless air. He pressed open the door, and there she was, as he had pictured her so often: her nightgown pushed up past her thighs, her mouth ajar, her hands stiffened. He stood there in the doorway, pretty sure that she was dead.

"Mom . . . ?" he said, and his heart quickened. The radio was still going. Her eyes were open as an announcer gave the weather, introducing a song. Her body seemed to be stiff, and he was prepared to put his fingers on her eyelids and push them closed.

He never did find out how many pills she had taken, how many different poisons she'd consumed. There was probably an autopsy report, but he never saw it. All he remembered was that when the pads of his fingertips touched her eyes, to close them, she opened her mouth, and an emptiness poured out. Her lips tried to form words. She gagged, her throat muscles suddenly beginning to work. One eye fixed on him while the other drifted off.

He always told himself that there was nothing he could do at that point. The doctors were unsurprised by her death; they didn't seem surprised that he hadn't saved her, but she herself had widened her eyes. "Don't make me go," she whispered, and her fist closed around his pinkie finger, the way an infant will clasp whatever is pressed into its palm. "I don't want to go," she said, and pressed her damp mouth against the side of his face.

For a moment, sitting there along the road, he recalled what her fingers felt like as they clenched tight and then, step by step, became dead. It wasn't like in a movie. The grip pulsed for a while, squeezing and unsqueezing, but it didn't stop. It kept on for some time, spasmodically, long after his mother had stopped making sounds, stopped breathing. The last part of her that moved was her legs, kicking out suddenly. Her feet flexed, shoving off, as if she were in deep water, trying to make her way to the surface.

31

June 4, 1997

It was going to be a short ride, at first. They were going to spend a few hours together. But now Jonah isn't sure how far, exactly, he's gone. An hour, two hours? He watches the speedometer, he passes cars and is passed by them, though mostly he stays in the right-hand lane. He can feel his steering-wheel hands and accelerator feet merging with the movement of the car.

Landscapes pass but don't really impress themselves on his brain, sliding through his eyes and out the back of his head—the painted lines, the signs with their shining reflector strip lettering, the barren prairie sod divided by fences for no clear reason, jagged buttes rising up, clusters of shacks, occasional cow or tree, thunderstorm. Jonah can feel the road beneath him, a taut string that his wheels are riding on, and he tries to put his mind in order. They cross into Wyoming, and Loomis rises up from dozing and presses his cheek against the cool backseat window.

"Where are we now?" Loomis says, and Jonah curls his fingers. He can feel the body of the car more than he can feel his own body.

"We're outside of a town called Torrington," Jonah says. "I'm still looking for an interesting place for us to visit."

Loomis is silent, gazing out, blinking. Driving, he says, makes him tired.

"I'm thinking maybe we'll head south for a while," Jonah says. "That might be better."

Loomis considers this for a moment, his face stern with sleepiness. "Okay," he says.

It's probably early afternoon when they get off the interstate and onto the back roads. Loomis is sleeping again, and Jonah has settled into the unconscious posture of the long-distance driver, which is itself a kind of sleep, a kind of hypnosis.

It has begun to occur to him that, officially, he might be considered a kidnapper. Especially with those small-town, St. Bonaventure policemen. Especially with everything he has heard about Judy Keene. And he's becoming nervous. It doesn't yet seem that he has done anything criminal—Loomis isn't unhappy, he thinks, Loomis had come with him willingly. *Just for a ride, just for a day together.* But at the same time, as he looks out at the road, he can't help but worry about what might be happening back in St. Bonaventure. She might have called the police by now, he thinks, and he imagines a search party, focused at first on the immediate area but then tracking in ever-widening circles; authorities will begin to transmit information about a "missing child" to policemen in other towns and other states. Maybe he is exaggerating.

So far Loomis himself hasn't questioned anything, and maybe there's nothing to question. He was glad to see Jonah. Jonah had been away on a long trip, but he'd come back to St. Bonaventure just to visit Loomis. Just to see him one last time.

He isn't even sure when the idea of taking Loomis for a drive had occurred to him. Was it the moment when he arrived back in St. Bonaventure after his long trip? Was it when he found himself, that June morning, parking his newly purchased used car in the alleyway behind Judy's house? Was it the moment when the opportunity presented itself, the moment when he stood, hidden at the edge of Judy Keene's yard, watching as Loomis lifted up rocks along the fence to look for worms and insects, the child's face stolid and scientific as he bent down?

"Loomis," Jonah had whispered, when the child came close to the shadows of the lilac branches, and the boy had looked up, startled.

"What are you up to today?" Jonah had said, and tossed another dog treat into the neighbors' yard. By that time, after so many visits to Judy's house, the neighbor dog had come to know him, to see him as another food bringer, and though the animal made Jonah tense, he felt fairly secure. It was chained to a clothesline. It didn't bark, as it had the first few times.

"Hello," Loomis said.

"Hi," Jonah said. "I came back to visit you. I missed you."

"You did?" Loomis said, curiously.

"Yes, I did. I'm sorry I was gone for so long. I actually missed you a lot."

"It's been boring around here," Loomis said, and Jonah glanced in the direction of the house. He could hear the television turned up, a chorus of people singing some old-fashioned song—"June Is Busting Out All Over." Maybe that was the moment.

"Would you like to go for a little ride?" Jonah had said, without really thinking. "Maybe go on a picnic or something? I have something important I want to talk to you about."

"Oh, really?" Loomis had said, and then he'd given a little shrug. "Okay," he said, and when Jonah reached down, Loomis held his arms up with a kind of gentlemanly dignity, allowing Jonah to lift his body over the fence.

They trusted each other, Jonah thinks. It just seemed like the right thing to do, for both of them. *Let's spend a day together,* Jonah had said, and if Loomis had said no he would have accepted it without question.

But Loomis had wanted to come with him, he thinks. He observes in the rearview mirror as Loomis breathes experimentally on the rain-cooled window, then draws an *L* through the condensation with his finger. When Loomis glances up, Jonah smiles.

"Is it a lot longer?" Loomis says.

Jonah is still trying to formulate the scenario in his own mind. Where, exactly, are they going?

"I don't know yet," he says. His eyes focus on the car in front of him and he pinches his mouth tightly, considering. He can feel the tires revolving against the seamless highway, the river of wind parting before the car's prow, rushing in flapping pennants along its sides.

———

It is almost two when they stop in the small town of Straub, in between Wyoming and Colorado. Fuel and food. The gas station they pull into is part of a national chain, done up in bright, unpleasant yellows and oranges, the windows adorned with signs for beer and soda and cigarettes, the rows of gas pumps sheltered under a long aluminum canopy, high enough for a semi to rest comfortably beneath it. Jonah gets out and inserts the nozzle into his gas tank, compressing the trigger on the handle, watching the face of the pump as the dollars and cents and gallons begin to tumble upward, numbers rolling on an axis like the slots in a gambling machine. It had stopped raining quite a while back, but the air is green-smelling, full of pollen and stirred-up dust.

When he finishes pumping, he opens the back door and leans in. Loomis is awake, but bleary, his eyes still thick with sleep, the imprint of the car seat on one side of his face.

"Do you want a pop?" Jonah says, cheerfully.

But Loomis gives him a solemn look. "I'm not supposed to drink it," he says. "It's bad for my teeth."

"Oh really?" Jonah says, still smiling hopefully. "Wouldn't you like to try that red cherry kind?"

"No thank you."

"Okay," Jonah says. There is a minor deflation. "What about some juice? Or . . . chocolate milk, maybe?"

"Juice would be fine."

"And a snack?"

"Okay."

Inside, Jonah scopes the aisles. He finds a juicelike drink in the cooler, and picks out a variety of foodstuffs—some beef jerky for him, chips, a mass-produced pastry with cherry filling, peanuts, bright orange cheese-cracker squares with peanut butter spread in the middle, sunflower seeds, candy. A plush, cross-eyed toy dog that giggles and says "Do it again!" when you press its belly. A set of eight crayons and a coloring book with robots.

He sets all this on the counter, and the old man at the cash register watches him carefully, looking hard at Jonah's scars. Jonah is used to being watched carefully.

"How's it going?" Jonah says.

"Not bad," the man says. He appears to be in the late stages of alcoholism—gaunt, with nicotine-stained yellow-white hair and rosettes of blood vessels on his cheeks and nose. "Is this all for you today?"

"I also have the gas," Jonah says, and he glances out, looking at the numbers on each of the pumps. "On three, I think." He watches uncertainly as the man begins to ring up his items. "A little something to keep my kid entertained. I'm on vacation with my son."

"Is that right?" the old man says.

"Yes," Jonah says, "I think that's right," and the man fingers his purchases, turning them slowly to find the bar codes, touching the cash register buttons with his old, soft fingertips. Jonah thinks: *My wife died recently, and my son and I decided to take a trip for a while. Just to get a change of scenery, you know? Get our heads clear.*

"I haven't been in Colorado since I was a little kid myself," Jonah says, as the man rubs a candy bar vigorously across the electronic eye that reads the prices. "I was born here."

"Well," the old man says, "welcome home then." And Jonah smiles tightly even though the man isn't looking at him.

———

He tries to remember what his mother said about Colorado. Had they lived there together once? Or was that something that had happened to her before he was conceived? He tries to remember the various stories she'd told him—many of them lies, no doubt. As they cross back out onto the highway, Jonah lets her cross his mind, letting her out of the small compartment that he relegates her to on most days. Her bare feet walk across gray, mossy stones, those long toes gripping delicately, the nails painted red. He tries to get a good look at her expression, to guess at what she might be thinking, but her long hair droops around her face.

I think we'll always be lonely, you and I, she says softly, and he presses his teeth against the inside of his lip. That's not the direction he wants to travel.

"Hey," Jonah says to Loomis, who is gently dangling his legs over the edge of the backseat, who has cautiously taken a single bite of a cheese cracker. Loomis lifts his head, raising his eyebrows expectantly.

"How would you like to sleep in a tent?" Jonah says. "Does that sound like fun?"

———

Even now he's not sure how far he plans to go. He's not a kidnapper, he thinks, and in many ways he may even be doing Troy a favor. He remembers what Troy had said during one of those long conversations they'd had that past winter, when they were trying to become friends.

"I think I'm about to get fucked," Troy had said. "I think I'm going to lose my kid."

"How could they do that?" Jonah asked.

"These lawyers," Troy had said, "they can do whatever they want to a person like me."

"Oh," Jonah said, but he hadn't believed it then. He didn't realize it was true until later, when he'd talked to Crystal that one time.

"Oh, Jonah," she'd said, "things aren't going so well for Troy. I guess his mother-in-law is going to get custody of Loomis for a while. Even after he gets off parole. Isn't that terrible?"

"Yes," Jonah had said, holding on to the pay-phone receiver, which felt like a bone in his hand. He could picture the time he'd seen Judy and Loomis at the supermarket, how she'd had Loomis sitting in that uncomfortable child seat, with the humiliating strap of a sort of seat belt around Loomis's waist. Judy was fat but not jolly; her jaw had a squared-off, somewhat militaristic quality, and she seemed to be angry about something as she looked at the ingredients on a cereal box. Loomis was more subdued than Jonah had ever seen him, sitting there, staring at his palm, and he didn't look up though Jonah had liked the idea of their eyes meeting, of exchanging a secret wink.

He remembered what Troy had told him. "I know I've screwed up," Troy said. "But I love my son, you know? I do." And Jonah had nodded. He could imagine the three of them, driving south. A beach in Mexico. A tourist restaurant that he and Troy would open together. *Maybe we could just leave,* he thought, but he knew how Troy would respond. That ironic cock of the eyebrow, that grimace. As if the world beyond St. Bonaventure were some science-fiction planet.

The campground appears about an hour and a half later, eight miles off the highway, along the eastern side of the Rockies: LITTLE ICEBERG LAKE RECREATION AREA. PRIVATELY OWNED AND OPERATED. CAMPING, FISHING, CANOE RENTAL.

"This looks nice, doesn't it?" Jonah says, and Loomis peers over the lip of the window, his fingers brushing the nipple of the door lock, his eyes serious as they bump down a narrow, poorly maintained dirt road toward what appears to be an old outhouse that has been converted into a guard station.

When Jonah stops, a teenaged girl with short brown hair and a long, acne-ravaged chin comes out of the structure carrying a clipboard. She collects fifteen dollars and when Jonah asks for a "secluded" spot, she consults her clipboard grimly, directs him to Lot 23B. She hands him a photocopied, hand-drawn map, which shows a curving maze of roads lined with numbered boxes. She circles 23B.

Little Iceberg Lake is not a particularly popular destination apparently. It is four o'clock in the afternoon, but so far only four recreational vehicles are parked in the front lots, one of them so ancient and bedraggled that it might be haunted. Circles of rust dot its white, aluminum sides, and a tattered awning near the door is hung with limp wind chimes. Several of the windows are broken—repaired with duct tape and translucent plastic, or not repaired at all, shards of glass still hanging from the edges of the frame. Beyond it is a wooden hut—a set of bathrooms and showers and a pay telephone—and then a trail of tire ruts that leads into the evergreens. They pass a few campsites before reaching 23B: two motorcycle men, long-bearded tattooed gnomes sitting on stumps in front of a small bonfire; four college boys, unpacking a polished black Jeep; a family at a picnic table, all blondes of different sizes and genders, eating watermelon; a man and a woman—twins, perhaps—both with their hair plaited into braids, playing Frisbee in an open area. At the far end of this road, a post has been branded with the numbers and letters, *23B*, and Jonah pulls up beside it. There is a small picnic table, one leg manacled to the earth by a thick, rusted chain, and a campfire pit, encircled by a ring that appears to be a section of a sawed-off metal drum barrel. The ground is grassless, trampled bare.

"We'll pitch our tent here," Jonah says. "Then we can make a fire."

———

Things seem to be going well for a while. It is interesting to put the long, flexible tent poles together, and Loomis enjoys the patient project of threading them through the eyelets of canvas, the struggle to erect the frame, bending the poles until the canvas skin stretches taut across them, staking the hollow, flat-bottomed balloon of tent to the ground. He is involved in unrolling the sleeping bags inside the structure, pleased by the way the late-afternoon sun glows against the nylon membrane of canvas, the way the opening zips and unzips. It keeps both of them occupied and engaged, and then they drive to a small general store where they can buy marshmallows and hot dogs and ice.

"Are you having fun?" Jonah asks, as they turn back onto the road that leads to Little Iceberg Lake.

"Uh-huh," Loomis says, but he looks at Jonah guardedly. He is holding the paper bag containing the foodstuffs in his lap, very formally, as if bearing a religious icon. "Jonah," he says, at last. "Does my grandma know where we are?"

"Of course," Jonah says. "I called her when I was at the gas station, and she said it was okay. She said that she's glad you're getting a nice vacation. She said you should just relax and enjoy yourself."

"Oh," Loomis says. For a moment, his gray eyes cloud with concern, uncertainty.

"I have some important things to talk to you about," Jonah says.

"Oh," Loomis says.

"But first we have to look for wood. We have to find enough good, dry wood to keep a campfire going. Doesn't that seem like the best plan?"

"Yes," Loomis says. He shifts in his seat as they are driving, fingering the seat-belt strap.

They walk along the wooded area behind the tent, picking up sticks and bits of fallen brush. The evergreens slope down to a creek, which apparently feeds into Little Iceberg Lake, and they stroll along its banks in the twilight, listening to the soft, swallowing plunk of frogs as they flee into the water at noisy human footsteps. Jonah's arms are laden with dry wood, and Loomis wanders out in front, scoping the pathways. They look enough alike, Jonah thinks, that no one will question the fact that they are related. Actually, he thinks, they *could* be father and son. Loomis looks from side to side and when he sees a bit of fallen wood he strides toward it confidently.

"That looks like a good piece," Jonah says.

"I think so, too," Loomis says, and bends to pick it up.

Jonah will have to call Troy eventually. Troy will probably be freaked out about it, probably angry, but then he will see the logic of it. Even if they'd parted on bad terms, even if he thinks of Jonah as a liar and a sneak, he will have to recognize that Jonah has done a very loving thing. He has rescued Troy's son. Whatever else has happened between them, that will have to count for a lot.

They will come to an understanding, Jonah thinks. He'll explain it all. A few days, a week, and they'll all meet together.

All this comes to him dreamily, as if it's a fairy tale he read long ago, some movie he'd seen as a child on "The Wonderful World of Disney." He vaguely remembers the scene: a little boy and a young man standing with the kindling they've gathered, among the Ponderosa pines and their puzzle-piece bark, the crisp carpet of needles beneath their feet, light stabbing through the boughs in milky shafts. The boy and man face each other hesitantly.

"Loomis," Jonah says. He adjusts the bundle of wood he is carrying, first cradling it and then bracing it against his hip. Finally, he sets it down on the ground. "Listen," he says. "There are some things I want to discuss with you. I was talking with your grandma, and she, well, she was saying that it might be good if you stayed with me for a while. She's old, you know, and I think she needs a break for a little bit. Now that you're out of school for the summer and everything."

"Stay with you?" Loomis says, at last. "For how long?"

"Let's get a fire started," Jonah says, "and then we can talk about it. Okay?"

———

Building a fire is fun. Loomis is fascinated by the process—the biggest log in the center, surrounded by a tepee of branches, the twigs and bits of bark around the circumference. They spend a lot of time building this structure, and then Jonah hands him the box of matches.

"Just drop the matches around the edges, where the kindling is, okay?" Jonah says. He helps Loomis pull the match head along the flint paper on the side of the box, but when the flame sparks, Loomis flinches and drops the matchstick quickly as if it has snapped at him.

"That's all right," Jonah says, encouragingly. "It's good to be cautious. You don't want to get burned." Then he takes another matchstick from the box. "Go ahead. Just do it slowly this time, now that you know what's going to happen."

Loomis takes the match between his fingers, his brow furrowing, his tongue clenched lightly between his teeth in concentration, reminding Jonah for a moment of Troy bending over his crossword puzzles. "Okay," Jonah says, and Loomis surprises him with the neat, expert flick of his wrist. A hiss—and then Loomis is holding up the flame, his wide, astonished eyes catching the flicker of light. He grins.

"That's perfect!" Jonah says, and his breath hitches in his throat, at the purity of Loomis's pleasure. "Now put it on the kindling. That's right . . . get that little stuff burning." He hestitates for a moment, then rests his palm very lightly on Loomis's shoulder, a shudder of tenderness moving up his arm. "That's right," he murmurs. This is the closest he's ever felt to another person.

———

In the movie, the man and the boy had gone up into the mountains to have a serious talk. He remembers it clearly. The man had a beard and bright blue eyes and wore a flannel shirt. The boy was troubled, moody.

They saw a moose crossing a stream. They sat around a small fire in the darkness, and the man played his harmonica for a while.

Jonah thinks of this movie as they sit around the fire they have made together. Loomis is roasting a hot dog, proudly holding his long, sharpened sapling over the flames. Jonah hums a few notes, experimentally, then stops. He can't think of any songs, not really.

Instead, he finds his thoughts drifting toward his mother again, his mother on the day of his grandfather's funeral, how sane and sober she'd seemed. She'd put on makeup, and plaited her long hair into a single, tight braid that ran down her back. She'd worn a black dress, and Jonah wore black pants and one of his grandfather's button-up shirts, one of his grandfather's neckties, which she'd knotted for him. He can recall her fingers moving beneath his chin, the brush of her brisk knuckles against his throat. The gentle finality as the tie was cinched around his collar.

Later, back at the house, they'd sat at the kitchen table together, and she spoke to him as if they were equals, as if they were brother and sister, drinking wine in the late afternoon. She reached out and touched his cheek.

"He loved you a lot, you know," she said. And Jonah had watched as her eyes grew a film of water, as she looked past his face, out the window. "It's kind of dangerous, to be loved that much by somebody. It's hard to recover from it. It's not as if you're going to run across someone else who feels that intensely about you."

"I know," Jonah said, uncertainly, and she ran the pads of her fingers along the back of his hand, making a sigh that slid into his heart like a fishhook.

"Loomis," he says at last. The silence has been extending for a while by that point, the night pressing down on the little circle of fire. He recalls the bearded man in the movie, the way he took the harmonica from his mouth and sat solemnly for a while, watching orange flecks lifting off from the campfire and winking out in the braid of rising smoke. And then he remembers what the movie was about. He remembers what the man had said. *Son,* the man had said. *I have some bad news. Your father is dead.*

"Loomis," Jonah says, and clears his throat. He tries it out: "Son?"

But unlike the boy in the movie, Loomis doesn't lift his head. Instead, he focuses on the little stuffed dog, and presses it.

"Heh, heh, heh," the dog says. "Do it again."

Sparks rise with the smoke in little eddies above the flaming logs, and Jonah cannot really get a clear sense of Loomis's expression as the orange light shudders across the boy's face. *Heh heh heh,* the dog says. *Do it again.* And then a pause. *Heh heh heh. Do it again.* Jonah waits, trying to imagine the exact right words. But Loomis just keeps pressing the dog's stomach, over and over.

32

June 4, 1997

At first it had seemed ridiculous. The policemen—Kevin Onken and Wallace Bean, the same cops who had arrested him—standing there on his doorstep, shifting earnestly from foot to foot, embarrassed to inform him that his son seemed to be . . . lost.

"Lost?" he said, and he looked at them, puzzled. This was St. Bonaventure, Nebraska; it wasn't the kind of place where children can get lost for long. "What do you mean?" he said. "You mean he wandered off?" He flicked his eyes from one cop to the other, aware of the suspicious way they were regarding him. Gauging his reaction.

"Oh, I get it," he said. "You think he's here?" And he gazed bitterly at them. The first image that struck him was of Loomis running away from Judy's place—trekking slowly across the lawns and alleyways and parking lots of St. Bonaventure, making his way toward his dad's. They would find Loomis halfway between, and for a second he was almost happy. He would talk to his lawyer, telling him how this Custodial Parent who was supposedly more qualified than he was had been neglecting his child. He pictured a courtroom scene, with Loomis at the stand, telling the judge: "I wanted to get away from her. I wanted to live with my dad again."

Onken and Bean stared at him sternly.

"You guys want to come in and search the place?" Troy said, and stepped back, as if to invite them inside. "I'm sure Judy Keene tried to insinuate that I came over and . . . kidnapped him or something, but I've been here all day." He lifted his pant leg. "I've still got the monitor on, guys. You can check and see if I've left the house. He may be headed over here, for all I know, but it's not my fault if he wants to get away from that woman."

"Troy," Wallace Bean said, and shifted his hams. "Mr. Timmens," he corrected himself, and it was the shift into formality that sent a sudden prickle through Troy's mind. He watched the movement of Wallace's jaw beneath the skin.

"I think this might be turning into a serious situation," Wallace said.

He sat in the back of the police car, with his hands folded tightly in his lap. It was ridiculous, he told himself. St. Bonaventure wasn't the kind of place where some crazy comes along and snatches a child out of a backyard. It wasn't even the kind of place where you could wander that far—a twenty-minute walk in any direction would lead you to the edge of town, to the hills and fields and prairie that surrounded the town for miles upon miles. They had told him they'd brought in trail dogs, and the air in the back of the car had begun to feel thick. There was no handle on the inside of his door, no knob that would unroll the window.

"Loomis doesn't like dogs," he said, even though it seemed beside the point. "He'll just hide from them." He looked through the metal netting that separated him from the men in the front seat. "Look," he said, "maybe someone should be at my house. That's probably where he's going. He's probably just trying to work his way back home."

But they didn't say anything. He stared at their heads. The shaved, tapered hair, the inner tube folds of flesh that were stacked up on the back of Wallace's neck, and he suddenly remembered that horrible story, that kid who was killed—What was it? Ten years ago?—knocked in the head and dying of hypothermia in the basement freezer. Joshua Aiken. What a stupid way to die! But Loomis was a smart kid, Troy thought, and cautious. He wasn't going to fall down a well or get hit by a car or eat some poisonous berries or something.

Loomis was fine, he told himself. He wasn't the type of kid who
would be lured into a car by some stranger. Troy breathed steadily
through his nose, in and out. "This is ridiculous," he said aloud, flinching at the memory of an old dream: Loomis at the top of a tree,
perched impossibly on a thin branch.

And then he thought: Jonah?

It had been almost three months since he and Jonah last talked. He
even remembered the date—March 18—because it was, Jonah claimed,
his birthday.

It was one of those late March days—neither winter nor spring, as
if the seasons were fixed; the days muffled, melting into one another,
the rain and snow mixing together.

Jonah appeared to be a little drunk. He wasn't quite stumbling, but
when Troy let him into the kitchen he held up a bottle of bourbon,
hesitating as he set it in the middle of the table, as if he were trying to
center on some particular target.

"Hey," Troy said. He hadn't heard from Jonah in some weeks, and
he wasn't sure what to make of this. He watched as Jonah sat down and
took a little sip from the bottle. Without thinking too much about it,
Troy went to the cabinet and drew out a highball glass. He picked up
the bottle and poured three fingers of the bourbon into it, set it down
in front of Jonah, who blinked at it, nonplussed.

"Thanks," Jonah said. He put his fingers around the glass, but
didn't bring it to his mouth. "Guess what?" he said, his voice a little
thick. "It's my birthday. Did you remember?"

"Well," Troy said. "Not really. I've had a lot on my mind, man." He
cleared his throat, then warily settled down into the chair opposite,
their old position since the beginning. "How old are you?" Troy said.
"What? Like, twenty-six?"

"That's exactly on the money," Jonah said with strained cheerful-
ness. He took a sip of the liquor and shuddered at the taste. "Twenty-
six," he said, hoarsely, then took another swallow. He was clearly not
used to drinking such stuff, and Troy wasn't sure whether to intervene
or let things play out. When Jonah set down his glass, a kind of moody,
melancholy hostility emanated from his downcast face.

"Well," Troy said, "happy birthday, man. I guess I should have gotten you a card or something."

"Ha," Jonah said.

In retrospect, Troy thought he might have been more careful, more gentle. But he was used to seeing people drink. He had spent a large portion of his life as a bartender, a professional presiding over the drowning of sorrows, and this particular stage of things was quite familiar. Jonah was intoxicated—depending on his tolerance, depending on how quickly he had been consuming the alcohol, he'd probably imbibed anywhere between four and eight ounces of bourbon. Not a lot, in Troy's estimation, but enough so that Jonah was now on a cusp, and Troy understood his hesitation. Soon Jonah would lack control. A few more swallows and he would make a firm commitment to true drunkenness; certain kinds of mental regulation and inhibition would become elusive—straight lines of self-consciousness would become more and more difficult to walk down, heel to toe. By Troy's estimation, Jonah was about three gulps of eighty-proof liquor away from this altered state. *Okay,* Troy thought. This had been going on for too long, sitting across the table from each other in these circling conversations. It connected in his mind with the circumstances of his parole, the days and days alone in this house, the empty rooms, the television playing in the background. He lit a cigarette, folded his hands expectantly.

"Okay," Troy said, "so," he said, and carefully poured a little more into Jonah's glass. "So ..." Troy said. "What's been happening? I haven't heard from you in a while."

"Not much, really," Jonah said, and then he sighed thickly with his lips, like a horse. "I guess I've been trying to figure out what I'm doing here."

"Uh-huh," Troy said, and gave him a small, ironic smile. "Tell me about it."

He felt a soft spasm of alarm, remembering this, sitting in the police car. He could picture the look that Jonah had given him, a kind of icy, endless gloom that he hadn't completely understood. Then he remembered

Crystal telling him—When? Back in May?—that Jonah had called her house, that Jonah had been asking about him. He wondered now what she had said. Had she told him that Judy had gained custody of Loomis? He would bet that she had.

"Wallace," he said now, speaking to the back of Bean's head as they traveled through the underpass toward Euclid. "Listen," he said. But then he realized that it was a very complicated thing to explain.

———

There's this guy who's kind of my half brother, he thought, and he could picture Jonah settling heavily into the kitchen chair across from him, the way they faced each other as they'd been doing for months, awkwardness emanating in thin, invisible waves. Except that now, without any apparent reason, Jonah had seemed so angry.

"I've been thinking about leaving town," Jonah said, as if this were something that would shock Troy, or make him feel guilty.

"Oh really," Troy said. "That doesn't seem like a bad idea. Back to Chicago?"

"Probably not," Jonah said. Troy observed as Jonah steeled himself to finish the last warm bit of whiskey in his glass. "Do you have any ice? I think maybe I'd like some ice in this."

Troy got up wordlessly and went to the freezer.

"I think . . . I think I just want to travel around for a while. I don't even know where." He paused as Troy dropped three ice cubes into his glass, observed as Troy poured another three fingers of bourbon over it. "There's nothing for me in Chicago," Jonah said. "I don't know whether there's anything for me anywhere."

"Hm," Troy said. He had known for a long time that it was best to remain neutral toward this kind of self-pity—a good bartender neither argued with it nor sympathized, but simply listened, simply asked noncommittal questions.

Jonah said that he might go to New Orleans, which had a lot of interesting history. Maybe he'd try Seattle, which he'd heard was a good city, and he'd never seen the Pacific Ocean. Maybe Arizona. Maybe he'd go back and visit Little Bow, South Dakota, where he grew up. "Make sure the graves are still there," he said. "Ha!"

Troy watched uncertainly as Jonah rolled the ham of his hand against his forehead. He was fairly drunk, in Troy's estimation, and the weight of his head slowly slid along the plain of his palm. "Listen, Jonah," Troy said. He thought for the first time in months about the letter that he'd tried to write to Judy, that pathetic, groveling letter, propped between the salt and pepper shakers on the table, along with the month's bills. For a moment, he half considered thrusting the letter into Jonah's hands, making him read it. *This is what it feels like to be really screwed,* he wanted to say. *This is what it feels like to be really trapped. At least you can drive away!*

But the letter wasn't there. He couldn't remember where he'd put it, and his face darkened. "Listen, man," he said. "I don't quite know what you want from me. I mean, let's say we're brothers. Half brothers. Whatever. What is this supposed to lead to? I've got a lot on my plate right now, if you haven't noticed, and you sit there like I'm *failing* you, or something. What do you want? Just tell me what you want."

He watched as Jonah shook the ice in his glass. Head down.

"I don't know," Jonah said. "I don't think it matters really. I think I'll always be lonely."

"What the fuck is that supposed to mean?"

And Jonah raised his eyes—a grim, bleary, furious glance that took Troy aback. "It's just something *our mom* used to tell me," he said, sharply, and then he let out a weird laugh. "You don't understand about her, you know."

"What?" Troy said.

"Oh, never mind," Jonah said. "People seem to think it's all either nature or nurture or some combination, but you know what? I think it's even worse than that. It's all . . . random. It's all chaos and luck and whether you're, like—" he cleared his throat. "Whether you're, like . . . stupid and cowlike, like *you*, or else you have some inkling of how deluded it all is."

Troy stared at him. *Cowlike.* "Don't be an asshole," he said. "You think I've had it so great? Well, I haven't, believe me."

But Jonah only bared his teeth. "You don't know," Jonah said, and his hand slurred in the air. "You don't have. Any. Fucking. Idea. You . . . You're just the baby in the basket. She always, our mother always used to say, *that's my baby*—and when I was little I always thought it was you, but it wasn't. It was just. Various babies. You were, like, I don't know, all *happy* somewhere else. I just wanted to change places with you, that's what I really wanted, if you want to know the truth. Because if I had your life . . . If I had your life, I wouldn't have fucked it up as bad as you did. I would have done better, you know? You had such a good chance and you just trashed it! I just wanted you . . . to be happy. That's all."

––––––––––

What do you say to that? Troy had wondered. If there was an understudy waiting in the wings to relive your life for you, could you doubt that they would improve on your performance? He kept his hands folded as Jonah took another drink of Jim Beam, as he drew a hiccupped breath.

"Listen," Troy said, softly. He couldn't help but feel sorry, he couldn't help but feel that Jonah was right. He had made a mess of his life. "Jonah, look, I . . ."

But Jonah's face remained in his hands. Was he crying? He shuddered when Troy touched his back, and stared up at Troy with wide eyes.

"I can't believe how bad I screwed this up," Jonah said, and his face twisted as if Troy had trapped him, as if Troy had finally, after hours of interrogation, broken his spirit. "You know, right?" Jonah whispered. "You figured it out, right? I never had a wife that died. I was never in a car accident. Our mom never got married to anybody. I'm not that person . . . I'm not anything."

––––––––––

It wasn't a shock, really. Everything he knew about Jonah seemed to settle and solidify. Of course he didn't have a wife, Troy thought. Of course he didn't have the kind of normal childhood he'd invented. He could sense the weeks that they'd spent together tighten and grow heavy in his mind. Of course he'd been lying the whole time, and there wasn't even any reason for it. Just fear, Troy thought, and, what, probably shame of his real life. He couldn't summon much outrage at the revelation. All he felt was a kind of dull, exhausted pity.

It was about four in the morning, and Jonah stumbled out the back door, tottered over the wet, muddy lawn. He grasped the tire swing and bent over, expelling a long, wet stream of vomit. His legs wavered for a moment, and then he sat down in a pile of melting snow.

"Jonah," Troy said. He stood there in the doorway, not sure how far the limits of his parole extended. Five yards, ten yards outside the house. He waded into the yard, trailing the electronic signals that his anklet might be emanating. He put his arms around Jonah, dispassionately, lifting him up. "Don't," Jonah whispered. "You win. Leave me alone." But Troy continued to pull his body across the yard, into the house: *You win, you win,* Jonah kept saying, even as his body grew slack.

———

Now, picturing this again, he could feel their lives locking into place, his and Jonah's.

"You guys," he said to the two policemen, "I think . . ."

But then he was silent. He could see the flashing lights of the ambulance parked in front of Judy's house as they turned onto Foxglove Road. Paramedics were running across the lawn, pushing a stretcher, and he could tell, even from a distance, that it was Judy.

"Oh Jesus, Jonah, don't do this," he whispered, but all he heard was Jonah murmuring.

You win.

You win.

33

June 5, 1997

A little bit after midnight, Loomis seems at last to be sound asleep. Jonah loosens his arms from around the child and slowly lowers him into the sleeping bag, letting his hand brush slowly across the soft cheek as Loomis makes a small, staccato whimper. "Shh," Jonah says. "Shhhhh," he whispers, as if he's letting the air out of himself.

He waits a while, until he is certain that Loomis is asleep, and then he steps outside of the tent to look at the fire. It hadn't gone as well as he'd hoped, and he still feels a little shaky, a little unnerved by how upset Loomis had become. He'd seemed to be taking it well at first, with the wood gathering and fire building, but then, as it grew later, Loomis had withdrawn more and more, and when Jonah had suggested that it was time for bed, his lip had quivered.

"I don't think I want to stay here," Loomis had said. "I'm not feeling very comfortable."

"Well," Jonah said, "we have to stay here at least for tonight. We're camping. I thought you said you'd like to sleep in a tent."

"I changed my mind," Loomis said, and Jonah's heart had quickened.

"You just have to try it out," he said.

"For how long?"

"Just a little while," Jonah said. "It's a vacation. Your grandma hasn't been feeling well lately, and so she asked me just to take you for a few days."

"I didn't even know that she knew you," Loomis said, frowning. "You said that I shouldn't tell her I was talking to you."

Jonah tried to smile. "I think you're a little confused," he said. "I mean, you know the situation with your dad, right?"

"My dad?"

"He got into trouble," Jonah breathed. "The truth is, Loomis, he and your grandma haven't been getting along very well, so I didn't want you to talk about me because I thought she would get mad about it. But the situation has changed. She needed someone to look after you, so I stepped in. At her request."

"Why can't I stay with my dad?"

Jonah sat there for a moment, nonplussed. "Loomis," he'd said at last, "he's still . . . having some problems. I don't want to worry you or anything, but your dad can't take care of you right now. He's in jail. That's why I'm here."

They looked at each other. At first it seemed okay—it was just a single tear, spilling over the edge of his eye, and Loomis wiped it away quickly. "I think I'm scared," Loomis said. And then, without warning, he began to weep.

Thinking of those sobs, Jonah still feels a little light-headed. He can't help but recall the sound of his mother's crying, the way his heart would tighten as he stood outside her door, his cheek pressed against the wall. It made you feel helpless.

He knows that he'll have to start making some big decisions soon, and he tosses a pinch of dirt into the fire, watching it spark.

They are surely looking for him by now. More than twelve hours have passed since he and Loomis drove past the St. Bonaventure city limits, and no doubt the police have been called. He guesses that probably everyone is very stirred up, though that wasn't his intention. He wonders if it is possible that he could even be arrested, even if he explained the circumstances, even though Loomis is his nephew by blood and they were just going on an outing. He imagines himself back in St. Bonaventure, in a courtroom, the judge ordering him to wear the same kind of monitor that Troy wears. Forced to sit in that old trailer, which would perhaps be a kind of justice.

He could still call Troy, he thinks. The fire is dying out, and he pokes at it with a stick, stirring the embers. There had been a pay phone near the entrance of the park, and he could walk down there, while Loomis was sleeping. He feels in his pocket: five quarters, three dimes, a few pennies. Maybe. He turns the end of his stick on the coals until the tip of it is orange. He looks at his watch, squinting, holding it close to his face. It's almost twelve-thirty.

Would Troy be in bed when the phone rang? He tries to project himself into that moment, to picture Troy rolling over to pick up the receiver—not fully asleep, surely, not with Loomis missing and all the worries that would be crawling like ants inside his head.

"Hello?" he would say, abruptly—Troy would no doubt be expecting bad news, and Jonah would have to pause.

"Troy," he would say at last. "It's Jonah."

Or maybe he would say, simply, "It's me."

He gets up and wanders toward the stake near their campsite, shuffling the road gravel beneath his feet.

"Troy," he thinks, hesitantly. "Hey, sorry to call so late. I figured you might be worried, so I just wanted to let you know that Loomis and I decided to go on a little trip together. I know I should have called sooner, but I didn't realize . . ."

No, no, he thinks. *Start over.*

"Troy, we need to talk," he says firmly. "I have Loomis here with me, and we've been talking some stuff over. He doesn't want to live with his grandma anymore, that's the thing. He wants to live with you and me. So we came up with this plan, you see . . ."

No, he thinks. Not right.

"Troy," he says, in a low voice, very calm and serious. "I'm just calling to let you know that Loomis is with me." And then he'll just have to cut Troy off, whatever he says. "Don't get upset. Just hear me out, okay? I need to know what you want me to do, because I think there are a lot of options that we might want to consider. But I really think . . ."

He takes a few steps down the gravel road, walking quickly into the darkness, aware of a hollow, fluttery feeling in his chest and legs. He looks over his shoulder at the hunched shadow of the tent where Loomis is sleeping, and then back toward the trail that leads to the pay phone. It's about half a mile, he guesses.

"I think I can help you," he says. "I know that you lost custody of Loomis, but if you just listen to me, if we just work together, we can all start over. I know it sounds crazy. I know that things haven't gone so well between us, and I know that I've lied to you in the past, but I swear to you that you can trust me. Just listen, okay?

"We'll let some time pass," he murmurs, in his mind. "Let's say about a month, or even two. Maybe they'll think your ex-wife took him. And then, when you're off your parole, we'll set up a meeting place. I think it should be in Mexico. Maybe near the beach, it'll be nice. I know you think you can't start over, but you can. We can both find some kind of job down there—I mean, there are bars and restaurants all over the world, and we're good at what we do. So we can just settle there for a while. You and Loomis and me. I know that it might sound outrageous, but maybe that's what you need. Maybe you just need to make a break. We can all start over, and there might be some snags at first but I think it will turn out okay."

He stands there in the middle of the road, two or three campsites down from his own, and there is only starlight, the galaxies hovering over him. Crickets. Cicadas. "It's better than just sitting there, and letting yourself get bulldozed over," he says. "You've gotten yourself into a situation now where you have to do something radical. It's like you're on a road, and you need to just pull over and . . . abandon the car. You just start walking away from the roads. Does that make sense?"

———

He waits for a moment, and finally, Troy sighs.

"How can I trust you, Jonah?" Troy murmurs at last. "Everything that comes out of your mouth is a lie. You lie when the truth would be easier."

And Jonah is silent for a while. *No, no,* he thinks. He listens to the steady churr of insects from the surrounding dark, to the even, rhythmic grinding of pebbles beneath the soles of his shoes. Over his shoulder, the fading campfire is barely visible in the distance.

"I realize," he says. "I've made some mistakes."

Then he starts over.

"Troy," he says. "It's me," he says, and Troy takes in a harsh breath through his teeth.

You scarfaced son-of-a-bitch, I'm going to kill you. The police are already looking for you and when they find you I hope they beat the holy shit out of you. You're going to go to prison for a long time.

"Troy," he says. "Listen, I knew you'd be angry but . . ."

Mexico? Troy says. *What is this, some kind of cheesy movie? Do you think you can just stroll across the border with a child you've kidnapped? And then what? Once you're in a new country you just call "olly-olly-oxen-free" and you're not a Class-A felon anymore? Do you think it's some sort of game to live the rest of your life as a fugitive?*

"Well," Jonah says. He looks around. The boughs of trees hang over him, observing, and a night creature—a frog or something—makes a deep, glottal, percussive sound.

And what is Loomis supposed to do when he grows up? What kind of life is he getting out of this plan of yours?

Jonah hesitates. *Start over,* he thinks again, but his mind gropes and finds nothing. What is he going to say? There is a long, unraveling space that he tumbles into.

He had imagined that the cluster of buildings with the pay phone was about a half mile away, but it seems as if he's been walking for a very long time. He holds his wristwatch up to his face, trying to make out the shapes of the hands on the numbers. He thinks of the flashlight, back in the tent next to Loomis, and wishes he'd brought it. It's very dark, and the moon doesn't seem to be anywhere in the sky.

Would the police really be looking for him specifically?

It sends a shiver through him, because he can imagine Troy's voice, he can imagine the policeman writing quickly with one of those short, eraserless pencils. "He's got a long, prominent scar along the left side of his face, from his eye, right across his cheek, all the way down to his throat. He's sort of a dirty blond, not quite six feet tall. Believe me, people will remember him if they see him."

He puts his hand to his chest, and he can feel his body vibrating as if there is a small motor inside him. What if he called Troy and the phone lines were bugged? What if Troy said, "Oh, yes, I think that's a good idea, I think we should meet," and all the while a policeman was standing there with a small machine hooked to Troy's phone, tracing the call? This is far-fetched, he tries to tell himself. Why would the police think Jonah had taken Loomis? Why would Troy, for that matter? They hadn't talked in months, and as far as Troy knew, Jonah was still in New Orleans, or someplace even farther.

But alone in the middle of the gravel road in the dark, he can't be certain of anything. Ahead, there is no sign of the buildings where he had seen the pay phone. Behind him, the campsite where Loomis is sleeping is no longer visible either. He scans the trees along the edge of the road, and can make out the glimmer of someone's campfire. The beam of a flashlight rattles against the treetops in the distance, then goes out. He can make out the sound of low voices from the shadows, someone still awake and talking, but he's not sure where they are.

Maybe he shouldn't call Troy, he thinks. Not tonight, at least. Maybe it should just be him and Loomis for a little while. A few days, a few weeks. He turns and begins walking back the way he came.

The campfire is almost completely out by the time he gets back. Only a few embers are pulsing out orange light through a crust of black ash, and he looks for his stick to stir them again. He doesn't know where he put it, and he feels a little sick as he casts around for it. It's as if his brain is actually moving around inside his skull as he tries to trace through the maze that he's somehow created for himself. He imagines sitting in a cafe in some Mexican village, drinking lemonade with Loomis, looking up as Troy comes through the doorway, his face solemn but respectful as he nods at Jonah, as Loomis leaps out of his seat. He imagines a nighttime roadblock, the cars ahead of him slowing, the cops running the beam of their flashlight along the body of his car, over his face, and he tries to twist the steering wheel, to accelerate. He imagines pulling up outside of Troy's house near dawn, opening the car door to let Loomis out.

Something rattles just beyond the edge of the campfire pit, and his thoughts stop. He can see the silhouette of a small child standing in the darkness.

"Loomis?" he whispers, but this child is shorter than Loomis. A toddler, he thinks, before he sees the yellow of its eyes.

A raccoon. It gazes at him as it stands there on its hind legs, its hands tucked close to its chest, and then it makes a slow, uncertain nod, bobbing its chin at him. Behind it, another one is backing tail-first out of the paper grocery bag where he and Loomis had left the remains of their supper—paper plates, half-eaten hot dogs, crumpled bag of chips. There are some other ones out there, too—four or five, he guesses. He can see their eyes.

"Shoo," he says hoarsely, but instead of approaching them, instead of waving his hands or stomping, he takes a step backward. That numb feeling, that stuff he doesn't think of, a mouth closing over his face. "Shh," he says.

None of them run away, though the one that backed out of the grocery bag stands up on its hind legs as well, holding the empty plastic wrapper that the hot dogs came in, nodding.

He puts his hand against the side of the tent, groping for the entryway. He thinks to retrieve the flashlight that he'd left there next to the sleeping bag that Loomis was curled into. He'll shine the beam of the flashlight on them, directly at them. That will chase them off, he thinks.

The opening of the tent is unzipped, and he crouches down with his eyes still on the raccoons, backing his way in. It's almost completely dark inside the little bubble of tent, and he runs his fingers along the edge of Loomis's sleeping bag, feeling for the flashlight, but it isn't there. *Damn,* he whispers, tracing his hands clumsily along the slick nylon floor of the tent, blind in the darkness. He doesn't want to wake Loomis up, and he takes extra care not to brush or bump against the child.

But when he puts his hand near Loomis's pillow, he draws in a sudden breath. Loomis's head isn't there, and when he presses his hand against the lump of sleeping bag, there's nothing but air inside it. No body. No Loomis. Disbelieving, he pats the sleeping bag harder and a tinny mechanical laugh rises up. "Heh heh heh," a voice says. "Do it again." He startles, lifting the bean-filled little toy by its string tail.

"Loomis?" he says. He turns in a circle around the tiny space, feeling around the circumference, clutching the sleeping bags, the pillows, as if Loomis were something tiny, like a key, that could be lost in the folds. Outside the tent, there is merely the soft, snuffling sound of the raccoons as they calmly go about their work.

34

June 5, 1997

Loomis has never been afraid of the dark, but in the woods it is harder to be brave. This is more dark than he's ever experienced, so he tries not to think too much about it. He holds his flashlight stiffly in front of him, pretending that the pool of light it casts is a dog he's walking. He likes this idea. A light-dog, he thinks, and it makes him feel a bit safer, even if it is make-believe.

He stops for a moment to look behind him, pointing the light at the bars of trees and tree shadows in his wake. The tent is somewhere back there in the distance, but he can't see it anymore, and he walks his pool of light around him in a circle. Twigs, pine needles, rocks. An empty can that says *Coors*. He listens intently to the steady, pulsing chirp of insects. He doesn't hear footsteps, though. He doesn't hear Jonah calling for him, and so he turns and continues walking, trying not to step on anything that makes a snap or rustle. There are plenty of people around somewhere nearby, he tells himself—he saw them as they drove to their campsite—but right now he only wants to put distance between himself and Jonah. If Jonah comes back and finds he's gone, Loomis imagines that he will try to catch him and make him sleep in that tent again.

He had slept for a little while, even though he was upset. Even though he'd started to cry, which is not something he likes to do. Some of the children in kindergarten cry over very small things, and Loomis doesn't really approve. But he hadn't been able to control his tears this time—he had been feeling very uncomfortable and nervous, and when Jonah said that he had telephoned Grandma Keene, he felt certain this was a lie. And then Jonah said that his dad was in jail. That was the thing that scared him the most.

At school, they teach you that Strangers, bad people, will sometimes pretend to be your friend. They might try to give you drugs, or pull you into their car and make you a prisoner. They might try to touch you in your private parts, and this is inappropriate. If this ever happens, they said, you should try to get away, and tell a grown-up that you trust, like a policeman or a teacher.

He is not really sure if Jonah is a stranger or not. All he really knows is that it is important for him to call his grandma, or his dad. He had woken up to the sound of the raccoons—five or six of them, bandits, tiptoeing and fingering through their campsite—and when he'd opened the zippered slit in their tent, he saw that Jonah had gone.

"Hello?" he said, and the raccoons ignored him, continuing their work disdainfully, as if they were aware that he was a child and they were adults. He held the flashlight in both hands, running it along the perimeter of the site. "Jonah?" he said. And when there was no answer, he hesitated for a moment.

Then he started walking.

He has been going forward for a while now when he pauses again. The forest is deep, he thinks, and it might be a long time before he can find a house. He thinks of fairy tales he has heard—*Hansel and Gretel, Little Red Riding Hood*—and though he's not afraid of talking wolves or witches, he wonders if there's any truth to those stories. Are there still woodsmen he could possibly encounter? Or are they extinct, like milkmen and cobblers? He pushes his light into the distance ahead of him, trying to see a pathway through the trees. He would like to meet a woodsman now, he thinks, and he imagines a man with a feather in his hat, a bow and a quiver of arrows swung over his shoulder, whistling along a path. He thinks about animals, too, about the book he had checked out of the library: *Wildlife of the Mountain States*. Colorado, he knows, is home to the lynx, an endangered species, and also to the black bear and the puma. The puma, also known as the cougar or mountain lion, crouches silently in the bushes or sometimes in trees when it is hunting. He can see the picture in the book, the tawny, large-eyed cat, and he can remember his grandma's voice as she read. "Movement, especially running, triggers prey instincts in mountain lions," and thinking of this he holds very still. He runs the beam of his flashlight along the boughs of pine trees above him, toward the star-lined lid of sky. He listens again for footsteps, for the sound of Jonah breathing. A gust of small insects passes across his face, alighting in his hair before he shakes them away.

He has been thinking a lot about his dad and mom. It has been a long time since they've spoken, but he thinks of them often. Dreams of them. Grandma Keene doesn't seem to know much about where they are. His mother, she says, had to go on a long trip, somewhere far away, and his father got into trouble. He can remember the night when the men, the police, came into his house, how he'd tried to hide under the bed as they pounded through the rooms. He can remember the bedskirt pulling back, the man saying "Come out from under the bed, sir," and the thick hand closing around his ankle. "Come out from under the bed, sir," the man had bellowed, and when he'd cried out they'd fired a gun at him. He remembers the sound, vibrating against the walls, and the way he'd curled up and stiffened, his rigid body pulled along the dusty floor like a mop as they dragged him out.

"Oh, geez," said the man. "It's a kid." And he could hear his father crying. His dad crying. "It's okay, Loomis, it's okay," his dad said, and he'd kept his eyes squeezed tightly shut.

He'd known—his grandma had told him—that his dad had been arrested, and had to go away for a while.

But he wasn't in *jail*! Like a robber or a killer. He had known that Jonah wasn't telling the truth, but that was the lie that was the worst.

That was the lie that made him realize Jonah was trying to trick him, and a mixture of fear and outrage looped around in the pit of his stomach. Maybe Jonah wasn't his uncle after all, Loomis thought. He didn't want to be on vacation. He didn't want to sleep in a tent. He thought of that terrible and frightening movie, *The Wizard of Oz,* which he swore he would never watch again. He remembered the moment when the girl was locked in a castle, and she saw her grandmother in a crystal ball. "Dorothy!" the grandmother was shouting. "Dorothy! Where are you?" It was the most frightening thing he'd ever witnessed—that poor grandma, trapped inside the ball, blind and plaintively calling—and he thought of this as he and Jonah sat there by the fire. He knew, suddenly, he knew in his heart, that his own grandmother didn't know where he was. She was looking for him. He couldn't help himself then; he began to cry.

He stands there as these memories pass through his mind. Then, very faintly, he hears a voice in the distance. "Looooomis!" someone is calling, and he tightens his grip around the flashlight.

And despite what he knows about the pumas, he begins to run.

————

When he comes at last to the clearing, the voice has fallen away into the distance. The beam of the flashlight has been rattling in front of him, bouncing off the ground and the trunks of trees, careening through leaves and the shadowy mouths that sprang out after them, shapes bending and elongating and tilting themselves when the light struck them, and Loomis fell a few times, tripping over a root or a branch and then pulling himself up to run some more.

"Loomis!" the voice says in the distance. "Where are you?"

He stops when the trees open up onto the campsite. There is a fire there, still high and flickering, and a larger tent, a kind of A-frame construction with poles that hold up an awning. The people are sitting in lawn chairs next to the fire. A man and a woman, both with their hair plaited into braids, both of them blond and darkly tanned, their skin almost leathery. The man seems to be dozing, and the woman points her feet toward the fire, sleepily. She puts a little pipe to her mouth, and draws deeply on it. After a moment, a long, curling stream of smoke trails from her mouth and nose and drifts into the air.

Loomis hesitates at the edge of a tree, watching as the woman stares at the fire. Then her eyes settle on him. They look at each other, both of them blinking, considering, like a cat and bird staring at each other through the glass of a window. Loomis watches as she touches her fingers to one ear and then another, as if adjusting them.

"Randy," the woman says, and the man stirs uncertainly. "Open your eyes for a minute. I think I see a little boy standing over there."

For a moment, Randy doesn't open his eyes, and Loomis doesn't move. It would maybe be possible for him to melt back into the shadows, to slip behind a tree, but instead he just freezes.

"Hello," the woman says in a soft voice, such as you might use to speak to a rabbit wearing human clothes. She doesn't look exactly like his mother. His mother had never worn braids, he thinks, but he steps a little forward anyway. There is something about her face—the turn of her mouth, the way her eyelids droop in a dreamy, unconcerned, smiling way—that reminds him of his mom.

It has been one year and three months since he last saw her—he knows because he has kept a record of it in his mind—and sometimes he is afraid that he will forget what she looks like. But he remembers her very clearly right now, and he looks at the woman hesitantly.

"Hello," Loomis says, still holding his flashlight-dog firmly, making it heel beside him. "I'm trying to find a telephone," he says as politely as he can. "I need to call my grandmother and tell her where I am."

The two of them, the man and the woman, exchange glances, and Loomis sees the man widen his eyes with amusement at the woman. He knows that they think he's funny—adults often do—because he is small for his age but doesn't talk like a baby, because he has a good vocabulary, because he doesn't act spastic, like some of the kids at kindergarten.

"No telephone here, little guy," the man named Randy says, and grins. "Kinda late to be out wandering around by yourself, don't you think?"

Loomis doesn't say anything. He doesn't like this person very much; he reminds him a little of his uncle Ray, who always wants to swing Loomis on his shoulders or wrestle with him even though Loomis has told him that he doesn't like to roughhouse, who teases him and calls him Little Professor Man, as if it is a joke to want to know things about the world. This Randy is of the same sort, and Loomis turns his attention back to the woman.

"Can you tell me where I could find a telephone?" he says, hopefully. "I'm a little upset right now, and I really need to talk to my grandmother."

"You're upset?" the woman says, and chuckles, gently. "Oh, you poor thing. Where's your mom and dad, sweetie?"

"I don't know," Loomis says. "That's why I need to call my grandmother. I'm living with her, and she takes care of me for right now."

"Okay . . ." the lady says, doubtfully, and she and the man named Randy give one another that private, bemused look again. "Are you camping around here somewhere?" she says, and Loomis is silent. He is aware that if they take him back to Jonah, Jonah will tell them the same lies. He will not be allowed to call his grandmother.

"Do you think there's a day camp around here somewhere?" the woman says to Randy. "Boy Scouts or something?"

"Escaping the Boy Scouts," Randy says, and chortles. "On the run. A refugee. He makes his way toward freedom."

"Stop it," the woman says, but Loomis can tell that she thinks Randy is funny. But she is at least kindly when she looks at him again. "Where did you come from, sweetie? Are you camping with somebody? Are you with a group?"

"My address is 508 Foxglove Road, St. Bonaventure, Nebraska," Loomis says. "The phone number is . . ."

"Name, rank, and serial number," Randy says.

"Shut up, Randy," the woman says, wrinkling her forehead. She sits up and gestures for Loomis to come closer. But he doesn't move.

"You can sit over here," the woman says. "It's all right. What's your name, honey?"

"Loomis," he says, and shifts from foot to foot. "Loomis Timmens."

"Loomis," she says. "That's an interesting name."

"Thank you," he says. He takes a step toward her, then thinks better of it. She seems nice, but he doesn't quite trust Randy.

"Loomis," she says, and he watches her cautiously as she stands up. "How did you get here, in Colorado, if your home is in Nebraska?"

Loomis hesitates. He looks down at the faithful spot his flashlight's beam is casting. "Somebody brought me here," he says carefully. "But

I don't think he asked my grandma for permission, and that's why I want to call her. I'm afraid she might be worried about me."

"Oh, geez," the woman says, and her face darkens a little.

And then, not far away, the voice of Jonah drifts out of the trees. "Loooomis," he is calling, and Randy sits up, cupping a hand to his mouth.

"He's over here!" Randy bellows.

Loomis doesn't know what to do when he sees Jonah coming through the trees, into the circle of campfire light. He thinks that maybe he should try to run, but instead he just stands there, feeling mixed up—scared, but also oddly guilty at the sight of Jonah's stricken, concerned face. He has never tried to run away before, and a part of him can't help but feel that he has been a bad boy.

"Loomis!" Jonah says, and looks nervously from the man to the woman. "I'm so glad I found you! I was really worried about you. You shouldn't wander off like that—you could get lost!" He lets out a sigh, and shakes his head humorously at Randy. "Wow!" he says. "What a relief! Thank you guys for finding him."

"No problem," Randy says, proudly, as if he'd casually saved Loomis from drowning.

"He's a little upset," Jonah says, and he tries to smile but a shudder runs down his face and across his shoulders, so that the smile doesn't seem quite real. "I'm his uncle, and I guess . . . I didn't realize that he'd get so scared. I just thought he'd like to go camping, you know? To go on a little vacation. Because, well, he's had a very hard time. His parents are gone, and . . . and his grandma passed away a few days ago, so . . ."

Loomis feels these words hit him sharp, deliberate blows, like slaps. He takes a step backward, clutching the flashlight to his chest. "You're lying!" he says loudly. He can't believe that someone would lie in such a way, and his mouth trembles with outrage. "You took me here," he says. "And you didn't tell my grandma! And she's *worried* about me." He wipes his face, aware that they are all staring at him.

Jonah's hand trembles as he puts it up to his face, up to his scar. The man named Randy lifts an eyebrow, uncertainly, his eyes moving from Loomis to the woman. But she is staring at Loomis, as if trying to make a decision.

"He's confused," Jonah says, but his voice wavers. "It was quite a shock."

"You're lying," Loomis says again, and he gazes up at the woman, because he knows that she will see in his face that he's telling the truth. She will not believe Jonah, he thinks. She will help him find a telephone. He watches her mouth growing small as she thinks. The woods seem to freeze for a moment. The darkness settles over the small circle of firelight like a lid over a box.

35

December 18, 2002

Troy wakes up to a gray light that could be dawn or dusk or afternoon, a pale cloudy day outlining the edges of the window shade. He sits up. Today is Little Man's twelfth birthday, he thinks, and though he knows it's a fact he has a moment of uncertainty, a free-floating gust of Rip van Winkle time in which he can imagine his son, aged four or six, asleep in the next room, his cheeks still soft and peach-shaped, his face solemn, pressed against the pillow, dreaming hard. "Little Man," he thinks: an old nickname they haven't used in years and years, coming back to him out of the past. He rubs his hands over his eyes. Hard to believe that his child will soon be a teenager; hard to believe that they're still here, in this same old house that Troy had grown up in, that they've managed, after all, to stay together.

He opens the shade and looks out to where a light snow is falling and imagines that it is probably near the end of morning, the beginning of afternoon. He was up very late, and he pads blearily down the hall, glances into Loomis's room. Loomis—Loo, as he calls himself now—has left for school already, of course. The days of shaking him gently by the shoulder to wake him, the days of packing lunches and making breakfast are long gone, and though he'd never relished pulling himself out of bed after a late night at work, he does miss that morning ritual a little. These days, Loo is like a considerate roommate. He rises to his own alarm clock long before Troy is even aware of morning, and most often he's already asleep when Troy comes home at night, his homework stacked neatly on the kitchen table, the dishes washed, the clothes taken out of the dryer and folded. It makes Troy nervous to think of Loomis growing up, moving away, growing distant.

He stares at himself in the bathroom mirror. Though he is only thirty-six, his dark hair has already begun to show some gray.

He is not crazy about the way time moves forward. Thirty-six is not old, he knows, but five years, ten years, seems like less than it used to. Loomis is in middle school now, and in ten years he will have graduated from college. You ought to make the time precious, he thinks, and he is pleased to see that Loomis has opened the presents that he left out on the kitchen table the night before—some books, shirts and pants, a new watch. A laptop computer—he'd had to juggle the finances a little for that one—and he smiles, imagining the look on Loomis's face when he unwrapped it.

When he opens the front door to grab the newspaper he sees that the mail has already arrived. He is aware again of that shudder of timelessness, that sensation of being unmoored. He could be twenty-five, or fifty. He could wake and find that actually Loomis had disappeared long ago and never come back, nothing left but a computerized age-progression photo on a card that advertised missing children. He could wake up and find that he himself was only twelve years old, listening to the refrigerator open in the next room, listening to the hiss of carbonation as his father cracked open a morning beer. There is a little snow on the ground as Troy extends his hand out the front door and sinks it into the mailbox. December 18, 2002, he thinks. That's where I am.

And the dates on the letters confirm it. Here, look: a few bills, some junk mail, a Christmas card. He glances at the return address, then down to where his bare foot has left an imprint in the dusting of snow on the stoop.

——————

He is halfway back across the living room when a voice calls out behind him.

"Troy!"

He is still sleepy enough, still deep enough in his head that it startles him badly. He whirls around, his hands coming up instinctively to shield his face, half expecting— What? An intruder? An attack? His eyes scope the room quickly before he locates the source of the voice: Here is Ray, sitting cross-legged on the floor behind the television.

"Jesus Christ!" Troy says. "What are you doing in my house?"

"Hey, Mr. Zombie Man," Ray says, and Troy slowly untenses. Ray is setting up a video game console, poking at some buttons on the controller. "You are really out of it, do you know that? I said hi and you strolled right past me like you were sleepwalking. What's the deal, man? Did you finally decide to start smoking weed again?"

Troy frowns. "No," he says, and he folds the Christmas card in half and puts it in his pocket. "I just woke up."

"You just woke up?" Ray exclaims. "Dude, it's one o'clock in the afternoon. What were you getting up to last night?"

"Nothing," Troy says. He shifts from foot to foot as Ray fiddles with some more buttons. The screen comes to life. There is the blast of heroic music, and a wrestling match announcer begins shouting.

"Geez," Ray says. "Look at this. This is fan-fucking-tastic. It's like the most realistic I've ever seen."

"Ray," Troy says, "what do you think you're doing?" But Ray doesn't look up. His eyes are focused on the screen as he starts up a game.

"It's a present," he says. "And not necessarily for you, my friend." Troy watches as Ray begins to flex and flinch along with the wrestlers he's controlling onscreen, his face hardening as the computerized action heats up.

"You didn't have to do that," he says, but Ray doesn't look up. "That's an expensive piece of equipment."

Ray only shrugs. He's not really that much different than he was when he was a teenager. He has a shaved head now, and a bristle of goatee, but his attitudes have remained the same, and even his body is as toned and neat as it had been when he was a stripper. He has never married, never even had a serious girlfriend. Looking at him, it would be hard to believe that he is a respectable business owner now, a member of the St. Bonaventure Commerce Association and the local Rotary Club.

"Look," Ray says. "I didn't buy it for you anyways, so don't worry about it." He glances up briefly, uncertainly, and their eyes meet. A myriad of things.

———

There has been some awkwardness between them lately. There have been more than a few times when they've had sharp words about the finances of the Stumble Inn, more than a few times when Troy has been made aware that he is, essentially, Ray's employee. "You're the manager," Ray used to say, when Ray first bought the bar from Vivian. "As far as I'm concerned, you run the place. Your decisions are my decisions." And mostly this had been true, but at the same time it was always clear that Ray was the *owner* of the bar. He was the owner, by this point, of four bars and one liquor store in St. Bonaventure and the surrounding towns. A local entrepreneur. They have never broached the subject of how much wealthier Ray was than Troy. No mention had ever been made of that valise full of drugs, which had been the original source of Ray's good fortune. It was clear that Ray was much shrewder with his income than Troy had ever been.

But even after all these years, Troy's social life still revolved around Ray and Loomis: a rock concert in Denver, a grade-school band concert in the tinny auditorium, a double date at a restaurant in which Ray and his girl played tag underneath the table, while Loo discussed species of birds with the woman Troy was supposed to be getting to know.

Troy watches as a tablet with the words GAME OVER hovers on the TV screen, and Ray smiles up at him sheepishly.

"Sit down," Ray says. "I challenge you to a battle, man."

———

Troy probably thinks too much about the past. He finds himself distracted by things he should have put out of his mind a long time ago—thinking about people like Lisa Fix, his old parole officer, whom he had dated for a couple of years after his release, before she'd left town for a job in Denver; or Vivian, who continues to sit regally at the same bar stool every night, Monday through Thursday, ever since her retirement. He can imagine how Ray would chide him: "What are you dwelling on that stuff for?" Ray would say. "How many years ago was that? Like, ten?" The truth is, he still thinks of these people almost every day—Judy Keene. Carla. Terry Shoopman. Jonah.

He lifts his head. Kick! Punch! Dodge! A couple of hours later, when Loomis gets home, Ray and he are still sitting there, and Troy hasn't won a single game.

Ray is the first to notice when Loomis walks in. "Hey, Birthday Guy!" Ray calls, and he holds out his hands dramatically toward the television screen. "Behold!" Ray says, and Troy smiles sheepishly, looking up from his seat on the floor into his son's face, as if Loomis is a grown-up and he is a small child.

"Hey," Loomis says, and he lets his eyes rest softly on Troy—as if to say "Are you doing okay, Dad?"—before he grins politely in Ray's direction. "Oh, my gosh," he says. "Uncle Ray, that's *really* cool. Thank you very much."

"You just have to remember that it's for you and not for your dad!" Ray says. "He's been sitting here playing all afternoon. I can't get him away from the thing."

"Uh-huh," Loomis says. He is reserved, as always, standing a little apart from them—still small for his age, though his shoulders are getting broader, his jawline is squaring off and becoming a man's. He waits there at the edge of the living room as Troy stands up. He allows Troy to hug him, to push back his messy bangs and plant a kiss on his forehead.

"Happy birthday," Troy says hoarsely, and Loomis accepts the fierceness of his father's affection with quiet dignity. He grunts a little, gasping good-naturedly as Troy squeezes him hard. "I love you, son," Troy whispers into his ear. "I love you so much."

———

After Ray is gone, a quiet settles over the house again. They sit at the kitchen table eating cake and ice cream, comfortable enough in each other's company. Happy enough, Troy thinks. He has tried hard to be a good father, and he knows that Loomis has made an effort to be a good son. They have had a solid life together, Troy thinks, though he wishes that they'd had a few more special moments, outside the routines of work and school, outside the rituals of watching television together and hiking out in the hills beyond the house. They don't argue about things. They seem to live their lives together smoothly.

Still, as they sit there at the table, Troy can't help but wish there was more time. He thinks about all the vacations they'd talked about and tentatively planned—to visit Washington, D.C., or Ireland, or South America—that they've never managed to afford. He thinks about the time he told Loomis he was thinking about taking some college correspondence courses, and Loomis had been so excited.

"We should just move someplace where there's a college," Loomis had said. "I wouldn't mind moving."

"Well," Troy said. "There's the money issue to consider. I can't just up and quit my job, right?"

And Loomis had shrugged. There was a deflation that Troy was aware of.

"I guess not," Loomis said, and Troy knew that he had said the wrong thing, that he had brushed against the edge of some different life that Loomis had fantasized about.

"You know, Loo," he'd said then. "I think it's a little late for me to become a different person."

And though Loomis had only been ten at the time, he'd made an irritable face. "Why do you have to be a different person to go to college?" Loomis had said. "Doesn't it sound like it would be fun?"

"Yeah," Troy said. "Sure." And he didn't meet Loomis's eyes. That was when their relationship started to change, he thought. When Loomis started to worry about him.

He had begun to be concerned about Troy's girlfriends. Suddenly, Loomis had recalled Lisa Fix and her pancake breakfasts, her stern help with grade-school math problems. "Whatever happened to her?" Loo said, and he had abruptly started to take an interest in the women that Troy went out with, even though no one serious emerged.

"Do you think you'll ever get married again?" Loomis had asked him once, trying to be casual, but it had taken him aback.

"I doubt it," Troy had said, as if it were a joke. "Who would I get married to?"

"I don't know," Loomis said. "One of these people you go on dates with, maybe."

"Any of them that you like in particular? Just give me a name and I'll propose."

"Oh, right," said Loomis, who had never liked to be teased. He turned his eyebrows downward, seriously. "What about Lisa Fix? She wanted to marry you, didn't she?"

"Ha," Troy said. "Did she tell you that?"

"No," Loomis said. "I just thought . . . you guys were together for a long time."

"I guess so. And we liked each other well enough. But, you know, I think Lisa Fix was interested in finding somebody a little more ambitious than I turned out to be." He considered for a moment, looking carefully into Loomis's eyes. "So what are you driving at, man?" he said, and ran his hand gently over the back of Loomis's hair. "You miss having a mom, I guess."

"Not really," Loomis said.

"Do you ever think about your mom? I know we don't talk about it much, and . . ."

"I don't know," Loomis said. "Not exactly."

"Oh," Troy said. He didn't think this was true, but what could he say? Over seven years have passed now since they last spoke to her, and still there was no word. Would it do any good to tell Loomis that he was fairly certain that she was still alive, that she was out there somewhere, in a new life? Would it do any good to tell Loomis that he still half expects the phone to ring, one of these years?

"You know you can talk to me about it, if you want," Troy had said, and Loomis glanced down at his fingers. "I mean, she's your mom. You've got to think about her sometimes, right?"

"I guess so," Loomis said. "I don't remember her that well. Besides," he said politely, "it's not like I want her to come back and live with us or something." And he paused for a moment, weighing his words. "I was just thinking that it might be good for *you* if you got married. I mean, I just want you to be happy, that's all."

And Troy had smiled, though Loomis's earnest, worried eyes made his heart hurt. "I am happy, son," he said softly. "I'm a very happy man."

He thinks of this all again as he watches Loomis stirring his ice cream, turning it into soft-serve. They have a good relationship, he thinks. They love each other. Loomis is doing very well in school. He seems content.

"So," Troy says, after a moment. "How was your day?"

"Fine," Loomis says. "How about you?"

"The usual," Troy says. "I slept until, like, one in the afternoon, and then Ray showed up, so . . ." He leans back in his chair, and then he remembers the Christmas card, still folded in the front pocket of his jeans. He puts his hand on it. "Actually," he says. "There was one thing." He smiles, awkwardly, and draws out the somewhat crumpled envelope. "Looks like we got a letter."

"Oh?" Loomis says.

"From Jonah Doyle."

Loomis says nothing. His eyes widen, then he looks down to his bowl and gives his ice cream another stir. This is another thing they don't talk about very much. They don't talk about what happened on the day that Jonah took Loomis to Colorado, the day Judy died. It's not something Loomis remembers very clearly, or at least that's what he says. Troy is aware that he has brought up another issue that might make Loo worry.

"Hm," Loomis says. "I thought he was in jail."

"No, no," Troy says. "He's been out for a while, actually. I told you that."

"No, you didn't. I don't remember you ever telling me that."

"Really?"

"I don't think so, Dad."

"Oh," Troy says. "Well, he's not in jail. He's been out for a little while now, I think. I could have sworn that I told you."

Loomis gives him one of his concerned, watchful looks. He has gotten Troy to cut his smoking down to almost nothing, and he has lately been taking note of Troy's bouts of insomnia. "You know," he has said, "sleep is really important for your health." And then: "Are you worried about something, Dad? What do you think about when you're up so late?" Now, looking at the card from Jonah, he pinches his mouth as if it might be another bad habit that Troy is acquiring.

"Why would he send us a Christmas card?" Loomis says. "That's kind of *weird*."

"I guess," Troy says. For Loomis, Jonah Doyle is a distant and somewhat unpleasant memory, little more.

"I want to go set up that laptop," Loomis says at last. "I have to tell you, that's the best present I've ever gotten in my life." He gives Troy another hug before he vanishes into his room.

Maybe it *is* weird, Troy thinks, as he sits there. Maybe his whole life is weird. He can imagine what Ray would have to say about it, or anyone in town for that matter. The event, as ultimately minor as it was, had caused quite a stir around St. Bonaventure, and people still referred to it as a "kidnapping." "That kidnapping that happened a few years back," people would say. It had been in the newspaper—even a small article in the *Omaha World Herald*—and folks in town had been pretty stirred up about it. Even now, customers at the bar would occasionally ask after Loomis— "How is he doing?" they would say, softly, as if he might still be suffering from the trauma. And Troy could only shrug. "He's fine," he would say, cheerfully. "Smart as a whip. Doing excellent in school. A really great kid."

He would listen as people expressed their outrage toward Jonah. "I hope they lock that guy up and throw away the key." Troy would nod.

What could he say? He seemed to be the only person in town shocked by the harshness of the sentence, the only person who'd blanched at the idea that Jonah should have been charged with felony murder for Judy's death, certainly the only one who had mixed feelings about the charge of criminal child enticement, which is what Jonah eventually pleaded guilty of, among other things. Even Jonah seemed to think that he deserved what he got.

Troy, on the other hand, didn't know what to think. There were too many things that he didn't quite understand, too many small, unexplained mysteries that had never been answered.

He had visited Jonah a few times in prison. There hadn't been a trial— since Jonah had pled guilty to all of the charges leveled against him— and this was another thing that Troy found inexplicably upsetting. It was as if Jonah was happy to go to jail, as if it were a fate that he had been waiting for, and he remembered sitting there at the table in the waiting room of the prison as Jonah shuffled in, wearing his gray prisoner outfit. Their eyes met, and Jonah seemed almost comfortable. He sat down across from Troy, and his gaze was steadier than it had ever been.

"Hello, brother," he said softly, and Troy felt a shudder go through him.

"Hello," Troy said. They sat there across from each other, and Troy tried to think of what to say.

"I guess you must be pretty mad at me," Jonah said at last, but there was an edge in his voice that suggested it was Jonah who was angry with Troy. "I was kind of surprised when you said you were coming to visit, you know? I mean, I really made a mess of everything."

"Yeah," Troy said. "In a way. But—I don't know—I suppose that I just wanted to talk some things over. There's a lot of stuff that we never really got . . . resolved, if you know what I mean."

"Like what?"

Troy shifted in his chair. The room they were sitting in was a small enclosed space, with glass windows on all sides. A guard stood outside the door with her arms folded, examining her fingernails distractedly, glancing occasionally to where they sat at the gray metal table. He sighed. What *did* he want, after all? He was aware once again of that feeling of having disappointed Jonah. *If I had had your life,* he thought.

"I don't know," Troy said at last. "I suppose I thought I'd get the real story. I mean, not just about Loomis but about . . . our mom, and everything. I'd like to get the real story about you, too."

"So would I," Jonah said, and smiled a little, a kind of private joke that eluded Troy completely. He had no idea what Jonah was thinking.

"I don't know, Troy," Jonah said. "I guess I had this idea that if I found you and put all these pieces together I could sort of solve the past—like it was a puzzle, you know? It's just that now I've kind of realized that it really isn't going to help me at all."

"Well," Troy said, and he sat there, puzzling, trying to find some coherence in what Jonah had said. "I guess I just don't get it, Jonah. I mean, I don't even understand what you're doing here. You didn't even try to defend yourself or explain yourself, and I guess that troubles me. Even if you were trying to kidnap Loomis, which I don't think you were, why didn't you just run away when you got caught? You just sat there with Loomis and those two people and waited for the police to come. That doesn't make any sense to me."

And Jonah had only shrugged. "I was depressed," he said. "I really didn't intend . . ." he said, and then he stopped as if checking himself. "I don't know what I intended, actually. It was just that—I didn't have a lot of energy left." He looked down at the table for a moment.

"You know," he said. "I don't really think I can explain myself to you, Troy. I'm sorry."

Perhaps that should have been enough. Does it matter that he'll never know what really happened?

He's not sure—but he nevertheless has found himself going over the small mysteries of his life—following rumors he hears from time to time about Carla's whereabouts, talking to detectives in Vegas and Lake Tahoe, sorting through the little scraps of information he has gathered about his biological family. It's become a kind of hobby, trying to put things together, these empty blocks in his life like squares in a crossword that he can't complete.

They keep him occupied, these projects. They are the sort of things that keep him up late at night—"worries," Loomis calls them, but Troy finds it interesting, and he's even had some successes over the years. He knows, for example, a little bit of the truth of his biological family. He has seen the grave in Little Bow, South Dakota, where Joseph Doyle was buried, and he has read the obituaries and death certificates. He has a copy of the article from the *Little Bow News*: "Boy Attacked by Family Dog," which he had taken along with him the last time he'd visited Jonah in jail.

They had maintained a cordial if distant relationship up until then. Mostly, Jonah would send him short, oddly formal letters, usually talking about the books that he was reading. He had gotten a job in the prison library and seemed very pleased about it. "I'm in the process of really learning a lot about myself," he had written, and he signed his letters: "All the Best to You and Yours."

But when Troy had shown him the Xerox of the article from the Little Bow newspaper, he had grown silent for a long time. He turned his hands over, palms up, and stared at Troy.

"I think I told you about that once," he said, coldly.

"You did?" Troy said. "I don't think so."

"It's not something I really want to talk about," Jonah said, and a few days later Troy had received a short letter in the mail.

"I'd like to take some time away from our relationship," Jonah had written.

———

It has been almost four years since that last letter, and after Loomis has disappeared into his room, Troy sits for a while in his easy chair in front of the television with the sound muted, turning the Christmas card over in his hands. The return address is printed on the back in Jonah's tiny, neat cursive: 2210 Hickory Street, Kingston, Jamaica, which seems as if it could be a joke. Troy had been a big Bob Marley fan, back in the day; Troy and Carla and Ray used to fantasize about living in Jamaica. But it seems to be serious. He turns the card over, and there is a Jamaican postmark over a Jamaican stamp.

And when he opens the letter he sees that it's not a Christmas card after all. It's just an ordinary card, a photo of a gnarled tree and a beach and a sunset—a scene from Jamaica, he guesses—and when he opens it he finds an old Polaroid: a picture of him and Loomis from years ago, the two of them standing in the backyard, Troy bent down on his haunches with Little Man beside him, his arm thrown around his father's shoulder. Loomis looks to be about five, and though the color has washed out a little, though there are some smudges along the edges, the two of them look brilliantly happy. He turns the photo over, then looks at the small block of carefully inked letters in the center of the card.

Dear Troy,

I have settled here in Jamaica for a while, perhaps permanently. I am doing graduate work at University in Information Science though I also am seriously considering the possibility of pursuing Medicine.

I found this photo while cleaning out some old files and notes and thought that you should have it back. I have changed a lot over the years but I am still not very good about saving pictures.

I hope you are well.
My Best to You and Yours,

Jonah

He sits there for a while, reading it over a few times, aware of a vague discouragement settling over him. What had he been expecting, after all? Some kind of confession? An explanation? A reconciliation? No, he thinks, and it occurs to him that all Jonah had wanted was evidence that his unhappy life wasn't his own fault—*If* he'd had a different mother. *If* he'd grown up in a different place—some kind of proof that he was unlucky, which was not what Troy could give him.

Still, despite everything, Troy can't help but feel that he's luckier than Jonah understands. I'm a lucky man, he would tell Jonah.

Lucky. He was a man who'd almost lost the person he loved most in the world, but he got another chance. The most amazing thing in the world. Don't worry about me, he wants to tell Loomis. I got you back. The best thing that could ever happen to me has already happened.

36

March 18, 1971

When the second baby comes, Nora is better prepared. She is in a hospital in Chicago, and no one is planning to take her baby away. She is safe. The doctor is a gentle, balding man who wears a clownish bow tie and calls her "Mrs. Gray." She has a house, and even a little room where they will put the new arrival, the crib they assembled together a few weeks ago, the tiny blankets and stuffed animals and rubber-nippled bottles lined up on a shelf. She isn't alone. Gary is sitting outside in the waiting room, nervously smiling at the mounted television, and even though he isn't the biological father, he will protect her because he loves her.

This is almost the way it is supposed to be.

———

Through most of her pregnancy she has been able to focus her thoughts on this new baby; she has been able to project herself into a happy future, to slide into the brightness of it as if she herself is being born, the elements slowly unblurring like a developing photo: child, husband, house, tree, mother. She promises herself that she is capable of having a happy life. She promises this new baby that it will be fine, it will be fine, she will be careful. She will steer their lives as neatly as she can.

But once the contractions start, she finds herself losing hold of the path that she has been trying to follow. It seems that she is shrinking: her fingers growing shorter, pulling back into her knuckles like a turtle's head into its shell; her hands withdrawing into her wrists, her wrists withdrawing into her shoulders, her entire body slowly gathering itself toward a central point. A shimmering nurse orbits along her line of sight, and she squeezes her eyes shut, pulling a stream of breath through her teeth. A force gathers at her middle and grips.

She had thought that she didn't remember anything about that first birth, but she remembers these pains clearly. Hard to believe they'd ever left her, and for a moment she is back in that hospital, back in the Mrs. Glass House, giving birth to a baby she will never see. *I've changed my mind,* she thinks. She remembers whispering it, *I've changed my mind, I've changed my mind,* pressing her head from side to side against her pillow, even as they wait at the edge of the room to take her child away.

She is crying a little, and the nurse's hand appears above her face to run a cloth across her forehead and eyes.

There is still a little space between the contractions. They are far enough apart that she can cling, briefly, to the single line that she's been following: the future, the new baby, the house, the tree. But it's hard to stay on track. Even as she dozes fitfully, even as the nurse's hand touches her wrist, adjusts a tube.

It's hard to believe that this is how it's done. That this is how we get here into the world, by accident or design, the microscopic pieces of ourselves borne by fluids and blood and growing into a tiny kingdom of cells inside someone else's body. It seems so difficult to become alive. So improbable.

Something cold is pressed between her lips, and her mouth works soundlessly. How can it be possible? she wonders. How can you come to understand your life when even the beginning is so complicated: a single cell imprinted with the color of your eyes and the shape of your face, the pattern on your palm and the moods that will shadow you through your life. How can you be alive when every choice you make breaks the world into a thousand filaments, each careless step branching into long tributaries of alternate lives, shuddering outward and outward like sheet lightning.

For a moment, she can feel it. She can sense herself dividing, multiplying, splitting into particles. She can feel the baby inside her, and the absence of the baby. She can sense the child that she had given away, lingering curiously over her, even as its physical body sleeps dreamlessly in a warm bed, in a pretty house at the edge of the sea. She thinks again of that house in the Winslow Homer painting, that landscape that had struck her so suddenly when she'd seen it: *Oh, that's where my baby lives,* she thought.

The child would be four years old now, almost five, and in the second before the next contraction she walks up the path toward that house. Wayne Hill is sitting in the grass with their child—a girl? No, a boy. A sturdy little guy with dark hair and Wayne's blue eyes, who waves when he sees her. Wayne and their son are sitting there eating Popsicles, and Wayne grins playfully, his mouth blue from the food coloring. He's wearing his navy uniform, and she lifts her hand, swinging her knapsack full of books. She works part-time in a small library. She takes courses at the college when they can afford it. But they are happy, and he sometimes tells her how grateful he was that she trusted him. He tells his buddies about the day he'd rescued her from the Mrs. Glass House, how brave she'd been, in the middle of a snowstorm, five months pregnant and climbing over the fence where his car was waiting.

And then her body clenches again, and for some reason she finds herself thinking of a memory from her childhood. That balloon, she thinks, squeezing her eyes shut. That yellow balloon her father had bought her at the fair when she was six. *Babygirl,* he said, *this is for you, because you're special,* and he tied the string around her wrist. She had never seen a helium balloon before, had never known that something could float like that, like magic.

She was standing in the yard when the knot around her wrist had unloosened. She remembers it clearly—the balloon, unmoored, lifting up. She'd clutched for the string but missed, and it kept rising and rising, shrinking, listlessly disappearing into clear expanse of sky.

She couldn't believe, back then, that things could be lost forever, that they could be irretrievable. She stood out there in the yard for most of the afternoon, shouting at the sky, commanding it, stomping her foot.

"Come back!" she called, and held her arms up, pleading. "Come back! Come back! Come back!"

She just wants a second chance, she thinks. She just wants to be able to think a moment before she takes another step into her life, to pause and trace along the edges of the people that she might become, but already they are putting a plastic mask over her face, already they are talking to her about breathing and bearing down, and she doesn't know what she wants yet. She doesn't know.

You Remind
Me of Me

A Reader's Guide

Dan Chaon

A Conversation with Dan Chaon

Q: This is your first novel, following two collections of short stories (*Fitting Ends* and *Among the Missing*). Was it difficult to make the transition to the longer form?

Dan Chaon: I found it very hard at first. I love the short story as an art form in its own right, and I want to continue to be a short-story writer. I am not one of those people who think that short stories are just practice ground for young writers to work their way up to writing a novel. Writing short stories is not necessarily good practice for writing a novel, because they seem to me to come from different parts of the brain.

 When I first began writing, I tended to be more interested in poetry. I didn't start out thinking in terms of "narrative" and "story." My earliest impetus for writing was simply observing the strange things I happened to notice in my everyday life, situations that struck me as compelling, anecdotes I'd heard, images, words, metaphors. A lot of the time, with stories, I'll start out with a title and try to dream myself into the story that it evokes—a kind of subconscious exercise in which I'm trawling for some kind of entryway into narrative. As a short-story writer, I usually just start at the beginning and write through to the end. You'll have some basic ideas—a character, or an image, or a situation that sounds compelling—and then you just feel your way around until you find the edges of your story. It's like going into a dark room . . . you stumble around until you find the walls and then inch your way to the light switch. With a novel, on the other hand, the walls may not be there. You may be in a dark field. There may not be a light switch. You can't stumble around blindly as easily and find your way out. You need to understand the scope and shape of the world you are writing about in a way that you don't often have to think about in a story.

But I didn't know that at first. Going into the novel, I was pretty ignorant about the process, and I just had a kind of vague idea of a general theme I wanted to write about. I knew a few things about the situation and some aspects of the characters' lives, but I didn't know much else.

So my first draft was a minor disaster. I couldn't get a grip on the structure, for one thing. I tended to go off on tangents and get lost as I was writing, and I realized that the problem was that I was trying to write it as if it were a very long short story. In my mind, I had as a model the kind of short, "perfect" novel, like *The Great Gatsby,* which takes place in a self-contained period of time and follows a direct line of chronological action from beginning to end. But this conception didn't work for me at all. I had too much chronological time that I was trying to cover and too many different character threads that needed to be fleshed out. The truth is that even in my stories I don't generally think in direct lines, and what I had come up with was layer upon layer of summary, flashback, and interior monologue—a big rambling mess, with almost no scene at all. I was very lucky to have had an editor like Dan Smetanka. He was very patient and really helped me to see how to begin to restructure the material—how to think in terms of novelistic scene, rather than short-story scene, and how to begin to find an overall shape for the material.

Q: The structure of *You Remind Me of Me* is quite complicated, using multiple points of view and a fractured chronology. Why did you decide to write the novel in this form?

DC: I started with a more traditional structure in mind. The first draft was in first person, from Jonah's point of view, and started at the beginning of part 2, when he arrived in St. Bonaventure. I saw the action of the book taking place over a period of three or four months. But as I was going back and trying to rewrite, one of the first things I realized was that Jonah's perspective was so distorted that he wasn't capable of telling big parts of the story that were interesting to me. I was curious about what Troy was thinking. And then I became interested in Nora's side of the story. And as I started to write about these different characters, I became interested in the ways in which their lives and their viewpoints contrasted and bounced off one another, particularly because the characters had such distinctive—even contradictory—senses of reality.

The other thing was, as I said, the first draft of the novel tended to be pretty heavy with summary and flashback. At the suggestion of Dan Smetanka, I began to dramatize the important events in the characters' lives: the dog attack; Nora's life in the maternity home; the first time Troy smoked pot. And as I began to accumulate these little dramatized scenes—each one almost like a self-contained story—I realized that my original concept of the structure wasn't going to work. Those months that Jonah spends spying on Troy in St. Bonaventure weren't really the only center of the action of the book. That was only one layer, and there were other times and other layers that, in my mind, were concurrent and interpenetrating—almost as if we had six or seven television sets all tuned to different stations, but each of the programs was secretly connected to the others.

After I'd accumulated enough of these fragments, I ended up establishing a skeletal structure for myself to work with: The novel is made up of three parts with twelve chapters each. Once I had some of those initial chapters in place, like support columns, I saw how they could be arranged to create suspense and how they could reflect off one another in interesting way. That collage aspect was actually eventually one of the most fun parts of the book for me because it allowed me to discover interconnections between the time lines and characters that I might not have found if I'd written the book in a more straightforward chronological way.

Q: It's surprising to hear that your conception of the novel didn't actually begin with the dog attack. It's hard to imagine the novel without that central opening incident—but it sounds as if the opening chapter didn't come until somewhat late in the process of writing.

DC: Well, the idea of Jonah's facial scars was around from the very beginning of the story. One of the first lines I wrote was, "I like for people to look at my scars." And in early drafts there were long first-person monologues from Jonah's point of view. He talked about the dog attack, but it was never really dramatized. I think that a big breakthrough for me was a discussion I had with Dan Smetanka about it. He was like, "This is the most compelling material you've written so far, and yet it's all in flashback and summary. Why don't you sit down and write ten pages where you dramatize the moment of that dog attack?" And when I did that, it really transformed my concept of the book and how I was going to put it together. The dog started out as this very abstract violent incident in the past, but it ended up that the relationship between the boy Jonah and the dog Elizabeth brought me to a much deeper understanding of Jonah's mental life. And Elizabeth the Doberman became an important figure in the book in her own right, and actually one of my favorite "characters" in the book.

Q: You have written before about being adopted. Can you talk a little about how your own experiences with adoption informed the writing of the novel?

DC: It's such a hard question for a fiction writer to answer.

So let me answer the easy part first. Yes, I was adopted. My parents adopted me when I was a six-month-old infant. I grew up in rural western Nebraska in the late 1960s and '70s, the oldest of three children—all of us adopted, none of us genetically related. We knew we were adopted, but we didn't make a big deal of it. Generally, I was very comfortable with the idea, though I did wonder, sometimes. In some ways, I guess, the *experience* of being adopted probably fed into a lot of the issues of choice and fate and circumstance that I find myself writing about frequently. Growing up, I was sometimes aware of the sense that there was another life out there that I might have had, or even multiple lives. What if I'd been adopted by a different family? What if my biological parents had kept me?

I grew up in a very working-class family—neither of my parents graduated high school—and they were not bookish or artsy in the way I wanted them to be. I fantasized that my biological parents shared more of my interests. I imagined that they were writers or actors or maybe rock musicians.

But the truth was, I didn't really start thinking about being an adoptee in any serious way until I was married and became a father for the first time myself. It struck me that my son was the first person I'd ever met who was related to me by blood. And I also realized that I didn't have any medical information about my biological family.

Finding such genetic information was much more complicated than I thought it would be. I ended up becoming involved with an adoption search group and learning a lot from them about the many issues involved for adoptees, birth parents, and adoptive parents. Eventually, I ended up getting in touch with my biological father—and developing a relationship with him.

Meeting my biological father answered some of my questions, but not as many as I imagined. I had always thought that the traits I clearly didn't receive from my adoptive parents must have had their basis in heredity. Yet, as it turned out, my biological father was very much like my adoptive father—both of them even worked as electricians! In some ways, it would have been easier to believe that the two of them were brothers than to guess that I was the son of either man.

"Maybe it's not nature or nurture, either one," my wife said to me after I'd met my biological father for the first time. "Maybe you just invented yourself. Why is that so strange?" And it may have been that comment that ultimately formed the seed of *You Remind Me of Me*. I began to think about it: Do you invent yourself? How much does nurture matter? How much does nature matter? And out of these thoughts, I had the idea of the character who eventually became Jonah—this literally scarred person who is involved in this kind of intense search for identity, while at the same time trying to escape his past.

At the same time, I really wanted to avoid direct autobiography in this book—maybe *particularly* in this book. So while I was drawing on this fairly intense personal experience as I was writing, I was also creating entirely fictional characters and situations. I was worried about hurting the feelings of both my adoptive family and my biological family, and so I was especially careful that no one would mistakenly identify themselves as one of the characters. Ultimately, there are very few direct correlatives between my life and the events and people portrayed in the book.

The one exception is Mike Hawk in chapter 11, who is based on a real person.

Q: That's interesting. The idea of "reality" seems to be a big issue in the book, and I wanted to go back to the comment that you made earlier. You said that you thought that the individual characters had "distinctive—even contradictory—senses of reality," and there were points in the novel where I had the eerie feeling that everything happening was a dream—that Troy and Jonah were feverish figments of Nora's imagination, for example. At the very least, people seem to live so wholly in their own individual perspectives that they have a hard time interpreting and understanding one another. Was that part of your intention here?

DC: Well, from early on I wanted to play around with the point of view. I started out with a kind of distorted first-person narrator, and I still had that kind of uncertainty and slippage in mind when I switched to multiple third-person perspectives.

I believe that one of the main ways we come to understand the world—and ourselves—is by telling stories. We narrate in order to understand our lives, to create order, and I imagine that many successful and happy people have a fairly clear sense of who they are and how they fit into the world.

But the characters in this book mostly don't. Jonah thinks he can invent a new life for himself through lies; on the other hand, Troy tends to accept the various definitions people place on him without much question. And Nora finds large parts of her own story slipping through her fingers, becoming indistinct and uncertain and, eventually, hallucinatory.

I suppose, as an adoptee, I'm more sensitized to questions of identity and self-narrative. Growing up, I was always fascinated by genealogy, and I was shocked that so many people I knew couldn't really trace their family lines beyond a generation or two. This may be true particularly in the Great Plains region where I was raised, where pioneers emigrated from the eastern part of the United States or from foreign countries, and very often completely lost touch with those that they left behind. But maybe this kind of disconnection is a part of the American experience in some ways. I'm fascinated by some of our social institutions—like the Orphan Trains, or the homes for unwed mothers of the 1950s and '60s, with their codes of silence and secrecy. Such institutions are almost like machines made to create a hole in the sense of self.

I guess it's that kind of hole or gap in the sense of identity that I'm interested in. There's something about this kind of alienation that I find profoundly sad and scary, which is why, I guess, there are so many ghostly and feverish elements at the edges of the novel. At one extreme are the fugue states that Nora experiences, so that she literally can't remember weeks and months of her life—she can't remember how she got pregnant with Jonah, for example—and those Nora chapters [13 and 19] were probably the creepiest for me when I was writing them. But I think nearly all the characters have these kinds of gaps and holes in their lives one way or another.

Q: One of the gaps in almost all of the characters lives is the absence of a positive mother figure. It seems as if there isn't a single "good" mother presented in the entire novel. Why is that the case?

DC: Well, I think Judy is a good mother in a lot of ways. She's a good grandmother, at least. But I know what you mean. I realized that this was an issue as I was writing, and I ultimately wasn't sure what to do about it. It wasn't entirely intentional—but by the time I was deep into the book, the pattern of lost and elusive and unreachable mothers had become really deeply entwined into the texture and mood of the book. If I'd tried to inject a "positive" mom into the book, it would have felt somewhat dissonant. In fact, at one point Troy's adoptive mother had a much larger—and more positive—presence in the novel, but I felt that she actually unbalanced things—or at least diluted the mood in a weird way. I'm not entirely working from a point of view of naturalistic realism, in any case, so I don't feel like I have a responsibility to be fair and equitable. Ultimately I decided that, for this novel at least, we just had to live with my world of bad moms. I'll make it up to the moms of the world in another book, maybe.

Q: The issue of responsibility is an interesting one. Do you feel as if you're expressing a certain kind of moral and social vision of the world through your work? How do you think novels are culturally significant, meaning how do you think they impact the world, if at all?

DC: It's a hard question. I guess I do have a moral and sociological perspective, but ultimately I don't think of what I do as rhetorical discourse. Instead, I think of it as very private communication between a writer and a particular sympathetic reader, a small, shared attempt. "To capture that trickle in time," as Alice Munro says at the end of one of her wonderful stories. "To rescue that one thing from the rubbish." The writers I admire, and the writers I aspire to be like, have this remarkable ability to enter into the consciousness, almost by stealth, reader by reader. There are certain stories and novels that I read over and over, ones that have deeply enriched my understanding of and experience of the world, and which have great personal significance to me—works that accompany me through my life almost as spirits that hover at the edge of daily consciousness; they are part of my thinking. If I have an ambition to influence the world, it is to have written something that a reader, a specific individual, will carry with him or her, something that he or she will love and remember. One of the aching and beautiful things about Michael Cunningham's novel *The Hours* is the way it suggests that a book might have the power to gently enter the lives of various people over time, over a century, and that those people the book touches become spiritually connected in a kind of chain. That's not necessarily cultural significance, but to my mind it's much better, much more lovely and hopeful, and much closer to what I think art is supposed to do.

Q: One final quick question—how do you pronounce your name?

DC: Dan?

Q: No—your last name.

DC: I'm just messing with you. It's pronounced "shawn"—much easier than it looks.

Reading Group Questions and Topics for Discussion

1. What is the meaning of the title of the novel? Who reminds who of whom? What aspects of themselves do characters recognize—and fail to recognize—in one another?

2. To what extent is St. Bonaventure a familiar, realistic version of the Midwest? To what extent is it a "fairy-tale" setting? What are some of the fairy-tale elements of the novel?

3. Why do the characters, especially Troy and Jonah, have such a difficult time changing their hard lives? What does Chaon want to communicate to the reader about the nature of suffering? Does your own philosophy differ from his?

4. There are several points in the novel when Nora thinks, "I've changed my mind." And in the last chapter, Chaon writes: "How can you be alive when every choice you make breaks the world into a thousand filaments, each careless step branching into long tributaries of alternate lives . . . ?" What role does freedom of choice play in the course of the novel?

5. Judy Keene has a critical role in the novel's plot. What are her motivations? Does Chaon intend us to see her as a villain in the story, or is her moral stance presented sympathetically?

6. There are many ways that Chaon creates suspense in the novel, but the most obvious one is the time structure. How would the book be

different if events were in chronological order? Are there any mysteries left unsolved by the end of the book?

7. Is Nora a "bad mother" or a "victim"? How responsible is she for what happens to her sons?

8. How much humor is there in the book? Of what kind? Is there enough humor to balance the sadness of the characters and their situations? What are some of the funniest moments?

9. In the end, Jonah seems almost glad to go to jail, and he rejects Troy's overtures of reconciliation. What has changed for him? Does he simply give up? What did he want, ultimately, from Troy and Loomis that he couldn't get? Does the novel hold out hope that Jonah will eventually find some kind of stability, or do you see him as a person who is never going to find what he is searching for?

10. What is the emotional effect of ending the novel with Nora giving birth to Jonah? How would the novel be different if it ended with chapter 35? If Loomis were *not* rescued?

PHOTO © BETSY MOLNAR

Dan Chon's book of short stories *Among the Missing* was a finlist for the 2001 National Book Award. In addition, the collection was listed as one of the ten best books of 2001 by the American Library Association, *Chicago Tribune, The Boston Globe, Las Vegas Mercury,* and *Entertainment Weekly.* It was also cited by *Publishers Weekly, The Washington Post,* and *The New York Times* as one of the notable books of the year. The collection has been translated into several languages.

Chaon's stories have appeared in many journals and anthologies, and have been included in *The Best American Short Stories* for 1996 and 2003; *The Pushcart Prize* for 2000, 2002, and 2003; and *Prize Stories 2001: The O. Henry Awards,* where his story "Big Me" was chosen as the second-prize winner. His first collection of short stories, *Fitting Ends,* was published by Northwestern University Press in 1996 and has been reissued by Ballantine Books (2003) in a revised edition.

Chaon lives in Cleveland Heights, Ohio, with his wife and two sons, and teaches in the creative writing program at Oberlin College, where he is the Houck Associate Professor in the Humanities.

About the Type

This book was set on the monotype in Garamond, a typeface designed by the French printer Jean Jannon. It is styled after Garamond's original models. The face is dignified and is light but without fragile lines. The italic is modeled after a font of Granjon, which was probably cut in the middle of the sixteenth century.